The Natanleods

Book 11

Daughter of the House
Part 1

By
Sunbow Pendragon

Text copyright © 2019 Sunbow Pendragon

ISBN: 9781707897902
All rights reserved

No part of this book may be reproduced or transmitted in any form or by any means, electronic or mechanical, including photocopying, recording or by any information storage and retrieval system without permission in the form of writing from the copyright owner.

This is a work of fiction. Names, characters, places and incidents either are the product of the author's imagination or are used fictitiously, and any resemblance to any actual persons, living or dead, events, or locales is entirely coincidental.

Acknowledgements

My Friends and Fans, I present to you Book 11 in the saga of The Natanleods. When I began to write this series, I had no idea it would eventually encompass so many volumes. I am grateful for all those who have read the tale, and offered their encouragement and support to keep it going. The Land is truly a magickal and mystical place! May the tale never end! Blessed be.

Table of Contents

Table of Contents
Acknowledgements..3
Table of Contents...4
Prologue..5
Chapter 1..7
Chapter 2..30
Chapter 3..46
Chapter 4..63
Chapter 5..82
Chapter 6..106
Chapter 7..128
Chapter 8..147
Chapter 9..169
Chapter 10..187
Chapter 11..221
Chapter 12..246
Chapter 13..265
Finis...275

Prologue

The former Amazon Commander, Ashara, sat on her porch, sipping fine whiskey and smoking a small sikar after her day's work. Most of it had been seeing to the small aches and pains of the former troopers there, but sometimes she was needed to perform counseling. They would come to her to talk about the days of war, about the blood they had spilled and the deaths they carried. Ashara's experience helped them feel comfortable talking to her, and they found relief for their mental anguish afterward. That day had been a long one, she had attended to two of the most strenuous counseling sessions yet since taking up residence here in the retirement village. At length, she finished her whiskey and stubbed out her sikar, ready to retire for the night. Entering through her front door, she paused to close it behind her, not bothering to lock it due to the constant patrols provide by those who found sleep elusive. When she turned to walk to her bedroom she found a visitor had arrived by magick, and when she saw his face, her breath caught in her throat a bit.

"My Lord Drake!"

"Greetings, Commander Ashara," he intoned. "I need to speak to ye about yer trainee Brianna. She has undergone a bit of a trial, and could use a talk with her trainer."

With that, he disappeared from her sight. She blinked, and suddenly found herself in her bed, the candle extinguished, the stars twinkling through the open window. Had she dreamed the entire thing, she wondered, smelling her breath. All she could detect was the slight scent of mint from the tooth powder she used, and she shook her head to clear it.

"What is happening?" she asked herself, rising from the bed and walking to the necessity. When she returned, she quickly examined the room, finding no trace of entry.

She experienced similar visions over the next two weeks, a single visit each sevenday, until she was convinced that she was needed at the Capitol city. Telling her neighbor she would be gone for a few days, and asking him to look after her chickens, she packed a small bag and dressed her horse for the journey. As she mounted her horse, she realized it was five days to the Solstice, and wondered if that had anything to do with her visions. Putting spur to her horse lightly to urge him into a comfortable canter, she turned his head toward the Capitol city and let him go at his best pace. Her route took her along an easy road, where she found guardhouses and inns in plenty, and so did not have to sleep outside, for which she was grateful. It was the morning of the Solstice when she found herself just outside the back gates of the Capitol, and she could hear the sounds of the party beginning already. Urging her tired horse forward, she entered the city and made her way up to the High Lord's Barracks, eager to find out what her visions were all about.

Chapter 1

"Happy Solstice, Father!" Erinn wished in the spirit of the day, tapping his cup against Drake's.

"Happy Solstice, my son!" Drake returned, clearly in a jovial mood. "We will have hungry folk to feed soon, we'd best get busy with this pig!"

"Indeed so!" Erinn laughed with him. Together, the two began the process of measuring, grinding and mixing two huge bowls of herbs and spices. When they were full, the men took the bowls of rub mix to the meat, washed their hands once more before beginning, for one could never be too clean around wild pork meat. As they worked together, starting from each end of the carcass and applying the rub liberally as they proceeded, meeting at the mid-way point. Once the pig was rubbed, sturdy Knights came to heft it onto the spit, then others brought the next pig and the process of rubbing it thoroughly with the remainder of the mix began once more. Drake watched with satisfaction as the next pig was hoisted up onto the sturdy spit, and the counterweights were wound and dropped, sparing everyone the onerous task of turning. One only had to baste from time to time, and everyone volunteered for that task gladly, simply for the opportunity to stand next to the roasting pig and take in the scent. "Now we have that task accomplished, what else needs doing?" Erinn asked, turning to Deborah. The High Lady simply handed them each a sweating, cold pitcher of brown ale, and a pair of sikars.

"Go on with ye, sit in the shade by the river and cool yerselves. Ye have worked aplenty for today, I think!" she laughed.

"Ye are the kindest woman I know," Drake replied smoothly, exhibiting some of the charm he was famed for. "I thank the High Lady for her indulgence. We will enjoy these to the fullest!"

"See that ye do!" she mock-ordered before dissolving in merry laughter, almost dropping her own cup of cold white wine. The young Dame, Brianna happened to standing right beside her to provide a quick hand to assist, something Drake complimented her for at once.

"Nicely done, young lady."

"Tha...Thank ye, My Lord," she answered, stammering due to his sheer presence and reputation.

"My dear, ye may drop the honorific," Drake chuckled warmly, offering her a pipe loaded with fragrant Herb. "Today *is* a holiday!" he went on persuasively. Deborah smiled, but said naught. She remembered how Drake had welcomed her into the family, so many years ago, and how confusing it had been at first, considering his reputation for violence. Sensing Brianna's growing discomfort, she moved to reassure the young woman by inviting her to return to the house with her.

"Sister, would ye come and help me for a bit?" she asked, putting herself beside the younger woman as a supportive presence.

"O! I would like that!" Brianna answered at once, glad for the distraction. Drake's eyes were so blue, and his presence was so magnetic, it was hard to think of anything other than him while he stood there. Deborah was well aware of the effect Drake had on women, she had experienced it herself during her early courtship with Erinn. Drake had attempted to sway her affections, testing to see if her love for Erinn was true and strong. While Deborah had not felt any desire for Drake in any way, she remembered that his magnetism could not be denied.

"Come then, I am ready for more wine."

"I am too!" Brianna echoed, slipping out from underneath Drake's gaze and joining Deborah as she walked away. When she thought they were far enough away, she turned to Deborah with gratitude. "Thank ye, My Lady. Yer Father-in-law is very magnetic and most attractive as well, I have always thought so. I hope my saying so is not offending ye."

"Not at all, my dear," Deborah laughed, pouring more wine for the both of them. "What ye are experiencing happened to me as well, when Erinn first made his interest in me known to his father. Drake tried seducing me, more than once, in an attempt to ascertain whether my love for Erinn was real or contrived. 'Twas very interesting to see him work so hard, for little reward. I simply told him he was not the Natanleod I was interested in."

"And he just ceased his pursuit?"

"Of course, he is a man of the Land. When a woman tells him no, he takes that seriously. After that, our relationship became much friendlier, and has continued to mature to this day. He is an amazing individual, his skills are without question, and his abilities are without limit, or so it appears. I admire him a great deal."

"He says similar things about ye," Brianna pointed out.

"Does he?" Deborah smiled, laughing softly. "He is very kind to do so. To have someone of his great achievement and accomplishment pay such compliments is a humbling matter in every way. However, ye will need a bit of instruction and coaching to avoid the pitfalls he intends to put in yer way. He would mean no harm to ye, of course, his intent would be only to ascertain yer fitness to join the House. However, since he likes ye a great deal already and has spoken endlessly about yer coming marriage to

Arthfael, ye have little to worry over. If ye just continue to act naturally around him, just be who ye truly are, ye will come to no harm from his probing. If it becomes overly pervasive, ye know how to deal with it. Ye are an Amazon, just tell him to leave off."

Brianna's eyes opened wide at Deborah's counseling, and then a smile spread slowly over the young woman's face. "I see! He means to test my mettle as surely as if we were in the arena then?"

"Aye, and ye can show no weakness in this regard, my dear. Treat him as ye would any man."

"I shall!" Brianna declared, a determined expression appearing on her face. Deborah hid a smile, meaning to speak with Drake later about the entire matter. She wanted to make her thoughts clear to both the High Lord and his ascended Father about how she felt concerning Arthfael's coming courting of Brianna.

The day continued forward; bright, clear and warm, lifting people's spirits as the sun continued its journey across the sky. At the family house in Dragon Valley, the guardian Knights broke out their instruments to play happy tunes meant to set toes tapping. It did not take long for Erinn to invite Deborah out onto the dancing square, and soon Arthfael and Brianna followed suit. Drake watched with interest, noting that the young couple moved well together, seeming to perform the steps and spins in good harmony. On the next set, he asked Deborah to join him in a stately tune, meant to allow folks to regain the natural rhythm of their breathing.

"As always, my dear, ye are most graceful and skilled on the dance floor," Drake complimented as he guided her through a complicated series of footwork.

"Thank ye Father," she answered with a soft laugh. "Are ye practicing in anticipation yer next set with Brianna?"

"Practicing?" he snorted with humor. "I have been dancing for a great many years, my dear. I hardly need to practice."

"How much dancing do ye get to do in the higher realms?" Deborah asked innocently, smiling wide as she did so. "After all, ye have no assigned tasks, no usual schedule relegated to ye. Ye can do as ye please, as long as the Lady has no work for ye. Is that not so?"

"Ye know I cannot discuss my life in the Ascended realms, my dear," Drake responded with a sarcastic laugh. "But if anyone would understand how life is there, 'twould be someone like ye."

"I wish ye would cease these cryptic comments Father," Deborah spoke forthrightly, knowing Drake preferred it that way. "I have plenty to occupy my mind, I need no unsolvable puzzle to keep it working. I shall continue however, to consider all of the remarks ye have hidden within our conversations. I hope someday ye will be able to help me make sense of them."

"I hope so too, my dear," Drake replied, his voice taking on a very intense tone. "I wish only the best for ye and Erinn. I would do everything in my power to keep ye from harm."

"From what harm?" Deborah inquired, then laughed. "Ye cannot answer, I know. I shall try not to drop hidden questions in my speech with ye."

"I shall try to do the same, despite my every instinct to continue," Drake told her. "I truly look upon ye as a *Daughter of the House*, a circumstance I find to be remarkably agreeable. I never thought to have a son, and after I knew Erinn was mine, I hoped he would find someone true of heart. Goddess bless me, he did," Drake finished, a tear running from the corner of his eye.

"O, Father!" Deborah said softly, offering him a handkerchief. "I love ye too."

"See, ye know what I am trying to say, even though sometimes I do not express myself well," Drake chuckled wryly, dabbing the water from his eyes. "What am I about?" he questioned, chuckling harder at his own foible. "Today is the Solstice, a happy day! I love this day, and I shall allow myself to enjoy it! What say ye, Daughter, will ye join me in another pipe?"

"Gladly Father," Deborah smiled, embracing him.

The day grew warmer all over the Land, even up as high as Tarana's district. The people happily shed the heavy woolen garb usually necessary to be comfortable at such heights, donning lighter more colorful clothing in its place. In the Forestry District, the Druids tending the trees walked among them, thanking them for their shelter, and the lumber necessary to build.

Out in the Grasslands Distract, Cadoc celebrated with his people at the new location of his fortress, where water ran in plenty and the sound of the waterfall filled his house. He stood with Nathan on his party grounds, watching the people celebrate, while talking with the Druid innkeeper.

"How goes the building?"

"Very well. Yer people work hard, I often have to make them cease their labors when the day is done. With such industry, surely we will finish the inn before next Spring, right on schedule. Yer blessed Father Lord Inglin, would be so pleased, at least I think so from what I remember of him."

"I think ye are right. He fought very hard against the Nagas alone for so many years. I know that when "The Commander" of the Black Dragons came to him and offered aid, he was most grateful. He also told me it was weeks before he realized he was dealing with Drake Natanleod, so complete was the disguising glamour he wore. I remember Father pulling an aged flask of whiskey from the cabinet one day after the Dragons had departed our district, and muttering to himself that he "should have known," all along that Drake was not dead. Raad's laziness and apathy certainly worked against him in that regard, he simply never ascertained the truth, nor did he seek Drake's corpse."

"A foolish decision," Nathan pronounced as he enjoyed the wine from Cadoc's grapes. "Someone like Drake Natanleod should never be discounted, nor underestimated. His resourcefulness and abilities alone would mark him as someone who posed a great danger to anyone else's rule. Raad was a fool. Allying with Secundus only proved that, as the second son of Julius was consumed by his lust to rule. Secundus would have just let him do all the work of the war, then he would have taken him captive and fed him to the Nagas, assuming the High Seat for himself. I think Julius saw all of that on the horizon when he took up Drake's training in the family arts."

"It could be, Julius was known as a man of vision and prophecy," Cadoc nodded. "I only know I am grateful to be a friend of the Natanleods, and the beneficiary of their patronage."

"As we all should be," Nathan sighed. "If the war had gone the other way…"

"We would not be having this conversation," Cadoc smiled faintly. "Come my friend, let us change the subject. Today is the Solstice, a happy day!"

All over the Land that day, and through the next, the people offered their thanks and reverence to the Goddess who sponsored them. Feasts were prepared, tents were set up, extended families gathered from far and wide and everyone stayed up late into the nights. Stories were told, the old tales of the Crossing and the establishment of the Land, of the War with the Nagas and how Drake secured victory with the Lady's help. Songs were sung, dancing music played and courtships were begun as well during the two days of the Solstice celebration.

At the High Lord's house in the Capitol city, the holiday dawned bright and clear. Millicent gave instructions that the outdoor kitchen should be prepared for use, that the dancing floor should be set up and that the regular musicians be called for. She and Gwendolyn supervised the preparation of a grand meal, all self-served from a line, of which the entire

House came to partake. Everyone was in good spirits, and when the aged Amazon Commander Ashara appeared in the midst of the party, Millicent saw to it she was quickly installed into a guest room.

"Thank ye, Madam Millicent, but the barracks would do," she smiled warmly.

"Nonsense! Ye are retired, ye belong in the House, not in the Barracks. I must ask, what brings ye home?"

"I have had a most startling series of dreams, in which the High Lord asked me to return," Ashara told her without blinking. "I had the same dream for many nights in a row."

"When ye say the High Lord, are ye speaking of Erinn?" Millicent queried.

"Nay, 'twas Drake," Ashara nearly whispered. "He appeared right in front of me. I can only think 'twas a dream, for he is departed from the Land, aye?"

"He is Ascended, Sister," Millicent comforted her, slipping an arm around her shoulders. "He may come and go as the Lady chooses."

"So, 'twas not a dream after all," Ashara breathed. "He was really in my room, asking for me to be here. What has happened to Brianna?"

"Dame Brianna?" Millicent asked, casting her mind over the name and coming up with the correct image. "She is with the High Lord on patrol of the Land. I believe they are taking the day at the family house, under Dragon Mountain."

"I see," Ashara mused. "I must go there at once!" she announced. "Can ye help me?"

"I can," Millicent smiled warmly. "Remember, ye will feel the bite of intense cold as ye travel quickly."

"As I recall, that house has a fine bath, with plenty of hot water," Ashara chuckled. "If I am needed, I should be about the Lady's business," she continued.

"Ye are like Drake, admiring of alacrity in every way."

"I have seen the effects of apathy," Ashara reminded her with a sigh. "I adopted the attitude of getting things done quickly very early in my life. My Commander, Laegarda, insisted on alacrity and did not mind backing up her orders with physical persuasion if necessary. Her cane was always tapping at my feet to get me moving. Up 'till she took me on as her squire I always thought that she just carried that thing for show."

"Not entirely," Gwendolyn put in at that moment, bringing Ashara a cup of wine and a snack. "Laegarda had a short leg on the left side, and usually wore a boot to compensate for it. However, 'twas uncomfortable to wear for long periods and so she would occasionally walk bare of foot. She needed the cane then, for certain. She learned to use it as an offensive weapon. On her last day I watched as she was deprived of her blades, then used that cane to kill several Naga priests with it before they overcame her and slew her. Jovita picked up the banner then, and assumed command, as we all knew she had been trained to do and we won the day. I think that Raad gained another scar because of their close encounter during the battle, right over the eyes. 'Twould have been just like Laegarda to train Jovita to cut a man over the eyes, so that the blood would run down into them, which stings like mad. 'Tis often just enough to allow a woman to either escape, or slay her attacker, and Jovita certainly used it several times that day!"

"I remember that!" Ashara smiled. "Come Sister, send me to Brianna. I think she needs me."

"I think ye are right," Millicent smiled. Putting aside her cup, she summoned her abilities and opened just the right-sized portal for the older woman to walk through, closing it behind her when she appeared on the other side.

"Commander!" Drake greeted happily, truly glad to see her. "To what do we owe the pleasure of yer company?"

"I have come to celebrate the day with ye, My Lord," Ashara smiled, bowing a bit. "Ye have summoned me, after all."

"Indeed I have," Drake grinned, handing her a full pipe of fragrant Herb. "The young Dame is in need of yer counsel, she was attacked by a fellow trooper on this patrol. While he has been dealt with by the Goddess, Brianna's condition is safe, thanks to my daughter in law's skill as an herb wife. She needs someone to talk to that she truly trusts, and I could think of no one more suited to that role. I shall have the Captain's quarters vacated for ye, so that ye will be comfortable."

"No need, I am not in command," Ashara grinned. "I shall be quite comfortable in one of the bunks, if I can sleep on the bottom.

"Nonsense, ye will take the fourth bedroom upstairs!" Deborah's voice entered the conversation, leaving no room for argument. "Ye are our guest, Dame Ashara. May I call ye Sister?"

"I would be honored, Sister," Ashara chuckled. "I need some wine."

"Come with me then," Deborah laughed, offering an arm to the older woman. It did not take long for the older woman to be served, then take upstairs and persuaded to change her warrior clothing for something more comfortable and cooler. Deborah helped her don one of her signature sun dresses, adopting the classic way of twining it about the body and tying it in place.

"Ye look well, Sister!" Deborah remarked, walking about the older woman as she finished tucking in the tied ends. "I wish ye could teach that to some of the younger women."

"One either has the knack of it or not," Ashara sighed. "I can do it, but my trainer could not. I ended up helping her dress for warmer weather every year. I am an expert at this!" she laughed, sipping her wine a bit before sobering. "Is Brianna well?"

"Aye, she is, and free of any encumbrance due to her encounter with Titan," Deborah assured her without missing a beat. "I attended to the matter personally, she will be well."

"She is very special," Ashara replied intensely. "When she came to me, she got down on her knees and begged for my help. We talked for hours about her attitude and her abilities, and then I took her into the ring for a good trial. After two hours, I agreed to help her. She is magick with a blade, Madam, I have never seen anyone with better control or more precise hits. She could be a Commander if she settles down and continues on with the life I showed her was possible."

"Ye are that impressed with her?"

"She is fierce and strong, her heart is that of a lioness, My Lady!" Ashara declared. "Have ye taken her on a hunt?"

"Nay, but perhaps I should," Deborah mused. "I think I might be in the mood for game birds tomorrow. Perhaps the young Dame might join me on the hunt?" she thought out loud.

"Take her along, ye will not be disappointed," Ashara urged. "If I could go too, I would, but my old bones will not let me trudge over hill and dale in search of prey anymore."

"Thank ye for the recommendation," Deborah smiled. "But, we have discussed business long enough. Ye have come to celebrate with us!"

"I have indeed, Madam. Happy Solstice," the older woman grinned and lifted her cup to tap Deborah's.

Throughout that night, Arthfael hovered close to Brianna, trying not to but unable to help himself. He was truly drawn to her as a moth to her flame, he simply wished to talk with her as often as possible. Finally, Erinn walked to his side and asked for his son to walk with him, just to give the young woman a moment. Timing his talk with Arthfael to coincide with Ashara taking Brianna aside for a private talk, Erinn counseled his son.

"My son, do ye recall our talk about how best to approach yer pursuit of Brianna?" he asked quietly as they walked away from where she stood with Ashara, Arthfael glancing back over his shoulder as they did so.

"What?"

"Do ye recall our talk about how to best court the Amazon?" Erinn reiterated, in a stronger tone. Arthfael was momentarily reminded of Drake in both expression and tone, and it brought him out of his distraction.

"What? Aye, ye said not to hover around her," Arthfael answered, then immediately, the young man blanched. "O dear. I have been doing just that."

"Aye, which is why I wanted ye to walk with me," Erinn chuckled. "Let her breathe, boyo."

"I do not wish to push her away," Arthfael answered intensely.

"Then back away yerself, and give her room to breathe. Let her have time to think and speak for herself, ye are dominating all conversation with her every time ye are around her. My son, she is reaching out for yer Mother's counsel, I think 'twould be best to allow it to happen, aye? Especially in light of recent events?"

"O, ye are right," Arthfael sighed despondently. "This courting business is complicated."

"Of course 'tis, but how else to show a woman ye are truly interested?" Erinn asked in return, offering a pipe to the young man to help ease his distress. Afterward, he clipped two small sikars and they sat on the porch to smoke them, enjoying the quiet, warm day. As he sat there smoking and sipping the delicious ale in his cup, Arthfael suddenly had a realization. He had all the time he needed to court Brianna, there was no need to hurry. A chuckle escaped him and he turned to Erinn, a look of wonder on his face.

"Father, thank ye for this lesson," he said quietly, not wanting to break the mood of the moment. "I shall remember that I need to take a pause from time to time, just to consider. Smoking a short sikar like this one provides just such a moment."

"I find it relaxing, and helpful if I need to think," Erinn replied simply. "The Lady provided a blessing when She brought tabac into the Land. Which reminds me, I need to go out to the new tabac farm to see how our new venture is proceeding. Perhaps ye would like to accompany me there on a side trip, as we return to the Capitol this Autumn after our work in the desert?"

"I would indeed, Father!" Arthfael agreed enthusiastically.

"Good, 'tis time ye begin learning the business of ruling. 'Tis important that ye do, in case yer brother decides not to return to us."

"Do ye think he would not?"

"I know not what my son is capable of at the moment. He caught me completely off guard by following Ishmael into the desert," Erinn admitted without hesitation. He was not overly proud of his intelligence, unlike past High Lords of the family, and was more than willing to admit mistakes when he made them. "I had to alter my entire vision of the future within days of his departure, and I am still refining it as time goes forward. Ye have responded very well to the entire situation, despite losing yer way early on in yer relationship with Tiamat. I noted ye have not done so with Brianna, ye are not obsessed with her."

"I agree," Arthfael nodded. "I feel the same intensity of emotion, but without the obsessive part. 'Tis enough for me to spend what time is contrived for us, rather than continually being depressed when we are separated."

"I feel that way about yer Mother," Erinn told him truthfully. "I never get to spend enough time with her, but we make our off-time as pleasant as possible. When we can contrive for privacy, 'tis like a Mother's Holiday for us."

"I can see that now in my relationship with Brianna," Arthfael smiled faintly. "I feel as though we never have enough time together, and I look forward daily to our talks and walks. I always feel better afterwards, as if I have learned something more about her."

"Ye have," Erinn chuckled. "Come on, we should return to the others. We would not want them to come looking for us."

"Why not?" Arthfael asked innocently. For his answer, Erinn simply embraced his son by the shoulders, slipping an arm around them as they walked back to where the others were now gathering to hear Deborah tell a tale.

While Deborah told her tale, Ashara listened as Brianna spoke her heart about everything that had transpired during her travels with the High Lord. As she related the attack by Titan, she found herself feeling very composed and distant from it, as if it had happened to someone else. Ashara watched her face as the realization dawned on the young woman that she had passed through a heavy trial and gained maturity as a result.

"O! I remember when you told me that someday I might be able to see hurtful incidents as something to be learned from! I think I have done that with this entire thing about Titan! I feel as if I am looking at it from the outside, as if it had happened to someone else!"

"Ye see?" Ashara chuckled, embracing her firmly, feeling as if she were a dear auntie to the young woman. "Ye are gaining maturity at last, because ye have learned to be introspective. Ye understand that incidents like this simply happen to help one deal with fears from past lives, or from this life. Consider this thought, ye will no longer fear being mishandled by a man and any man who would consider attacking ye should pause and think again. Yer totem is the lioness, embrace Sehkmet's influence in yer life."

"I shall, Commander Ashara! I see yer words as the Goddess' work!" Brianna vowed sincerely, embracing the older woman again. When Arthfael and Erinn rejoined the crowd, she went directly to his side and pulled him off for a private talk. Ashara watched, sipping her wine, wearing a look of satisfaction on her face. At last, she thought, Brianna has accepted who and what she is. 'Tis about time, she chuckled to herself as Drake filled her cup once more.

"Is she well?" Drake asked quietly.

"Brianna? O aye, she is quite well. Ye should expect to see her rise like a lioness from this point on. Ye know, she is like Sekhmet. She has a fiery nature, and is fierce in her passions. And she talks about yer grandson a great deal."

"Does she?" Drake grinned a bit, handing Ashara a sikar. "They do seem to enjoy each other's company a great deal," he remarked.

"I see that as something good," Ashara commented. "She has been alone most of her life, and knows very little about how to express her emotions. Her reticent nature is not unlike Prince Arthfael's, as I see it."

"They have found common ground to talk," Drake answered softly. "Such an occurrence is always the first step towards friendship."

"Friendship is more important than love," Ashara observed.

Drake simply chuckled and offered the older woman a fond embrace, for he saw her as a friend and swordsister in every way, making sure she had a full cup until she refused more.

As the people gathered around bonfires that night to hear their local storytellers, a pair of men washed up on the southern beaches of the Land, just a mile or so away from Erasmus' port city. They did not know each other, nor did they even see each other as one went directly to the city, while the other stood on the beach assessing his surroundings. From what he could see, the shoreline was rich with life; fruit trees swayed in the breeze, laden with their burdens. He recognized pomegranates, oranges, lemons and limes, as well as mangos, papayas and bananas. After many days floating among the ruins of the ship transporting him from Acre to Constantinople, he was hungry for the taste of the fruit and so helped himself to the plenty until he could eat no more. A stream bubbled close by, offering fresh water to ease his thirst and he drank deeply, noting the sweet taste of the water.

"I have reached a paradise of sorts!" he thought to himself. "I can see no signs of civilization here, perhaps if there are people, they are the simple type. I might be able to set myself up rather well, if they will accept my story as truth. Let us see if my persuasive skills are still intact," he laughed himself. Making his way off the beach, finding game paths and other tracks through the dense tropical forest, he soon gained one of the main roads on which patrols of Knights and Dames toured the Land. The road was broad and flat, paved with good stone, like the roads around Rome. Much effort and organization had gone into the project, he thought as he walked along, finding the way easy. He wondered just how intelligent the citizens of such a place would be, and then laughed to himself. He had executed his schemes in the heart of Roman influence without detection or punishment, and so he thought himself quite clever with his ability to lie and deceive.

He had not counted on the Lady of the Land however, as most of the folk in the Land were quite capable of discerning the truth of people's words. However, due to his ego, he missed the signs that would usually indicate that his lies were not being believed, right from the very first village he entered. He found the square in the center and stood within it, making his first announcement of opportunity through employment.

"I mean to purchase the largest tract of land available hereabouts," he called out to the gathered crowd, who could hear the lie in his words. However, it was against the Lady's Law to do harm if no harm was being done, and since everyone knew he was lying, they saw no harm in allowing him to continue. Most of them thought he was diseased somehow, and so sent for their village healer to tend him. The man, whose name was Liam, shook off their help, explaining he was not ill.

"I am not sick!" he shouted at them when they came with their bags and tinctures. "I am offering ye all employment and riches!"

"We have all we need," the village leader told him with a gentle smile. "If ye persuade the High Lord to grant the plot to ye, we will be good neighbors for ye. 'Tis no need for strident words or shouting, good brother. We have called the Healers to tend ye, ye are clearly not of the Land and are feeling ill."

"I feel fine!" the man said. "I do not need such help. If ye are not interested in my offer, I shall simply take it to the next village. Good day!" he said in a haughty tone, shaking off the concerned hands of the healers and walking away quickly.

"Poor man, he is not well," the eldest of them murmured. "Insisting on lying like that just shows how ill he is. We should contact the High Lord at once, and inform him that someone from outside the Land is wandering about telling mistruths. We must keep him from doing any harm."

"If those are the worst lies he can tell, he poses little danger to anyone," the village headwoman laughed aloud. "Goodness, what blatant falsehoods he was spouting! Are they so ignorant outside of our borders that they cannot hear such lies?"

Liam continued on his way for weeks, telling the same tale at each village and finding their reactions to it infuriatingly helpful. At each village, healers were called to attend him, even though he insisted he was completely well. He managed to escape them each time, thinking himself fortunate in every instance, not knowing that they could help him be free of his mercenary and lying ways.

Finally, he found himself at Cadoc's capitol in the Grasslands District, where he took a position in the market square and made his pitch to those who would listen. Laughter erupted from the crowd when he finished, and everyone came to congratulate him on the wonderful joke he had involved them all in.

"I am not joking!" he screamed out at length. "I am deadly serious! What is the matter with all of ye? Do ye not like wealth?"

"We have all we need, and to take more would be harmful," the magistrate told him when he was brought before her. "I do not wish to trouble My Lord Cadoc with this, as ye are clearly a liar. Ye will leave our city at once. Knights of Cadoc, come and escort this man out of our District! Take him to the High Lord, at once!"

"High Lord?" Liam objected, his voice breaking a bit now that he was caught and fear was setting in. "I have done no crime!"

"Ah, but you have," the Magistrate Colleen replied in a serious tone. "Ye have been traveling about the Land, telling all manner of lies in an effort to deceive folk into giving ye gold in large amounts."

"But…how…"

"When ye floated onto the beach below the Port City, ye left behind yer world, and entered ours. Ye have come to a place where lying is considered a terrible crime, for all the harm it does. When a person lies, they cannot be trusted. How can we all live together in harmony without trust? Aye, ye must be taken to the High Lord's house to await his disposition. I shall write a report, and suggest that the severity of yer crime be dealt with empathy, since ye are not of the Land."

"The Land?" the man cried out, now in much distress. "What are ye talking about? 'Tis only one world, the one we live on!"

"O my goodness, they do not teach spiritual truths very well in yer world, do they?" the Magistrate laughed a bit. "Knights of the Land, ye should restrain him, for yer own safety. A liar cannot be trusted, everyone knows that."

"Aye, Madam Colleen!" the Captain of the group agreed, taking a pair of light manacles out of his pocket and walking to Liam's side. "Stand easy and ye will not be harmed. I am using steel manacles, not the iron ones unless ye prove ye need them. If ye will extend yer arms, so I might simply put them on, all will be well."

"I am not letting ye put those on me!" Liam screamed, having been chained up many times. He had never experienced the light weight of steel, he only knew cruel and filthy iron restraints. He had seen fellow prisoners die while shackled with iron as something about the metal poisoned people's blood and they died in great pain.

"Very well, if ye will not simply allow it, ye will be forced for the good of all. Brothers, if ye would please restrain him?" he called to his group and they fell upon Liam, quickly subduing him sufficiently to allow the Captain to fasten the restraints in place. Once they were on, the Knights released him and put him back on his feet, stepping away into formation. Liam snapped the chain between his wrists tightly and swiftly, thinking there might be a weak link. He found however, the manacles were in good repair and held him easily. They were much more comfortable, he noted, than any he had ever worn before, and so he relaxed a bit, thinking this experience might actually be different. Perhaps this ruler might be susceptible to his gilded tongue, as so many others had been in the past. How the Magistrate knew that he was lying mystified him, but he pushed that aside and concentrated only on surviving the experience to come. Once he was properly restrained a horse was brought for him and he was ordered to climb aboard, which he managed at length. It was a good thing the horse was well trained, for the man had no skills and was barely able to keep himself in the saddle. At length, one of the Knights simply climbed up behind him and took over the reins, for which Liam was very grateful. They stopped that night before the sun went down to make camp by a flowing stream, a small hot spring steaming beside it. They allowed Liam to use the thing first, since he felt the most pain from the day on horseback, but a guard was placed close by to remind him of his status. Several days later, they arrived in the Capitol city, taking Liam directly to Ulric for disposition.

"So, ye cannot be trusted to tell the truth," Ulric mused aloud, reading Colleen's report. "Such is a very serious crime here in the Land. Ye must be from outside not to know this," he continued, glancing up and making eye contact with Liam. The Outlander squirmed a bit under his assessment, feeling as if Ulric were looking into his very soul. "Very well, ye will await the High Lady's word on the matter. I shall take yer case to her at once, and she may wish to see and talk with ye. I would caution against practicing deception with her."

"What is the matter with all of ye?" Liam asked softly, still not understanding his situation. "I am simply a common business person, pursuing my business in the usual way. Ye are acting as if I have done some great crime, which is hypocrisy at best. No one tells the truth, not even the Pope."

"I see the Magistrate's assessment of ye is entirely correct," Ulric sighed. "Ye feel completely at ease with yer mistruths, and think everyone practices the same evil. Ye are clearly not of the Land, and here by error. I am certain the High Lady will right the situation as soon as she talks to ye. I would advise being truthful with her, she is impatient with liars and manipulators."

"She is a woman, a natural liar," the man proclaimed, earning himself a slap across the face from the War Duke. Liam fell to the ground, a huge red mark slowly forming where Ulric had struck him.

"We do not talk about our women that way," he growled. "Especially the High Lady whose reputation is without stain or blemish. Of all the people in the world who should not point fingers at someone accusingly, I am astonished at yer own hypocrisy! Come, I am tired of talking to ye already. The sooner ye are out of the Land, the better. I feel dirty just standing next to ye," Ulric remarked, shuddering visibly. Liam said nothing, after all, he thought Ulric and everyone else he had met so far were insane. He wanted to escape this place, even floating out on the ocean would be better than being around such strange and frightening folk. He did not resist as Ulric took him in charge, the escorting Knights handing him the key to Liam's manacles before departing the War Duke's office. In return, Ulric called for his squire to find quarters for the men, so they could remain overnight.

"Thank ye, My Lord War Duke!" Cadoc's Knights said gratefully. "The ride here was a long one, with such a fabulous liar along. None of us slept very well."

"Ye are most welcome, and thank ye for yer service, gentlemen," Ulric responded before turning to Liam. "Ye, come with me at once. We will get this over with before Supper. Ye might have a long trip ahead of ye tonight."

"Where?"

"Back to the port city, and onto a ship leaving the Land, if the High Lady is in a forgiving mood," Ulric told him seriously. "If she is not, 'twill be all the worse for ye. Hurry up, my wife is waiting supper for me. I would not wish to make her wait."

"Ye are all insane!" Liam shouted, finally at the end of his patience. "No one is so severely punished for a simple mistruth!"

"In the Land they are," Ulric responded in a grouchy tone, pushing him in front of him. "Move yer ass, today has been a long day."

Liam did not dispute Ulric's orders, especially in light of the look on his face and he nearly ran down the hallway, fearful of what might happen to him otherwise. Ulric's grin could barely be contained, the man was craven and cowardly in all regards. How else to explain his constant lying, he wondered. Finally, they reached the main floor, where Deborah stood just outside the kitchen talking with Reeves. It was all concerning what she wanted done while she was gone, escorting Olga and her husband Hodor to their new land grant.

"My Lady!" Ulric called. "If I may intrude, we have a matter of dispensation to deal with here."

"O?" Deborah asked, turning to regard the War Duke and his prisoner. She could see the dark aura around Liam clearly as he walked towards her, and was on guard.

"Aye, My Lady. This man has been attempting to deceive people and manipulate them into giving him their gold or labor, according to Magistrate Colleen of the Grasslands District. Within her report, she remarks that he is a fantastic liar of epic proportion."

Deborah frowned, she despised liars and thieves. "Is this so?" she asked Liam, turning her grey eyes upon him in an assessing manner. "I should warn that like most people in the Land, I can hear any lie ye are telling. Unlike most however, I can hear yer thought process too, and I feel the evil within ye. Remember that as ye answer."

"Ye are all insane!" Liam blurted, unable to hold it back. "I want to leave this place as soon as possible, before I go mad! Let me go, at once!"

"Very well then, if such is yer desire," Deborah answered, a cold smile on her face, for she could feel his malice growing. "My Lord War Duke, arrange escort for this man back to the Port City, and see to it he is put on the first ship that has proper quarters for a criminal such as him. I want him gone from our shores before morning."

"Aye, My Lady," Ulric nodded, glad the man was leaving, for Liam's malcontent was now affecting him. "Come then maggot, we must return to the Barracks, where I shall arrange yer passage back to the port."

"Maggot?" the man objected in a hoarse tone.

"Ye are a criminal in the Land, having been named so by the High Lady. Ye should be accorded no other name," Ulric growled, dragging him down the stairs most ungently. When he walked through the common area, he saw part of the Phoenix Guard standing there and a smile crossed his face.

"Excuse me, Sub-Captain," he called out. An older woman turned, and Ulric realized that the Goddess was at work, for the woman was one who had suffered under Secundus' torture and survived.

"Dame Lillian, are ye and yer group assigned to a task at the moment?" he asked.

"Nay, My Lord War Duke," the woman answered in a quiet, but stern tone. "What service might we be?"

"This man has been exiled for his lying ways. The High Lady has ordered him taken to the port city and put on the first ship leaving the Land. Would ye provide him proper escort?" he asked, humor evident in his tone.

"Of course, My Lord," Lillian answered, and now Ulric noted that her tone was more feral than before. "I would be happy to assure that such a criminal is exiled from the Land. May I take a few sisters along with me, just to assure he arrives quickly?"

"Of course, assemble what force ye wish," Ulric grinned. "Be sure ye requisition proper traveling supplies. Ye will be camping out, most likely."

"We will also find shelter in a guardhouse or two along the way," Lillian answered. "I look forward to visiting with long absent sisters and brothers."

"Excellent, so it serves everyone's purpose. I see the Lady's Hand in it all then. Depart as soon as ye have assembled."

"My Lord, what is the man's status?" Lillian asked quietly.

"If ye mean to ask if he is a slave, ye know well that slavery is forbidden here in the Land."

"So he is to be simply put on a ship? What of the gold for his passage? How shall that be acquired?"

"Dame, he is a condemned liar and a potential thief. As such, he has no legal status in the Land, except as a criminal. Criminals have no rights whatsoever, except to their proper punishment."

"Aye, My Lord!" Lillian answered, offering the proper salute. "Thank ye, My Lord, for clarifying his situation for me," she grinned in a most mercenary fashion. "Come maggot, the Port City awaits ye. Steel yerself, yer fate will not be the easiest one," she laughed.

"What are ye talking about?" Liam asked in confusion. "I simply wish to leave this insane country, and all of the crazy people living here!"

"Come then, we will arrange for that," Lillian told him, taking him in hand without removing the manacles.

"Remove these restraints, I insist!" Liam demanded, earning a hard slap across his face for his trouble.

"Silence, Criminal! Ye have no right to insist upon anything," she chuckled. Liam was shocked into muteness as she attached a collar and leash to him, then simply led him away as if he were property.

Five days later, as the sun set, Lillian and her troupe of Amazons arrived at the gate of the Port city, with their captive in tow. Lillian had enforced this upon him, due to his constant griping and complaining initially. Liam had even attempted escape, finding himself quickly and easily captured by the experienced Amazon. He could barely walk due to his weariness, for that day, Lillian had simply tied a rope to his collar and made him walk or run behind her horse. He could barely stand, which made him easy to deal with in every way.

"Ho there, who approaches the city of Erasmus?" the gate guard called out.

"I am Dame Lillian and these are my troupe!" she called back. "Tell me, is there a sale proceeding at the dock?"

"As a matter of circumstance, ye have arrived on a most fortuitous day!" the man laughed, looking at the wretched man behind her. "Ye have a captive, I see."

"Aye. He is a criminal, a fantastic liar and manipulator. The War Duke has given orders he is to be put on the first ship leaving. He has no rights whatsoever."

"Come then, and let me take ye to the ship where the sale is happening," the man laughed. "My shift is over for the day."

The man took them directly to a huge, three-masted ship with two levels of gun decks. As they approached, they could hear the auctioneer's voice, calling for bids.

"Ye cannot sell me!" Liam screamed out, suddenly aware of their intent. "I am a free man!"

"Ye gave that up when ye began lying in the Land before ye knew the Law," Lillian responded shortly. "No one gave ye permission to speak!" she went on, slapping him hard across the face.

"Hmm...a feisty one," the man escorting them noted. His name was Longines, and he recognized the Amazon in front of him, very well. "Come, the Captain holding the sale might purchase this one for herself."

"Noooo!!!" Liam moaned out as he was led along, fighting the leash the entire time. Nonetheless, he was led up the ramp and onto the deck of the huge ship, where the auctioneer noted him at once.

"Ah! We have a new piece of flesh to sell!" he called out with a laughing tone. "This one has not been a slave very long, has he?"

"Nay, he has been a free person up 'till now!" Lillian called back, her tone rich with humor. "However, his new master or mistress should know he is an epic liar!"

"Ah, but he will not be for long, I think!" she heard and a large, handsome, dandified man of Iberian blood stepped forth. "My goodness, what a handsome slave! He looks perfect for my ship. I even have room for him close to me. How much do ye want for him?"

"He is untrained," Lillian told him. "Let the auctioneer sell him!"

Liam was unceremoniously led up to the block, his rags were stripped from him and he was sold completely naked, except for the collar he wore. When the sale was complete, the Iberian captain had won a new slave and Lillian had a huge bag of gold in her hands. She watched as the ship cast off, and heard the first round of instructive punishment handed out to the slave on board before turning to her companions.

"Well sisters, it appears we shall be staying the night!" she laughed. "Perhaps we could seek rooms at the guardhouse?"

"Come, we have extra rooms aplenty!" Longines told her. It did not take them long to walk from the dock to the guardhouse, and soon they were all escorted to the guest rooms and invited to remain for supper. Longines, however, went to Lillian with a special request.

"Excuse me, Dame," he began carefully.

"Aye?" she asked, turning her deep green eyes upon him.

"Yer name is Lillian, aye?"

"Aye, how would ye know that?"

"Ye were at Secundus' fortress," he ventured in a quiet voice.

"Aye, what of it?"

"I was there the day Drake led the Army up the mountain to Raad's fortress to liberate the Amazons. I watched them bring ye out of Secundus' chambers. Madam, after ye were taken in hand by the Healers, several of us ventured into what remained of Secundus' chambers before the fire took it all. I still burn with anger and shame at what we saw in there, the whipping frame, the manacles on the wall, and the rape bed on the floor. What ye endured from him should not have been done to any woman, anyone," he continued, shuddering openly. Lillian could say nothing, she had long ago let go of all of the memories and pain of those days. To hear Longines describe the room where she had suffered being the object of a sorcerer's "affections" brought back thoughts long ago put aside. "I always hoped that ye and I would meet again under friendly circumstances, Madam," he continued cautiously, seeing that she was listening to him. "If ye will come upstairs to my room, I have two steaks and a half cask of very special red wine to share with ye. The view from my room is quite spectacular, and includes sights of the harbor not usually seen. The view from my window is better than My Lord Erasmus' in my opinion."

Lillian's face creased into a small smile, and she walked around him slowly, assessing his form, coming back to face him toe to toe. "A view better than Master Erasmus' own? Such a sight should be quite an experience."

"I hope so Madam," Longines smiled, seeing her fall into the word game with him. "I keep the windows in my room very clean, so that the salt spray does not impede watching the waves. As well, my room has a separate suite. Ye need not sleep on the sofa if ye choose not to, if I may be so bold as to suggest. I would enjoy spending time talking with such a wise and experienced swordsister."

"And this view cannot be experienced in any other room?" Lillian inquired, the smile remaining on her handsome face.

"Nay, Madam. The sights from my room are quite unique, especially after the sun sets and the stars can be seen. I have a lovely extension outside my windows, where I like to sit and smoke a sikar. I often cook out there, if the weather permits, and sometimes, I even sleep out there to enjoy the cool of the breeze on a hot Summer's night."

"Intriguing," Lillian remarked. "Very well, I shall accept yer invitation after I enjoy a bath and a change of clothing."

"I have a marble tub in my room that ye are most welcome to use," Longines offered, extending his hand. She took it, running her hand up his arm and liking the musculature very much. They walked up the stairway to the mid-level, where the Commander's quarters waited and he opened the door for her, inviting her inside. The room was quite spacious, and he had not misled her, she could see the doors of two separate suites facing each other across the space. Between them stood a series of tall, clear, glass windows that she could see were very thick, but the view of the harbor could be clearly seen through them.

"My goodness," she gasped a bit, for the beauty of the view could not be denied. "Ye were right to say that yer view is better than Erasmus'! What a fine room!"

"I am very blessed, Madam," Longines replied, pouring wine for them both and offering her a cup. "I shall go and start yer bath, if ye wish."

"I would like that. The sooner I am clean, the sooner we can talk," she smiled warmly. "I have never bathed in a marble tub before."

"I like the experience," Longines smiled, glad she was there. "The water seems to stay much hotter for much longer, and I can actually soak for an extended period. As a Commander yerself, I am certain ye understand the benefit of doing so. Ye will find a pipe over there in that small drawer, help yerself. I shall return apace," he said warmly, walking to where the huge tub for two stood and turning the tap to allow hot water to begin filling it.

Lillian sipped her wine, enjoyed the pipe and as she did so, the thought of remaining at the Port City for a few days appealed to her. After all, the War Duke had ordered them to bring the slave with alacrity, he had said naught about returning with alacrity. She reckoned they had time to relax a bit, and so allowed herself to do so. Three days later in the morning, she bid Longines a fond farewell privately, then rejoined her troupe for the ride back to the Barracks.

"Ye look relaxed," one of them commented with a grin as she walked to her horse and mounted up.

"I think being by the ocean appeals to me," Lillian remarked coolly. "I am thinking of asking for a transfer to this guardhouse. I have always wanted to live by the ocean, and now might be my opportunity. I have never slept better."

With no further remarks on the subject, Lillian gave the order to move out and they galloped out of the city gates onto the road home. Without the encumbrance of the prisoner, they made better time returning than going. They only camped out one night, rising early and riding late into the night to arrive in two days just before midnight's turn. Lillian wasted no time making her request for transfer, answering in succinct terms when Ulric asked her reason.

"I have found something there I wish to pursue, My Lord."

"Something? Or someone?" Ulric smiled, having already received a report from the guardhouse. "Longines is a good man, I approve of yer choice, if I may be so bold."

"Thank ye, My Lord," Lillian answered simply, without rancor. She knew that rumors flew around the Barracks like the breeze blew through the forest, having been in the Amazons for nearly six decades.

"Do ye need anything?" Ulric asked, nonplussed.

"Just my horse, and what is in my room here, My Lord. I shall begin packing and saying my farewells at once. I wish to return quickly, so as to begin my new term of service. It might be my last one."

"Madam, ye are nearly seventy years of age," Ulric pointed out. "Ye served during the war, and suffered some of the worst humiliations and abuses. If anyone deserves an early retirement, 'twould be ye."

"My lessons were easier than some," Lillian told him, a tear trickling down her face at the memories of those lost. "But Secundus met the fate he had earned, and now his punishment can truly begin."

"Indeed, he has been roasting for many years already, if Fate is just," Ulric grinned.

"Fate is just another of the Lady's personas," Lillian replied seriously. "Thank ye, My Lord, for yer willingness to grant my request. I truly appreciate it."

"Ye have earned every consideration, Madam," Ulric replied, just as seriously. After she left, he quickly penned a letter to Erasmus, informing him of the change of personnel. As well, he briefed the former pirate on Lillian's past service, ending with his personal request.

"She has enough tenure and experience to be a Co-Commander, if Longines will accept it," he finished. "I suggest that since his quarters were originally designed to house a united pair of Commanders that she should be granted her rank upon arrival."

Erasmus, the elderly Lord of the Port City and a former pirate captain himself, loved parties and celebrations of all kinds. Upon receiving the War Duke's missive, he began planning for Lillian's arrival and elevation ceremony without consulting Longines in any wise. The best part of a party, he reckoned, was any positive surprise that could be arranged and so when Lillian rode through the gates several weeks later all was in readiness.

"Greetings Dame Lillian," Longines greeted her personally at the gate on the day of her arrival. "Be ye welcome into the Port City guard."

"Thank ye, Commander. I have my transfer papers with me," she said coolly.

"Good, I admire efficiency," Longines complimented professionally. "If ye will enter the guardhouse, we will get ye settled. Squire, take the Dame's horse to the stable, if ye please?"

"Thank ye Squire," Lillian added to the young woman who came to take her horse in hand. The two entered the guardhouse, where the entire complement of the place waited to welcome their new Co-Commander. Erasmus was with them, and ready for the party afterwards. When Lillian was brought into the common area, they all erupted in applause, and shouts of welcome, for everyone was happy to have such an accomplished woman among them.

"What, what is this?" she asked, turning to Longines.

"The War Duke suggested that ye might agree to share the load of command with me," Longines answered simply. "Ye are free to choose how ye will, but as ye can see, everyone is happy to see ye here."

"Share command?"

"Aye, I have Dames here as well as Knights, and there are certain areas of the city where my men are not welcome to enter. If I have a Dame as a Co-Commander, those difficulties will no longer encumber my duty. Besides," he went on, turning to face her and continuing in a more quiet voice. "The burden of command is a lonely one. I shall be thankful for the Lady's gift of yer presence. I have enjoyed our conversations a great deal."

Lillian looked at him, measuring his words for false intent and finding none. "Ye are serious!"

"I am, and ye need do naught but command, if 'tis yer preference. Ye have yer own room, and ye may keep yer own schedule."

"I accept," she answered without hesitation.

"Good!" he smiled, offering her the grip. "Now we can go on with yer welcoming party, as Lord Erasmus has arranged. I hear he has brought in an entire steer."

"Welcoming party?"

"Ye will find yer new Lord to be a bit of a merrymaker," Longines smiled broadly. "All of us who were redeemed from our lives as pirates by the kindness of the Lady are the same way. I suggest ye simply let yerself enjoy it, ye have certainly earned it."

"I shall take the smaller suite," she replied coolly, changing the subject.

"I have had it cleared, cleaned and redecorated just a bit," he told her. "I hope ye will be comfortable in yer new quarters."

"Thank ye, Commander," she replied a bit uncomfortably, for she had never shared command before.

"Let us establish our forms of address now, in private? Ye will address me as Sir Longines, and I shall refer to ye as Dame Lillian. Will that suffice?"

"I like that," she ventured a smile. "My suggestion is that we meet every morning over caffe and treats before parting for our various daily responsibilities."

"I like that idea, and of course, we should end the day sharing supper too, so as to exchange news of our daily work."

"Agreed!" Lillian smiled.

"Come, let me show ye yer new quarters," he invited, taking her bag off the floor and walking to the door.

Chapter 2

After the incident with Liam, and Lillian's departure, the House readied itself for another leaving. After her return to the Capitol City, Deborah had taken two days to rest up a bit, allowing the patrol extra time to assemble. On the day they left, Deborah's patrol was fully supplied and ready to march before the sun was completely above the tree line. Within the group were Olga and Hodor's family all nestled into a comfortable wagon for the trip. The long train of Knights and Dames, as well as the supply wagons holding food, gear and clothing for the extended patrol followed after them after Deborah opened the portal to allow them a quicker trip to the property granted to the new citizens of the Land. Once through, it was just a few miles to the acreage. It took just a half day to arrive, and when they did, the young family piled out of the wagon to see their new home. Whoops of delight could be heard from the boys when they saw the broad stretch of river flowing through the property and Hodor's pleasure at seeing the rows of trees heavy with fruit could not be mistaken.

"By Thor's beard! Look at those orchards!" he exclaimed at length, coming to stand before Deborah with gratitude and respect. "Ye have granted us a kingly property! Thank ye, we will make it bloom!"

"I hope so, Master Hodor," Deborah smiled at his enthusiasm. "As ye can see, it has lain abandoned for many years and will need much work."

"I and my family will change that!" Hodor vowed, offering an embrace of friendship and respect. Deborah gladly accepted it before turning to the patrol and issuing her orders.

"Make camp my friends, and set up the outdoor kitchen in the best place for it! We will eat and retire early tonight, so we might be up early in the morning to begin our work! Quartermaster, break out the ale and get a keg into that cold water! Foragers, be about yer work, and let us get a few lines into the water as soon as we can? Fresh fish is always a delicious meal!"

"Aye, My Lady!" she heard a reply and looked up to see Aldridge and his group of Druids, come to welcome the family and be of what assistance they could.

"Elder Brother!"

"Younger Sister! 'Tis good to see yer smile, it truly lights the day!"

"My goodness, a fine compliment, Master Druid," Deborah laughed softly, offering an embrace. "Ye have a silver tongue."

"I have been accused of being smooth in my speech, My Lady," he laughed with her as she produced a bundle of small sikars, handing it to him. "Ye would have to ask the women about having a silver tongue," he laughed harder while making the double entendre.

"Master Aldridge!" Deborah cried out in mock-distress, laughing harder as well. "To speak to me in such a way, with my husband not present! I should be embarrassed!"

"Nay, My Lady, 'tis I who must bear the burden of embarrassment. I have clearly overstepped. Forgive my crudeness?"

"I can never be angry with ye, Master Aldridge," she smiled. "I thank ye for bringing yer Druids along, we will need some counsel as to which trees should be cut for the new house. I have boards and nails aplenty for the inside finishing, but the outside must be provided from the trees onsite."

"Is it not fortunate then, that a flood washed over this area several years ago, and a great swath of trees were left standing. They have been slowly curing since then, and should be perfect for the purpose."

"The Lady is truly kind to provide lumber in plenty," Deborah smiled. "Perhaps yer Druids would join the fishing party?" she laughed, indicating the riverbank. As his eyes followed her finger to where the camp was laid out, he was surprised to see many tents already up and that the rest would soon follow. Those whose shelters were ready were down by the river already, stringing long poles and setting bait on hooks, ready to vie for their supper. Deborah took up a seat on the bank just above the line of fishermen, Aldridge by her side, sikars in hand, watching their eager contest. Squires brought buckets to the water's edge, filling them with the cool river water in anticipation of the catch, and it did not take long for the first bite to bend a pole nearly to the water. The fish that rose out of the stream was a huge rainbow trout, and every person holding a pole salivated over catching one like it. Deborah granted the first catch a sikar as she admired the huge fish before it was whisked away to the kitchen to be cleaned and scaled.

The sun slowly sank as they caught more and more fish, some large, some small, but most of them the perfect size for one person's meal, until the cook called out they had sufficient fish for that night. With great reluctance, they all pulled their hooks from the water, whispering a silent thanks to the Lady for the meal and for the pleasure of fishing. That night was merry as they cooked their supper, then sat to eat together, listening to a short tell by Deborah afterwards.

"Good night my friends," she called out after finishing. "I am ready to retire. We have a long day tomorrow, we have many logs to cut and haul up the riverbank. We will use as many of the war horses as necessary to speed along the work, they have all had some training as work horses, aye?"

"Aye, My Lady," Tristan, one of the newer members of the Black Dragons spoke up. Ulric had chosen the man to act as Sub-Captain of the troupe due to his diligence and fortitude, not to mention that he was brilliant with two swords in hand. He was also extremely handsome and well-built, and there had been a few incidents requiring him to be disciplined over his treatment of women when he had been drinking. However, he had put aside drink for an entire six months to prove to Ulric he was not bound to it. He had embarked on a self-improvement campaign as well, attending classes at the Druid Shrine in the area, signing up for a course at the University to study geology, and he had also attended Deborah's cooking classes in the city. Over time he had proven he could be trusted, and women warmed to his clever talk and deep tenor, as well as his watchfulness around those smaller and slighter than himself. He was quite protective of such folk, and finally Deborah took the opportunity to ask him about it.

"My older sister was as fragile as I am stout," he replied simply. "She was constantly attacked and abused, until I was old enough and big enough to make it stop."

"She has passed," Deborah noted with empathy.

"Aye, of the wasting sickness," he sighed. "I felt helpless as I watched her wither away, her fighting the entire time to live. It took a long time for me to get over her death."

"I am sorry, I hope she will be reborn into the Land a healthier person," Deborah offered quietly. Tristan had turned to her, a strange expression on his face, and then a slight smile had appeared as he answered.

"Thank ye, My Lady. 'Tis likely we will not know each other in such a case, but she deserves a proper chance at life after everything she went through. Surely, the Lady will be kind?"

"We can only hope so, Sir Tristan," Deborah answered. "The best way to honor her is to offer good service, and to love the Lady's Law."

"I do," he smiled, turning to her. "In any other place, I would now be a prisoner or a life criminal due to my errors of youth. Here in the Land, I have the opportunity to win forgiveness simply by working for it honestly."

"Indeed, the Lady loves an honest man," Deborah quoted out of the writ.

After supper she watched him stand by Tyrion's side to take command subtly but firmly, and she stepped away from it, knowing she must.

"Come my friends, let us attend to the first posting of the guard so that others may get some sleep!" he called out, gathering the Knights and Dames to him. For her part, she simply walked to her pavilion where Calla nervously waited to serve. She had never been a valet or an attendant of any kind, and while she had been briefed about her duties, she was still anxious.

"Good evening, My Lady," she greeted.

"Good evening, Calla," Deborah returned. "I am going to change into something a bit more comfortable. I would like a cup of wine please, and would ye set out pipe and Herb? 'Twill be my custom to retire in such fashion as often as possible on this trip."

"Thank ye for that, My Lady. I shall remember," Calla replied, making the note on a wax tablet before going to fetch the requested items. She set them on the table where the small pillow sofa was laid out, lit a lavender candle and poked the small chiminea to wake the fire a bit. When Deborah appeared, she was wearing soft, warm house clothing, a robe, thick hose and fluffy slippers, looking very comfortable and at ease. She sat at the table, found the loaded pipe and smiled, especially when she saw the wine poured and the carafe at hand.

"Thank ye, Calla. Ye have done everything exactly as I like it," she complimented. "Ye may retire for the night, I like to sit up a bit to relax my mind before I sleep."

"I can do no more for ye?"

"Not tonight. Sleep well, yer service has been exemplary today," Deborah told her honestly. She had done naught except give the order to the young woman to make her pavilion ready, when she returned she had found it completely set up and ready for her use. Calla had even lit incense so the place would have a good scent, despite the smell of horses and sweat all around her.

"Good night, My Lady," Calla responded wearily, trudging off to her cot and making herself ready to climb in.

Once she was alone, Deborah sighed, lit a sikar and let her mind reach out for Erinn's, so far away in the desert.

"Husband?"

"Ah, my wife," she heard his thoughts, and a smile appeared, for he was also drinking wine and enjoying a final sikar. "Are ye well?"

"I am well, are ye?"

"Indeed, the work continues on here, and we are making good progress. When we leave here we will not only have regained everything lost due to time and error, but we will have put the entire project back on a proper schedule. I am very pleased. Arthfael has lost all of the weight he gained during his indolence as well, he looks lean and trim once more."

"That little roll around his middle was not flattering," Deborah agreed.

"I shall remember ye dislike such a look," Erinn chuckled warmly.

"Ye have no need to worry," Deborah answered, just as warmly.

They continued on in such a vein, speaking as married folk do when separated by great distance and responsibilities until they could no longer continue. Wishing each other a good night, they allowed their mental link to dispel. Turning to her nightstand, Deborah put aside her empty cup, snuffed out her sikar, rose and walked behind the screen to attend her nightly ritual. Using the rosemary mouth rinse, she swirled it over her teeth and gums for long moments to assure her mouth was completely clean. After spitting it out into the necessity bucket, she rinsed with clear water and swallowed, enjoying the taste of the tincture and recognizing the benefits of introducing rosemary oil into the body in such a way. Finally, she was able to lay down, pull up the blanket and quilt, lay her head on the pillow and close her eyes, falling asleep nearly at once.

At the Oasis of Palms, in the Serai, Arthfael came awake in early morning, feeling a bit spent after the Solstice celebration. It had been two days, he realized, but he still felt tired. It was only after he recalled his diet for the celebration that the realization hit him, he had indulged in so much rich food, wine and sikars that his body had returned to a toxic state.

"I wonder if I still have any of Grandfather's tonic?" he wondered out loud, turning to his night table. A wave of relief washed over him when he saw the phial, and then another one when he saw a considerable amount of it remained. Remembering the dosage from before, he poured water and added a few drops, not as much as he had taken before however. He reckoned his body was not in such a toxic state as it was the first time, and did not wish to experience any more of the effects than necessary. He was just about to drink it when a knock sounded on his door, and Aasimah's voice called through.

"Young Prince, I have yer morning tray. The day will be hot, and I have brought yer usual light first meal."

"Just fruit and yoghurt?"

"Aye," she laughed.

"Thank ye Madam Aasimah. Yer foresight is appreciated," Arthfael called back as he opened the door. "I can take the cart, I have some exercises to perform before I start my meal."

"Very well, Young Prince," she answered, inclining her head with respect. She liked Arthfael, very much, and thought his match to Brianna was far better than the one with Tiamat.

Once Aasimah was gone, Arthfael finished taking the tonic, experiencing the effects within a short time. It was over quickly and relatively painlessly, and soon he was sitting to consume his tea, bowl of deliciously ripe melon and the shimmering bowl of yoghurt flavored with vanilla bean. Finishing the entire portion easily, he felt content and rose from the table to clear his dishes, returning them to the cart and pushing it outside close to the wall so as not to impede the passage of others. Now, it was time to dress for his work day, and so he donned his typical wear which mirrored Erinn's quite closely. The only difference was that he had yet to add the light chain mail beneath, as he had not had time to have one made to his specifications. Anyone who saw him thought he wore the practical black clothing well, the cut and style complemented his athlete's physique quite well, but he was not so vain as to be overly concerned with that aspect. He liked that it fit well, and did not interfere with any of his movements, nor did it chafe or bind. It was a hot set of clothing to wear, and throughout the day, he would eventually shed the thick shirt and work bare-chested, as so many of the other workers did. Even they would seek the shade of the many palm trees growing about in the midst of the day, when the sun was at its fiercest. Erinn had long ago adopted the practice of the desert folk to deal with it, ordering the camp to begin work before the sun rose in order to work in the cool. A three hour rest period at mid-day provided them all a chance to eat a meal and even take a short nap before returning to their labors, ending just before sundown. The next crew took over then, working throughout the night to resupply all of the work stations and the camp kitchen too, so that work could go forward with alacrity the next day.

Once he was fully dressed, he took a last look in the short mirror just to make certain he had buttoned everything necessary. Departing and leaving the door open a bit to indicate he wished to have his chamber serviced, he walked to the common room for another cup of tea, finding Erinn there conversing with Sylvene and Brianna.

"The rains are coming so early?" he heard his father repeat with a question in his tone. "Is the priestess certain?"

"She came to me this morning in great distress, My Lord," Sylvene told him with complete seriousness. "Apparently, the Lady has decided this area needs a time of rainy weather, which puts an end to our working season. She indicated there might be flash floods in the distant hills, where a certain individual makes his remote and secretive home."

"I see," Erinn answered, his face tightening a bit at the mere mention of Ishmael's existence. "Very well, give the order. The camp is to be put to bed and the workers should depart at least a week ahead of the rains. We should also assure that our friends among the desert dwellers are warned and that they have accommodations should they need them."

"My Lord, 'tis my understanding from the locals that the High Lady has seen to that need already by establishing one of her emergency shelter retreats close by." Sylvene smiled. "And the Serai is sturdy enough to withstand a bit of rain, even if 'tis a month's worth."

"Are ye suggesting the entire camp be closed down, Captain?"

"I am, My Lord, except for the small contingent of Knights and Dames who will remain to guard supplies and such. I have already elevated my second Myrtle to temporary Captain until my return."

"And Captain, do ye intend to return?" Erinn asked, a slight smile on her face. He knew well that Thomas de St. Germain had presented Sylvene with a ring of pure silver, decorated with a huge, nearly black amethyst cut into a pleasing shape. He had even already come to Erinn, asking about which of Nathan's inns he would recommend for a getaway for the two. The High Lord was certain that Thomas meant for this trip to act as an engagement gift, and so he had recommended the Emerald Lakes Inn.

"My Lady and I found the remoteness of the place to be very conducive to conversation and relaxation on our last outing there," Erinn recalled with a sigh. "The fishing is good too, and there are full hot spring facilities there now too. I think Sylvene would find it a perfect place to simply relax, I know my lady did."

"Thank ye, My Lord," Thomas had replied, a warm smile on his face. He was truly a man of the Land now, having nearly forgotten his life among the Templar Knights and the Crusades in the Holy Land. All he wanted now was to feel complete, and Sylvene's presence provided that for him. "I am glad to finally be at peace, at home."

"Ye are home," Erinn smiled, offering him the grip. When Thomas pulled his arm away, he found himself holding a large package of tightly pressed and very fragrant Herb. It even smelled potent, and a wide grin passed over Thomas' face. He had never smelled anything quite as good, and he reckoned that Erinn had gifted him a rare sample of the Herb grown in the family valley, under Dragon Mountain. There was even a simple wooden pipe included with the package, as well as a voucher for Nathan's Inn at the Emerald Lakes.

"I *am* home!" he thought with glee, tucking it away.

Now, Erinn turned to Sylvene to give his orders as to the disposition of the camp.

"Very well then, send the workers home and close down the camp. Everyone non-essential is to return to the barracks or their homes, including ye and Dame Brianna, Captain."

"Aye, My Lord. May we ride with yer party back to the Capitol? I have something I wish to discuss with ye in private."

"Of course, my door is always open to ye, or at least my tent flap," Erinn chuckled. "I wish to leave on the morrow, get to yer work."

"Aye!" she agreed, turning to Brianna. "Dame, proceed as we have discussed, and in the order we discussed it. When ye have finished, return and assist me in packing for our leaving. I shall be glad to see green trees in abundance again!"

"I too, miss the greenery," Brianna sighed. "However, I have come to love the desert's wild and stark beauty, in every way."

"Good, then perhaps ye will not mind returning next year," Erinn proposed.

"I should be honored, My Lord," the young woman smiled.

"Dame, go and pack our things. I have a feeling the High Lord is in haste to return to the Capitol."

"Not yet, but the rest of the Knights and Dames are, except for ye and Dame Brianna, Captain."

"What service may I be?" Sylvene asked at once.

"I have two very important side trips to take before I go home," Erinn told her, dropping the volume of his voice. "We shall discuss all of this over supper. Ye will bring the young Dame, so that she can be acquainted with the schedule I wish to keep."

"Very well, My Lord," Sylvene nodded.

"I shall send the young Prince for ye at the sixth hour tonight. Please dress comfortably, 'tis a hot night."

"Indeed, My Lord," Sylvene nodded. "Come Dame, we have work to accomplish."

"Aye Captain," Brianna answered, turning to follow. Erinn watched the two walk off, finally noticing Arthfael sitting at a table, enjoying a final cup of tea. He walked over, took a seat and signaled to Aasimah he was ready for his morning meal.

"Good morning, my son. How much of the news have ye heard while sitting here?" Erinn inquired, wanting to test the young man's observational skills.

"I know we are shutting down the work site for the rest of the year, and that ye have invited Captain Sylvene, Sir Thomas and Dame Brianna to ride with ye on the way back to the Capitol."

"Ye are coming with us as well, my son. I have a few stops to make before I can relax for the rest of the year. I must visit Alom's tabac fields to see what progress has been made in assuring a constant supply of good leaf for the Land without having to depend on the whims of ship captains. I hear that our friend has made considerable headway, and that he has his first small harvest ready. I would like to see it for myself. What most people do not know is that he also brought caffe plants with him, and the last letter I had said they were thriving. I hope to see a small harvest from both crops, but we will see what the Lady's will is on the matter."

"Will we be camping along the way?"

"Aye, for most of the time, the outdoors will provide what we need. I have so much to teach ye, my son, and ye are already older than I was when Drake finished my schooling."

"I am a fast learner, Father."

"So ye are, my son. Have ye eaten yet?"

"Aye, I had my first meal in my room," Arthfael confirmed.

"Good, my meal should be here shortly. As soon as I have eaten, I want to go straight out to the work camp. I want to assure everyone has their final pay in hand, as well as hand out special rewards to those who have worked the hardest."

"Is such always the practice for the High Lord?" Arthfael asked.

"While I am High Lord, 'twill be," Erinn grinned. "I saw yer Grandfather be generous with those around him, as well as how much they loved him for it. I have been without, I know what hunger and want is like. Ye do too, which will help ye be generous in the future."

"I hope so, Father. I hope if I do come to rule, I shall be as wise and generous as I have witness ye be. I feel most fortunate to be called yer son."

Erinn smiled warmly and offered him the grip, which Arthfael gladly exchanged with him. "I do look forward to visiting with Alom, he has a very unique perspective on things, being from so far across the ocean. O, my plate is here!" he smiled as Aasimah put the platter down and he saw the stack of golden brown griddlecakes. "Thank ye, Madam. Those look delicious!"

"Ye are quite the flatterer, but ye are welcome nonetheless," Aasimah answered with a smile. "Enjoy yer meal. Will ye be checking out of the Serai?"

"Aye, as soon as we return from the work camp today," Erinn told her. "Send the bill to the House in the Capitol, if ye would please?"

"Of course, My Lord," she smiled. "We look forward to yer return, and if we can get away for the holidays, a visit to yer home for the Winter Solstice?"

"Ye and Master Othello are always welcome in my home," Erinn told her truthfully. She smiled wide and left him to eat his meal, which the High Lord did with gusto. Once he had finished, he brought his plate into the kitchen and handed out largesse to those employed there, thanking them for the fine service they had rendered during his extended stay. By the time he had returned, Arthfael was waiting at the bottom of the stairs.

"I am ready to begin my day!" Erinn announced, fishing a pair of small sikars out of his pocket and handing one to his son. "Let us go and tend to it. I would like to be out on the road just after noon. I long to find a cold running stream and some green trees!"

"Dangling a line in the water to fish for supper sounds like a fine idea to me!" Arthfael agreed enthusiastically. The two clipped and lit the tabac, then disappeared from the common room of the Serai, reappearing just outside Sylvene's pavilion. Erinn noted the huge tent being struck, Brianna directing the process with alacrity and skill, something the High Lord appreciated in all regards. As he looked about, he could see the process in motion; Sylvene's attention to duty was clear, she had already given the orders necessary to accomplish the High Lord's will. Erinn and Arthfael simply walked through the area, helping wherever they could and wishing the workers a good trip home while passing out their pay and some small tokens of the High Lord's esteem. As the stream of workers headed out swelled to include them all, Erinn finished passing out his gifts and thanks. After they were finished, they gratefully returned to the quiet of the Serai to pack their things and dress for the journey.

"Are we ready Father?" Arthfael asked, casting his eyes about the room one last time to make certain they had retrieved every possession. His eyes fell upon a stone, a huge piece of clear agate that Brianna had found on one of their walks, and he hurried to add it to his luggage so as not to leave it behind.

"I am ready, are ye?" Erinn called back, already packed and now lighting another sikar.

"I am," Arthfael called back, walking to where his father stood waiting.

"Good, I dislike waiting," Erinn told him with a grin. Out of the room they went headed for the common room and their farewells. Othello and Aasimah waited along with the rest of the staff, receiving the last of Erinn's largesse for their service.

"Thank ye all very much. As always, our stay has been made better due to yer excellent service," Erinn told the group.

"Thank ye My Lord," he heard their collective response. "May the Lady watch over yer travels," one of the senior staff added.

"Thank ye, good folk," Erinn smiled. "Farewell to all of ye, until we meet next year."

"Farewell, My Lord!" he and Arthfael heard them say all together. With a final wave, the two men walked up the stairs and out into the bright sunlight of day, which belied the approach of the coming rain. It did not take them long to walk to the stables, where their horses waited already dressed, Sylvene, Brianna and Thomas de St. Germain aboard.

"All is in motion, My Lord, and my second has taken up her responsibilities," Sylvene reported. "I am free to travel with ye."

"I am sorry for the delay," Erinn called out with a grin. "But, we will make good time now. Let us ride hard and fast to find a green place to camp this night!"

"Aye, My Lord!" Sylvene agreed. "Lead us out!"

"Come then!"

He climbed aboard, settled himself in the saddle and took up the reins, urging his steed into a traveling canter and out of the gates of the Serai. As soon as they were away from the Serai, Erinn called a halt, opened a portal and they found themselves close to the crossroads, where they could make the turn for the Capitol District. The miles just fell away under the hooves of their horses, and as evening approached they found a perfect place to spend the night. It was a small clearing in the midst of thick, young trees, where a small river bubbled and splashed in an elbow curve around the clearing. The grass in the clearing was thick, bearing ripening grain heads that made the horses pull at their bits to be at it. Erinn grinned and slid off his horse, leading him to the center of the glade.

"I think we have found a nice place to spend at least two nights," he proclaimed, removing the voluminous robes that had made working in the desert tolerable. Once he was down to his undershirt, he continued. "Ah, my skin can breathe again! Now, let us unpack our tents and get set up quickly. I shall assist with that, so we can get our lines in the water faster. Hurry, I am thirsty too!" he laughed.

"But Father, we have naught to drink!" Arthfael pointed out.

"Such is no difficulty for me," Erinn smiled, snapping his fingers. A full keg appeared and lowered itself into a shallow pool where the water flowed around, which would keep it cool. "I suggest we hurry," he laughed. It did not seem to take a long time for tents to be spread out, erected and pegged into the ground for security, as well as to tend to their tired horses. Once their basic needs were seen to, Erinn gave the order to drop lines in the water. For himself, he simply took a cup of the cool ale and sat on the bank of the river watching them, glad to be out of the desert.

"Ye've found a fine site to camp on tonight, boyo," he heard his father's voice say. Turning, Erinn saw Drake emerge from nothingness into full corporality, a smile upon his handsome face. "May I join ye?"

"I am glad to see ye," Erinn responded, "calling" a cup of ale from the keg. When it filled itself, it floated over to Drake's hand and he snatched it from the air carefully, saluting the Goddess with the first few drops.

"Thank ye, my son. The ale is good here in the Land."

"Aye, I think so," Erinn agreed, and Drake could hear his weariness.

"Ye have labored hard this year so far," he noted with concern in his tone.

"We are going the long way home," Erinn told him, enjoying the fragrant tabac. "I want to visit Alom's tabac works to gauge his progress in growing both it and the caffe plants he brought with him. I am hopeful we have finally secured proper supplies of both products. 'Twill give me time to spend with Arthfael, time I had hoped to spend with both of them, preparing them for taking on more responsibility. Now, I shall be watching over his courting of Brianna, as well as the final stages of Sir Thomas' pursuit of Sylvene. Ye should see the ring he is intending to offer her, 'tis nothing short of stupendous."

"I hope he used emerald for the stone," Drake replied in a somewhat distracted tone. "Amazons seem to have a particular love for green stones."

"Which is what I told him when he came for advice, however, it appears that Sylvene is an unusual woman. Ye should see the color of the Amethyst in her ring, 'tis nearly black," Erinn chuckled. "He has proven to be a fine addition to the Land's population, his loyalty is without question, and his dedication to hard work is complete. He would make a fine Commander."

"I hoped he would. We need his advice on how they fight wars out there," Drake told him simply. "I have always thought to be forewarned is to be for-armed. Thomas has fought in their 'Crusades', which represents their latest military strength and tactics. Ye should engage him in conversation concerning such things."

"I have, and it seems that in the outside world, they are depending more and more on machines and projectile weapons, wandering away from the traditional weapons," Erinn reported. "Barbarity is common, and their warriors have become little more than mindless soldiers, fighting whatever war they are sent off to without considering the consequences of serving either side. 'Tis all very worrisome, their tactics are becoming more and more savage."

"Let them come," Drake growled, a puff of steam appearing from his nose. "They will find that dragons are very savage when provoked."

"Indeed, not to mention Phoenixes," Erinn chuckled. "Look, someone has finally gotten the first bite in their fishing derby!" he went on, pointing at the riverbank. Sylvene's pole was bent all the way to the water's surface, and her merry laughing could be clearly heard as she battled the huge fish. Thomas stood at hand with a huge club, in case it was one of the catfish the Land's rivers were famous for. Erinn and Drake wandered down to the scene for a closer look and as the battle raged, Drake's face creased into a huge smile.

"I think she has hooked a sturgeon!" he shouted out with delight. "Such a fish makes a very fine meal!"

Sylvene was now battling the fish, due to its tactic of relaxing and sinking to the bottom of the river, remaining nearly motionless. Sylvene thought for just a moment it had slipped the hook, at least until she pulled on the pole and it bent to the water's surface once more.

"I think I have a big one!" she called out. "I shall need assistance getting it onto the bank! Who will help me?"

Nearly everyone ran to do so, Drake included, and within a short time and with considerable coordinated effort, they managed to pull the huge fish from the water. It was a male, and from the size of it, it was one in the prime of its life.

"O my," Sylvene cried out, nearly weeping. "I need to return him to the river! Their breeding season is upon them, and he will make a fine father to the next generation. What say ye all, will ye help me?"

"Ye have made a wise and merciful choice," Drake intoned. "Worthy of an Amazon! Stand back, I shall assist."

Striding to the riverside, he knelt beside the gasping fish, which was easily three times as long as a man. With his great strength, the former High Lord cradled the fish carefully in his arms, then gently pushed him back into the river, until he was standing waist deep in the midst of it. All of them watched as he spoke to the fish and moved it through the water, until it began to struggle a bit against being restrained. Drake allowed it to swim free, and with a final splash of its huge tale, the sturgeon disappeared beneath the surface of the water.

"Let us bait our hooks again, and walk downstream a bit," he suggested with a grin. "I would almost wager a school of beautiful rainbow trout awaits just beyond that bend."

Once they had all moved to the new spot, Drake's prediction was proven correct. Within moments of Thomas' line hitting the water he was rewarded with a huge fish that it took considerable effort to bring to the bank.

"Thomas, what a fine catch!" Sylvene complimented, granting him a peck on the cheek, right in front of them all. "I wonder if a larger one awaits?" she laughed, baiting her hook and casting it into the water. It was Arthfael's line that was hit next however, and his fish was equally large. Erinn saw they had plenty for that night's supper, and called an end to the fishing session.

"Come my friends, we have plenty for our meal," he called out. "Let us get these fish cleaned and rinsed out, I want to get back to camp for another cup of ale before I start supper."

"Ye are cooking tonight, My Lord?" Brianna asked.

"I am, Dame Brianna," Erinn smiled warmly at her. "Would ye care to be of assistance?"

"I would! I need to learn to fry fish nice and crispy like ye do," she declared with a grin.

"Excellent! Perhaps ye would also agree to keep my mug full while I work?"

"It if means my mug will be full as well, of course, My Lord," Brianna answered with a bright smile. Erinn realized she was playing a bit with him, and so engaged her.

"My dear, if ye would keep my mug full, I would be most appreciative, I assure ye," he answered in a full and sonorous tone. She looked up at him, met his eyes, and a slow smile crept over her face.

"Ye pick up on the word game quickly, My Lord."

"I have found that to do so is to my complete advantage, my dear," Erinn answered, keeping his voice low and warm. Deborah often responded well to such tones, and Erinn was curious to see if Brianna would as well. "I have won over more than one noble by doing so."

"If ye spoke this way to yer lady while ye were courting her, I can see why the two of ye are together," Brianna answered carefully. Even as she did so, her heart was pounding a bit, she was breathing a bit faster than usual, and she felt flushed. Not even Arthfael made her feel such intense emotions, she noted, and she wondered if it had anything to do with Erinn's age and experience.

"My Lady made it very easy to speak with her," Erinn smiled, sipping his ale. "We soon found that our minds and emotions were in complete accord. I hope ye and Arthfael find such a relationship between ye. 'Tis most satisfactory, in every way."

"Have ye always been able to hear each other's thoughts?" Brianna asked without considering the question first, being a very curious young woman. As soon as the words were out, she realized that she had overstepped and made to apologize, only to have Erinn offer her an embrace, chuckling all the while.

"Ye have naught to apologize for, my dear," he told her reassuringly. "I am glad ye feel comfortable enough to ask me such a thing. It means ye regard me as something other than just the High Lord. Perhaps ye might even begin to see me as yer Father-in-law as yer relationship with Arthfael continues forward?" he smiled winningly. Again Brianna felt the power of his presence, a famous Natanleod trait, one that had been both benefit and bane to the family. She found it difficult to think at first while engaged in casual conversation with him, but that her anxiety soon eased as they spoke. A realization crossed her young and intelligent mind.

"I have always wondered why people feel so comfortable with ye, even those who have never met ye," she finally smiled a bit after a few moments. "I think I understand it, yer family has a very magnetic aura and ye use that to help ease the anxiety of those ye talk with. Am I thinking correctly?"

"Ye are a very, very smart young woman," Erinn complimented without confirming anything. "I think I finally understand how my father feels about and treats my lady, as if she truly is his daughter in many respects. Age does truly bring wisdom," he laughed softly. "Come, let us fill our cups again, then wash up and don aprons. I am getting hungry!"

"O aye!" Brianna agreed, feeling as if she had passed some test of character. Once their hands were clean and aprons donned, the fish were brought to them, with thanks to the High Lord for his cooking skills. The rest of the patrol retired back to the river for a quick swim, enjoying the chill of the water even more due to the heat of the Autumn day. By the time they finished, Erinn had finished preparing the fish and was showing Brianna the secret to properly breading them.

"First, they must be dry," Erinn explained as he worked, Brianna paying close attention. "Next, into the beaten egg they go. Remember we have seasoned this liberally with salt and pepper, as we have the flour, so that we create layers of flavor," he quoted Deborah, since he was using her technique. "Once they are coated, pat the excess flour off, then back into the egg quickly before rolling them in the breadcrumbs, and then right into the hot bacon fat for a good sear on each side. They will be tender and juicy if ye do it this way."

"It smells delicious!" Brianna remarked with a grin. "And so do those papas ye have frying. O my! We have no bread to go with the meal!"

"I can fix that!" Drake put in with a chuckle. "Ye have left me naught else to do, I might as well make the biscuits. I shall use the High Lady's recipe too, so everyone will enjoy them!" he laughed.

The scent of cooking food drew the patrol members close as the sun sank behind the trees, and soon they were sitting about a rude table made from a flat stump to share their meal. Conversation flowed as did laughter as they enjoyed the simple fare, then quickly cleaned up afterwards, allowing the dishes to air dry in the foldable rack. Erinn began to yawn in more rapid succession, as did everyone else, until finally he rose to wish them all good night.

"I shall raise the protective dome over us so we all might sleep well," he told them. "I care not if we remain here another day, in fact I might encourage it, if we cannot locate another camp within a half day's ride. But we will attend to that in the morning. Good night."

"Good night, My Lord!" he heard them all reply as he trudged into his tent to make ready for sleep.

Chapter 3

While Erinn traveled across the Land on his way home, Deborah was completely involved with her task at the Obsidian Spire Temple, and at Olga and Hodor's house. After Aldridge and his group of Druids arrived, the work started in earnest. The very next morning, they were dressing war horses in work harnesses, cutting the huge, drowned and dry trees, then hauling them out of the swampy area where they had waited years to be used. While they did so, others leapt to the task and cleared off the old foundation of the house, exposing it to the sun's light for the first time in many years. As they stood there looking it over, Deborah felt a rush of familiar energy and Drake appeared out of the fog.

"Good morning Father," she greeted without surprise. "I am glad for yer presence so early in the morning. We need yer Engineer's eye here."

"I should be only too happy to assist, my dear," Drake smiled.

Walking to the site, he circled the foundations looking it over carefully, Hodor with him as a dowser, looking for flaws and cracks that would render the place unusable. On the second circuit Drake frowned as he came upon one area, closest to the river bank in the front of the house. It was cracked badly, and showed evidence of the fierce fire that had destroyed the original building. He called Hodor to the place and when the huge Viking man saw it, he looked at Drake with alarm.

"We cannot build on this foundation," he pointed out practically. "At least not a permanent house. If the river floods, this flaw will allow the house to flood easily, not to mention the storage area beneath."

"Ye have a keen eye for engineering," Drake complimented him, handing him a sikar. "Do ye indulge?" he asked afterward, a grin on his face as if challenging the man.

"I have tasted tabac before, My Lord," Hodor grinned, taking the sikar. "But, it has been a very long time. Thank ye!"

"Let us find a better site for the place then, and see how many of these stones we can reuse. I might have to fetch a few more, if we do not have sufficient reserves."

"Is there a quarry close about?" Hodor asked, unknowing of Drake's abilities.

"Nay, but such circumstances present no difficulty to me," Drake laughed a bit. Hodor looked at him, very puzzled. He knew naught of Drake's true abilities, and no one had entertained him with tales of Drake's dragonish tendencies. The former High Lord said no more about it, instead redirecting everyone to begin taking up the stones carefully, keeping as many intact as possible. Any of the broken pieces were taken aside and piled neatly to be used for landscaping or gardening purposes later. Finally, the old storage area appeared, a vast chasm in the ground, and they could see that no supplies remained. Drake smiled mysteriously when Hodor asked about filling the place, merely saying it was time to start the cooking fires for supper.

"But…" Hodor made to object, only to have Drake hand him another sikar as well as the flask in his pocket.

"Ye are not in the outside world, my friend, and anything ye can imagine could be possible here. Ye should simply allow yerself to believe it."

Hodor stopped talking then as if Drake had slapped him sharply, and he met the ascended being's eyes levelly. "I have always had difficulty simply accepting things as they are, My Lord," he admitted quietly as Drake lit his sikar with a fingertip flame. "I shall try my best to lose that impediment."

"Good man, now, come and help me decide what meat to use for supper. I am thinking ham, since I know 'tis a huge one in the ice wagon."

"I enjoy a good slice of ham," Hodor answered simply, a huge smile growing on his face. He was beginning to like this man, and he rarely took a liking to anyone so quickly. He wondered why he felt that way, at least until he spoke with Olga later that night.

"We have found ourselves a good place to call home," he said quietly to her as they tucked in their sons, as well as Olga's grandmother.

"I think so too," she agreed quietly.

"What do ye think of the one they call Drake?" he asked.

"Him? He is very different than anyone I have ever met!" she remarked seriously. "Have ye noted the air of confidence around him, as if he can do anything he sets his mind to?"

"I have," Hodor nodded. "I like that about him, but he has a way of talking about things here, as if we are not on the Earth anymore."

"I do not believe that we are, husband," Olga said after they had left the boys and grandmother to sleep the night away in the wagon. "I believe that when we crossed over that reef, and washed up on the shore below Erasmus' city that we crossed into a blessed realm of sorts. The old tales are filled with stories of such places, even Valhalla is reputed to be *between the worlds*, or so my mother taught me."

"Are we dead then?" Hodor asked as he walked beside her, his arm around her waist.

"I think not," Olga laughed softly. "I do not feel dead, do ye?"

"Nay, in fact I feel more alive today than I have in many years. I was looking at my face today, and I swear I look younger!"

"I know I look younger," Olga rejoined, laughing a bit. "I know I am not younger in years, however. I cannot explain what is happening to us."

"It must be the magick of this place," Hodor said at length, taking his time to think over the situation. "My dear, I think ye have hit on the explanation for it all. We are not on the Earth we knew at all, we are in a much, much better version of it, as if we are close to Valhalla."

"I for one, am very grateful for that," Olga finally said as they prepared for bed themselves. "The world we left behind is a savage, brutal place, and getting more so all the time. The Mother Goddess is being forgotten, She is being written out of history, as are all the other Old Gods. Here, I think we will find that the old ways are valued most, a situation I find most agreeable. Our sons will not have to go a'Viking for land and goods, they will find an honest living here. They will find good opportunities to make that living too, and nice women for wives. I could ask the gods for no more, and I am truly grateful to be here."

"I am glad to be here too," Hodor said as they pulled back the quilts and laid down to snuggle for sleep. "The gods have been kind to us, and we must be of service to show proper gratitude. The Land has provided us everything we have ever wanted."

"Aye, husband," Olga yawned. "Good night."

Once everyone was sleeping, Drake emerged from his tent, a determined expression on his face. He took a moment to stretch to his full human height, changing as he did so, until his dragon-self stood in the same place. More stone was needed to build a proper foundation and storage room below the new house, and his abilities could make that happen much more quickly. Launching himself into the air silently, his wings unfolded and the first few strokes brought him up to clear flying height and he made for the closest quarry. It would have taken a wagon days to get there and back, but Drake made several trips that night, stacking stones carefully and strategically around the new house site they had divined earlier. As for payment, he simply left a huge bag of gold, the device of a black dragon embossed on the outside. Everyone knew Drake used such a device commonly, and the quarrymen would understand that the stone had been taken for some purpose of the Land. As for the huge hole left by the former house, Drake used his huge arms and claws to raze it completely, then he brought in load after load of good fertile dirt, thinking since there was a southern exposure to take the best advantage of it. The area would make a good garden plot for the house, he thought, leaving the area behind the house for fields and outbuildings. The view would not be obstructed by having a kitchen garden right here, he thought with satisfaction as he dropped the last load of dirt on to the spot and quickly leveled it. Finally, he returned to the new house site and excavated the hole for the new storage area before weariness overtook him and he returned to his human form. Dawn was just breaking over the hills as he surveyed his progress, a smile of satisfaction on his face.

"There now, they should be able to proceed without delay. Good, I admire alacrity, in every way!" he chuckled, returning to his tent and disappearing within. He did not emerge until first meal was nearly on the boards, and by then his work had been discovered by the entire camp. Hodor and Olga were the only ones who were surprised at finding the huge stacks of stones piled about the work site but they were doubly surprised to find the huge hole in the ground had been filled and leveled, and that the new foundation had been roughly excavated. As Hodor walked about in amazement, he kept detecting the scent of sulfur on the stones. Finally Deborah provided an explanation that simply shocked him.

"Sulfur?" she questioned, beginning to laugh merrily. "I see that my Father in Law has been busy overnight. We must be thankful to the Lady, She has provided plenty of materials for the building of yer new home so that we will have no more delays."

"What would make ye think of yer Father in Law when ye smell sulfur, My Lady?" Olga asked.

"O! I forgot, ye do not know about him," Deborah laughed softly. "My Lord Drake Natanleod is half dragon by birth, his dragon form is more natural to him than his human form. It allows him to do great feats of strength and magick that no one else could possibly attempt."

Olga's mouth made a perfect, "O" and Hodor's face went completely white as Deborah made her explanation. As if for punctuation, they heard a great roar and a shadow crossed the rising sun as a huge Griffin flew above the trees.

"What...was...that?" Hodor breathed in awe and shock.

"I am certain ye have never seen a Griffin," Deborah stated. "At least not 'till now."

"But...they are creatures of myth!"

"Valhalla is a place of myth," Deborah rejoined. "One must pass on to verify the truth of its reality. Ye have seen a 'myth' in real life, and the longer ye remain here in the Land, the more 'myths' ye will discover to be real. Just wait 'till ye see yer first Unicorn! They are truly beautiful!"

Olga's eyebrows rose speculatively, and Hodor's face adopted a hopeful expression. He had always wanted to see the one-horned horse of legend, just to say he had seen it. "Where would one go to see such wonders?"

"I have found they come to ye when ye are least expecting them to," Deborah chuckled. "As last night's visitation proves in every way. I need to get to the kitchen tent, when my Father in Law rises from his meditation, he will be epically hungry."

Hodor's brow wrinkled a bit and he looked at Olga for explanation, only to have her shrug.

"I would imagine being a dragon would be a strenuous experience," she ventured, turning to Deborah.

"O, 'tis not being in dragon form that causes such a hunger, 'tis the work he did while in that form," Deborah chuckled a bit. "Look, we have enough stone and porcelana to finish the project and he has provided the space for your storage and cold rooms. How many men and days would it have taken for us to do that, without his help? He has done that much work, and so his appetite will be vast. It only makes sense, if ye think about it with a clear mind. If ye will excuse me?"

"Of course, My Lady," Hodor nodded. His mind whirled a bit, thinking that a man might actually be able to adopt such a huge animal form and control it. He knew other skalds and shamans who claimed they could spiritually control their totem beasts, but he had never heard of them actually becoming that beast. It roused his curiosity a bit, especially when Drake appeared looking fresh and extremely well rested.

"My daughter, tell me ye have caffe ready?" he asked in a jovial tone.

"I do, if ye will sit to partake?" she invited. "I also have a few treats to hold yer appetite at bay. Ye have had a busy night."

"I have no idea what ye are talking about," Drake replied in an aloof tone, although the hint of humor was clear. "I rested well."

"After yer work was done, I would imagine ye needed such a rest," Deborah rejoined, and suddenly, Olga and Hodor were treated to a fine example of two people engaged in a friendly game of words. "After all, yer advanced age must be considered while ye are here in the Land."

"My age is no impediment, on any level of existence," Drake rejoined in a mock haughty tone. "Here in the Land, I can do more than my share of work on any day ye ask me to," he went on with the familiar boast.

"Is that so?" Deborah countered in a comic, measuring tone. "I can see ye have already done quite a bit of work today, or at least since the moon reached midnight."

"Someone had to step in, since the task was suddenly so much bigger than planned," Drake defended himself, a broad smile on his face as she put the mug of caffe in front of him, along with a plate of treats. "I simply did what ye could not do, while giving ye the opportunity to rest and relax. Ye, my dear, work entirely too hard!" Drake chuckled. "Thank ye for the caffe and the cookies, they are both welcome and delicious as always. Tell me ye are making griddle cakes?"

"As if I would not make such a meal for so many hard workers?" she laughed merrily. "One cannot expect people to work hard on poor feed."

"Indeed not, and we all know what a generous woman the High Lady is," Drake smiled warmly, ending the friendly exchange. "I shall wait my turn though. Ye should feed all those who will be working today first. I shall want at least another mug of this delicious brew before I am ready to feast upon yer light and fluffy griddlecakes."

"Ye have such a way with words, Father," Deborah laughed, offering him an embrace. "Perhaps ye should teach a quarter at the Temple, instructing the young men in how to manage the word exchange with young women?"

Drake laughed merrily as he amended his caffe. "I am not patient enough for such a role."

"Ye did well with Erinn."

"His mother is responsible for that," Drake sighed, remembering Fleur fondly. "I had naught to do with him 'till he was almost ten years of age. I had no idea I was a father."

"But ye stepped into the role very well," Deborah told him honestly. "He has matured into a fine High Lord, as well as a good husband and father. Ye did well to train him so quickly, once ye knew he was yers."

"His lessons did not have to be as strenuous as mine," Drake replied in a rare moment of self-reflection. "Erinn was easier to train than I was. He wanted to learn what I was teaching him. Julian gave me no choice, I had to learn if I wanted to avoid pain."

"It must have been very hard," Deborah offered after a moment of fighting against her outrage. Children's youth should not be stolen from them, and they should be offered a range of opportunities to excel, she thought to herself.

"Yer childhood was also stolen from ye," Drake acknowledged. "In the most horrific way I can possibly imagine, even now as an ascended being doing the work I do. I have seen things and done things since leaving the Land that would shock ye, I think."

"Ye know very little shocks me, Drake," she answered and he could hear the emotion in her tone. She had even used his name, rather than the affectionate title she usually used. "My memories are still intact, unlike Arthfael's."

"He has remembered nearly all of it, ye know."

"I know it, we have talked about his experiences in the pits," Deborah sighed. "I had to tell him everything in order to get him to trust me enough to do so, however. I think that in doing so, I might have actually triggered some of his memories. We have had some very interesting mental conversations."

Drake's expression turned from slightly humorous to one of awe and wonder. "I had no idea ye were counseling him."

"I would not make a huge matter of it," Deborah smiled in return, filling his caffe cup once more. "Counseling is all about discretion and privacy."

"Indeed, and I shall not ask ye about yer discussions," Drake smiled.

"Ye have no need to ask," Deborah pointed out with a wry chuckle. "Ye can simply look into people's memories to learn what ye wish to. Is it not so?"

Drake was silent as he stared at her, again astonished at her perception and intuition. "How is it ye know that?" he asked softly. "I have never told anyone about that."

"Ye forget, I am a truthsayer too," Deborah smiled, her eyes turning slowly amber. "Ye need not be concerned that I know, I have never revealed such a talent to anyone, not even yer son. I would imagine it comes in very handy, in yer line of work."

"And what line of work do ye suppose I am involved in?" Drake asked, testing her.

"I can see ye doing the same secret work ye did during the war, but on a much expanded scale," Deborah replied without hesitation. "I would think yer ability to extract truthful confessions from people comes in very handy as well in such work. If the Universe was under a state of martial law, someone like ye would be essential to keep it in order."

"I cannot discuss it," Drake replied at once, and she could hear the steel in his tone. "My dear, 'tis much too easy to talk to ye. Even I can be lulled by yer easy acceptance of general talk. Veronica had the same talent, she was very easy to talk to as well."

"I count it as something I need to perform as High Lady," Deborah replied. "It should not discomfit ye in any wise to know what I can do. 'Tis due to yer encouragement all along to develop all of my abilities to the fullest. If ye wish to blame anyone for having them, ye should look to yerself first. Have a good day, Father," she replied coolly, picking up his plate and taking it to the dish sink, immersing it in the hot, soapy water. Drake followed after, both to continue their conversation as well as to get more caffe.

"I do not think it a bad thing, ye having such abilities, my dear," he said to her as he stood behind her. "And ye are right about me encouraging ye all along, but ye can hardly blame me. How often does a man get to see a Phoenix woman developing right in front of him? If anyone would appreciate such a thing, 'twould be me, being dragonborn. Ye will excuse my reaction, but ye continue to astonish me daily."

"If ye can be put into a state of wonder by such things, they must be rare," Deborah replied elegantly. "Thank ye again for yer efforts overnight. I was concerned we would fall behind, having to send out for porcelana and stone."

"We would not wish the High Lady's project to be delayed, in any manner," Drake chuckled merrily, bending to kiss her cheek with great affection.

"Have a good day, Father."

"Ye as well, my dear."

Deborah quickly washed the plates and flatware in the sink, rinsing them and setting them in the rack to dry before immersing the next round of plates and flatware in the sink. Wiping her hands, she removed the damp and spotted apron she had used to prepare the first meal of the day, placing it in the hamper for later washing. She wanted to get at the work of the day, and when she arrived at the house site, she found Aldridge there directing the work of all: Druids, Knights and Dames.

"Good morning, My Lady," he called out cheerfully as she approached, inclining his head with great respect. "I hope I have not overstepped by beginning the work. I think the day will be quite warm, so the sooner we begin, the better."

"I agree, Elder Brother," Deborah answered quietly, her respect for his abilities quite clear from her deference. "I appreciate ye doing so, it leaves me free to do what work is mine and mine alone. I must go and inspect the spire for spiritual damage. The Nagas may have done something to defile it permanently. If so, it must be taken down at once and 'tis fortunate indeed we have a dragon at hand to help us with such a task."

"My Lady's wisdom of such matters is appreciated," Aldridge replied. "Ye are truly one of Ramona's daughters, Spurious had no part in yer creation," he whispered.

"It matters not, I am what I am," Deborah replied humbly. "If ye will excuse me, I must go to my work."

"Aye, My Lady. Are ye taking Olga with ye?"

"I am, I wish to understand her abilities a bit better. She may need a sister here at her new home, to help her learn more about how to work with the Lady's energies here in the Land. We will see. I am not certain she knows much about what she can really do."

"Elanor will be here soon, are ye certain ye do not wish to wait?" Aldridge asked. Deborah rose to the tone of challenge in his tone at once, doing so with cool authority.

"My Lord High Druid, if I cannot see to such a matter then perhaps I should not be High Lady," she proposed. "Are ye challenging me?"

"Not I, My Lady," Aldridge answered at once, bowing his head a bit to show respect. "I simply thought ye might wish her assistance as High Priestess of the Lady."

"If I need her assistance, I shall certainly call for it," Deborah replied strongly, and as Aldridge watched, her hair sprouted dark red streaks.

"Of course, My Lady," Aldridge deferred. He watched her walk away, noting her graceful strides as her hair lost the auburn streaks. Her mood had calmed quickly, he noted, a grin appearing on his face, it was clear to him her mastery over her abilities was nearly complete. There had never been a High Lady quite like her, he knew that due to his examinations of the Land's history.

Deborah walked away from Aldridge, calming herself nearly instantly as she pulled a short sikar out of her inner pocket, clipped and lit it to help her relax. Her eyes searched among those working until she found Olga, making directly for her once her eyes found the woman.

"Olga!" she called out in a friendly tone to gain her attention and the woman stood at once, waiting for Deborah's approach and inclining her head respectfully once the High Lady was close enough. "We have work to do, ye and I. If ye will come with me, I would like to tend to it."

"Of course," Olga replied, putting aside what she was doing at the moment. They walked together out of the camp, Deborah handing Olga a sikar of equal length to her own and lighting it for her. "Thank ye, My Lady. I do enjoy smoking the tabac."

"I find it soothing, and that it helps me focus my thoughts," Deborah replied easily. "I am not certain we can do this ourselves, I shall know more once I am closer to the spire. If I think we need further assistance, I shall certainly call for it."

"Of course," Olga nodded. "What should I do?"

"I shall instruct ye as we go, as I have never done this before. I have woken Temples however, and really, how different could this be?" Deborah replied reasonably.

"I am still new to the Land, and all of the magickal possibilities here," Olga replied. "I was considered to be quite accomplished among my people, but I realize now I know very little comparatively. I look forward to expanding my knowledge."

"Good, such an attitude will serve ye well in yer life here in the Land," Deborah smiled. The grassy path they walked was wide and level, Deborah could feel the paving stones beneath the thick grass and moss. It would take very little effort to scrape off the years of accumulation to reveal the roadbed, which Deborah had heard was beautiful pink granite. The trees bent over the sides of the road, obscuring the entire view as they walked along, chatting companionably. It was fine to follow the path as it bent in gentle curves from time to time until suddenly, the view opened up and the tall obelisk of pure black obsidian was revealed. Olga's eyes opened wide in amazement, the thing had to be twenty feet tall, she speculated. It was carved on all four sides from the tip to the base in flowing designs that resembled runes, she noted, but she could not read them despite her training. The "runes" appeared to be painted with gold paint, Olga noted, wondering if it was actually gold leaf she was seeing. Deborah stopped at the edge of the clearing to remove her shoes, nodding at Olga to do the same.

"If ye will wait here a moment and let me assess the situation, sister," Deborah advised. "I know not what to expect."

"Of course, Sister," Olga agreed, marveling at the sight before her.

Deborah closed her eyes and summoned her full set of abilities, changing from her human self into the flaming Phoenix that marked the rise of her powers. Olga gasped at the sight, the Phoenix was a powerful totem in her old belief system, one that signified wisdom and advanced magickal abilities.

"My Lady…"

"Do not be concerned, Daughter of the Land," she heard the response, realizing that Deborah was temporarily housing the presence of the entity known as the Lady. "Ye are here to see something of a mystery," the words flowed out of Deborah's mouth. "As for the Phoenix ye see in front of ye, if ye are of good heart, ye have naught to fear."

"I only wish to serve," Olga answered, finding the words coming easily to her.

"Good then, stand back. Hold yerself in reserve. She will need yer help returning to the camp," she heard within her mind. She hesitated only a moment before focusing her attention on what Deborah was now doing, thinking to herself this was a challenge. The Lady had thrown down a gauntlet of sorts, and Olga was determined to rise to it.

Deborah, now fully enflamed so as to appear as a living Phoenix, strode forward and laid her hand upon the obelisk. Olga felt as if a wave of pressure passed over her as the High Lady did so, Olga closed her eyes and imagined herself absorbing the energy that engulfed her. It took only moments for her to regain her balance, and when her eyes opened, the sight that awaited her astonished and amazed her. There was the Phoenix fully displayed, overlaying Deborah's body so as to appear she truly had wings and hair of flame. Olga struggled for calm, this was truly beyond anything she had ever experienced, and she felt a very light touch of a hand on her shoulder. Turning, she saw no one, but the sensation remained and she used it as a focus for her own abilities. As she did so a shadowy bear appeared where Olga had been, as if Great Ursus Herself had come to watch and ward. The appearance of the huge bear did not startle the High Lady, she found it comforting. Deborah smiled and stepped to the obelisk laying her right hand upon it softly, the words of invocation coming easily to her.

"My Lady Mother, cleanse this tower and make it ready for Thy Use once more!" Olga heard. A crack of thunder sounded followed by a flash of lightning that touched the top of the obelisk, while Deborah's Phoenix form continued to provide a steadying energy. The graceful language on all four sides began to glow, the light of it growing intensely as it continued to build.

"Let the Light replace any Evil within!" Deborah called out. Olga's eyes widened in shock and amazement as the tower began to glow from within, and then the most shocking thing of all occurred. Ghostly entities began to emerge from the stone, some wreathed in beautiful silvery light, some cloaked in velvet darkness. When they emerged, they were grappling with each other, as if in eternal conflict, and only Deborah's words halted it.

"HOLD!"

Fire wrapped around the spirits, separating their conflict and keeping them from reengaging one another.

"Ye have battled each other long enough!" Deborah called out. "Now, 'tis time for ye all to receive yer rewards! Keepers of the Light step forward!"

Twelve of the spirits answered her command, those wrapped in silvery light, and came to stand before her, kneeling as one.

"We have kept our vow," the most elegant one spoke out in melodic tones. "The spire has not been used for the purpose *they* intended," the spirit continued, pointing at the others.

"Ye have served the Lady well all these years," Deborah replied, a gentle smile on her flaming face. "Now, ye may go to yer reward. Ye have earned that much, and more."

"O! Thank ye!" the spirits all said at once, their faces reflecting great joy. With a wave of the High Lady's hand a stairway appeared that led upward and upward, and the spirits of Light ascended it, quickly disappearing in the clouds. The ascending stairway disappeared then, replaced by a descending staircase, guarded by a solitary figure all in black.

"Knight of the Land, come forth!" she called out and the figure walked to her, kneeling as soon as it was close enough.

"I have come to do the Lady's Will," the figure intoned, pushing back the hood that covered his face. His voice sounded very familiar to Olga, and she suddenly realized that this was Drake, come to attend to the fate of those spirits wrapped in velvet darkness. A smile appeared on Deborah's face as she turned back to the others still waiting to hear their fate.

"All of ye who came to despoil this place, 'tis time for ye to receive yer rewards as well. Ye have earned further punishment for yer crimes, up to and including the deaths of most of those who lived here, which ye accomplished in the most horrific way possible. Ye burned them to death, confined in their homes. They had to watch their children perish and were unable to stop it. It was Raad's order that allowed it, but ye did not have to follow them to the letter, and so, ye will share in his fate. Begone to what ye have earned! Knight of the Land, do yer duty!" the High Lady intoned.

"Aye, My Lady, and gladly so with this group!" he growled, pulling his blade. Deborah noted the blade glowed brightly as soon as it left the scabbard, something she had never noted before, and her interest was piqued. Drake strode to the first entity, which writhed and howled within the magickal constraints put upon it by Deborah. With a single swing, he simply took its head, moving on to the next one and repeating his actions. One by one, each of the dark beings were beheaded, and afterward, Drake simply kicked the body down the stairway, tossing the heads after them. As soon as they had all been dealt with, the stairway disappeared, leaving the ground exactly as it had been before. As soon as the stairway disappeared, Olga returned to her human form, feeling a little spent. She could barely believe what she was seeing. It was as if she stood watching an epic event from her own mythology, and again she wondered just exactly where she was.

"Thank ye, Knight of the Land," Deborah called out to him, her voice warm and gracious. "Now, if ye will please provide the guard, I shall attend to the spire."

"Aye, My Lady," he agreed, taking up a guardian stance.

Deborah walked to the spire, and circled it clockwise, touching each side in turn as she did so. When she pulled her hand away, the fire from it ran up the sides of the spire, and the strange runes began to glow brightly. As Olga watched, the gold seemed to flow out of the letters and then over the entire surface of the spire, suddenly being absorbed within the stone, until the black surface sparkled and gleamed with sparkles.

"Consurge! Evigila!" she called out the ancient words used to evoke the energies of the spire. Using those words, she commanded the energy of the spire to awake and arise, and as Olga watched, the spire lit from within as if it were a lighthouse on the coast. It glowed subtly, ripples of energy coursing up and down the edges, and a quiet hum could be heard. A smile appeared on Deborah's face and she returned to the ground, having been floating a few inches off the surface. "'Tis done!" she called out and the fire surrounding her withdrew suddenly. It was good that Drake was right there to catch and support her, and Olga came to be of what assistance she could be.

"Take her other arm and support that side," Drake instructed quietly. "We must get her back to the camp, to her tent, at once. Prepare to travel quickly."

Olga nodded once as she took up her position opposite Drake, helping to support Deborah while her energies flagged. Drake opened the portal and they stepped through, arriving back at the camp. Olga felt the brief bite of the cold as they traveled through, something she was not expecting. When they arrived back at the camp, Deborah's energies gave out completely, and Drake simply picked her up, carrying her to her pavilion and laying her own on her bed.

"Calla!" he called out sharply, and the young Dame appeared. When she saw Deborah she gasped and nearly ran to her side, looking at Drake for instruction. "She simply needs to sleep," he told her kindly. "I shall leave her with ye."

"I shall tend to her, My Lord," Calla agreed easily.

"Thank ye," Drake smiled genially, turning to Olga. "Is there drink about?"

"Aye, My Lord," Olga replied. "If ye will come with me, I shall take ye to it."

"I am very thirsty, and she will need a huge meal in a few hours. Is there a cook in the camp?"

"Aye, we have Cyrus from the Barracks kitchen with us," Olga replied.

"Good, she should not have to work for an entire day," Drake told her, his voice stressed and anxious. "Waking a spire like that alone, she should know better!"

"Has she done it before?" Olga asked innocently.

Drake turned sharply, stopping suddenly, to stare at the Viking woman, his mind working rapidly. At length, he began to chuckle merrily and resumed his walk to the kitchen tent. "Ye are right, she has not. I am worried about her, and so am over critical. It must be due to my intense hunger," he laughed a bit. "Thank ye, my dear, for keeping me from making a bit of a mistake. Will ye join me for a snack?"

"I am a bit hungry myself," Olga admitted, suddenly hearing her stomach rumble. "Perhaps ye might explain what just happened while we eat?"

"When Raad's forces came here, 'twas with every intent of taking over that spire for their own nefarious purposes. The twelve priestesses in charge of keeping it safe did their duty, they stopped twelve evil Naga priests from inhabiting the stone itself by engaging them in spiritual warfare within the stone itself. They stood as a force of Light, keeping the evil from taking it over. If the Nagas had succeeded in taking this place for their own, the war would have turned out completely differently. That spire acts as both sender and receiver of energies, they would have been able to open a huge gate here, right on this spot next to the Elan. With the ability to bring in as many of their own as necessary, I and Hadrian would have quickly been overwhelmed, no matter what we did to stop it. Those twelve women are no less than heroes of the Land, and I am glad they have been rewarded for doing their duty."

Olga's brow furrowed as she gave the matter a bit of thought before speaking. "My Lord, how is it possible that the tale of these priestess's work has gone untold?"

"No one in the Land understood what happened here, 'till just this morning," Drake told her sadly. "Not even I knew, and I was here mere hours after the event. All I found was burned out homes, with their residents still inside. The spire was as ye first saw it, despite being as it appears now for most of my life up to that point. I could never reckon it out, and the Lady did not supply any explanation other than what was done was necessary."

"Then I see it as the Lady's Will that Deborah is here to do this," Olga spoke out. "She is the Land's historian at the moment, aye?"

"Aye, she is researching the entire history, as far as I know," Drake chuckled. "Including all of what transpired during the War, known and secret. I would say ye are right about her being the correct person to be here at just this moment. Now, where is that food? I am practically starving! Must I go hunting?" he complained good-naturedly. Cyrus heard him, and with a chuckle, he brought Drake an antipasto and a bowl of lentil soup. The former High Lord ate with his usual gusto and good manners, until the bowl and plate were completely empty.

"Ah, thank ye, Cyrus!" Drake said, bringing the plate and cup to him. "I feel much better and ready to work!" he went on, handing the man a sikar of good size.

"Thank ye, My Lord, for remembering that I enjoy this size of sikar," Cyrus acknowledged humbly.

"What are ye fixing for supper?" Drake asked quietly.

"I am preparing grilled chicken, with saffron rice, fresh bread and a mixed green salad," Cyrus told him.

"Ah, delicious, I am hungry again already," Drake laughed, taking his plate and bowl to the sink. "If ye need aught, ye have only to ask," he said in a conspiratorial tone.

"Is the High Lady well?"

"Aye, just tired after her exertions," Drake assured him. "She will truly enjoy the chicken ye are preparing."

"Thank ye, My Lord!" Cyrus replied with relief, wanting everything to go well.

Once Drake had washed his hands and rinsed his mouth, he left Olga with Deborah and joined those working on the foundation. They were even now finishing the clearing of the hole his dragon-self had dug, using the flat sides of the shovels to pack and level the dirt. Drake watched for a bit as barrows of river gravel were trundled into the hole, then spread out in a goodly layer in preparation for the stones, providing both drainage and a leveling aspect. Drake walked among them to pass around sikars, as well as his thanks for their work so far before picking up the first stone himself and laying it in place. A pass line formed then, starting at the stack of stones and ending with Drake, who set each one carefully before adding the next one until they had three courses set in place. Drake looked at the wall and nodded, they would need a few more courses of stones to bring the height of the storage cellar to the proper level. It appeared a dragon would be needed again that night, he reckoned as they continued to bring stones to be mortared into place.

By the time the sun began to set that day the walls of the foundation stood almost to the top of the hole, and Drake ordered the work to continue until the walls of the foundation stood twelve feet high. They only ceased because there was no more stone to use.

"We have done good work today, my friends," he complimented as they cleaned up the work site. "And whatever Cyrus is cooking for supper smells delicious! Let us clean up and get to it!"

"Aye!"

Just a bit later they were all seated and enjoying the deliciously tender and juicy chickens, stuffed with saffron rice and vegetables before being slowly roasted whole. Cyrus had even made desert-style flatbread to go with it, having spent time in the desert to learn how to make the delicious alternative to the golden loaves usually served. Everyone enjoyed the lighter meal, especially since it was quite hot, and looked to be even hotter the next day. After supper, Drake retired to Deborah's pavilion, where Calla watched over the High Lady's slumber.

"Have ye eaten, Dame?" he asked courteously.

"I have, My Lord. She has not flinched a muscle, nor made a sound since I tucked her in. Is she well?"

"Aye, but she is in a recuperative sleep, a deep one. She did something epic, something she should have asked for help to do. But being herself, she sees no limits, no boundaries to her abilities. If I had been granted such gifts..."

"Ye do not envy her, do ye?" Calla asked frankly, then gasped at her temerity.

Drake laughed a bit before he answered. "Ye are like her, willing to push boundaries in order to gain knowledge, which would make ye an Amazon in every way. I do not envy her, but if I had been granted such gifts, my job during the war would have been much easier. It gives me pause."

"My Lord, I have heard many tales of yer exploits during the War with the Nagas," Calla replied. "Some of them seem quite fantastical to me for a long time, up 'till we met. Now that I know ye, they do not seem quite so unbelievable, such as yer being able to adopt a dragon's form upon command."

"Of all my abilities, my dear, ye have picked the one that takes the least of my skills," Drake laughed heartily. "After all, being a dragon is very natural to me, being only half human."

Calla laughed with him, believing he was simply joking, at least 'till many days later. She was working with the Druids, helping to clear the orchards when she saw a huge dragon fly over. She thought nothing of it, at least 'till she saw the dragon stop, hover, then stoop sharply, taking a huge elk right off the ground. The dragon flew off with its kill and Drake appeared several hours later from that direction. She noted he was walking much slower, as if he had consumed an enormous meal, and then she made the connection. Her conclusion was proven out as he passed her, for there were flecks of blood still on his goatee.

"My Lord, ye might wish to wash yer face one more time," she suggested quietly as he passed her.

"O?" he returned in a muchly muted voice. "Did I miss something?"

"Aye, a glance in the mirror will help ye," Calla suggested.

"Thank ye, Dame," Drake said, smothering a belch. Handing her a sikar, he nodded to her and walked slowly away, finally gaining the command tent. A cot awaited within, and he took advantage of it, resting comfortably while the huge meal slowly digested.

It was not until the next morning after waking the spire that Deborah was fully awake. She decided to take a longer rest to regain her strength and lose the dizziness that always accompanied a recovery period. While she rested, Drake took command, so that the work continued to go forward. When she finally returned to work three days later, much had been accomplished. The cellar was ready to be finished, the garden plot was being plowed and harrowed, and the orchards were being pruned carefully, so as to maintain as much of the fruit already growing. In short, all was proceeding satisfactorily, and as she walked the work site, she passed out compliments and largesse to show her appreciation.

"Ye have all been working very hard," she noted with a smile. "Perhaps we should call a Mother's Holiday for the morrow? What say ye?"

Chapter 4

"A fine idea!" Drake's voice boomed out. "And what shall we roast for the feast?"

"A pig!" he heard the collected response.

"Ah, my favorite meal!" Drake laughed. "Very well. I shall return apace, make a firepit ready. I am going to bring a big one," he chuckled.

"Very well, Father," Deborah smiled. "Shall I go with ye, to provide an archer in reserve?"

"Are ye saying I am likely to be injured?"

"Wild pigs are notoriously ill-tempered when being pursued," Deborah countered, a grin on her face.

"I have no intention of hunting wild pigs, my dear," Drake laughed. "Is there more ale?" he asked in a much quieter voice.

"As much as ye will require to properly baste yerself, and the pig," Deborah laughed uproariously.

Drake's face assumed a sad appearance, as if he were deeply hurt and offended by her words, but his laughter was merry and bright, once he let it loose.

"O my dear, ye are a clever woman!" he proclaimed, disappearing. Deborah smiled wide, then returned to her pavilion to don a lighter garb for the day. It was warming quickly, and there were no clouds floating overhead. Once she was dressed, she called Calla to her, offering her a sundress out of her own collection, reckoning that the young woman did not have such things.

"For me?" Calla asked.

"Aye, and I want ye to keep it," Deborah told her with a smile. "Come, let me show ye how to don it, it takes a bit of a knack."

Calla had no difficulty donning the dress, managing the long coil of silk, twining it around her without using the ties. Deborah was impressed, not many women had the ken of such things. Calla looked astonishingly changed once in the dress, her beauty was fully revealed. She resembled as Persephone, Goddess of Spring, to Deborah, who thought that if she donned a tiara woven from flowers and grasses it would complete her look perfectly.

"My goodness!" Deborah smiled, handing her a mirror so she could see herself. "Ye are as beautiful as Persephone!"

Calla stared at the image in the mirror, unbelieving of what she saw. The young woman rarely used a mirror when dressing, thinking it a vain exercise but now as she looked at herself, she thought of having one installed in her quarters.

"My Lady, is that me?" she asked in wonder.

"Aye, my dear. I am doing naught magickally. What ye see is what I see, how ye truly appear. Ye are stunning and lovely! Stay beside me for a while, the men in the group will react to ye now very differently than before. Have ye played the word game very much?" Deborah asked kindly.

"Nay, My Lady. I have had little use for it up 'till now," Calla admitted in a small voice.

"Since yer Mother is not here, nor any of yer sister Amazons, I shall help ye, if ye will allow it," Deborah offered at once.

"Please, My Lady? I do not wish to make a mistake now. I am just starting to be liked, after a very rough start."

Calla was referring to her arrival in the Barracks two years earlier. An orphan girl adopted by the Amazons, she was recommended for service to Ulric by Ashara personally. Calla had no idea of the recommendation, even to the present day. Deborah knew the story of how she had come to improve herself, and let her mind run over it. She had been walking through the Barracks when she had overheard Ulric and Ashara talking.

"I tell ye, My Lord War Duke, if she could just rise above her isolation, she could be a great warrior. I cannot help her at the Fortress, I must have her here to help motivate her. She is already better than most of the young women there, and in fact has been pestering every advanced trainer there to take her on. I like persistence, but her attitude is atrocious and she will not listen to me. In other words, she knows how good she is and will not work hard to make herself better. I think she believes she is so good, she does not need further training of any kind. Here in the Barracks, she will find the challenge she needs to improve. No one here will tolerate her bragging, at least I hope not. I hope she finally accepts, because she is told often enough, that she is a little loudmouth. Even I think she is a pain in the ass, and everyone knows about how my attitude was when I first arrived at the Fortress."

"I have heard ye were a pain in the ass from Athena," Ulric pointed out.

"She was right, I am a pain," Ashara had laughed. "But I use it better now. Just keep matching her up with competent swordspeople who will not tolerate her big mouth and bragging ways. I think she will tire of it, eventually, and come to me finally for the help she needs."

"And if she doesn't?"

"Yer the War Duke," Ashara had laughed merrily. "Ye do with her what ye would do with any warrior who doesn't work out. Ye send her home. She returns to the Fortress, where we will deal with her."

"Very well, send her," Ulric had agreed, trusting Ashara's experience.

Now, Deborah and Calla emerged from the pavilion, wearing their silk dresses as well as head coverings against the burning sun. The entire camp went silent as they walked through to where the men were setting up the firepit, erecting the spit over it. Even Olga was struck speechless, for upon seeing the two of them, she would have sworn they were older and younger sister. All work stopped and pairs of male eyes suddenly saw Calla's beauty, wondering why they had never seen it before. Deborah observed the reaction and stepped in to dispel the tension.

"My goodness, have ye already built the firepit in such a short time?" she asked in a merry tone. "Ye have all been very busy while we were gone. Yer preparation will assist when the meat arrives, and ye have my thanks."

"We...we were happy to help out, My Lady," one of them finally said, tearing his eyes away from Calla. "We best go and gather firewood so as to have it at hand. Come my friends!" he called out, finishing settling the spit into place. "Besides, I bet that river water will not feel so cold today! 'Tis blessed hot!"

While all this transpired, Drake flew through the air, looking for a prosperous farm. He intended to purchase a pig, so as not to go hunting for one, nor to call one unexpectantly from the Capitol House's cold room. Besides, he thought, a bit of unexpected gold in any house would be a blessing for certain. It did not take long for him to find a very beautifully tended farm, and he landed in the heavy trees that surrounded the place to change form. When he gained the front door, he knocked and waited on the doorstep for a long time before someone answered. The door opened and a heavily muscled man appeared, carrying a cudgel.

"What do ye want?" he asked roughly. Drake was not offended at all, he knew that some of these outland farmers rarely saw others, preferring the solitude of their own company.

"My name is Drake Natanleod, and I am looking to purchase a prime porker for a little supper I am preparing. Would ye have such meat available?"

The man stared at him, peering at his face and blinking several times in disbelief.

"But...Raad had ye declared dead!" he finally blurted out.

"So he did, much to his own dismay," Drake chuckled. "However, the reports of my demise are completely wrong, because I am very much alive and well. Now, as to the pig?"

"But Sir, I know ye!" the man said, lowering the cudgel a bit. "I served with the Army during that time. Ye *did* disappear for a long period."

"Indeed I did," Drake chuckled. "And 'twas very fine to rest and heal up while being perfectly safe for once. After all, who goes looking for a dead man?"

"O Sir!" the man finally put the huge club aside. "I am very sorry, I believed the rumors and I quit the Army! I came here and took up farming, so as not to have to fight any more. I am disgraced!"

"Nay, not at all!" Drake disagreed. "And besides, look at this place! I have rarely seen such a finely kept land grant! Ye have done well, and done service for the Lady and the Land. Ye have naught to be ashamed of. What is yer name?"

"My name?" the man asked, his brow furrowing as he thought. "O my goodness, I have not heard my own name for so long, 'tis hard to remember!"

Drake smiled faintly, he had heard of such things before, especially in those who had experienced the worst of battle. He liked to think of it as a heavy recuperation period, in which the mind put aside those memories it found difficult to deal with, and as the body healed the mind followed. The healers called it war fatigue, and it caused heavy depression and sadness in those it affected. Some even became so overcome with fear they lost themselves completely, and only the best Healers for both mind and spirit could bring them back to themselves.

"Hamman! My name is Hamman!" the man finally said, a brilliant smile appearing.

"Well Hamman, do ye raise pigs?"

"I do sir, and I have several I could sell!" the man answered. "If ye will come with me, we will go have a look at them."

"And perhaps ye might have a mug of ale to spare as well?" Drake asked. "I have gold."

"I shall take no gold from ye for ale, Drake Natanleod!" the man declared. "However, I shall take gold for the pig."

"Done!" Drake agreed with a smile. Hamman took him down to his cellar to fetch a pitcher of ale and two cups before taking him down a smoothly dressed stone-lined path, lined on each side by neat stone walls standing six feet high. "Ye have done much work here in the time ye have occupied this place," Drake commented.

"After I left the Army, felt guilty," Hamman admitted quietly. "When I found this place burned out and abandoned, I could see that it had been beautiful and prosperous at one time. I wanted to see if I could make it so once more, and so I set about it. I found milled lumber in an outbuilding, enough to build a small barn. I lived in it for that winter, slowly exploring around to see what resources the land might provide. My Lord, there are veins of brilliant silver here, of a quality I have never seen before. Gold runs through the property as well, and I only mine a little bit when I need to make a purchase. The water is sweeter than any I have ever tasted, and there are wild ponies up in the hills above me. The forest teems with deer, elk, and game birds of all kinds, the small pond behind the house has enough current for me to raise trout. I have been blessed to be able to stay here all this time. I know I do not hold the grant for it, I always meant to walk to the village and apply for it. Perhaps ye might be forgiving?"

"I am not High Lord of the Land," Drake replied in a soothing tone, for the man was a bit distraught. "However, my son is and he does sometimes listen to me. I shall speak for yer right to hold the grant, if ye wish to apply for it."

"Ye…ye would do that for a deserter?"

"Ye are not a deserter," Drake smiled gently. "Ye gave yer oath to someone, and then that person was declared dead. No more could be asked of ye, and I would never disparage someone who can make a dead farm bloom like this. Do not let it concern ye any further, ye owe me naught."

"O! My Lord!" Hamman cried out, overjoyed. "I have wanted to make this right for many, many years. I thank the Lady for arranging it so I could speak with ye personally, so I could explain. Thank ye!"

"As I said, 'tis over and done with between us," Drake smiled. "Ah, we are at the pig pens! My goodness, look at the size of them! Ye raise good pigs!" he marveled. He was right to do so, for the man's pens contained huge pigs, as big as any at the High Lord's house. "They must average about fifty stone each! Which one would ye suggest?" he asked enthusiastically, sipping the excellent apple ale.

"Come with me, let me show ye the best I have," Hamman gestured and Drake followed, foaming cup in hand. Into the main sty they walked, and Drake noted how clean it was. He could see no manure or pools of urine anywhere, the barn smelled of grass hay and cedar shavings and each animal had a large, clean pen with fresh water and a bucket of cooked grain mixed with chunks of apples. Hamman led him down a short corridor to the end sty, turning with a flourish of his hand. When Drake stepped in front of the sty, his eyes grew large, for the pig standing there was prodigiously huge.

"I have four like this one, My Lord. He will easily dress out over seventy stone. How big is yer supper?"

"We are building a new house next to the Temple below, the one that borders the river Elan," Drake told him. "I was planning on two pigs, but with one that size, I shall only need one. How much do ye want for him?"

"How are ye planning on getting him to the river? Do ye have a wagon?" Hamman asked suddenly.

"Transportation will be provided, ye need not worry," Drake smiled mysteriously. "Unless ye would like to loan yerself and yer wagon to me?"

"I cannot leave the farm for so long, 'twill take at least two days to march to the river," Hamman told him honestly.

"Ye needn't concern yerself, the Lady will provide the way," Drake told him. "Now, as to yer payment for the pig. Ye will take this small bag of gold, aye?" the former High Lord went on, handing Hamman a bag of gold the size of one of his feed buckets, which held three gallons of liquid. The man's eyes went wide with surprise, he tried to hand the bag back, thinking Drake was overpaying.

"Ye are giving me too much, My Lord. He is not worth that much, even if I could take him to the Capitol market!"

"Ye are mistaken, my friend," Drake chuckled, pressing the bag back into the man's arms. "I have a butcher friend in the city who would gladly pay this much and more for such meat. Ye do a fine job out here, but ye need help, I think."

"Company would be nice, and I have learned a great deal about how to properly put good weight on a pig. Come, let me show ye my smokehouse."

"Smokehouse?" Drake inquired, very interested.

"Aye, I think ye will appreciate this," Hamman laughed a bit. Stopping at the house to put the gold on the table, they continued on to a small shed where fragrant smoke trickled out of a small chimney. "I have always loved salted pork, as everyone does in the Land," he began. "However, one does grow tired of it when 'tis the only meat about. I remembered watching the red people of the Northern District catch salmon, then use salt and smoke to preserve it. The taste of such a thing is unforgettable, and I recommend it highly. I thought I could do the same thing with pork, and I spent a summer with the red people to learn the technique. My Lord, a smoked ham is to be experienced, here, let me cut ye a piece."

"Ye can just eat that without cooking it first?"

"Aye, My Lord. 'Tis completely safe to eat. I know, I eat it nearly every day!"

"Hmmm…I shall mention yer process to the High Lord. I would imagine he will wish to come and inspect the place himself," Drake smiled.

"Thank ye My Lord!" Hamman smiled broadly. "Do ye want to take him on the hoof?"

"The pig? Aye, I shall simply take him with me," Drake told him. Hamman's brow wrinkled again, he had no idea what was about to transpire, but he did as he was asked, fashioning a quick halter from stout rope and fastening on the pig's head. The animal was used to such treatment and made no resistance as he was restrained then led out of the sty. "Ye have them trained very well," Drake commented.

"I do not like to cause them undue distress during the slaughter," Hamman replied quietly. "When 'tis their time, I take them out of the sty and far enough away so the others cannot hear them, just in case I miss my first stroke. I try to give them the easiest death I can, I think the meat tastes sweeter due to that."

"I agree with ye that an easy death is the best one for a meat animal. I shall slay this one on the spot, so 'tis as fresh as possible for our feast today. Thank ye Hamman, I am glad the Lady brought us together once more. I shall return, and hopefully bring my son along with me to see yer fabulous farm. May the Lady be with ye."

"May She be with ye as ye travel, My Lord," Hamman returned, offering the grip. Drake shared it with him before taking up the pig's lead rope and walking off with him, headed for the woods. Hamman watched as he gained the edge, turned and waved once more, then disappeared into the depths. He wondered just how the former High Lord was going to get that pig to the river in time for supper. The question only bothered him until he reached his house and saw the bag of gold on the table. Plans for it began to swirl around in his mind as he picked it up, taking it to his bedroom and stowing it in a chest under his bed.

Drake and the pig quietly walked into the forest, until he was far enough away from Hamman's house to open a portal. He reckoned the man had experienced enough shock for one day and thought to spare him the sight of instant transportation. During the war, Drake had hidden his magickal abilities for the most part, so that most people would not be able to identify him easily. Very few in the Army had ever seen him disappear or turn into a dragon, at least not right in front of them, he thought seriously. Such things could give a man heart arrest if he were not properly prepared for them, he reasoned.

Once he was far enough away, he took a moment to prepare the pig for the journey. "Brother Porcus, we must travel quickly," he warned the animal. The pig glanced up at him momentarily, then simply relaxed, showing no signs of distress when the whirling aperture appeared and they stepped through. Once they were through, Drake simply led the animal to the camp, proclaiming he had brought supper.

"I shall deal with his death," he volunteered his services. "I shall work quickly, and cleanly."

"Thank ye, Father," Deborah said gratefully, not liking how pigs generally met their end. It was that final squeal that always made her cry, even though she knew they were being slain mercifully. Drake sent everyone away, however Calla remained.

"What I am about to do is not a pleasant thing to see," he warned her.

"I am an Amazon, but I have never seen death," she replied stoically. "I must test myself in some manner, to know how I will react if the day should come."

"Very well then," Drake nodded, understanding her reasoning. "Please, do not speak until the deed is done. I must concentrate."

"Aye, My Lord."

Calla trailed him to where the pig now stood quietly, as if it understood its situation. As she watched, Drake approached the pig, knelt in front of it, and put the blade down so it could be seen. The pig flinched a bit and looked up at Drake, as if meeting his gaze. What happened next was quite extraordinary, as the former High Lord began to speak with the animal. More astonishing still was that the pig spoke back, aloud, so she could hear it.

"Brother Porcus, 'tis yer time. I shall make it as quick as possible, so ye will feel the least pain I can manage. I can even offer ye a sleeping potion, if ye prefer."

"I would prefer that, wouldn't ye?"

"I would," Drake answered honestly. "I have felt my share of pain, 'tis never pleasant."

"Then I shall take the potion first," the pig made its choice. Drake wasted no further conversation, simply drawing a bowl of water from the river, taking the phial from his pocket and sprinkling in a few drops. Setting it down in front of the pig, he nodded and stepped back, allowing the animal to drink its fill. Calla felt strange about the pig's death now, and she wondered if she would be able to enjoy the feast at all as she watched the animal slowly lay down, close its eyes and fall asleep. Drake was over him within a few steps, and the deed was done, the blood staining the ground.

"Great Mother, take this blood and use it for Thy purpose. Brother Porcus, thank ye for yer life, and for the nourishment ye will provide the people. May ye be reborn," she heard him intone and a single tear dropped upon the pig's body from his eyes.

"Ye are sad to take a life!" she realized.

"Of course. The taking of a life is a heavy burden, my dear, even in war. Ye must kill to win yer cause, but 'tis not a pleasurable experience, in my opinion. I kill only when I must, and I make it the best death, whenever I can."

"But Sir, ye are an Ascended Being, surely, ye do not participate in death?" Calla asked, unable to help herself.

"It seems my war goes on, even in the higher realms," Drake said enigmatically. "And there are many kinds of death. But let us not linger over that. If ye will assist me in dressing the pig, we can get this meat on the spit! Have ye ever dressed out a pig before?"

"O aye!" Calla assured him. "But many months has passed since I did."

"Well, come along then and help me!" Drake chuckled. "I am an expert in such things, having done them many, many times. Ye see, the favorite meat on a Natanleod man's table is pig."

"Why is that?" Calla asked and Drake glanced up at her. She was deadly serious about her question. He decided to answer her question in the same light, to test her reaction.

"Pig skin provides the best opportunity to get a ken of what 'tis like to slice through human skin, my dear. Ye are aware of our family's occupation with learning the truth, at whatever cost to the enemy, aye?"

"So, 'tis true then. A secret workroom exists below the High Lord's house in the Capitol?" Calla asked in return. "I would like to see it someday, if 'tis permitted," she continued and Drake could hear the truth in her words.

"Why would ye want to know such a thing?" Drake inquired at once.

"It contains a vast array of weaponry, the like of which I have never seen before," Calla answered in far-off tone and Drake began to wonder about her. "Would ye show it to me, My Lord?"

"The workroom is no longer mine to command, my dear," Drake told her. "Ye will have to gain the permission of the current High Lord."

"Would ye help me speak to him about it?" she asked humbly, kneeling at once. "I would so like to see it, truly."

"Very well, on the next opportunity when we three are within speaking distance, I shall open the door for yer question, young Dame."

"O Sir, I thank ye!" Calla replied with great enthusiasm. "I am very so grateful! How may I serve ye to compensate ye?"

"Just help me dress out this porker, and then, we will work together to make the rub to season it. Have ye made spice rub before?"

"Spice rub? Is that why the meat in the Barracks tastes so good?"

"Aye!" Drake grinned, extending his hand to her to help her up off the ground, where she had been helping him dress the pig. "We must deal with the entrails."

"I shall go get a shovel," Calla offered, only to have Drake smile.

"Bury them? When the scavengers are always hungry?" he asked in a fierce tone. Closing his eyes, he reached out with his senses, finding a pack of wolves nearby. "Brothers and sisters of the wild, I have fresh entrails for ye," he sent out with his mind and heard their receptive thoughts respond with joy.

"Thank ye, Brother of the Dragon. We have many pups this year. They must learn how to eat a fresh kill. We come."

Drake turned to Calla, gesturing for to stand back, and he used his abilities to lift the meat off the ground. He and Calla walked away, the meat following them, floating magically all the way to the cook tent, where Deborah had a clean preparation table laid out. As they walked away, Calla turned back to see about seven large adult black wolves emerge from the edge of the wildwood. She stopped to observe as they led a large group of pups all about the same age to the pile of steaming entrails, then she watched as the pups attacked it hungrily. Their feeding was messy and noisy, she thought, but then they were still young and learning.

"As ye are," she heard in her mind. Starting at the voice, she looked up to behold one of the lead female wolves standing apart from the rest, staring at her. "Ye do not flinch to see their feasting?"

"Such is yer way," Calla thought back. "No one should fear it."

"But many do. Ye are more fearless than the rest."

So saying, the wolf rejoined her pack, standing to watch the pups devour the meal left by Drake's work.

"She is right, ye know," Drake's voice startled her out of her reverie. "Ye are very fearless, but still young and learning. Have ye any idea of who yer people are?"

"Sir, I do not remember much of my past," she answered honestly. "If I had not been found by the Amazons, I might have perished in the burned out village they found me in."

"I see," Drake mused. "I do not mean to cause any pain. I am a very curious man, and ye are a bit of a puzzle to me."

"I have always been told that my curiosity will be the death of me," Calla laughed outright. "I have the need to know things."

Drake took a moment, subjecting her to a deep assessing gaze, which she stood unflinching for. "I have a way to discern yer parentage, if ye would be willing. 'Twould only take one drop of yer blood."

"I shall consider it," Calla returned confidently. "Perhaps I do not wish to know these things. Perhaps 'tis why the memories were taken from me."

"Take yer time to think about it," Drake replied casually, although he was now burning with curiosity about just who this young woman might be. She reminded him of Hadrian, with his constant and burning curiosity to know everything.

Now they were at the cook tent, where Deborah had everything prepared. The morning was still young as Drake quickly selected the ingredients he wanted, passing them through the mortar and pestle while explaining to Calla what each one was for. She absorbed his teaching while Deborah watched their interaction, wondering what Drake was about with the young woman. He was clearly interested in her for some reason, and when she excused herself for a few moments, she went to her father in law to ask about her.

"Father, what is it about Calla that has piqued yer interest?"

"Her curiosity, her thirst to learn everything, and an odd fascination with weaponry of all manner, including that used in the workroom," Drake explained succinctly. "If I did not know better, I would think she was a scion of our family."

"How do ye know she is not?" Deborah asked simply.

"I do not, but I can find out," he grinned suddenly, his mood lightening. "Would it not be amazing to find yet another hidden member of our family?"

"So, now I understand," Deborah nodded.

"I was not pursuing her!" Drake insisted, a grin appearing on his face.

"I never implied ye were, Father. But for someone like ye to take such an interest in someone like Calla, I had to ask."

"Of course, o one of the burning curiosity," he laughed outright, offering her a warm embrace. "Please, tell me ye have plenty of cold ale on hand? I feel especially thirsty."

"Ye usually do after being a dragon, and performing a perfect death," Deborah answered, mock-seriously, handing him a foaming mugful.

"Ye are the kindest woman I know, except for Jovita, of course," he complimented, saluting the Goddess with a drop on the ground before drinking with great thirst. "Ah! That puts heart back into a man!"

By this time, Calla had returned and Drake put her to work helping him sprinkle and rub the spices and herbs into the meat, her paying attention all the while. Finally, the carcass was properly prepared and Drake called for assistance to take it to the spit. Several men stepped up to do so, and soon the pig was turning slowly while being basted with Drake's sauce, made from all the trimmings, what remained of the rub mix, honey and a generous portion of red wine, slowly simmered into a thick liquid. It did not take long before the air around the camp was heavily scented with the odor of roasting pork. Everyone's minds turned to side dishes to fill out the meal, and Deborah organized several foraging parties.

"Let us see what the Goddess provides for our meal," she suggested with a gentle smile. "I am certain She will be generous."

Once most of the people were out of the camp, Deborah opened a portal to the High Lord's house in the Capitol city to call for a few fresh supplies, just in case. Her list to Millicent included eggs, cheese, fresh bread and butter, as well as a large bowl of salad greens. Of course, Millicent also included a premade container of the barley salad that everyone in the Land loved, as well as some of the white wine Deborah preferred on hot days.

"How is the weather there?" Millicent asked as the supplies floated through the portal.

"The morning is cool, but I can feel the sun's heat behind the fog," Deborah told her. "Be sure to send a full cask of cold ale through? Father will be very thirsty today, for certain. He has been a dragon, and given a pig a perfect death."

"I shall be sure to send the brown ale then," Millicent replied with a chuckle. "He prefers that when he has been shedding blood."

"Oddly, so do I," Deborah returned.

"Most people in the Land feel the same way, my dear, whether they have been fighting or simply working hard," Millicent laughed a bit. "I find it no wonder that Caius Ironhorse became proficient at brewing, and eventually perfected the recipe for the brown. He had to shed his share of blood and more. No one was a harder worker, either."

"We all miss him, but he is with his lady and working to better himself in the Lady's realm now," Deborah responded kindly.

"Aye, I do miss his grouchy self," Millicent said, wiping a tear away. "O, the basilica is nearly ready for its first harvest, which ye usually use for pesto. I know ye like to be here when 'tis made, to oversee the drying process. Erasmus' delivery of olive oil was very timely, it just arrived this morning."

"I must compliment the Lord of the Port City on his efficiency," Deborah laughed a bit. "Just remind everyone not to add the oil to the part we are going to dry."

"I never forget after the last time," Millicent laughed aloud. Deborah had been so busy one year she had simply turned over the process to a group of women in the kitchen who should have known the technique. However, they were not as familiar with how certain foods take to drying, and so they made the pesto with oil instead of with water before taking it out to dry in the warm sun and breeze. When Deborah had checked it several hours later, it was beautiful and bright green but still a wet paste. She had simply gathered up the few pans laid out, returned it to the kitchen and ordered them scraped clean. All of the warm pesto had an extra bit of cool olive oil added to it, then it was packed away in ceramic jars with locking lids and stored in the ice room. Deborah had continued the process of allowing some of it to freeze like that after using it during the Harvest Feast the same year, finding it completely fresh tasting and wholesome in the middle of a cold and frozen Winter.

"I shall not be there in time, I think, for this batch. Put Emelia in charge of it, I think she is ready to show her knowledge."

"Aye, My Lady, should I allow her to choose her own team?"

"Within reason, aye. We do not wish this to be seen as favoritism or nepotism."

"Of course not!" Millicent snorted. "Not in my kitchen!"

"I shall see ye soon, my friend," Deborah answered with a laugh. "The task here is proceeding well."

"I know, I felt the spire waking," Millicent answered, her voice filled with pride for Deborah's accomplishments. "It does sponsor strange dreams, and sometimes past life memories too."

"Is that so? I did not know that," Deborah answered, filing away the information. "Thank ye again Millie, for staying on for the harvest. I shall miss ye at my side next year."

"I shall be happy to be missed," Millicent laughed heartily, and then their communication ended.

Once the portal closed, Deborah gave instructions to immerse the cask in the shady part of the river. "Be sure to put some of the white wine next to it, if ye please?"

"Aye, My Lady," Tyrion agreed easily. He liked serving under her command, thinking she was a smart and capable woman. She watched him simply put the small cask on his shoulder and walk it to the river. Tyrion noted at once that the cask was already cold so he found a nice spot where a huge willow hung over the river, providing ample shade to assist in keeping the liquid cold.

From that point on, Deborah walked about the camp, stopping to chat briefly with those who had already distinguished themselves by their labor and attitude. They merited rewards such as vouchers to Nathan's inn, or to Pints, Pitchers and Barrels, or even Antonina's house in two cases, and each one was passed out in an envelope. Deborah reckoned such giftings were better off done without attracting undue notice from the others, it was no one's business what rewards she was handing out, after all. By the time she had walked through and around the camp, supper was well on the way to completion, and the scent of roasting pork filled the air with a delicious odor. By sunset that night, they were sitting down to the full meal, listening to the river sounds as they enjoyed their plates. Even as big as that pig was, barely half remained after the meal, due to their hunger. The cook told Deborah not to worry, he had plans for all of the leftover meat.

"Very well then," she responded, handing him a large bag of treats and sikars. "I look forward to tasting the products of yer industry. Ye have a long night ahead of ye, if ye are planning to do what I think ye are."

"I am going to smoke the ribs in sweet and spicy cherry glaze," Cyrus told her. "I think the hams will be good for our first meal in the morning, and the rest of it I can shred and make into handpies. If we still have more, I would imagine a family in the area would welcome such a gifting."

"Ye are right about that! But will ye not need assistance in finding such a family?"

"Ye needn't worry, My Lady, I shall see to it all as I watch over the smoking process."

"Ye *do* have a busy night ahead of ye," she smiled handing him a bundle of sikars.

"Thank ye, Madam. These will help pass the time!"

Deborah nodded, noting that she felt calm and very relaxed, unusually so. As she had passed through the camp, she had casually asked how everyone else was feeling, only to receive nearly the same reply, that they felt good about how the project was going and that they were not feeling any discomfort or pain while working. As she walked back to her tent, content and tired, she found Drake waiting for her outside and invited him to join her for a last sikar.

"Ye look very relaxed," he noted with a gentle smile.

"I feel at ease, which I do not completely understand," Deborah smiled faintly. "I am never this way."

"When did ye notice?" he asked, clipping one for her and lighting it. Deborah perked up at the question, and he watched her mind engage on the puzzle.

"As I look back on it, 'twas just hours after the spire woke," she finally responded to his question aloud, a trace of wonder in her tone.

"I am not surprised, the spire has a way of smoothing emotional energy, and putting people at ease. 'Tis why this place was a place of healing. I truly regret not being able to save the small Temple building here, as it was built in the classic style with columns and a lovely fountain in the atrium."

"Perhaps we should rebuild the Temple, but not on the original spot," Deborah mused as she exhaled the fragrant tabac smoke. "The land here is fertile enough to support a small Temple, as well as a Druid Shrine."

"Originally, the place held a united Temple and Shrine complex embracing the Spire between them," Drake told her. "Both sides used the Processional way on different occasions, and the High Priestess and Elder Brother of the Temple were usually a mated pair. We should speak with both Elanor and Aldridge about it, and if they think 'tis a good idea too, we should do that right away."

"We?" Deborah inquired with a chuckle.

"I mean our family, my dear," Drake laughed with her, noting his lapse. He had actually issued orders, as if he were still High Lord, and she his Secretary, and the both of them laughed heartily, enjoying the joke. "I meant no disrespect, ye know."

"Of course not, and yer input is always welcome, Father," Deborah smiled, patting his hand in a reassuring manner. "I shall always think of ye as an elder High Lord, ye know, and there are days I miss being yer Secretary."

Drake laughed merrily and embraced her, loving her kindness and ability to make the best of any situation. After finishing their sikars, Drake wished her goodnight, taking up the guard position outside her door despite the magickal shield she had put into place. When she found him there in the morning, she simply greeted him with an embrace, knowing he had done so due to his love for her.

"Good morning," she said quietly, for the rest of the camp had yet to rise.

"Good morning, daughter," he returned. "The night was quiet and warm, I had plenty of time to think."

"Then the time at guard duty was well-spent, despite being unnecessary."

"Ye may think it unnecessary, my dear, but I think otherwise," Drake responded, as he usually did. "I would not be sleeping in any case, and the time was spent in deep thought. I feel rested and ready for my day, which should start with a nice big cup of hot caffe."

"Come then, I have supplies in the pavilion for that. We need not bother anyone, except my valet."

Calla was already up, dressed and making the brew, much to Deborah's approval. The young woman had shown herself to be very organized and able to anticipate her needs better and better daily. Quietly and expertly, she laid out the morning table for them, then stood at hand to be of any assistance. After the first cup, Deborah sent her out to the cook tent with the request for first meal and the young woman was quickly back, bearing a full tray of sweet biscuits and jam, along with a note asking for her patience.

"All will be prepared soon, the night has gone well. The only task I was not able to accomplish was finding a family to accept what we cannot use this morning."

"I shall deal with that!" Drake volunteered at once. "Which will leave the High Lady here at the camp to oversee the work!"

"Thank ye Father," Deborah replied gratefully. They shared the tray of treats, then enjoyed the handpies delivered by Cyrus, who waited nervously for her assessment.

"Cyrus, these are completely delicious!" she said after enjoying the first bite. "Ye have used papas in the mix for these, and I have never done that. I shall in the future, and I shall insist that ye get the credit for yer suggestion in the Barracks Kitchen cookbook!"

"Thank ye, Madam," Cyrus returned humbly. "But we have been using these for some time in the Barracks, and 'twas Klietos' idea."

"Very well then, he will get the credit. But, I shall add a notation that ye were the one to first introduce them to me."

"Thank ye," Cyrus replied, bowing smoothly. Turning to Drake, he continued, "My Lord, when ye are ready to come for the meat, 'twill be cold and packed for travel."

"Thank ye, I appreciate alacrity," Drake grinned, offering him the grip. Off Cyrus went to begin preparing the second meal of the day, leaving Drake and Deborah to finish their caffe. Drake quickly drained his cup, took up his weapons and donned his cloak, preparing for his duties that day. "I shall see ye later, my dear, and I shall bring the meat for supper. I feel like hunting."

"Enjoy yer day, after ye have seen to yer volunteering," Deborah smiled.

"Ah, such duties are no burden," Drake smiled. "There should be no hunger in the Land, unless one seeks it."

"Especially where children are concerned," Deborah agreed, giving him a kiss on the cheek. "Good day. May the Lady be with ye as ye go about yer business."

"Good day, may She stand beside ye throughout yer duties, my dear."

With that, he simply disappeared in front of her, reappearing in the cook tent, somewhat startling Cyrus. "O!"

"Sorry brother, I meant no harm. I merely wish to be about my business so as to return before sunset," Drake told him in a calm tone. "Where is the package?"

"Over there, within the empty wine cask immersed in the river to keep cool," Cyrus pointed.

"Good, now that I know where 'tis, I shall not have to bother ye later. Good day, Cyrus!" he said with a grin as he winked out of sight.

"I wish I could do that," Cyrus said in a quiet, wistful tone, for he was one of those in the Land with little to no magickal abilities.

Drake only traveled a short distance, reappearing in the woods just outside of Hamman's farm. He reckoned that such a man would have a good idea of those in the area needing a bit of help, and after a bit of searching, he located him just emerging from his smokehouse.

"Ah, my friend Hamman!" he called out, and a startled man turned to meet his eyes.

"O my! Ye have returned!"

"Aye, with many thanks for the meal ye provided for a very hungry group of people," Drake grinned. "However, we have eaten our fill, and still have plenty to share. Would there be a family in the area who would take this meat?"

"I have a good idea of at least two families who could," Hamman smiled wide. "Come, I was just about to go and visit them. We were going to discuss putting their sons to work in the pig pens, and some of their daughters to clean my house from time to time. Ye have provided a way for me to ease their pain at having to ask for help."

"Are they in great need?" Drake asked, his concern for them very clear in his tone.

"Actually, one of them is. The father of the family is ill at the moment, and their farm is falling behind schedule a bit. His children are young, but willing to work hard to make sure they eat this Winter."

"Take me to that family then," Drake decided in mercurial flash of insight. "I think they need my help more."

"I was going to visit them first, My Lord," Hamman smiled. "But, where is yer wagon?"

"I am Drake Natanleod, I do not need a wagon," was the amused answer he received. "Take me to them, if ye please?"

"But Sir, they live half a day's walk from me!" Hamman objected. "I must remain to care for my animals!"

"As I said, being who I am, such things do not concern me. If ye would simply step back a bit, I shall make myself clearer."

Hamman did Drake's bidding, wondering what he was about, at least until the swineherd watched the man become a huge black dragon. Hamman nearly fainted with fright, knowing that dragons were possessed of uneven and uncertain tempers, and that they ate a great deal of meat, no matter what kind.

"Be not afraid, my friend," he heard in his mind, and recognized Drake's voice. "I am still me, despite the change of shape. Climb aboard, let me make our travel to be of service much faster!"

"Ye would allow me to ride?"

"Of course, why else would I travel this way?" Drake laughed into his mind, dipping a wing to allow him to mount. "Settle in between the wings, ye will find a natural seat there in the shoulder blades. Grip tightly with yer knees, as if ye are riding a semi-trained horse and take hold of the bone ends ye will find to steady yerself. 'Twill be a short trip."

Hamman scrambled aboard, finding the natural seat Drake described and wasting no time settling into it. There were indeed natural hand grabs there, which he employed when Drake launched into the air after a brief warning. He was snapped back a bit by the force of leaving the Earth, and the sound of the wings beating to gain height sounded more like thunder to him. Once they were above the trees, Drake leveled off and began to glide more than fly, using the warmer air to assist him.

"My Lord, what a *marvelous* experience!" Hamman shouted out, laughing a bit with sheer joy. "I shall never forget this day!"

Drake held off laughing with him until they landed a short time later, using the thick screen of the trees surrounding the small farm to hide the dragon landing. When they appeared on the verge, they were again themselves, and the farmer there recognized Hamman at once, calling a greeting to him.

"My friend! What brings ye so far from home this morning? Is all well?"

"Aye, my friend Xeneon," Hamman smiled wide, offering him the grip. "I have brought a friend along today however, I hope ye do not mind."

"I am not used to strangers on my land," Xeneon growled a bit.

"Then let us become acquainted so as not to be strangers to one another," Drake offered smoothly, stepping forward to offer the grip. "I am Drake Natanleod, and Hamman tells me ye are going through a bit of a rough time."

The man looked first at Hamman, then to Drake, distrust obvious on his face. "Drake Natanleod is a dead man," he stated flatly.

Chapter 5

"I am clearly *not* dead, and yer name is not Xeneon, is it?" Drake asked with a half-grin. "Yer name is Xelion, and ye are mated to a very good friend of mine, the last Mother of the Obsidian Temple, Hellen. Do ye think I am dead, old friend?"

"DRAKE!" the man shouted happily, dropping his cudgel and coming to embrace his old friend. "When ye fell that day, I believed what Raad spread around about ye, and so did Hellen! She will be so happy to see ye, perhaps it might help perk her up."

"What is amiss?" Drake asked at once.

"She has been failing a bit every day for a long while now, My Lord," Xelion answered quietly. "Her mind is still sharp, but she has the trembles badly. She can barely cook due to it, I must do all of the knife work."

"Take me to her," Drake implored, his face wreathed with distress. "I wish to see my old friend."

Xelion put his cudgel on his shoulder before turning to walk back to the house, just a short distance away. Drake followed after, as did Hamman and soon they were inside the cozy cottage. Two young girls stood at the sink washing the morning dishes, and two large dogs lay quietly in front of the small hearth.

"Ye still have them?" Drake asked quietly.

"Her dogs? Aye!" Xelion confirmed. "Ye remember their names, aye?"

"Aye, she is Enodia and he is Cerberus," Drake chuckled, going to kneel in front of the dogs to give them a friendly pat or two. "How are ye two? Taking good care of yer mistress?" he asked them directly, speaking with quiet woofs and barks.

"Aye, Drake!" Enodia answered within his mind, coming to greet him with a friendly lick on the face. "Ye have been gone a long time!"

"I have not been missing, but ye and yer mistress have," Drake chuckled. "May I go to her?"

"Go, ye might be the only one she will see, except for family," Enodia mentally encouraged him. With an affectionate pat to both animals, Drake rose and walked confidently into the darkened room.

"Who is that?" he heard her ask at once, very alertly. "I think I have not heard those steps for a long time."

"Indeed, my dear," Drake intoned with great respect. "Hellen, 'tis Drake."

"Come back from Hades again, have ye?" she laughed outright. "I knew Raad was premature in announcing that ye were dead. I also knew ye would turn it to yer best advantage, I am glad my intuition was right."

"Why have ye been in hiding all these years?" Drake asked.

"Raad wanted all of us Elder Sisters sacrificed to his demonic masters," Hellen answered at once. "I knew he would burn the Temple of Sight, and that he would attempt to overcome the Spire's guardians. Please, tell me he was unsuccessful?"

"Most decidedly so," Drake chuckled. "In fact, twelve of yer sisters stood to fulfill their vows to keep the Light of the Spire safe against the Nagas and their evil. My daughter-in-law has just re-awoken the Spire, releasing them all to their fates and judgments."

"What? Daughter-in-law? What are ye saying, ye have a son? O my!" she gasped as a realization hit her. "Fleur was not sick with the wasting sickness at all! She was with yer child! No wonder she was so ill! How is it ye were able to keep that from *me*?"

"I knew naught of him 'till age nine," Drake told her honestly. "Fleur kept all knowledge of his parentage away from everyone, apparently."

"And?"

"He is a good man," Drake told her, letting the love for his son show in his tone. "Despite all odds, he has matured into a fine and fair High Lord, especially with Deborah by his side."

"Deborah?" Hellen gasped again. "Veronica's daughter? Ye were supposed to…"

"I know what I was supposed to do," Drake answered, a warning growl in his tone. "But when I beheld her in her crib, even dirty and abused, I could see she had a golden heart and I had mercy. I wanted to take her from there, but being dead has its disadvantages. I could not give away knowledge of my being alive to Raad by taking her, he would have known 'twas me. If he hadn't, Secundus would have, and they would have been able to find not only me but what Black Dragons I could muster. I made a choice, one life for many, and I feel the guilty pangs for it, knowing now what she had to endure. I shall tell ye she has won my heart, and that her abilities as High Lady must be seen to be believed. She has been revealed as a Phoenix, one of Ramona's Daughters."

"Is it so?" Hellen smiled. "So, Ma'at was right! A Phoenix had been born in the Land!"

"Aye, both of ye completely right, even though none of us knew what it meant."

"I was sure 'twas Julia or Ma'at!" she smiled, then winced a bit.

"So, ye have the wasting disease? How long have ye known?" Drake asked kindly, sitting across from her.

"Since before the War began, my boy," Hellen smiled beatifically. "I have had a good life, I have two daughters I have passed much of my knowledge onto, and I even managed to write a journal of my life while here in seclusion," she told him. "The Lady has been most kind, and if I am to meet my end this way, I must face it with courage."

"What if ye needn't meet yer end?" Drake proposed softly, feeling the Lady's energies building within him. "What if ye were to be offered a healing?"

"Ye are no healer," Hellen pointed out with a smile.

"I may not be, but many of my family are," Drake pointed out. "I carry the ability within me, and as an Ascended Being, I should be able to pull that ability forward."

"*Ascended?*" she asked, startled.

"Being dead has its advantages," Drake grinned. "I was able to rest, relax and meditate as I healed from the encounter with Secundus. While I did so I kept my mind on my promises to all, including the Black Dragons, about what I meant to accomplish. The Lady favored me with Her gifts, as She always does our family, and so the Commander of the Black Dragons rose to take Drake's place and finish what he had started. Julius' training, however harsh, made all the difference and I found myself doing more and more incredible feats of magick. I had to hide all of them, so as to avoid being openly sought out by Secundus. Raad's offer of great reward for my death, and that of the Black Dragons was very amusing, as it kept increasing every year. I even thought of turning myself in, just to collect the reward!" he laughed, hoping she would too. Instead she fell into a coughing fit, and when Drake offered her his kerchief, it came away bloodstained. "The disease has made great inroads," he noted.

"Aye, it should not be long now," Hellen answered, gasping a bit to regain her breath.

"If I could heal ye, would ye accept it?" Drake asked softly.

"I would," she said, managing a smile.

"Good then, if ye will allow me to touch ye?" Drake asked, in the best manners of men in the Land.

"If ye are certain about doing this," Hellen smiled faintly. "Ye know how debilitating healing this way is for people, aye?"

"I have some idea about that," Drake chuckled. "Try to relax, 'tis a mystery to me what is about to happen."

"Very well," Hellen nodded, closing her eyes and laying back on the thick quilts. Drake stood there for a few moments, allowing the energy he was feeling to rise up. Before he could touch Hellen he heard a distinct popping sound and looked up, seeing Deborah arrive, wreathed in flames.

"Stand back, Knight of the Land. 'Tis my task ye are undertaking, I should be about it."

Hellen opened her eyes and gasped, startled at what she saw. A gorgeous woman, enveloped completely in living fire licking around her outline. The fire however resembled long, fiery feathers, rather than its usual appearance, and Hellen could not stop staring.

"Lay back Elder Sister," Deborah advised kindly. "Relax, and accept the Lady's gift."

"I would willingly do so," Hellen agreed. At the first touch of Deborah's fiery fingers, Hellen gasped a bit, but not from any pain. It was more the realization of prophecy, manifested physically in front of her that caused her shocked reaction. Ma'at had said a Phoenix would manifest in the midst of Raad's war, but no one had understood her words at the time. In fact, they had all looked at Elanor with expectant eyes, only to have her laugh aloud.

"I am no Phoenix! The High Priestess' prophecy does not talk about me."

"Then whom?" Ma'at asked in wonder.

"The Lady's Will has yet to manifest," Hadrian had finally said. "We must be patient 'till it does. As Father always said, one can never anticipate the Goddess, or how She attends to Her work. But, when this Phoenix does manifest, we must know who she is and where she is. Drake, this falls to ye."

"Me? Brother, I am a dead man!" Drake had laughed aloud, the wounds from that battle still visibly healing. "I can do naught at the moment. I am fortunate to even be here, talking to ye."

"I know it well, ye should have read Raad's letter, offering me the opportunity to surrender now that ye were dead," Hadrian chuckled. "I am very glad 'twas just a letter I read, if he were standing next to me, I might have slain him just to stop him from gloating."

"Let him gloat," Drake growled a bit. "He has done his worst to me, now let him reap the rewards he has earned by doing so. I shall fulfill every promise I made, to all of those who are dead or captured. I shall not rest 'till I do, or 'till I am truly in the Lady's realm. Raad will die at my hand, and no other, that I vow."

All these thoughts now ran through Hellen's mind as she watched thin lines of fire trace over her body, as if in search of something, finally congregating around the large bulge on her left side. As she watched, the tendrils of flame sank into her skin, and she could feel the warm within her, and then a dull pain in the tender area where the bulge had been growing for years. Hellen glanced up, finding Deborah's eyes amber and warm, reassuring her all was well. She relaxed once more, finding that upon doing so, any pain receded, replaced by a feeling of warm well-being. Deborah's flames worked quickly, and as Hellen watched, the lump began to reduce bit by bit, 'till no more could be seen.

"O My Lady!" she cried out with joy, pain free for the first time in twenty years. "I am so very grateful to be healed!"

"Thank the Goddess for it," Deborah intoned, the flames suddenly abating, leaving her a bit spent. Drake was there at once to support her, for which she was very grateful.

"Ye have done good work today, Daughter," he said soothingly to her. "Let me carry ye back to yer pavilion, so ye may rest."

"O my!" Hellen's startled voice rang out across the room, and both of them looked up to see her standing in front of her mirror. Drake's eyebrows arched tall in surprise, Hellen looked about twenty years younger to him. Deborah's healing had been more thorough than ever before, and Drake now understood where Artos' abilities came from. "I have been given a full healing! She truly is one of Ramona's Daughters! Thank ye, Great Lady of the Land, for Yer favor!"

"Ye are most welcome," they all heard the whispered response, as if it were carried on the wind.

"Friend Xelion, come and greet yer wife!" Drake called out in quiet tones and when the man arrived his face turned first white with shock, then joyous when he saw that his wife was fully recovered.

"By the Lady! My wife will live!" he shouted out, coming to catch her in careful embrace. "I must go to the Temple as soon as I can to thank our Goddess!" he said, pushing her away just enough to look her over. Only then did he see the real healing that had been done, for Hellen's face and hair were twenty years younger. "What miracle is this?" he whispered. "She has restored two decades to ye!"

"I know not, except that a Phoenix is capable of channeling great amounts of divine energy, husband. I have never heard of such a healing being done before, not in all my years of studying."

Drake looked at Deborah, his eyes wide with astonishment and glistening with pride for her accomplishment. She met his gaze, smiled, then fainted into his arms, he barely catching her due to the suddenness of it. "Ye have done a miracle, again," he whispered as he lifted her. "Is there no end to yer abilities?"

"Who is she to have been so blessed?" Hellen asked.

"The daughter of Ramona," Drake answered. "Naught else matters about her."

"Ye are right about that," Hellen stated, nodding as she realized the truth of it due to her gifts. "I am glad ye did not end her life."

"I could not do what I meant to, and as I said before, I continue to feel guilty each time I am reminded of that day. I lost track of her soon after, so that the next time I saw her, I could not place her right away. When her identity was revealed to me I even thought about counseling my son against wedding her. I tested her, much to my embarrassment, and she proved to be earnest in her love for him. She resisted my every charm, every suggestion, and even refused to play the word game with me at all, such a woman's loyalty is a welcome addition to any marriage, aye?"

"And she is High Lady?" Hellen asked.

"Aye, and no one has filled the position better, not even my own mother," Drake answered truthfully.

"So, Ma'at's prophecy proved completely true. *The people will love her as one of their own.*"

"They do, ye know," Drake smiled. "I should get her back to her pavilion, where she can recuperate. Be well, Hellen. In yer kitchen, ye will find a small, wet barrel that needs to be opened right now. I hope what is inside will be a welcome addition to yer meal tonight. I shall return in a few days with some of the Black Dragons, I can see yer farm needs more than a bit of repair. We will make it all right again, and now that I know ye are here, I shall assure that help reaches ye. The Temple below is to be rebuilt and staffed, someone of yer knowledge and experience would be a welcome addition there."

"I shall think on it," Hellen smiled faintly. "I would like to meet the High Lady, when she is up to it."

"I would imagine she would be happy to meet with ye as well," Drake replied. "Good day all!"

So saying, he disappeared taking Deborah with him. Hamman suddenly found himself back at his farm, right where Drake had found him.

"I need a cup of ale," the farmer thought to himself. "Today has been one fraught with marvels!"

Back at the camp, Drake appeared with Deborah within the confines of her pavilion, where he found Calla in the process of tidying and cleaning the place.

"O my! What has she done now?" the young Dame asked with great concern as Drake gently laid his daughter in law down and stepped back.

"A great healing," he said. "She must sleep now. I shall leave her to ye, and take command of the camp. She would wish the work to continue. Watch her carefully, and if anything seems amiss, send for me at once."

"Aye My Lord," Calla agreed easily, already turning to loosening Deborah's garb in preparation for removing it, making it easier for the High Lady to sleep comfortably.

Drake strode out of the camp, his own clothing altering as he walked, until he looked ready for common work.

"Good morning all!" he called out as he approached the kitchen tent. "The High Lady has already performed her work for the day and needs to rest. I shall take command for the day, if ye will allow?" he smiled.

"Of course, My Lord," both Tyrion and Tristan nodded. "Where shall we begin?" asked the former.

"What needs doing next?" Drake asked in return, accepting a cup of caffe from Cyrus. It did not take long for a list of work to be made, assignments handed out and then they dispersed to accomplish as much as they could for the day.

Halfway across the Land, Erinn felt his wife's powers emerge even as far away as he was and a smile passed over his face, knowing she was about to do something stupendous. He was granted a vision of what she was doing, healing an older priestess, and a wave of pride and love washed over him. As he sat there, Arthfael noted the change of expression on his father's face, and he experienced a bit of a realization. His father was in magickal communication with his mother, and he wondered what was transpiring. Brianna saw his face adopt a slightly dreamy expression, and she quietly inquired.

"My Lord Prince?"

"My Mother's Phoenix abilities are at work, she is doing a healing by fire, or so it appears to me. Would ye like to see it?"

"Stop!" he heard as he reached out his hand, and the wraith of Sasha appeared between them. "She is not ready for such a thing, her abilities are not as honed as yers."

Arthfael snatched his hand back quickly, as if he had been slapped. Brianna's eyes grew wide as the apparition appeared, spoke and then disappeared, leaving them both a bit startled.

"I shall describe what I am seeing," he offered, regaining his aplomb first.

"I would like to know," Brianna agreed, settling in to listen. Her wonder quickly grew into awe as he described the healing of Hellen, the shrinking of the huge lump on her side, and the reversal of her aging. He was just finishing the tale when Erinn knocked on his door and entered.

"I had no idea my Mother could do that!" Arthfael concluded, his own tone awestruck.

"One must wonder if there are any limits to yer Mother's abilities," Erinn chuckled. "My son, I should go to her. Can I leave ye here overnight, under Sylvene and Thomas' supervision?"

"Of course," Arthfael answered at once, knowing what his father was subtly asking. "All will be well as we await yer return."

"Good. I want ye to walk with Alom tomorrow, and learn as much as ye can about what he is doing. Take whatever notes are necessary to organize yer thoughts. Dame Brianna, would ye please provide security?" Erinn asked quickly.

"Of course, My Lord," the young woman nodded.

"I would also like ye to learn as much as possible, so when I speak to the both of ye next I shall have a complete report."

"Aye, My Lord, I shall do my very best," Brianna acknowledged.

"Very well, I shall see the both of ye on the morrow, bright and early," Erinn smiled, disappearing from their sight.

"My Lord, 'tis late," Brianna said, turning to Arthfael regretfully, for she wanted to remain. "I must consult with Captain Sylvene as to my duties for the night."

"I shall see ye in the morning," Arthfael replied, even though he wished for her to remain. "Sleep well, when ye do."

"Thank ye, My Lord," she answered professionally. He watched her walk away, waiting until she was well gone before breathing a heavy sigh. Turning to his own duties, he found his wax tablet and stylus, setting them out so he could see them in the morning. Quickly he undressed, attended to his nightly ritual and settled into bed, adopting a meditative posture. The next thing he knew, the sun had just tinged the sky light pink. He noted light purple streaks running through it, and knew the day would be a hot one. Rising, he dressed quickly, making his way to the kitchen tent and quickly assessing what was on hand. He was missing an important element, and a splash from the nearby creek inspired him to fashion a quick spear. Brianna was just finishing her guard shift, and as she passed by the last station, she observed the young prince standing bare-chested with his trous rolled up to his knees in the midst of the creek, holding a spear. At once she noted his chest, broad and strong, with the characteristic rippled muscles in the midsection that attested to both his heritage and his commitment to work. He was alertly staring at the water, holding the spear at the ready, and she guessed his intent at once. Strolling to the waterside, she took up a guardian post, silently watching his pursuit. He did not even see her, or notice her, so intently did he watch the surface of the water, waiting for just the right moment. Finally as the chill of the water began to bite his toes a bit, a huge brown trout swam right between his feet. Arthfael's reaction was quick, and with a victorious cry, he pulled the flopping fish from the water impaled on his sharpened wooden spear, quickly dispatching it while thanking it for providing first meal that morning. He carefully set it up on the bank, then repositioned himself, waiting for the next fish to swim by. Brianna was very impressed, she had rarely seen anyone spear fish out of a stream before, and the gentle way he handled the fish afterwards touched her. Realizing she was behind her time, she almost ran to Sylvene's tent to make her report, so as not to delay the superior officer's day.

"Dame!" she heard as she reached the pavilion's entrance.

"I am here, Captain!" she panted out.

"Good, I thought ye were going to be late!" Sylvene answered, throwing sarcasm into her tone. "Ye know I despise tardiness."

"Aye, Captain!"

"What is for first meal?" Sylvene asked, testing her.

"The young Prince is spearfishing in the creek at the moment, Captain," the young Dame answered at once. "I would assume he is thinking fried trout, papas and eggs."

"Ye would be assuming correctly, Dame," they heard his resonant voice confirm from behind her. Sylvene, Thomas and Brianna turned quickly, seeing Arthfael's approach. He carried with him three large trout, already cleaned and scaled. "Who will assist me this morning?"

"I shall!" Thomas volunteered at once.

"As shall I," Sylvene laughed a bit. "Dame?"

"I am very hungry, I would be happy to help!" she laughed along with them. "Where would the best place be for me to start?

Sylvene grinned and pointed to the bin where the papas were stored. "Ye can start by scrubbing a dozen or so of those, Sister."

Without another word, the young woman bent to the task, taking up a large colander and filling it with some of the purple roots. Walking to the river with a stiff brush in hand, she bent to the task, emptying the colander into the river and scrubbing each root carefully until it was free of any dust or dirt. Once it was clean to her satisfaction, each one was returned to the colander, then the entire thing was given one more rinse before she returned to the cooking area. Thomas and Sylvene were working there together, and it was an easy relationship. Brianna had a prime opportunity to watch a well-matched couple work together, and she liked the picture it presented. They moved around each other easily, adding words to help direct the other to avoid colliding in the small space, and they asked questions of each other in a comfortable manner. When they were close to each other, there were no excessive displays of affection, but the warmth between them was a palatable force.

"Is that what being in love means?" she wondered to herself as she pulled out a cutting board and a chopping blade in preparation for seeing to cutting the papas. "I wonder what 'twould be like to feel that comfortable with someone."

Turning her attention fully upon her task, she made short work of cubing the papas into bite-sized squares, all approximately the same size. She liked onion with hers, and so sprinkled a few of dried ones out of the packet included in the packed stores they had with them. Almost at once, the scent of cooking tubers and onion filled the camp with a delightful scent, bringing compliments from both Sylvene and Thomas.

"Yer doing a good job there, Dame," Thomas complimented smoothly. "Someone taught ye how to do that very well."

"I learned from the High Lady," Brianna replied quietly, not looking for recognition.

"Well then, ye have had the best teacher possible," he smiled. "Have ye had caffe yet today?"

"Nay," she answered, continuing her work.

"May I bring ye some?" he asked.

"Thank ye, Sir Thomas. I would appreciate a cup," she answered with respect. He was back with it within a short time, and she found it amended according to her tastes. "My thanks again, the cup is perfectly amended."

"I have been observant then," Thomas smiled back at her.

"Ye have been watching me amend my caffe?"

"I have learned that being observant of a woman's habits is beneficial in every way, Dame," Thomas answered elegantly. "I mean no harm by it. 'Twas only meant to show friendship."

"I accept it in that light," she answered with a grin.

By this time her skillet was smoking hot, so that when she tipped the colander filled with cubed papas, a great sizzling noise resulted. The scent of their cooking soon filled the tent and the noise brought a smile to everyone's face.

While she worked on that aspect, Arthfael quickly ran to his tent to change his clothing, since he smelled of fish innards and sweat. He walked back to the area quickly, noting the smell of cooking papas.

"Those smell wonderful, Dame!" he called out with a grin.

"Thank ye, My Lord Prince," she returned, a grin on her own face. He found Sylvene and Thomas now washing the fish free of any remaining scales and offal, patting them dry as they laid them on the clean board. Arthfael turned to the stores, finding both maize and wheat flour available. He mixed them in the right proportions to make them tasty, adding salt and pepper into it. Next he returned to the river, where he opened the cold barrel to find the dozen eggs they still had with them from the last trading session. He cracked a few of them one by one into a bowl, scrambling them and mixing them until the liquid was golden yellow throughout. With the addition of salt and pepper, he reckoned he was ready to begin cooking the fish as soon as Brianna had the papas cooked. It did not take long before she proclaimed them nearly done, and when she did, Arthfael began the process of dipping the fish into the egg, then into the flour, then back into the egg, then back into the flour, tapping off the excess each time. By then his skillet was ready, the bacon fat smoking a bit as he slipped the fish into it, listening to the crackling as the fat hit the flour. He did a fish at a time, due to the size of the pan, and he made certain to feed everyone else first before filling his plate with the remainder. Sitting among the others, he dug in with real appetite, enjoying the simple meal among friendly folk.

"My Lord, the fish is quite delicious!" Sylvene complimented after the first mouthful. "I have rarely eaten a better meal!"

"Thank ye, Captain," he answered simply and humbly.

"I quite agree with the Captain," Thomas chimed in. "Yer family seems very gifted where cooking is concerned."

"I have watched and asked questions as my family has cooked before," Arthfael answered quietly. "Cooking is not that difficult a skill, if ye simply pay attention, and practice what ye see. I know I enjoy it," Arthfael smiled as he answered. "What should we do for the rest of the day?"

"The High Lord left no order for us to advance our progress along the road," Sylvene answered in a musing tone. "I believe we should just remain here, awaiting his return."

"We should go hunting then," Brianna suggested. "I love fish as a meal, but I heard ducks and geese honking during my guard shift early this morning."

"I saw deer tracks on my shift," Thomas put in. "But, most of the does are now nursing fawns and the males are very protective. We should seek easier prey."

"I suggest we find a farmhouse and negotiate for bit of beef," Sylvene added her opinion. "The High Lord brought a pig from somewhere, there must be farms about the area. We should split into two teams then."

"I shall take Sir Thomas and go across the river," Arthfael assumed command of the situation. "Ye and the young Dame will go in the opposite direction. We will meet back here around noon, with whatever meat we have bagged, if any. We might be able to barter for eggs and cheese too, if we find a farmhouse."

"Good idea," Sylvene nodded. "Let us clean up our camp, put things away and be off. "I think 'twill be hot again today, and the chill of that river will be welcome after pushing our way through the underbrush."

It did not take them long to wash up their dishes, and tidy up the camp, including adding a layer of lime to the latrine area. Once all was clean and organized, they split up into their agreed pairs and departed in opposite directions. As soon as the men were out of sight, Brianna turned to Sylvene with a conspiratorial wink.

"Captain, I am certain I heard geese last night," she said. "I propose we go and find them. Perhaps we might find the Lady's generosity will extend to a nice fat bird or two for supper. I for one, have had my fill of fish for a few days."

"Let us find them then," Sylvene nodded. "I shall let ye lead, since ye are blessed of Artemis."

Sylvene was referring to the young woman's genius for tracking game, which had surfaced soon after Jovita arrived with the young girl sitting behind her saddle. Brianna had lived with the Commander for many weeks due to her night terrors, which continued even after she asked to be moved to the common barracks. The young woman had slowly gained mastery over her fear of the dark, of strange noises and beds, and most especially of small places by exposing herself continually to them, so as to learn to deal with the fear. Soon after, the young woman's ability with weaponry was proven to be considerable; she was quick to learn what she wanted to, discarding anything she thought useless to her pursuit of perfection. The first time she had picked up a bow and arrow, mere months after her arrival, it was as if she had always held them. Jovita had been completely astonished to see her string the bow as if from memory, then load and shoot a nearly perfect center shot on the closest target.

"Who taught ye to do that?" she had asked the young girl. Brianna had looked up at Jovita with startled eyes, answering in a small voice.

"I am not certain, Commander. Did I do it wrong?"

"Come with me, young one," Jovita had entreated, holding forth her hand. Walking with the young girl, the Commander of the Amazons showed her how close her arrow had come to scoring a perfect shot. "I have never seen anyone pick up a bow and arrow for the first time and shoot like that. Ye are blessed of Artemis, a sister to the Lady of Wild Things. The Amazons are fortunate to have one such as ye among us."

Her memories continued to play forward, and she recalled from that point on, Jovita worked to expose the young woman to every piece of weaponry in the armory. Daily, the two had worked in the arena, the Amazon Commander seeking to find her specialty but finding that Brianna was bred for war and weaponry. In the process of building her up, however, Jovita had inadvertently let loose the young woman's ego. It had taken until Ashara's intervention in the barracks to resolve it.

Now, Brianna stooped to examine the ground, locating the distinct tracks of many birds; geese, ducks, pheasant and even grouse. Her mouth was set on roasted goose, and so she struck out for the marshy area they could see from their vantage point. Sylvene followed closely behind, on guard for any rogue bear or wild pig that might be about, knowing their uncertain temperaments could spoil any hunting trip very quickly. Brianna made a direct approach to a place she could use as a blind, it was heavy with cattails and reeds, as well as a large stand of brambleberries. Sylvene knew that in the Autumn, the deer would come here to eat the berries, knowing they were safely screened by all of the underbrush. They could hear quacking and honking coming from the small river, and found a place where they could crouch to observe. Brianna carefully parted the heavy reeds, and they beheld a hunter's delight. There seemed to be dozens and dozens of birds floating there in the gentle current, and Brianna quickly looked them over for potential prey. It was obvious to her which pairs of ducks and geese had young, but she could see there were un-mated birds floating among the others. Such a thing was not rare, even though Brianna knew that such birds mated for life, they sometimes did not find mates in time to breed, or their mates were lost to predators. The loss of their mates must be devastating to them, she thought sympathetically as her eyes continued to scan the scene. As she did so, a huge goose floated by, and she could see it was feral. Someone in the area had lost one of their house geese, she thought with a smile, for it meant this one might just serve her cause. Such animals seemed to have a harder time finding mates in the wild, and Brianna's opinion was simply that since they had been raised by humans, they had no idea how to be wild geese. Trying to pursue a mate without knowing what to do would be fruitless, she reckoned as she watched the huge grey bird float by, concentrating on the surface of the water, looking for small fish or large insects. Brianna prepared to make her shot, beginning by taking an arrow from her quiver and attaching a line to it. Pulling her bow from her back, making no discernable sound to Sylvene's sensitive ears, Brianna loaded it and slowly pulled it back, aiming it at the floating grey goose until she had the perfect shot lined up. The arrow shot from the bow, striking the goose in the neck, severing the vein running there and killing the bird instantly. Brianna pulled on the line attached to the arrow's butt, and within a few moments, they had their bird without getting wet in the cold morning water.

"Sister!" Sylvene commented with a grin. "Ye *are* truly blessed of Artemis! We did not even have to go swimming this morning, and I did not relish the necessity of having to do so. We will be back in camp before the men, and have plenty of time to laze about! The day will be hot, and I suggest digging out our sundresses!

"I agree, Sister!"

The two women quickly took up their catch, quickly field dressing it right there on the bank. Leaving the entrails in a neat pile on the bank, the both thanked the goose for its life, and for the nourishment the meat would provide. With one final rinse of the carcass in the cold river water, they were on their way back to camp, and the sun was barely an hour above the trees. Once they were back, they quickly heated some water, sponging themselves free of any sweat and blood from the hunt. Afterwards, they dressed in the bright silk sundresses created by the High Lady, for the sun was already beginning to warm the air. They waited and waited for Arthfael and Thomas to return, finally helping themselves to a cup of cold wine each to ease the thirst raised by their hunt, and by the heat of the day. That was how the two men found them when they finally did return with scratches and tiny tears in their clothing from pushing through the brambles all that morning.

"Ye two look very comfortable," Arthfael grouched a bit as the two women handed them each a cup of the cold wine. "Did ye have any luck?"

"Aye, we have a nice fat goose for supper!" Sylvene smiled. "Our young huntress brought it down, and we did not even have to swim for it!"

The two men stared at Brianna for a moment, looks of wonder and awe clearly reflected in their faces, and they asked for the tale of the hunt. Brianna gave it to them very professionally, barely acknowledging how rare and perfect her shot had been.

"The young Dame is too modest," Sylvene offered when she was done. "She took that goose out at twenty paces, and even thought to attach a cord to the end of the arrow before shooting. Her shot was perfect, and with the cord, all we had to do was pull it to shore! She is a sister to Artemis, as Jovita declared all those years ago."

"Congratulations," Arthfael offered at once, extending his forearm to exchange the grip with her. "Twenty paces over water, and ye did not even get wet! What a shot, I wish I could have seen it!"

"Where is yer contribution for tonight's meal?" Sylvene asked with a grin.

"We foraged on the way back from spending hours chasing shadows," Thomas offered at once, pulling the full bag from his back. "We have wild onions, plantain leaves, wildflowers and look! We even brought honey!" he laughed a bit, rubbing his arm where two large welts were even now forming.

"O my!" Brianna exclaimed, looking at his arm. "Ye got stung for yer trouble!"

"Any pain is well worth such a prize!" Thomas smiled wide. Brianna put her wine aside at once, reaching for one of their service bowls and walking to the riverside. Kneeling down, she found an area that was nice and muddy, the kind that would cling to the skin once it dried a bit. Scooping up a bit in her palm, then another, she sorted out the small pebbles, adding the clayish dirt to the bowl with sufficient water to keep it moist. Returning to where Thomas stood, she asked him to extend his arm, slathering the cold river mud all over the beestings in a very thick layer. "Keep that on 'till it dries Sir," she instructed from experience. "The mud will pull out the venom from the beestings, and help reduce the swelling. I have been stung for my efforts to secure honey from wild hives, I learned quickly what to do about it."

"Ye are very practical," Thomas complimented, noting that the pain was already receding. "Thank ye very much, Dame. The pain is already less."

"Ye should not move that arm around much, at least not 'till the swelling goes down," Brianna continued professionally, her own experience guiding her. "The goose will not be difficult to cook, but we should see what edibles you have brought with ye! I would wager we will have a royal meal tonight!" she laughed a bit, the wine helping to relax her.

"I can help with that!" Arthfael volunteered at once. Sylvene and Thomas exchanged a glance, knowing they were the acting chaperones.

"We should get to it, before the sun climbs any higher," Brianna replied. "We would not want anything to wilt before we can eat it!"

"Take the produce upriver a bit," Sylvene instructed. "I am certain ye can find a nice calm place to wash and sort out everything. It should not take ye too long to do so," she went on, adding her suggestions without being overbearing.

"Aye, Captain," Arthfael answered, a slight smile on his face as he heard the subtle instructions in her words. "We should not be gone overlong."

"That should give me time to wash up a bit!" Thomas put in. "I shall not bother with the medicinal pack on my one arm, however. I might need assistance getting dressed."

"Ye will have all the help ye need," Sylvene smiled warmly.

"Yer assistance would be greatly appreciated," he answered.

Brianna and Arthfael started to feel a little uncomfortable as the intense emotions between the two surfaced. They turned to take up the two large bags of foraged goods, put one each over their shoulder and walked away from the camp, following the small stream. They walked a goodly ways up the river, to nearly where Brianna had first spotted the river fowl on her sentry shift. There was a depression along the river, a natural bowl they quickly piled large stones around to deepen enough to provide a basin to wash their produce. The water smelled clean, and Brianna even went to the extreme of tasting it first to assure its purity.

"The water is clean, My Lord Prince," she stated with a smile, keeping their relationship professional, her usual approach.

"Thank ye, Dame," he answered in keeping with her attitude. Quickly, they emptied the foraging bags, sorting everything into piles to take a quick assessment of what they had. Brianna grinned, for there was a goodly amount of wild asparagus gathered, as well as mushrooms, wild onions, wild artichokes and finocchio bulb. There were wild turnip and mustard greens too, enough for everyone to have a generous amount.

"Ye have brought a great deal of produce, My Lord," Brianna commented as they rinsed and scrubbed everything clean. "Are we expecting company?"

"One never knows, Dame," Arthfael chuckled. "There are travelers and merchants on business trips, one must be ready to offer hospitality, after all. 'Tis also the possibility of my father's continued absence past today. I have noted that when my parents have an opportunity to be together, they usually stretch it out for as long as possible."

"I would imagine their opportunities to be alone together are relatively rare outside the Capitol city," Brianna speculated. "It seems to me that if ye are married, ye would want to be together as much as possible."

"I see it the same way," Arthfael nodded as he put aside the last of the wild onions. Turning to the pile, he pulled out the mustard and turnip greens, beginning the process of washing each leaf free of any dirt remaining. Their time together seemed very short indeed as they worked together, chatting companionably the entire time, finally rinsing out the bags and returning the clean produce to them for their walk back to the camp. Sylvene and Thomas were just finishing setting the cooking fire for the night as they returned, and the produce was taken to a shady spot close to the river to await its cooking.

"A cup of wine for the both of ye?" Sylvene asked.

"I would enjoy a nice cold cup!" Brianna declared. "And as soon as we have our meal ready to cook, I think I am going swimming! The day is getting hotter as it progresses!"

"So 'tis, young one," they heard and watched in astonishment as Drake Natanleod suddenly materialized out of the shadows, having been sent by the Goddess to do Her work. "Good day! I hope I am not intruding?" he smiled.

"Sir!" Arthfael greeted him with a smile. "Ye are always welcome! Are ye thirsty?"

"The day is hot enough to inspire thirst in anyone," Drake chuckled. "Ye do have something cold about, aye?"

"Right this way, Sir!" Arthfael invited. Together, they walked to where the cask of wine stood in the cool shade, about a quarter of the barrel immersed in the swirling river water. It did not take long for Drake to be holding a cold cup, and after the first drop or two was poured out for the Goddess, he sipped deeply, quickly draining the vessel's contents. With a grin, he held it out for more, and it was quickly refilled, only to be drained once more.

"Ah! 'Tis fine to sip a good vintage on such a warm day!" he smiled, holding forth the cup once again. Arthfael gladly did so, enjoying his Grandfather's company a great deal while they talked of pleasant things. Finally, Sylvene walked to him, inclined her head to show respect and addressed him.

"My Lord, why are ye here?" she asked plainly.

"Ye are a true Amazon, my dear," Drake chuckled. "Always curious about the underlying causes as to why things happen the way they do. I am simply here because my son is not. I am not saying ye and Sir Thomas are not fine chaperones, but Arthfael is a Natanleod, and they are different than most folk in the Land. Besides, I hear 'tis a goose needing to be cooked! I love cooking wildfowl!" he volunteered himself subtly.

"We would be honored, My Lord," Brianna stepped forward at once. "If I may assist, so I might learn as well?"

"Yer assistance will be very welcome, young Dame," Drake smiled winningly. She felt the power of his charm wash over her, her cheeks flushing a bit in response. Arthfael was beside her at once, assuming a protective stance as he did so. Drake smiled inwardly, thinking the two young people would make a fine match. "I hope ye will also help us, young man?" he turned to Arthfael to ask.

"I would be honored."

"Good then! We should get that goose rubbed down soon, so the seasonings have time to flavor the meat properly. Have ye decided what to do with all of the foraged goods ye have on hand?" he asked with a grin.

"If we had more eggs, we could make beautiful fritters, My Lord," Brianna sighed.

"Ye are only lacking eggs for that?" Drake asked alertly.

"Aye Sir, we have flour and olive oil aplenty!" Brianna assured him.

"Good then," Drake grinned, making a subtle gesture with his left hand. A wicker basket of large brown eggs appeared, suspended by its handle, which Drake grasped deftly out of the air before it could fall. "Will this be sufficient?" he asked.

"My goodness, there must be five dozen in there!" Brianna assessed quickly.

"The hens at the High Lord's house are generous layers," Drake chuckled, knowing Millicent would note the missing basket at once. He was sure she would contact him later to scold him for theft, and anticipated the word battle they would play as a result. "Now, let us see what we can use," he went on, gesturing to where the produce lay out in the shade. Drake's face broke out in a smile and he nodded in satisfaction. "We have enough for not only the egg fritters, but 'tis also sufficient produce make a nice soup too. Well done, Sir Thomas and Arthfael!"

"Thank ye, My Lord!" the two called back.

"Dame, would ye please fetch me a bowl, if ye have one?" Drake asked.

"Of course, My Lord. We have a cutting board and knives set up in the cooking tent already."

"Good, we can begin cooking at once then," Drake smiled. Quickly, he chose what he wanted for his batter, reserving the rest for another usage, taking his bowl filled with greens and other produce to the shelter of the tent. Setting them out in the order he wanted to use them, he laid them out neatly, then washed his hands. "Dame, would ye please put a large kettle of water on to boil?" he asked, turning to her. "Hot water in a kitchen is a necessity, especially for washing hands in between ingredients."

"I agree with ye, Sir," Brianna responded, going to the task. It did not take long for the water to steam pleasantly, and after washing his hands up over the wrists, Drake began to put together the rub mix for the goose. Brianna washed just as thoroughly, as did the rest of them, so they could be of as much assistance as possible. After the goose was rubbed with the spices and salt, inside and out, the younger couple retired to the river for a swim. Sylvene retired to the tent, leaving Thomas there with Drake. A short time passed in silence as Drake sat beside the cooking fire, basting the goose to keep it moist, until finally Thomas cleared his throat.

"My Lord," he began.

"Go on," Drake encouraged, knowing what the man had to say was likely very important.

"Captain Sylvene and I have been talking a great deal while assigned to this detail," Thomas began, his voice low and intense. "We originally made plans to be married at the High Lord's house, in the Barracks among our friends, but our feelings have changed recently."

"And so?"

"We would like to be together in a more official capacity sooner rather than later," Thomas let it spill out, his emotions raw about it.

Drake grinned wide at once, putting aside his pan of basting sauce. Once his hands were free, he extended his right hand to the man in front of him, offering his congratulations.

"I can understand yer haste," he said quietly. "Sylvene is an attractive woman, and well skilled in every art she has pursued. If ye ride to the east about twenty miles, ye will find a small Temple where ye can contract for yer ceremony," he grinned. "Here is the silver to offer the priestess, a pack of ten sikars, some Herb and o, take this voucher for one of Nathan's inns for yer honeymoon. 'Tis good for a week's stay at any of them. I never had the chance to use it myself," Drake said quietly, handing it to him. "My felicitations upon yer joining. May the Lady bless yer union with peace and joy for all days."

"These are kingly gifts!" Thomas marveled, tucking them away. "What inn would ye recommend?"

"For Sylvene?" Drake asked in return, taking a moment to consider before answering. "I would take her to the coastline, to the Inn of White Sands. I know Jovita would have enjoyed our stay there."

"Thank ye, My Lord!" Thomas whispered in suppressed excitement. "I would not have such things to offer her without yer generosity! Our new life will start out on a very good note!"

"As it should, Thomas de St. Germaine, man of the Land," Drake smiled warmly. "Ye have shed everything from out there, and embraced the Lady's way completely. May ye be happy in yer new life! Ye should be off soon, if ye are to arrive at the Temple before dark," he suggested.

"O!" Thomas exclaimed suddenly. "I forgot about the younglings! Sylvene and I were tasked to watch over them!"

"I am here," Drake pointed out seriously. "Surely, 'tis the Lady's providence that such is the case? If I were not here, yer wedding would have to wait. As 'tis, ye can go without guilt, as they will be watched over by myself."

"But we gave our word," Thomas hesitated. His reluctance disappeared in the face of what happened next, as the Goddess materialized beside Drake.

"Aye, so ye did. I have sent someone whose word is impeccable, so that ye will feel free to go," She pointed out gently. "Ye have done well, Thomas de St Germain, to embrace yer new life so completely. I can arrange for yer older memories to leave ye, so that ye will cease to be reminded of what ye left behind, if ye wish."

"My Lady, ye have no need to remove them," Thomas smiled warmly. "They seem to me to be but faded dreams, I must work hard to remember them. Names and faces are disappearing from my memory too, for which I am most grateful. I am a man who has been blessed with a great gift, and I do not intend to misuse it."

"I knew ye would understand, once yer mind was free," the Lady smiled benignly. "May yer union with Sylvene be all ye both need and require for mutual happiness."

"Th…Thank ye, My Lady!" Thomas smiled, bending the knee out of respect and love.

"O, get up!" She laughed, offering him a hand to assist. "Go on now, surprise yer lady with all the news. If ye ride hard, ye will be married before midnight."

Thomas' only answer was a wide and excited grin, giving his face a very youthful appearance for a few moments as he nearly ran to the pavilion to relate the day's happenings. When the two were seen next, they emerged from the tent, their bags in hand, dressed for travel. It did not take long to inform Brianna and Arthfael as to the situation, and after exchanging hugs between the women and the grip between the men the two were off.

"Ye are a good hierarch," Drake said quietly to the Goddess beside him as he watched the intended couple spur their horses to a full gallop, headed in the direction of the small Temple.

"I reward those who deserve it, and let justice fall upon those who do not honor my Laws. Oftentimes, both expressions are circumvented by the forces who seek to do evil, but sometimes they do finally reach those for whom they were intended. Thomas is one of those, and I am glad he is redeemed from the false religion taught out there. He is too good of a man to leave among such savages."

"It continues to degrade?"

"Constantly, as if people were de-evolving in some way," the Goddess sighed heavily. "As ignorance is continually enforced by religion, and dogma replaces truth in teaching, the mind loses its ability to reason clearly. Those who support the agenda of evil certainly would not want people thinking for themselves, 'tis why they use such tactics. Ignorant people, people led by fear and intimidation, are much easier to control than those who can think for themselves and reason despite their emotions. The enemy wishes to enslave Creation, so as to harness the power of the elementals for itself, diminishing the reach of the Light. People like Thomas prove to me that all hope is not lost, and that that world out there is filled with good folk who only wish to do good deeds and live well. Why others believe they are entitled to more is beyond me, when simply having enough should suffice. Even I do not fully understand what drives people from time to time, and I do not lay all of it at the feet of the enemy, since people have free will to choose. Why they would choose evil is the question that continues to evade answer in my mind, when choosing the Light is so much more beneficial to all?"

"The answer to such a question is beyond me, My Lady," Drake admitted without hesitation. "I wondered that often during the war, when the fate of battle put me against a former associate. I could not and still do not understand what makes people willingly choose evil over good."

"Someday, we will all understand," the Goddess sighed. "Watch over them Drake. Arthfael may be an understated member of the family, but his passions run deep. He reminds me of ye, actually, in that regard."

"I shall be very diligent then," Drake chuckled deep in his throat.

"Ye should not be overly proud of yer past, ye know."

"I am well aware I am no angel, My Lady," Drake returned without hesitation. "And much of what I did was in the interest of winning a war I had no business winning," he continued in defense of his actions. "I needed as many allies as possible, and father always said that women would be my best friends when times were hard."

"He was right about that," the Goddess laughed a bit. "I shall leave ye to yer duty."

"Farewell, My Lady. I believe I shall enjoy this duty," Drake laughed with her. Once the deity had departed, Drake took a deep breath and set himself for his next duty. Turning, he walked to where the two people sat beside the small stream and squatted down beside them.

"It appears ye are now under my tutelage," he said quietly. "I shall tell the both of ye right now that I consider ye both adults and completely capable of conducting yerselves in an upright manner. Ye both know the rules, and the usual manner in which relationships are handled in the Land, I am only here to watch over ye and to keep ye safe. I do not expect I shall have to watch every move ye make, nor monitor everywhere ye go, am I understood?"

"Aye, Sir," Arthfael agreed quickly.

"Aye, My Lord," Brianna added.

"Good then, we shall enjoy our time until the High Lord returns then," Drake nodded. "Now, I must return to basting that goose, before it dries out! I hope someone will bring me a cup or two while it roasts?"

"I shall!" Brianna agreed at once.

"As shall I," Arthfael chuckled.

The rest of that day was spent relaxing and watching the goose skin turn golden brown and crisp. When it was finally finished, their plates were quickly loaded before the three of them walked to the riverside to sit for their supper. It was very pleasant to sit and listen to the river's music, the rushing fall of it over rocks and into small pools while eating the deliciously cooked meal.

"O Sir!" Brianna remarked after nearly half her plate was gone. "I have never eaten such a well-flavored bird! I shall use this method every time, from now on!"

"I am honored, young Dame," Drake smiled warmly, liking her.

When the bird had been reduced to a meaty carcass, Drake directed Brianna to bring him a kettle of water from the river. She watched in fascination as he set the water to heat over the fire, chopping and adding the last of the onion, carrot and finocchio bulb as aromatic components, starting a hearty soup for morning. The carcass was quickly divested of every scrap of flesh remaining, then it was tossed into the depths of the small river, an offering of thanks to the scavenger children of the Lady. Drake smiled to see both of his charges attend to the clean-up of the camp without further direction, and as the sun set all was in readiness for the next day's activities. It took two pots of tea between the three of them to settle their supper, while Drake conversed easily with the younger people, answering their questions as they were asked.

"Grandfather, why did ye not try to slay Raad before the war's end?" Arthfael ventured.

"O, I tried boyo," Drake sighed heavily. "In fact, 'twas that very thing that got me caught and imprisoned and I was introduced to Ishmael ben Cain for the first time. Would ye like to hear as much as I can tell ye without his presence?"

"I would!" Arthfael answered with a huge grin on his face.

"As would I!" Brianna echoed.

"Very well, 'tis a short enough tale, without Ishmael's input. I always forget a vital detail or two, especially about his contributions," Drake chuckled. "It happened just after my discommendation was handed down by Hadrian," he began, letting his mind wander over the events of the past. "Raad heard about it and before I could stop him, he captured Ironhorse and most of the older Black Dragons. He sent me a letter, written in their blood, telling me to surrender myself or he would start bleeding them dry, one by one, starting with the oldest and frailest of them. I could not, would not allow it to happen, not when I alone could stop it and so I made my way to the fortress he was occupying, high up in the mountains. Presenting myself at the gate, I was taken directly to him, a great prize of war," Drake continued, a strange smile crossing over his face. "I was given to Secundus, who began his campaign to kill me slowly and painfully at once. When he finished with me that day, I was tossed into one of the holding cells below and left to recover as I could. It was then I met Ishmael, he was in the cell next to me and he was slated to be bled for the Naga's cause next. I used what magick I could summon to disguise his presence within the cell, so it appeared he had simply vanished. As soon as his 'escape' was reported, we were able to slip away, as they left his cell door wide open. He bent the bars of my cell to allow me to slip through, and we helped each other escape. As soon as we were outside and away enough, I simply collapsed from the effort of using the last of my strength and magick to conceal us. Ishmael carried me into a cave and secreted us within, allowing me the time to recover and heal. We made our return to the fortress a few days later, finding Raad in the process of bleeding the next of the elder Black Dragons. It hurt me, but he was already on the road to the next life, and so we used his death to cover the escape of the rest of the Dragons. I shall always remember the smile that appeared on his face as he saw us leaving, and since my ascension, I have had the chance to speak to him about it. I know that he feels he was of service to his fellow

Black Dragons, and his presence in the Higher Realms is proof enough that the Lady loves him."

The two young people stared at Drake as the scene he described played out in their fertile imaginations.

"My Lord," Brianna finally said, her voice filled with respect and awe. "I have heard that ye fought a secret war during those times, that yer sentence of discommendation was a mere ruse that allowed ye to work without being observed too much. What ye have just told me only confirms those tales; I thank ye for sharing it with me, and for everything ye did to overcome Raad and his Naga allies. Because of what ye did, we are all free."

"As it should be, young Dame," Drake grinned. "Now, ye two should be abed. Sleep deeply, as I shall be on guard all night. I think I shall enjoy a sikar for the first part of my shift. Good night."

There was no arguing with his tone, they stood and respectfully wished him a good night before preparing for sleep. Wishing each other a good night after attending to their nightly routines, Brianna allowed a discreet kiss on the cheek to pass between them, which Arthfael counted as somewhat of a victory.

"Good night, my…Arthfael," she said quietly.

"Good night, Brianna," he answered, letting his feelings enhance his rapidly deepening voice. "Sleep well."

"I hope ye do too," she answered, turning to where curtains created a partition between their beds. He watched her walk through them, and once she was out of his sight, he sighed heavily. Turning to his own screened sleeping area, he quickly attended to cleaning his mouth once more, using the rosemary rinse to finish. Once his head was on the pillow and the covers draping him lightly, he was asleep within moments, resting quietly throughout the night.

Chapter 6

"Arthfael!" he heard the barked order in his dreams, and sat straight up in bed, shaking off the covers as he did so. "Get up, 'tis dawn! Ye have work to be about, boyo!" Drake finished.

"What?" the young man answered in a dazed voice.

"Get up!" Drake repeated, more harshly. "The sun is up over the treetops, 'tis time to be up and about!"

"Aye Sir!"

Scrambling out from under the blankets, Arthfael dressed quickly as he heard Drake repeat the urgent summons to the young Amazon across just across from him.

"Dame Brianna, 'tis time to be up and about! The sun is rising!"

"Aye Sir! I have just finished my morning prayers to the Goddess!" came the ready response. "I shall be dressed momentarily."

Before too much time passed, both young people stood before Drake, fully dressed and ready for their day. After a quick inspection, he pronounced them properly accoutered for the day.

"We will have our first meal, which is ready," Drake told them, taking full command. "Afterwards, we will go on a bit of a walk to aid with our digestion

"Very well, Sir. I am ready!" Brianna pronounced.

"As am I!"

"Good, let us get to it then!" Drake grinned. Walking outside, the scent of the soup Drake had put to cook overnight hit their noses, and their stomachs growled in response. The former High Lord had caffe ready, a welcome cup of warmth after the long night, which they sat to enjoy while listening to the river's music. After they had consumed two bowls of the delicious soup each, along with the rest of the biscuits from the night before, there was very little left to put away, and so it was piled into one of the soup bowls and left by the river for the scavengers to enjoy. Drake reckoned the bowl would be empty by the time they returned to camp, somewhere around noon by his estimation. Once everything was washed and put to rights, their food had settled enough for Drake to order them out into the woods for a long run, starting slowly and building to a swifter pace by the end. He was gratified to see Brianna's conditioning was every bit as good as Arthfael's, the two of them took very little time to recover their breath after the intense run.

"Good, ye are both in very good shape!" he complimented, handing them each a water flask. "Now, I want to eat from the Lady's Abundance tonight, and we used all of the foraged goods on hand in camp. Here are three bags for each of ye, including me. We will walk together, and I shall test yer knowledge of foraging."

The day was already hot, but the forest shade cooled them as they walked along, talking about how to use what they found. Their bags filled with wild edibles; garlic, onions, finocchio bulb, greens of all kinds, and they even found an early stand of fall gallinacci mushrooms too. Their orang-ish flesh and frilly edges promised a rich and delicious supper, everyone in the Land enjoyed searching for the elusive mushrooms every Autumn. As they walked along they came upon a small farmhouse, with a large flock of hens. The older woman and man working in the house garden came to greet them, and willingly bartered several dozen large brown eggs for a share of their foraging, plus a silver coin or two. Drake was certain to pass the man of the house a sikar or two, inquiring quietly if the lady smoked as well.

"Ye'd best leave me one or two more for her, just in case," the man chuckled a bit. "She's a good woman who works very hard, and asks for so little. I want to have one for her if she wishes."

"Very well," Drake grinned, handing him two packages, one of the larger size he enjoyed, one of the smaller ones that Deborah liked to smoke. "Just clip off the end before ye light them, and remember not to pull the smoke too far down into yer lungs."

"Ah, thank ye for the reminder!" the older man laughed. "Ye don't remember me, do ye?"

"Should I?"

"Aye, my name is Lightfoot."

"Lightfoot?" Drake ask incredulously, peering at the man intently. "Is it possible that ye survived the battle of Demon's Pass?"

"Ye see the evidence in front of ye, Drake Natanleod," he heard the man laugh in answer, and heard the echo of a more youthful man. "Do ye not believe yer own eyes?"

"By the Lady, 'tis ye!" Drake laughed in delight. "The fastest runner in recorded history! Ye outran the avalanche!"

"In a way, aye. I was able to get out far enough ahead to find shelter in a cave. When the entrance was covered over by ice and debris, I found my way out through miles of tunnels. When I emerged at the base of the pass, I was astonished to see the devastation caused by the avalanche. It was clear to me that Secundus' demon army was no more, and so I simply walked away from it all. I wandered the Land for a bit, 'till I found this place, a burned out shell of a house and barn, and this beautiful lady in the midst of it, burying her former husband. We've been together ever since, rebuilding the farm to how ye see it now."

"Ye have done a fine job too!" Drake declared, looking around the place. "May I be introduced to yer lady?"

"Aye. Bernice, will ye please come and meet our guest?" he called to her. She came to him at once, her hands dusty from the garden, and her apron filled with produce.

"I am very happy to meet ye, My Lord Drake," she smiled.

"But we know each other!" Drake realized. "Ye used to be a priestess in the Obsidian Temple! I remember ye could read people's illnesses simply by touching them, so sensitive were yer abilities."

"I can still do that," Bernice smiled benignly. "But not for everyone anymore. I simply do not have the strength I used to."

"Who does?" Drake smiled warmly. "I am glad to see the both of ye alive and well, after all this time. Thank ye for the eggs, they will make a fine meal in the morning!"

"The war, 'tis over, aye?" Bernice asked suddenly.

"Aye, 'tis over," Drake told her. "However, our enemy is tenacious, and we still find the occasional small conclave from time to time. 'Tis good then, that my son has inherited my abilities, and that his wife is who she is as well."

"Wait, what?" Bernice asked in a startled tone. "Son? Have ye adopted then?"

"My abilities would not fully pass to an adopted son, my dear. Ye are well aware of my true nature, ye would understand this. Erinn is my natural born son, Fleur of the Temple is his mother."

"Fleur? But, she is so tiny!" Bernice blurted out. "A child of yers would likely rip her to pieces, and she would never be able to bear another!"

"Ye are mistaken," Drake replied. "Not only did she survive his birth, but she lived to see him become Knight Commander, then War Duke, and finally now High Lord before she passed. I am very proud of him."

Bernice just stared at Drake, her mouth slightly agape as she processed all of the news she had just heard. "My goodness, I have been gone from the center of things for a long time. How old is yer son?"

"He is in his thirties," Drake told her. "As is his wife, Deborah."

"Deborah? Ye mean Spurious' demon child?" Bernice shrilled back, her tone reflecting horror. "But, ye were tasked to see to her passing! What happened?"

"When ye have the chance to meet her, ye will understand why I stayed my hand, my dear," Drake answered. "She truly has a golden heart, and she is the Phoenix the old High Priestess Ma'at prophesied of."

Bernice stared at him, unable to speak due to her shock, she had thought all of this over and done many years earlier. The news that the promised Phoenix had appeared in the person of Veronica's daughter was completely unexpected. Bernice sat down quickly, her mind spinning and her heart pounding, as she processed everything Drake had just told her. With a gesture, Drake produced a skin of wine and beckoned to Lightfoot for a cup, pouring her a draught and handing it to her. She did not even hesitate, she simply sipped a few times before putting the cup down suddenly and swallowing hard.

"Ye just manifested that skin out of the air," she pointed out.

"Dragons have such abilities," Drake answered seriously. "I have found that since my ascension that my dragon-self manifests more often than it did when I lived in the Land."

"Ascension? Ye did it?"

"I did, with the Lady's assistance," Drake smiled. "It can be done, as I said it could be. The Land is the perfect place to make such an effort, as 'tis a place of magick and mystery of every kind."

"By the Lady, ye have truly done it!" she answered as his skin began to glow subtly, taking on the appearance of polished alabaster, lit from within. "O Drake, I am so happy for ye! Ye have done something no one has been able to accomplish for many centuries! Congratulations, my dear friend."

"Thank ye, my dear!" Drake smiled brightly. "Now, I must get back to training my grandson and the young Dame there."

"Dame?"

"Aye, remember I promised the Amazons would be part of the regular Army?"

"I do."

"Meet Dame Brianna," Drake grinned and gestured with a flourish. "She comes to us from the Amazon Corps, personally trained by Commander Ashara's hand. She has proven to be an excellent addition, as have all the Amazons who have joined. I am glad to have them in our Army!"

"O my goodness!" Bernice grinned, finishing the wine in her cup. "I feel like celebrating. All of this good news, all at once! Husband, perhaps we should call our friends for a party tonight? We have so much extra cheese, and I could just make antipasto plates and a nice light soup, because of the heat. What say ye?"

"I like this idea," Lightfoot smiled.

"Ye have a good time," Drake put in. "I must get these two back to camp before the High Lord returns from his side trip. I almost forgot to introduce my grandson, Arthfael ap Erinn Natanleod."

"He is not yer natural grandson," Bernice pointed out.

"Nay, he is adopted, but he is a son of the House, 'tis no question of that," Drake chuckled.

"He is Raad's get?"

"Aye, and his mother was a Temple Priestess before Raad corrupted her. His start in life was not a good one, but the Lady is making that all up to him now, I think."

Bernice stood and put aside her cup, walking to Arthfael to stand in front of him, extending her hand. "My son, if ye will allow me to read ye?"

"Why?" Arthfael asked at once, hesitating. Drake grinned a bit, but said nothing, waiting for Bernice to explain.

"I am an empath and I see illnesses within those the Goddess allows me to. I have used the ability before to assess someone's character, ask yer Grandfather."

Drake blushed a bit, and a roguish grin appeared, but he did not flinch when meeting the old woman's eyes. "Her abilities are remarkable, and I wish she would have been available to treat Hadrian," was all he would say.

"Very well, I have naught to hide," Arthfael agreed. As soon as Bernice touched his arm, she recoiled, for the first memories she touched were those of the days in the pits below Raad's fortress.

"Ye were just a babe, how could he?" she whispered as she saw his torment and abuse. "O Drake, thank ye for rescuing him!"

"I could not rescue so many, I am glad he was one I could help," Drake replied humbly.

"Ye helped all of us, if ye won and forced Raad out."

"He is dead, and so is Secundus, along with the eldest of all the Nagas in the Land," Drake said, and she could hear the satisfaction in his tone. "Ye should come down to the Obsidian Temple, my daughter-in-law is doing restoration work there and giving a family a new home on the grant there. They will be in charge of the support farm to supply the Temple with fresh fruit and vegetables throughout the year, as well as producing Temple wine and ale. From what I understand, the man of the house is an accomplished brewer."

"And what of the Temple's guardians?"

"Released, along with those who came to despoil the Spire. Their eternal battle has been ended, and each group has gone to its proper reward for their deeds."

"Then I should return, if only to meet this extraordinary Daughter-in-Law of yers," Bernice smiled.

"Ye should indeed," Drake agreed, offering an affectionate embrace. "I should be going, we have supper to prepare, and the camp we are staying at to maintain. Be well, the both of ye. I look forward to talking again, soon. May the Lady be with ye."

"And with ye, My Lord," the two of them called in unison as Drake gathered up the two younger people and walked them back to camp. Nothing was said for a long time as they washed and scraped the produce they had gathered clean, then laid it out to dry in the waning sun's rays.

"Now, since ye two are going to be together, let us see how well ye work with weaponry. If ye are going to be together, ye should be able to work together without harming each other, aye? How do ye think the High Lord and the High Lady are able to work so seamlessly together, at such a fast pace?" he chuckled. Deborah and Erinn had worked together in the arena as a team right from their very first encounter with weaponry, and all he had done was simply guide their work. He had never seen two people more suited to one another, he thought with admiration as he recalled those early days.

Brianna put aside her weariness, they had walked miles that day, foraging the entire time. The short respite while Drake visited with his old friends had been just enough to allow their breathing to steady and slow a bit, she thought with chagrin. Now he marched them quick pace back to the camp, which she estimated was at least a five mile journey, so that when they arrived, they were breathing heavily once more. Brianna's legs cramped a bit, as she was not used to walking quite so much over open ground. When she bent to rub her calves, Drake's face grew concerned.

"Are ye well then Dame?" he asked, walking to her side. "Ye haven't rubbed up against a poisonous plant, have ye?"

"Nay Sir," she answered calmly, rubbing the backs of her legs to help forestall the contractions of her leg muscles. "I must admit, I am not used to walking over ten miles in a day. I must condition myself better, I can see that."

"A ten mile march is not uncommon during times of war, Dame," Drake replied in an instructing tone. "Everyone in the Army should be able to keep pace with me, as long as I am only working on the level of those here."

"Yer energies are still above most people, Father," he heard and turned sharply to see Erinn emerge from a whirling portal. "Dame, ye should take some willowbark powder for that aching. A hot bath would be helpful too, hmmm, perhaps I might assist with that?" he chuckled.

"Is yer wife well?"

"Aye, finally awake and eating ravenously," Erinn chuckled deep in his throat. "She told me I could return to my duty here, that she intended to eat a full meal then sleep the night away."

"She dismissed ye then?" Drake grinned.

"Apparently so," Erinn laughed heartily. "Now, what is going on here that the young Dame is so very sore and tired? Ye all look like ye've been pushing through the brush all day."

Arthfael, standing just off to the right of Drake, burst into merry laughter at his father's question before launching into the tale of the day's events. Brianna brought him a cup of cold wine from the barrel in the river, noting with astonishment that the level of liquid within it seemed unchanged from their first day at the camp. It was still very nearly full, and she also noted that the level of the liquid remained at the same point, even when she dipped out the pitcher for the High Lord. Likewise, she had also noted that the food rations for the horses had not diminished during their travel, which she found remarkable in the light of the fact she was responsible for feeding them nightly. When she returned to the group with the pitcher and the cups, she summoned up the courage to ask about her observations.

"My Lords, I have noted that our wine supply as well as the food supply for the horses are not diminished by their daily consumption."

"Surely, ye must be mistaken, Dame," Drake chuckled, testing her will.

"I am responsible for feeding the horses nightly, My Lord," she answered carefully, keeping her voice respectful. "I would note if their grain and hay stores were getting low. They simply are not, I know, I have been measuring the level of the wine daily and even after the heaviest consumption, 'tis still the same."

Drake chuckled harder, his tone truly merry as he offered her the grip, congratulating her on her observation skills. "Well done, Dame. Most people would not even comment upon it, thinking themselves quite fortunate to have the situation as 'tis. Ye continue to impress me, and such a feat is not easy anymore."

"I, impress ye?" Brianna repeated in a startled tone.

"Aye! Ye are one of those types that do not give in easily, ye are resilient and tenacious, as an Amazon should be. Yer stubborn nature, now that ye have it mastered, is an asset to ye now, as is yer drive to excel. Such a thing is very impressive in light of how I remember ye were before. Well done."

Brianna's eyes opened wide at the compliment offered by the former High Lord. "Th...Thank you, Sir. I am honored by yer words."

"And yer way of speaking has also improved," Erinn put in. "Before ye were telling us all how good ye are, now ye are showing us instead of bragging upon yerself constantly. And ye have also changed the depth of yer tone as well, yer voice is a bit lower than I recall before ye took training with Ashara."

"She said I sounded like an old fishwife at the market, selling her wares," Brianna laughed a bit. Drake laughed with her, hearing his own thoughts echoed in Ashara's words.

"Have ye ever been to the Port City, Dame?" Drake asked.

"I have not," Brianna told him.

"We will have to arrange for a visit," Drake chuckled harder. "I shall take ye to the market myself. Ashara's description of how yer voice sounded is not far off the mark."

"O dear!" Brianna said in dismay. "I am glad my voice sounds better now!"

"As am I," Arthfael put in. "The sun is going down, perhaps we should consider cooking our meal? I am very hungry!"

"Me too!" Brianna rejoined.

"Very well, wash up a bit, and we will begin. Since we are making egg patties and papas, it should not take overlong. Supper will be served shortly," Drake chuckled. He was right about the meal's preparation, it was done quickly by four sets of hands and soon they were all sitting around the fire, consuming their platefuls.

"Now, who is ready for some chess?" Drake asked, pulling a board out of his knapsack, always swung over his shoulder nowadays.

"I am!" Arthfael cried out with delight, enjoying playing the strategic game with his grandfather. Erinn turned to Brianna with a smile, offering his help with the dishes.

"If ye will wipe them and put them away, I shall wash."

"Thank ye, My Lord. Also, ye mentioned a hot bath earlier. Would that be possible?"

"With the Lady's assistance, all things are possible," Erinn told her gently. "We will see what resources we have available close about."

It did not take the two of them a long time to wash, dry and store the pan and dishes used that night. Once they were done, Erinn took her to the riverside to assess the bathing possibilities. Brianna waited hopefully, as her muscles were stiff and sore from the long day's walk and work along the way, until finally Erinn smiled. He had reckoned out how a bath could be arranged, if the elementals would be of assistance. Striding downstream just a bit, he saw the perfect place, a wide bank heavy with gravel where the water slowed a bit.

"I shall need a few moments to set myself," he told her quietly. "If ye will please refrain from speaking 'till I speak to ye?"

"Of course," she agreed readily.

Watching with fascinated eyes, the young woman observed Erinn step to where the rocks and gravel deposited in the heaviest layer. Forming a picture of a small round tub in his mind, something that would hold one person at a time, Erinn waited until he felt his spine tingle a bit before waving his hands in a circular motion over the rocks. Brianna watched in awe as the stones began to rise and swirl slowly, settling into something that looked like a natural tub one would find at a hot spring. Next, she watched him project gentle flames into the midst of the open space, heating the rocks until they steamed a bit. Finally, Erinn made a gesture to the river, asking for water to fill the tub and a small side rivulet opened to accommodate his request. He kept gentle heat on the rocks until the water was just right, asking the stones to keep it warm until Brianna finished her bath. When he finished his work, he could feel that the elementals were cooperating with him and that all was well.

"Dame, yer bath is ready," he turned to her with a smile to say. "The water will stay hot enough for ye to soak a bit, and here are some of my lady's best bath salts that I just happened to have with me."

"Ye used yer magick to call that from somewhere, and ye are using yer magick so I might have a hot bath," Brianna replied, the wonder of it all clear in her tone. "Why would ye do that for me?"

"I would do this for anyone in my Army," Erinn replied at once. "The health of the fighting people of the Land is my direct concern, being yer Commander, and hot baths are all part of that. Ye have worked hard today, my father's 'walks' can be most strenuous as I recall. I always enjoyed a hot bath after one of them, I still do. Enjoy and let the water provide the healing ye need."

"Th…Thank you My Lord," Brianna stuttered over it, feeling a bit uncomfortable.

"What is magick for, except to make our lives a bit easier from time to time?" Erinn smiled. "I made sure to include some lavender soft soap. We Natanleods, at least this one in any case, seem to favor the scent."

"Thank ye, My Lord," Brianna answered softly, blushing a bit as his charisma washed over her. His arm brushed hers in passing as he left her, and she noted at once the firmness of the skin, as if it were tightly drawn over a frame. The sensation also indicated strength and conditioning, and she noted his skin was well-tanned from exposure to the sun's rays. It left her breathless, as all contact with the males of the ruling family tended to do nowadays. She waited until she was certain he was gone before stripping and climbing into the tub, finding the water at the perfect soaking temperature. She was unaware that Erinn remained just outside of her sight to watch over her while she bathed, at least until she caught the faint scent of the sikar he enjoyed while doing so. Strangely, his being there did not alarm her, in fact it was a comfort to know she would be completely safe to relax and soak. When she finished, she felt compelled to say her thanks to the rocks and the water for their help, and felt a wave of emotional warmth pass over her, moving her to shed a tear or two due to the intensity of it. Wrapping up in her robe once more, she picked up her towel and returned to camp, passing by Erinn's sentry position.

"Thank ye, My Lord, for yer guardianship," she said quietly. "Only the scent of the sikar gave ye away to me though, yer stealth is truly miraculous."

Erinn smiled gently, rising from the rock he was seated upon to walk her back to the camp. "I hoped that the odor would alert ye to my presence without alarming ye. Ye should feel safe with me, I mean ye no harm whatsoever."

"I know it," Brianna responded. "And 'tis a welcome change from how I usually feel around men. In fact, yer family seems to be much different than is commonly thought in the Land. Ye are all seen as very distant, with the exception of the High Lady, of course."

"Think for a moment, my dear," Erinn replied in a friendly tone. "We rule, we must put a bit of space between our family and the rest of those in the Land. 'Tis the only way to keep one's perspective, so one can rule wisely by making good choices, ones not based on the emotions of the moment. When ye are in command, ye put that space there naturally, so that the troopers will treat ye with respect. I have seen yer natural leadership abilities at work, and I must say ye handle yerself well."

"Thank ye, My Lord. But without Commander Ashara's training, none of that would have ever emerged."

"Aye, and ye are wise to acknowledge that," Erinn smiled. "It just shows again how much ye have grown in the last year or so. I like to see individual progress in my Army, it means ye have yer own motivations to be there beyond wishing to serve. Humility is an excellent quality in a Commander."

Arriving back at camp, they found everything calm, except for Arthfael's delight at how the chess game was proceeding. It looked like he was about to checkmate his grandfather. Erinn turned back to Brianna, a smile of challenge on his face.

"Be sure to wake early in the morning, Dame," he advised quietly. "Ye might see something ye have never seen before."

"What might I see?"

"Wake early, and dress for the day before ye come out of the pavilion," Erinn chuckled mysteriously. Just then, Arthfael stood up and laughed uproariously, embracing his grandfather tightly.

"How did ye do that?" he asked. "I thought I had ye boxed into a corner, only to be defeated at the very last moment!"

"I have more experience than ye do, and I play for the end game, boyo," Drake replied with satisfaction. The game had been hard-fought, requiring more than the usual amount of concentration to achieve victory. "Ye did not make it easy, I must say. Ye are learning quickly, and soon, ye just might be able to beat yer father."

"We will see about that after yer time in the tub by the river," Erinn spoke up. "Come on then Father, ye owe me a game!"

Brianna sat up a bit watching the vigorous match, but due to her bathing earlier, she could not stop yawning and soon excused herself. Once under her quilts, she was asleep within moments and slept very well throughout the night.

Dawn was just lighting the sky when her eyes opened suddenly, responding to the faint sounds she could hear through the thick hemp-cloth walls of the large chambered tent where she slept. As she listened intently, she rolled out of bed, dressing quickly all the while until she realized what she was hearing. It was the sound of a sword exercise in full progress, she could hear the ringing noise as the blades passed by one another quickly. The High Lord's words from the night before surfaced in her memory as she reached for her boots, and realization dawned. It was he and his ascended Father exercising together with live weapons, and it was a sight she wanted to witness personally, as it was a rare opportunity. As she emerged from the curtained chamber, Arthfael emerged from his and their eyes met.

"Is that what I think 'tis?" she asked.

"If ye think 'tis the High Lord and his father working with blades, ye would be correct," he smiled. "Come, let us hurry. I wish to see it too!"

Now they could hear loud and merry laughter as they emerged from the pavilion's shade, into the growing light of dawn.

"O come now Father, ye can do better than that!" they heard Erinn's sarcasm. "Surely, all yer time in the higher realms has equipped ye to defend against my puny efforts!"

"Stop it!" Drake growled a bit, concentrating on what Erinn's very sharp blade was doing. "Ye are simply trying to distract me."

"And it looks as if 'tis working!" Erinn laughed harder, feinting to one side, then striking on the opposite one. Drake parried it away easily enough, his own face taking on a humorous aspect.

"Good one, my son!" he commented, barely breathing hard. Saying no more, he thrust out hard for Erinn's belly, only to have his blade parried away at the last moment.

"Good one yerself!" Erinn chuckled. "Honestly Father, the pace is so very slow. Could we please pick it up a bit? I am getting bored," he laughed merrily.

"Bored are ye?" Drake growled, but both of the young people present could hear the background of challenge in his tone. "Let us see then, if ye can honestly keep pace with me!"

The gauntlet thrown, the two men engaged in a furious exchange of measured blows, the sound of their blades resembling a chorus of small bells being rung vigorously. The sun continued to rise, and the first rays flashed off the steel, causing Brianna to throw up a hand to shade her eyes. Her desire to see all of the exchange in front of her was rewarded as soon as the sun's glare was sufficiently blocked, but when her eyes refocused, the two men were already a blur. She could barely make them out as separate bodies, so fast were they moving. The laughter continued, however as the blades struck against each other in harmless blows, and she looked up at Arthfael in wonder.

"I know," he said quietly, in awe himself. "I have seen this a few times now, and I stand in astonishment each time. How can they avoid cutting each other at such a pace, and will I ever be that fast? Those are the questions that consume me each time I see this. If ye join our House, ye will see this more often, and other manifestations of my family's special arrangement with the Goddess. Yer ability to adapt quickly and be reasonable in the face of surprising events will be tested often, such are the lessons I have learned since my adoption. As a Daughter of the House, ye will have to simply accept such happenings as the usual course of events."

"I have not agreed to such a thing," Brianna reminded him as the sound of the sword's ringing suddenly ceased, and the two men appeared out of their exercise, literally manifesting out of the glowing ball of light they had created around them. "I am intrigued however. My feelings for ye have naught to do with the rest of yer family, I care not if ye rule. I am not certain I would wish to do so, or if I even have the proper nature. I do know I enjoy being with ye, talking with ye is something I have come to anticipate daily. Ye are intelligent and thoughtful, ye take time to consider yer answer before ye speak, and yer care for the people and the Goddess is evident. Such things have been rare amongst the men I have met so far in my life, and I wish to continue our talks and our walks, if such is yer desire."

"I would desire no more of ye, 'lest ye were ready to give it," Arthfael replied intensely, reaching for her hand. "I am not one to force my affections upon anyone, as I have had it happen to me. Ye are completely safe in my presence, Dame Brianna."

"I feel safe in yer family's presence, which is an odd feeling. I have rarely felt safe in anyone's presence, let alone a male. I am sorry ye must pay the price for that now, a part of me wishes I could let go of my hesitations and fears now rather than later."

"As I said, I am in no hurry," Arthfael smiled, reaching for her hand once more. It felt good when she accepted it, their hands seemed to fit together nicely, in his opinion and the feeling of warmth made it even better.

As Drake and Erinn walked back to the pavilion, looking for a towel each to wipe the sweat from hands and brows, they noted the two standing there hand in hand. A smile crept over Drake's face, and he nudged Erinn to call subtle attention to it.

"Their affection grows," Drake spoke to Erinn's mind.

"So it seems," Erinn replied, still recovering from the extended and very vigorous sword session. "I am not opposed to it, after all, look at his face."

"I know, 'tis almost revolting, aye?" Drake's humor was evident.

"I think they make a nice couple," Erinn replied seriously. "She is nearly as tall as he is, walking together will not be a challenge."

"Walking together is not what concerns me," Drake replied in a worried tone. "They are both scarred in ways neither of us can imagine. If they are together, they must produce an heir."

"Deborah was just as scarred as they are, inside and out," Erinn replied, still serious. "As ye can see, we managed."

"So ye did," Drake replied with great affection into his mind, physically clapping him on the back. "Good morning ye two!" he called out aloud to the young people standing by the opening of the pavilion. "Who is ready for first meal?"

"I think we both are!" Arthfael answered for both of them.

"I could use with a steak!" Drake stated.

"Here is what I propose," Erinn spoke up. "I believe we are only a few miles from the crossroads that would take us to the Emerald Lakes. Let us pack our things quickly, and we will go quickly to the lodge there. We will see if Nathan's preparedness is as thorough as always," he chuckled. They quickly snacked on the last of the bread and slices of cheese before packing everything away and policing the camp completely. Erinn magickally sent the barrel they had been drinking out of back to the House in the Capitol city. When it reappeared at the head of the line, ready to be used, Gwendolyn who was taking inventory, simply added the numbered barrel to those marked for quick dispersal without further comment. Back at camp, the latrine area was dealt with as always, by covering it completely and sprinkling wildflower seeds over it. Erinn made sure to soak the dirt until it was muddy, to allow the seeds the best chance to sprout and grow before taking his leave of the place. One more inspection to assure they had returned the place to as pristine a condition as possible and then they gathered together in a tight group. Erinn opened the portal for them to lead their horses through, and then closed it behind them, taking a moment to recover before mounting his own steed.

"Come my friends, the Lodge is just down the road a bit. If I am correct, we will find everything we need there to be comfortable for a few days."

Urging their horses down the steep and winding roadway, they rode hard, arriving at the rustic log Lodge, perched on the edge of the Emerald Lakes, which provided an amazingly lovely view. It was late morning as the horses were quickly cared for and turned loose in the large paddock, their stall doors open to allow them entry later. Horses in the Army were trained to lock and unlock doors, just in case they were captured or otherwise unlawfully detained, they simply closed the doors after themselves, tripping the lock bar to fall into place.

Once the animals were fed, watered and brushed until dry, Erinn led the way into the large, lofted Lodge building, finding the usual note from Nathan hanging on the latch.

"Welcome, My Lord. Ye will find all prepared for ye within. I shall visit later today, to assure all is well."

It was signed simply with Nathan's rune sign, and Erinn found the key nestled within the envelope with the note. Once inside, he raised the dome of protection over the Lodge, thanking the Fae folk for their help. Closing the door behind him, Erinn turned to the group with a huge smile on his face.

"Ah, 'tis good to be indoors for a bit, aye?" he asked. "I am going downstairs to see what provisions are available, the rest of ye are free to choose beds and start the boiler for a hot bath. I intend to rest and relax today, for we will be back on the road tomorrow. I am anxious to inspect Alom's tabac farm to see his progress."

With no further words, Erinn descended into the cold room, opening the door that kept the food inside from spoiling too quickly. There was a note hanging from one of the shelves, addressed to him, and so the High Lord reached up for it, opening the tidily folded envelope.

"My Lord, I hope I have chosen a good piece of beef to send you. Thank ye for returning the remainder of the barrel, I have already distributed it out for the staff. Enjoy yer stay, Gwendolyn." A grin appeared on Erinn's face as he refolded the note, tucking it away in his pocket so as to remember the Assistant Kitchen Mistress' kindness. Walking directly to the back of the area, where the ice kept meat frozen, Erinn was delighted to find an entire steer frozen in two halves. His desire for a morning meal of steak and eggs resumed, and it did not take him long to divide one of the sides into two quarters, taking only one of them upstairs magickally. Once it was upstairs on the table, Drake helped him saw off a few rib steaks before snapping his fingers to return the frozen meat to the hook below.

Now they had the meat they wanted, and both men were practically salivating as they used cold water to quickly thaw the steaks enough to season them correctly. Meanwhile, Drake washed, pared and sliced enough papas to accompany the steaks, providing a goodly portion for everyone. He also mixed up rustic biscuits, pouring the batter directly into the baking dish instead of portioning it out by the spoonful. He reckoned to simply cut the biscuit into squares once it was baked, making it easy for everyone to serve themselves.

While they worked in the kitchen, Brianna and Arthfael worked in the lodging area, making beds up with fresh linens, blankets and pillows as well as starting the fire under the boiler reservoir. The day was beautiful and brightly warm as they worked, to take advantage of the slight breeze off the lake they opened the windows to allow the fresh air to circulate through the sleeping area. They had just finished their work when the scent of broiling steaks and frying papas hit their noses, and they practically ran to the kitchen area where Drake had caffe ready. The hot beverage tasted very fine as they waited for their plates, and the odor of the cooking food continued to tantalize them until they finally were served and seated. After a quick blessing, they all dug in with real appetite, as it was hours past their usual meal time. The steaks were perfectly rare, the papas crisp and tender, and the center of every egg bled the rich, yellow yolk over the food when it was cut into.

"Delicious, My Lord," Brianna complimented after a few bites. "I find myself quite astonished at how fine a cook ye are. Most men would not be interested in learning such things."

"Most men are not given the opportunity to do so," Erinn replied. "I had a thought recently and I mean to implement it at the Lady's School when I return. I think both the boys and the girls should learn the basics of cooking. Everyone should be able to cook themselves a meal, it just makes sense. No one likes to be saddled with the same chores day after day, and I would imagine that in a farm home, the women are tasked with the cooking chores most often. I know my mother was very grateful when my stepfather would volunteer to cook a simple meal, just to give her the break."

"A good idea, my son!" Drake put in. "I should have thought of that!"

"Yer time of rule was a busy one, Father," Erinn pointed out, wiping the last of the egg from his plate with his biscuit. "And I am glad ye left me some work to do, after all," he chuckled, as he stood to walk the plate back to the kitchen. Brianna was up before him, having also finished her meal, and before he could move his plate joined hers in hand. She stopped to pick up Drake's and Arthfael's too on the way, earning her thanks from both men.

"I shall take care of the dishes as my contribution to the meal," she offered. "The water should be hot enough at least to wash a few dishes, it should not take me too long."

"Good, I want to go fishing!" Arthfael piped up. "Perhaps ye would go with me?"

"I would be delighted, My Lord," she answered, smiling.

The rest of the day was spent simply lazing about, and when Nathan made his promised appearance, he found Drake and Erinn enjoying a sikar while battling over the chessboard on the lakeside porch.

"Ah, Nathan!" Erinn greeted him as soon as he rounded the corner. "As always, everything was perfectly prepared for our arrival. I must ask though, how 'tis ye always seem to know when and where I shall need shelter?"

"Ye are not the only one the Fae folk talk to," Nathan answered at once, his voice very serious. "I find one particular individual's information very useful in keeping track of ye when ye are traveling about."

"I see," Erinn grinned. "How long have ye known Oracia?"

"I was there when her sentence was carried out, a long time ago. I was one of the first ones who could hear her beyond the High Lord at the time. I am much more ancient than my looks would indicate."

"Oracia has been confined to that map how long?" Erinn inquired.

"Decades, My Lord," Nathan answered. "Her term of confinement will be a long one, as her crime was considered very grave."

"What exactly did she do?"

"She attempted to seduce Oberon on the eve of his wedding to Titania," Nathan answered without hesitation. "Apparently, she was wearing Titania's wedding ring and dress at the time, something that Oberon's wife would be very, very angry about. It did not help that Oberon was very drunk, and spoke up for Oracia, which only intensified Titania's resolve to separate them. She wanted her exiled or slain, according to the laws of the Blessed Realm, but the High Priest Blaise intervened and suggested that her knowledge of the Land might be of enough use to spare her. Oracia is someone who traveled a great deal, inside and outside of Oberon's lands, and her knowledge of places and paths is immense."

"I see," Erinn nodded. "I shall remember to be kinder to her more often. I have never heard the complete tale, and now that I know it, I feel badly for her. Is there no way for her to be released?"

"The terms of her confinement are specific, she is to live in a representation of the Land until she learns her lesson, but can never return to the Blessed Realm."

"How would one know the terms of that were fulfilled?" Erinn inquired.

"Anyone who knows Oracia understands the challenges she faces in overcoming her overly passionate nature," Nathan smiled faintly, and Erinn's intuition brought him the knowledge that Nathan and Oracia were likely more than just friendly. "She is loud and strident, her needs are unusually persistent. She needs someone she respects, someone strong enough to challenge her and not be put aside by her beauty and sensuality. Whoever wins this woman's affections will find himself with his hands completely full, and his life will be a whirlwind. I like my life a little quieter than that," he finished with a sigh.

"She is beautiful, and quite persuasive," Erinn agreed, sighing with him. "I feel fortunate to have found my lady before I met Oracia."

"Yer lady is formidable," Nathan answered honestly. "She has no difficulty in dealing with someone like Oracia, I would imagine."

Erinn's mouth curled into a smile as he recalled his wife's description of her first meeting with the Fae creature living within the huge map in his office. "Let us just say that they came to a quick understanding about who the High Lady is, and what she is capable of."

"As I said, yer lady is formidable," Nathan chuckled. "Will she be joining ye?"

"I know not, but 'tis unlikely, as we are both involved with our different projects this year," Erinn sighed. "I hope all is going well at the Obsidian Temple."

"Obsidian Temple?" Nathan asked, his voice reflecting concern. "Ye know about that place, aye? 'Tis said the spire is haunted by those who remained to defend it!"

"Perhaps 'twas, but no more," Erinn smiled. "My Lady has released those who struggled within the spire, and both Lightworkers and the enemy have received their proper rewards."

"Brrr…" Nathan shuddered, thinking of what might await those embracing evil. "I shall have to visit there soon, I did enjoy my service there."

"Ye?"

"Aye, I used to run the kitchen there," Nathan sighed heavily. "I did enjoy that, very much."

Erinn filed that away for future reference as Nathan toured the building quickly, taking inventory as he went. Before he walked out the door, he turned back to Erinn, list in hand.

"I shall assure this all is delivered before sundown tonight," he said as Erinn walked with him. "I think a storm will blow up tonight, I shall send along another cord or two of firewood. It might be cold tonight, especially this far up. Good day, My Lord."

"Good day, Nathan," Erinn replied respectfully. They continued relaxing, Erinn remaining in the shade most of the day while watching Arthfael and Brianna work at catching supper for the night. Brianna was actually the better angler, Erinn noted as he watched her catch fish after fish, until they had a dozen or so.

"We have plenty for our supper, Dame," he called out after the last, largest one finally was angled out of the water. "I am ready to preparing our meal, and I believe that Nathan's weather sense is about to prove out. 'Tis turning chilly as the sun sets."

"O, ye are right!" Brianna noted finally, now that she was done working. "I am ready for a hot bath, and then to be whatever help I might be to prepare supper."

"Good," Erinn smiled, appreciating her willingness to be of help.

"The Dame can bathe first," Arthfael offered at once. "I shall start cleaning these for ye, Father."

"Thank ye, my son," Erinn said with a tired smile. "I feel like I need an easy night and a good night's sleep."

"We will all sleep well indoors, I think," Arthfael speculated. "I think the night will be quite stormy."

By the time Brianna finished her bath and joined them, the trees were swaying vigorously, and lake's surface grew quite choppy. Arthfael went for his soak next, leaving the young woman to work with Erinn in the kitchen. She saw to the making of a salad, including creating a beautiful basil vinaigrette from the garden just outside the door. Erinn made quick work of frying the fish, Brianna watching intently as he did so, finally asking if she could take over for a bit. Erinn remained, wine in hand, to supervise and advise her, but soon he saw he was not needed and left her to it. Finally, he thought, I can step into a hot bath and just relax.

"I am going to bathe now," he announced, seeing Arthfael emerge from the steamy room. "The storm outside is intensifying, let us be sure to have the fire going well and plenty of wood inside before it gets dark?"

"I shall see to it Father," Arthfael offered at once.

"Thank ye, my son," Erinn smiled tiredly. Taking a cold pitcher of wine with him, he retreated into the tub room, where Drake was already soaking. "Where have ye been all day?" Erinn asked, slipping his clothing off and stepping into the hot water gratefully.

"I have been assuring that all the passages leading to that cave we found last year are found and sealed off," Drake told him quietly. "I do not want anyone else playing with cursed dragon gold."

"A wise precaution, Father."

"Ye look very tired, my son."

"I know it, 'tis why I wanted to come here. Sleeping inside will be more restful, as I do not have to remain on guard all night."

"If any guarding needs doing, I shall attend to it. I want ye to rest as much as ye can. Ruling is difficult if one cannot think clearly due to lack of sleep," Drake offered, his concern growing. "Ye did sleep some when ye were with yer lady, aye?"

"Of course we slept," Erinn growled, not liking being questioned about intimate matters.

"I am sorry my son," Drake apologized at once. "I am simply worried about ye. Ye are my only son, as far as I know. I had not thought to have such a gift granted to me."

"I am sorry to react that way," Erinn returned, his good nature returning rapidly as always.

"I should not have asked," Drake replied, grinning. "More wine?"

"Aye, I feel as if I cannot drink enough tonight. What is amiss with me?"

"It matters not. Ye are simply relaxing when ye can. My son, I was not going to mention this, but I found signs that someone has been up in the dragon's lair we found last year," Drake sighed, making a gesture. A knapsack appeared in his hand, one that did not appear to have lain in the cave overlong.

"Any idea who it might be?" Erinn asked, his emotions rising in alarm as he searched through the contents. In it, he found sticks of incense, a pouch of second grade Herb and a change of clothing, clearly already worn. "Someone is up there holding a ritual."

"Aye, and from the contents we can see, I can only surmise they are attempting to reopen the portal within that cave. Dragons make their lairs close to such things, in order to guard them for their own use. We have a Naga priest or priestess to deal with, I think, one of the younger acolytes that has escaped our notice 'till now. I do not wish to alarm either Arthfael or Brianna, but ye and I must go and deal with this."

"I agree," Erinn nodded.

"But not tonight, we will go in the morning so that the sun's energy will help us," Drake told him. "Ye need to eat a full meal, and get a good night's rest before we do any such thing."

"I had intended to do just that," Erinn chuckled. They soaked until that pitcher and another besides it was gone, and finally, Erinn pulled his weary self out of the water, wrapping up in the thick robe provided. When he and Drake emerged from the bath, the entire Lodge was pleasantly scented with the smell of frying fish and papas. Erinn's stomach rumbled loudly as he sat at the table, listening to the wind whistle outside. The fish was deliciously fried, the skin crispy and the flesh moist. The papas were perfectly cooked as well, tender and creamy inside, a nice thick crust outside. Brianna's salad set everything off well due to the delicious vinaigrette she had made, and once Erinn's plate was full, he set to cleaning it rapidly but neatly.

"Ah, I enjoyed that!" he said with a smile, finishing his plate and setting his flatware at an angle on it, to indicate he was done. Drake stood at once and took the plate along with his own to the kitchen, sparing Erinn the effort.

"Care for a sikar?" Erinn called after him.

"I would, but I would like to remain indoors to do so. Just listen to it out there, the wind is practically howling."

The force of the wind against the sturdy walls of the Lodge could be clearly heard while they indulged in the delicious tabac, talking quietly about what could be going on above them where the dragon bones lay in the deep cave.

"No one should be up there, we must assure that whoever is using the cave ceases doing so at once. 'Tis not a good thing to be around so much cursed gold, the temptation is too great. Secundus found that out, to his own dismay. He really thought he could overcome it, the fool," Drake sighed.

"What is it about this gold?" Erinn asked.

Drake sighed a bit, the time had come. "That skeleton is all that remains of the last dragon father, Nirvut the Black."

Erinn gulped as the words registered. "How did the gold become cursed?"

"Nirvut did it himself, as he was dying on the horde," Drake told him in a faraway tone.

"No one can touch it?"

"My son, 'tis not simply touching it that causes the curse to be invoked, 'tis the use of it. If it were to be used for art, or jewelry, or for honest purpose, 'twould be naught to fear from it. However, if the user decides to use it for greedy or evil purposes, the curse is released and the user slowly goes mad as Nirvut's warning constantly plays in his mind."

"A terrible fate, to be certain," Erinn shuddered. "Very well, we should probably do this at night, so that we have a bit of cover, aye?"

"I was going to propose that very thing," Drake grinned. "But, not 'till tomorrow night, when the dark of the moon occurs. I like to do this kind of work at such times, it just seems the proper time."

"I shall be glad to wait," Erinn yawned, stubbing out the sikar, which still held about half its length intact. "I am going to bed, Father. I cannot stay awake any longer."

"Go on then, my son," Drake encouraged, standing. "Do ye need help?"

"I can walk from here to my alcove," Erinn chuckled. "Thank ye kindly though, Father."

"I meant no offense my son, I simply wish to be of service to ye."

"I know it, I am just grouchy and tired. "Good night."

"Good night, my son. Sleep deeply."

"I hope so," Erinn chuckled wryly as he trudged away. Stopping only to say his goodnights to Arthfael and Brianna, who were just finishing cleaning up after supper, he continued on his way to where his bed awaited. Pushing aside the curtain, he entered the alcove, saw to his nightly ritual, stripped to his unders and climbed into the narrow bed, pulling the covers over him. It was good to be inside, he thought as his eyes closed, letting himself just fall asleep.

Chapter 7

Erinn woke very early, feeling well-rested and ready for the day. Seeing to his morning routine, he dressed quickly and pulling on his boots, stepped out of the curtained alcove. Drake was in the kitchen, and Erinn now could smell caffe brewing as he walked closer. A grin appeared, and he was glad for his father's presence, not just due to the hot beverage being ready, but because he relished the opportunity to share companionship with a peer. Drake's lust for life was one of those charismatic things about him that people respected and admired, his son was one of those who did so because of everything he had seen Drake be able to do.

"Good morning," he called out quietly, seeing they were the only two awake.

"Shhhh... look over there by the hearth. They must have fallen asleep talking," Drake chuckled softly. Erinn's eyes turned to the scene and a gentle smile appeared, for the two young people were leaning up against each other, back to back, their feet propped against the bottoms of the furniture. They shared one of the larger quilts left out in the common room, and Erinn could see that Arthfael had been the one to wrap them both up in it, assessing by how the folds were laying.

"How can they sleep like that?" Erinn whispered.

"They are young, they can sleep nearly anywhere, not like us poor older men, who must have a bed and a bath to be comfortable," he chuckled.

"O, and is yer advanced age telling upon ye?" Erinn questioned sarcastically, their word game commencing. "Really Father, gallivanting about as if ye were only fifty years old, aren't ye just a little embarrassed?" he laughed softly, taking the cup from his father's hand.

"I can still outwork ye any day or night," Drake replied with a grin, knowing his son was simply teasing him.

"Is that so?" Erinn questioned in return. "We will see who gets to the top of the cliff first then. If ye are still operating at full capacity, ye should have no difficulty overtaking me."

"Boyo, ye should be wary of challenging me like that," Drake growled a bit, and Erinn laughed merrily in response.

"Ye should have slept some last night, Father. Ye are as grouchy as an old bear this morning."

"Ye would be grouchy too if yer son were questioning yer fitness!" Drake answered, then covered a guffaw of raucous laughter. "Come on, let us go see what supplies we have in the larder for this morning's meal. We should let them sleep."

"Or we could have a pipe and a sikar while we enjoy our caffe," Erinn counter-proposed. "I am in no hurry, are ye?"

"Now that ye mention it, I would enjoy sharing the time with ye. I do not hear the wind howling outside, it might be safe to step out onto the porch and take a look about."

"Aye, but I heard naught to alarm me," Erinn replied.

"The way ye were snoring, 'twould be a miracle indeed if ye heard anything," Drake chortled, pulling two long sikars from his pocket and clipping them.

"My snoring?" Erinn chuckled merrily, producing a fingertip flame to light for both of them. "When ye were still High Lord, yer snoring would rattle the door to yer room!"

Drake smothered a guffaw or two as they walked outside, leaving the door ajar to let the young people know where they were. Stepping out onto the porch, Erinn looked about, his eyebrows quickly arching tall in surprise. The damage from the wind the night before was heavy along the shoreline; the fishing platform at the end of the dock had broken free and was floating away as they watched, the small boats moored to it now drifting all over the Emerald Lakes, capsized. Trees had fallen across the manicured lawn of the Lodge, their tops now in the water, but the building was completely intact. Even the stable was in good repair, only missing a shingle or two, but the horses inside were neighing and nervous.

"Look about ye," Drake said after assessing the scene. "Does this seem a normal storm's damage to ye?"

"It does not, just look at how the trees fell, completely missing both the Lodge building and the stable too. Someone wanted to send us a message, I think," Erinn speculated, his anger roused at the thought of a Naga being responsible for such a calamity. "I think 'tis time we find out exactly what we are facing, or more rightly, whom. Father, have you any idea?"

Drake's face drew up a considerate expression as he went through the list of possibilities. A name crossed his mind, and a frown appeared as soon as it did. "We should find out at once, so many of the elder Nagas simply disappeared. I hoped they had returned to their world, but it appears that at least one of them remains. If so, this entity will have taken possession of someone, both body and mind. Ye must be willing to sacrifice both in favor of saving the soul of the host. Ye are the High Lord, 'tis yer task ahead of us. I shall guard and ward, and if I must step in, I shall to ensure that whatever or whoever awaits us is rendered inert. Come, I am eager to see to it."

"As am I!" Erinn rejoined, taking a moment to gather his energies. When he felt himself empowered, he snapped his fingers and the black armor from the High Lord's house appeared. Erinn simply stepped into it and it closed about him, an impervious joining. Drake watched in astonishment, for the armor seemed to simply flow about Erinn's body until it adopted the perfect arrangement before setting into place.

"My Father talked about the armor adapting itself to its owner, and now that I have seen, I believe him. Ye see, the armor never manifested itself to me as it just did for ye. I have always had to command it to work with me. Ye are the true heir to the armor, and the rightful High Lord."

"Ye said that when ye handed me the ring," Erinn smiled fiercely. "Come and let us attend to our duty. I am eager to deal with this and return to seek relaxation. It should not require much effort to deal with this threat between the two of us!"

"Aye!" Drake rejoined, calling his own special armor to him. Together the two men opened a portal and walked through it, arriving just outside the collapsed entrance to the dragon's cave.

"I wish yer wife had not been so efficient," Drake complained good-naturedly, addressing his attention to the pile of vulcanized stones. "Accessing the cave is very difficult. We must climb up a bit."

"Ye have been here a few times already then," Erinn replied. "Father, ye should have come to me earlier. I should have been here from the first."

"I know it, and I apologize for over-stepping. Ye are High Lord, not I," Drake replied, somewhat abashed. "I have a tendency to simply act as I see fit, rather than wait for hierarchy. I have been cautioned about doing so in my current work, and have found it to be good advice."

"Ye seek to counter any harm being done, having been responsible for doing so all these years," Erinn returned. "It must be difficult to stop and ask for help."

"Ye see through to the truth of the matter, my son," Drake smiled faintly. "Come, the climb is not a difficult one."

"Why climb at all?" Erinn asked. "Would using magick alert whoever is inside the cave?"

"I know not, perhaps. 'Tis best not to chance it," Drake advised. The two of them roped themselves together quickly, Erinn leading the way they climbed up the short but challenging climb. Once at the top, they found a small hole in the rocks, barely big enough to wiggle through. Erinn glanced at Drake with chagrin before laying on the ground, stretching himself to his fullest and carefully worming his way through the small hole. Once he was through, Drake followed and soon they both stood on a ledge just inside the vast cave below them. They were in a place where they could see almost the entire expanse where the dragon's remains lay in repose, and the scent of incense filled the air.

"Someone is working," Drake whispered. "We must be cautious. I shall warn ye, the energies of the worker seem very familiar to me. I suspect we are about to encounter a possessed person, someone who very likely has no idea they are carrying a separate personality within them."

"Such a practice is disgusting, it violates the free will in every way!" Erinn whispered in outrage.

"Aye so it does, but the Nagas do not believe in free will, my son. They believe that free will is an aberration and that subservience is the natural state for anyone other than themselves. They are all bigots, believing they are superior to absolutely everyone, including the Lady."

"They believe they *are* gods," Erinn stated flatly, and Drake nodded agreement. As they stood there in the shadows, a droning chant resumed and a burst of flames as another handful of incense was added to the ritual fire.

"We must assure he is not planning a sacrifice," Drake whispered. "I shall take this passage, if ye wish to continue this way down. We will both arrive within moments of one another, and we will have whoever 'tis between us."

"I like this plan, 'tis good to know yer advanced age has not dimmed yer mind," Erinn chuckled.

"Not now!" Drake growled quietly. "Ye will make me start laughing, and much too soon. One must plan these assaults carefully, so as to have the best chance of success. The time for laughter is after the deed is done, not before."

"Of course, otherwise 'tis a show of ego. Very unflattering for a High Lord, aye?" Erinn chuckled deep in his throat. He was eager to be at the enemy, hoping that perhaps this one would indeed finally be the last one. Sharing the grip with Drake they parted, Erinn continuing down the path, following the faint footsteps in the dirt floor of the cave. It was long minutes later when Erinn rounded a corner, after stepping over the skeletons of small animals clearly sacrificed to whatever was being worshipped down here, and beheld the work in progress. There was a young man dressed all in black and gold robes, the sign of a Naga priest. His hood was over his face, and he was completely naked under the robe, which did not dismay Erinn in the slightest. The man held a golden cup in his hands, the outside of which held dribbles of red liquid, which Erinn assumed was blood. He wondered where the victim was, deciding it was better not to know.

"Hold!" he called out as the man made to drink from the cup. "Blood sacrifice is forbidden in the Land!"

"Not for much longer, aye High Lord?" he heard the response. The man put the cup down carefully, as if it held a precious substance, which it did since blood was held as the most sacred thing in the Land. "I am about to call my allies through this portal, and 'tis naught ye can do to stop me."

"How do you reckon that, since I am armed?" Erinn laughed.

"Ye have come alone, and I am not alone," the man answered, making a casual gesture. As Erinn stood there, the ancient bones of the huge dragon stirred and it rose on shaky legs to confront him. "See if ye can deal with *that* while I do my work," the Naga priest laughed merrily.

Erinn said naught, simply turning to the dragon skeleton and speaking to it in dragon tongue, which rose to his mouth instinctively, having never done it before.

"Go back to sleep, Great One," he spoke soothingly. "The time has not come for the dead to rise."

"I was called," he heard in his mind.

"By a possessed Naga priest," Erinn replied reasonably. "Ye would not wish to serve our enemy, aye?"

"I shall not be wakened by our enemy!" he heard the outraged response. "Ye are the High Lord, ye must deal with him!"

"I shall. But, ye will not help him, aye?" Erinn replied, seeing Drake emerge from a small cave exit, standing behind the Naga priest, completely unseen.

"I would not willingly do so," he heard and a smile appeared on his face.

"Then so be it. If ye are being bidden and compelled, let that compulsion be ended at once!" he spoke out aloud. With no further words, Erinn pulled his blade and moved to engage the Naga priest before Drake could warn him off. The older Natanleod recognized the spirit within the young body, his name was Enki, a name stolen from ancient Sumeria in a twist of mocking humor. This Naga had existed by moving as a spirit from body to body, discarding each as it aged and withered. It made him one of the most dangerous one of their kind, as he could possess anything living; plants, animals and people as well.

"Erinn, be cautious! He is Enki!"

"Enki?" Erinn replied mentally. "How could that be? He was supposed to have perished in the catastrophe that overtook Atlantis!"

"Enki came along during the Crossing, with Raad's ancestor!" Drake returned quickly. "It might take both of us to destroy him!"

"I am the High Lord!" Erinn replied aloud. "He is mine to deal with!"

Drake halted at his words, knowing he was right to declare himself. Instead, he put himself on guard, knowing that there were always hidden dangers in places such as these.

"He can possess anything living! Be careful, my son!" Drake called back as a group of empty-eyed people came rushing from a side tunnel, bidden by their master to defend him.

"Anything living?" Erinn thought. "I must battle him somewhere no one else can be affected then!"

At once a large whirling vortex enveloped him and Enki where they stood, and as Erinn watched in amazement, a large clear bubble formed around them. It completely encased them, even to the cave floor, which seemed to be part of the thing. They could see out, and people could see in, but they were alone within the bubble and no one could interfere. Drake saw it happen as he finished off the zombie-like followers called by Enki.

"Erinn!" Drake cried out in dismay, for his son was now sealed off from any aid he could provide. "Great Goddess, look after him!"

"I shall," he heard Her patient reply. "But, ye have little idea of what yer son can actually do. Ye doubt his skills and abilities, 'tis so?"

Now that he was finished with defending Erinn's back and had time to properly assess the situation, Drake was brought up short and he realized She was right. He did have reservations about what Erinn could do because the young man had not fought during the entire war. His son had not been pressed to the ultimate of his strength or skill by anyone, including himself. Drake glanced back at the bubble, saw it was within the same time as he was and grinned. Erinn had come up with the perfect battle arena to take on Enki, and now Drake did something that he knew would enrage the ancient, evil Naga. He withdrew a sikar from his pocket, clipped and lit it, then took the flask from his other pocket and prepared to watch the show, wearing an anticipatory grin the entire time. He even produced a chair to sit upon, which brought a look of alarm to the face Enki wore at the moment.

"Who are ye?" he finally asked Erinn.

"I am my father's son, Erinn Natanleod, the High Lord of the Land, the Lady's Anointed," Erinn introduced himself formally.

"Impossible!"

"Clearly not, unless ye need reminding of how children are spawned and born in the Land," Erinn chuckled, looking at Drake briefly. He noted his father looked very comfortable sitting there smoking a sikar and sipping from his flask. Turning his eyes back onto Enki, he hefted his blade and advanced quickly on him, forcing the Naga to produce a weapon magickally. It was over quickly, for despite Enki's soul having plenty of knowledge and experience in war and battle, the body he resided in was not trained, nor did it have the stamina to meet someone of Erinn's caliber. Drake was treated to a fine show of his son's skills nonetheless, for the Naga battled on until the body finally succumbed to its lack of conditioning. Erinn wasted no more words, simply and quickly beheading the body, watching it crumple to the ground. A brief thought crossed his mind, one of simple gratitude at being released from possession, and then it was over. Sheathing his sword, he was about to disperse the bubble or at least try, when Adalinda appeared in her human form, gorgeously arrayed in the house colors of black and purple, trimmed with silver and dark green.

"Thank ye, my son Erinn, for this gift. I have been waiting for a long time to have Enki's trial," She told him in round, resonant tones.

"I am happy to be of service, Great Queen," Erinn responded reverently. With no further words, Adalinda scooped up the head and disappeared with it, the bubble dispersing around Erinn as soon as She did so. He was glad of it, as he had really no idea how he had called it, and then he realized he hadn't called it at all, that Adalinda had provided it so his fight with Enki could be contained. As soon as the bubble dispersed, the headless corpse dissolved into a pile of dust, and Erinn realized that Enki had lived in that body for a long, long time. He turned next to the dragon's skeleton, which had settled in a jumbled pile. With a wave, the bones reassembled themselves upon the huge horde of gold, appearing as they always had. One more task remaining, Erinn turned to the golden goblet filled with sacrificed blood. Pointing a finger, he sent a burst of dragonfire to surround it, heating it until the liquid boiled and the metal melted. Once he was done, he took a deep breath and simply stood there, regaining his strength for a moment.

"Are ye well, my son?" he heard Drake's voice ask him.

"Aye, but I think I shall sleep well tonight. Did ye see the body crumble into dust?" he asked.

"Enki kept himself young by stealing energy from everyone and everything around him, boyo. 'Tis no telling just how long that body had been kept alive by his evil sorcery. "Thirsty?"

"Exceedingly so," Erinn replied. "I am ready for some cold ale and security. We are housed at the Lodge, it should be private enough for me to relax a bit."

"Boyo, ye made that look incredibly easy," Drake told him. "Ye will have to tell me all about it, once we get back to the Lodge. What say ye, shall we clean up the building quickly, then evaporate to the family House in the valley? We will be perfectly safe there, and ye can relax as ye need to. I think ye will find yerself exhausted in a short while."

"I already am," Erinn replied. "Come, yer idea is a good one. Arthfael and Brianna will help us get ready quickly and then we will use a portal to get there. I want to sleep in a familiar bed tonight."

"Good, if ye will allow it, My Lord, let me provide the means for our return to the Lodge?"

"If ye please, My Lord," Erinn responded with a chuckle. In a moment they transported from the depths of the deep cave to the comfort of the Lodge. Brianna and Arthfael were awake, a first meal of oat porridge was cooking and they were cleaning the place while they waited for their meal. When Drake and Erinn walked in, Arthfael noted the situation at once, and realized they had been at work.

"Father, are ye well?"

"I am, but tired my son," Erinn smiled. "Is there caffe?"

"Aye!" Brianna answered, taking one of the carafes and filling it for them, bringing cups and the amendment tray with her.

"Thank ye Dame," Erinn smiled wearily. She quickly poured his cup and prepared it as she had seen him do, offering it to him. With a nod he took it and sipped, then sipped again. A wider smile appeared, for the taste was as he liked it. Clearly, she had been watching closely, he realized. "The caffe is amended well, ye have been paying attention to how I prepare it."

"Ye are most welcome, My Lord," she replied softly. "I am going to finish cleaning up. I expect ye wish to depart this morning?"

"Aye, we will be traveling magickally to the family House for a few days' rest," Drake put in. "If ye wish, I can take ye directly to the Barracks, so ye might resume yer duties there."

"I have been assigned to this duty, My Lord," Brianna countered at once. "When 'tis discharged, I shall return to the Barracks, 'lest ye order otherwise of course."

"Ye are welcome to remain," Erinn spoke out. Brianna set out bowls of the oat porridge for them, finding she had cooked exactly the right amount of the grain, much to her delight. After they had eaten, she quickly washed up their bowls, cups and flatware, laying them on the clean towel to dry. She knew staff would be here later and wanted to make their job as easy as possible. Finally done, she draped the damp cloth she was using over the edge of the sink and walked away to gather her bag and cloak, preparing to leave.

"All looks fine, and I see ye have stripped the beds we used too," Erinn smiled at them. "Come, let us go home. I wish to see familiar walls about me."

Drake opened the portal for them and they stepped through, their horses arriving shortly after, looking slightly panicked as they had been simply transported from their stalls. Now they stood on the green expanse surrounding the family house, standing quietly according to their training but clearly confused. It took a bit of crooning and an apple for each to convince them to enter the stable building, but as soon as they were inside they relaxed, seeing familiar surroundings. It did not take long to install them, then open the stable door to allow them to graze outside for the rest of the day. Once the horses were tended, they walked from the stable to the house and into the door. Erinn felt himself relax at once, and made a bee line for the bath, lighting the boiler and allowing the reservoir to fill. As he stood there, he took a deep breath and reached out with his mind.

"Wife?"

"Husband? What is amiss? Are ye well?" Deborah responded at once. "Ye sound ill. I should come there at once!"

"Ye should come here, to the family house in Dragon Valley," Erinn chuckled. "I need a rest after today's activities."

"What has happened?"

"I shall tell ye all about it when ye arrive my dear. I am hungry for yer cooking, and for yer company," he added.

Where she was, Deborah suddenly could see him clearly and the evidence of his exhaustion was all over him. "I must put someone in charge of the work while I am gone. I shall cook the meal for ye and whoever is there with ye, and ye will tell me the tale when ye can. I am coming, my love."

"Thank ye," he responded simply, allowing their communication to cease. It was just too difficult to maintain at the moment, he thought as he heard the familiar noises the boiler made while heating the water within it. Ah, hot water will soon be ready in abundance, he thought with satisfaction as he left the room, finding work in progress in the common room.

"Look outside," Drake encouraged with a grin as he laid a fire in the hearth. Erinn briefly wondered why he would do so, it being mid-Summer and so glanced out the huge portrait windows that graced the common room. It was raining torrentially and as he stood there, he could see the ice in the rain. Thunder sounded over the building, followed nearly at once by a lighting's flash.

"What a storm!" Erinn commented with a grin. "We were wise to seek shelter, it seems. Who would want to be caught out in that?"

"According to the young Dame, the horses will need to be inside. She is out there attending to it, with Arthfael's help. I did not think either of them should go out there alone."

"What, ye think 'tis something amiss with the storm?" Erinn asked quietly.

"Not exactly amiss," Drake chuckled, directing his attention out the back window, where Dragon Mountain loomed in the distance. The storm did seem to be more intense over the lofty cliffs, and the lightning bolts were huge and brilliantly blue-white. Erinn looked back at Drake with questions in his eyes, and his father supplied an explanation.

"She took the head containing the last remaining traces of Enki's being. I suspect She is doing something with that energy, something great and positive."

"Such as?" Erinn inquired, unable to help himself.

"Reinforcing the barrier between the Land and the outside world," Drake answered at once. "I would do that, if 'twere me. We can never allow the Land to be invaded by the outside. They would misuse everything and anything here, not understanding what they were despoiling. It cannot be allowed. The Goddess' work here must go on, despite what the outside world does to itself. They are tearing each other apart out there, caught up in the never-ending quest for wealth and power. So many good folk will never have the chance to find their way here, I think, if I read the situation correctly out there. 'Tis simply constant war and conquest happening, all done in the name of one Father God or another. They all seem to be the same entity to me, but ye could never convince the people of the outside world of that. They all seem to think their "God" is the only true one."

"Which is ridiculous in the first place, since the Goddess rules, whether within or outside of the Land."

"I wish more people in the outside world would see that," Drake sighed heavily. "Thirsty?"

"Ye know I am. I *am* yer son, after all," Erinn chuckled, taking a seat on the sofa. "O my, that feels good," he sighed.

"Ye *are* tired," Drake observed. "I hope yer lady hurries along. I am concerned."

"I am just a bit tired, Father," Erinn half laughed as he sat there. "And besides, I have not seen my lady for a few days. If I must make a bit more out of my labors to call her to my side, I am willing to risk her wrath for it."

"Have ye looked at yerself?" Drake asked in return. "Ye look as if ye have not slept for days and days, working hard the entire time."

"Ye have described this Summer's working trip perfectly, Father," Erinn laughed a bit as his father set down a full cup of cold ale in front of him.

"Ye are doing naught but sit, drink and smoke after ye bathe," Drake ordered. "If I must cook supper to allow it, I would be happy to offer."

As they discussed and readied the house for Deborah's arrival, the High Lady was busy arranging for her temporary leaving. She went to Tyrion, the Captain leading the Army contingent assigned to her.

"Captain Tyrion!" she called out as soon as she spied him, working with those now laying the foundations for the new house and barn. Hearing his name called, he stopped his work, took up a towel to wipe his hands and stood up at attention.

"Aye, My Lady?" he called back respectfully.

"I must leave for a few days," she explained with a smile. "My healer's skills are needed to aid my Lord Erinn."

"Ye should go at once then, My Lady," he advised gently. "If ye will give me an idea of what progress ye would like to see when ye return, I shall see to it."

"Just get as much done daily as possible to aid in our raising the house walls soon," Deborah replied with authority. "If possible, I would like to start that upon my return. I see that the foundation is nearly complete, well done! Make certain everyone gets an extra ration of ale or wine tonight, with my thanks?"

"Of course, My Lady. The boards are here for the floor, and more are on the way for the walls. The Druids are of great assistance with some of the heavier work, magick can lift a greater load than a person can, after all."

"Aye, 'tis so Captain," she smiled at him, handing him a large bundle of sikars.

"Thank ye, My Lady. I have found these to be an excellent motivator and they are always welcome as a reward amongst those in the barracks."

"I find them an excellent reward for a day's hard work," Deborah answered honestly. "I should not be gone more than four days. I would advise simply keeping the schedule we have so far, and simply supervising their excellent work. I see we are almost ready to lay the floors, a good piece of progress in itself, but the sooner the walls go up the better. I shall leave it in yer capable hands, Captain. If enough is done, a Mother's Holiday will be called, with good beef on the spit and cold ale out of the cask. The entire camp will take the next day off as a rest day as well, 'tis Summer after all, and time for a bit of fun besides the work."

"I shall pass on that bit of information, My Lady," Tyrion answered, bowing low. She had given him exactly the motivator he needed to get the best work out of all of them, and when she disappeared in front of him, he knew she trusted his ability to command. Concealing the sikars within his shirt pocket, he returned to his place and took up his work again, waiting for the first man to ask what the High Lady's orders were.

"She instructed us to work hard for the next four days," he began when he called them to him and they stood around him. "The floor can be done within two days, easily and if we work in two crews, the walls can be constructed as well. If they are ready to raise when she arrives, surely the High Lady's orders will be well followed, aye?"

"Aye!" he heard their response and watched them all fall to working again with renewed energy. He knew that even if they did not get the walls raised, they could be in the process of building them when the High Lady arrived back at camp. Such would be amazing progress, considering they were just about to start laying the floor of the grand farmhouse. It eventually would be two stories, but for now, just the basement and first story would suffice to house the family over the Winter. The barn would eventually be expanded as well, but for now, they set it up with a small milking area, then a large common area where the cattle could shelter and sleep as a herd. A simple hay loft would store enough for them to get through the cold season, and there were other farmers about who could help out if they ran short. They spent the rest of that day and the next four working together for their common good, hoping their efforts would be sufficiently good to please the High Lady.

Drake had just clipped a sikar while Erinn sipped the ice cold ale in his cup when Deborah arrived, her healer's bag in hand.

"Greetings, Father. Husband, I am glad ye are sitting down. Ye look so very, very tired. What have ye been doing to exhaust yerself so completely?" she asked in a suspicious tone.

"My lady, perhaps ye would like to change yer clothing, and join us here on the sofa for a pipe and a sikar?" Erinn asked tiredly, wearing a smile. "I am certain we have white wine downstairs ready for yer cup."

"I am ready for a cup of wine, most certainly," Deborah agreed, assessing Erinn quickly, using her skills as a healer to do so. "Husband," she called to him mentally. "I am very concerned, what have ye done?"

"I shall tell ye all about it once ye have a cup in hand and a pipe too," Erinn smiled. "I suggest ye get comfortable, since ye volunteered to cook," he went on.

"I fully intend to do just that," Deborah replied tartly, rising. Drake stood with her, walking her to the base of the stairs.

"He has performed a great feat today, my dear. Ye will take care of him?"

"Of course, 'tis why he called me, aye?" she asked in return.

"He summoned ye?"

"I can be summoned by my husband, as any married woman can be," she replied with a smile. "Now, if ye will please move, unless yer advanced age makes that difficult, I shall see to changing my clothing into something more suitable for my duties tonight."

"Not ye too!" Drake groaned at her teasing, wearing a wide smile despite it.

"Where are Arthfael and Brianna?"

"Tending to the horses, although they should be back by now. I think I shall wander over to the stable and see what is keeping them," Drake smiled. "I shall return apace, to share that pipe with ye and my son."

"Be discreet and patient," Deborah advised. "They are both good people."

"Of course, but they are young and inexperienced. We wish to avoid mistakes at this juncture. 'Tis time for their chaperone to reappear," he smiled, winking out of sight.

Deborah continued up the stairs to the room she shared with Erinn while they were in residence at the family retreat, finding the beds dressed with clean sheets and pillowcases. Brianna must be responsible for this, she thought as she pulled a set of house clothing out of the clothespress, put aside her working clothing, sponged off the sweat of the day and dressed anew. A pair of comfortable slippers finished her outfit nicely, and after putting her hair back enough for cooking, she donned a robe and returned down the stairs. Drake had returned to the sofa, sitting with Erinn sharing a pitcher of ale while they smoked a pipe of fragrant Herb and she joined them, sitting beside Erinn in time to take the pipe after he finished his dosage.

"Thank ye, husband," she said quietly as their hands touched in passing. "What appeals to ye for supper?"

"If we had time for turkey, I would choose that," Erinn replied with a sigh.

"Turkey?" Deborah smiled. "It so happens that I know Millicent and Gwendolyn are thawing the cold room right now. I would wager she has an extra one or two roasting right now. Let me see if she has one that we could finish off," she smiled.

"Thank ye wife," Erinn sighed, taking the sikar his father handed him.

"Ye should go and bathe, ye will feel better," Deborah advised. "Use the rosemary salts, they will help energize ye a bit."

"Yer presence is inspiring, my lady," Erinn answered elegantly. "And I believe ye are correct that I stink and need a bath," he laughed a bit. "Father, will ye join me?"

"Daughter, do ye need my help?" Drake asked kindly.

"Go and bathe, I do not want him alone in there," Deborah answered mentally. Aloud she answered his question in a jovial fashion. "I think I can manage, Father."

"I have no doubt of that, Daughter," he answered with a smile. "Come my son, we are being sent away," he laughed, helping Erinn to his feet. Erinn allowed him to do so, a rare thing.

"Father," he heard Deborah's question in his mind. "Are Brianna and Arthfael well?"

"They will return to the house shortly. All they are doing is sitting and talking. I see no reason to spy upon them as they are both reasonable young people. Besides, I had a word with Arthfael privately and reminded him of his place in the world as well as his responsibilities. Brianna is naturally reserved and so I think we have little to be concerned about. I did tell them ye were here and to return to the house quickly."

"Very well, let us hope yer assessment is correct then, for everyone's sake," Deborah replied. Mentally, she sent her thoughts out to the Kitchen Mistress at the High Lord's house in the Capitol city, finding Gwendolyn the recipient of her summons.

"My Lady?"

"Gwendolyn, would ye happen to have an extra turkey on hand?" she inquired.

"My Lady," she heard a startled response. "How did ye know we were roasting extra turkey for supper? The part of the frozen stores where all of last year's turkeys and chickens was ready to be thawed and cleaned in preparation for the slaughter this year. Millicent left instructions they were all to be cooked, and so we are roasting them for supper tonight. The turkeys are about halfway done, and filled with a proper stuffing. I used plenty of walnuts, chestnuts and hazelnuts, knowing that the nut harvest this year will be epic by all signs."

"Ye are a treasure," Deborah sent back to her. "I shall need only one, but make it one of the largest ye have. We have hefty appetites here at the house."

"Of course, anytime yer family gathers, there are always hefty appetites," Gwendolyn laughed. "Take whichever bird suits yer needs, we have plenty!"

It did not take Deborah a long time to mentally scan the ovens to select her bird, opening a portal to summon it to her kitchen, pan and all. The oven was ready to receive it, and so with a subtle gesture she magickally opened the door and the roasting pan floated in, settling in the proper place. The door closed by itself as well, and soon the aroma of roasting turkey filled the common room. Erinn could even smell it in the bath and it spurred him to finish cleaning himself quickly, finishing by washing his hair, rinsing it clean of lather before leaving the tub and pulling the drain plug. When he emerged from the bathing room, the scent of roasting turkey surrounded him, and he began to anticipate that night's meal. He walked quickly through the common room to ascend the stairs, returning quickly, comfortably dressed and ready to relax.

In the stables, Brianna and Arthfael were sharing a few discreet kisses, both of them trying it out and finding they liked it. The young dame pulled away breathing hard, and she noted that Arthfael's breathing was also harder and faster than usual.

"I have no idea what is happening to me," she stated flatly, walking away to sit upon a convenient bale of hay. "I should not be feeling like this."

"Why not?" Arthfael asked, joining her and producing a pipe filled with Herb from his pocket. It had not been there before, he noted wryly, handing it to her. "Is it not usual for young people to be attracted to one another?"

"I am not just anyone," Brianna stated. "I do not mean that egotistically. I mean that because of everything I have suffered at the hands of men, it seems odd that I would seek affection from ye."

"I too, have suffered at the hands of men, and women," Arthfael pointed out softly. "Could it be that the Lady means to bring us together, so that we might comfort and help one another?"

She heard his words, and the honesty behind them. It caused her to take the moment and consider before answering. "I know not, I only know that I wish to be with ye, in whatever capacity that might manifest as. I do not know if we can be intimate, but if I were to be, 'twould be with ye."

His gasp at her stark frankness was clear, he sat there just staring at her before finally answering. "And I would never, ever insist. Even if we were to marry, 'twould be yer choice entirely when and where we consummated it. I would even agree to separate rooms and beds, 'till ye felt comfortable enough to come to me."

Now he heard her gasp at his frankness and they sat in silence for a long while, considering each other's words. The sound of the rain increased suddenly as a huge burst let loose, then a roll of thunder shook the building, followed quickly by a large bolt of brilliant lightning. When the flash dispelled, the rain slowed and ceased just as quickly as it had started, opening up an opportunity for them to run for the house. After exiting the stable and closing the door securely, they bolted for the house, barely gaining the porch before the next burst of rain let loose. They ran into the house, laughing with the joy of youth at avoiding being drenched, alerting everyone they had returned.

"The horses are tended, blanketed and bedded down," Arthfael announced. "I am ready to bathe, change into comfortable clothing, and help cook our meal if I am welcome in the kitchen!"

"Ye are always welcome in my kitchen!" Deborah smiled fondly, loving the young man just as much as if he were her own blood son. He beamed a smile, offering an embrace which she gladly shared with him before beginning her work. "Why don't ye go downstairs to see what vegetables we have on hand? I was going to make a salad, but the way 'tis pouring out there, I have no desire to go out into the garden patch. We will make do with what we have," she told him.

"Aye Mother," he smiled, taking a basket in hand. "Dame, would ye like to come with me?" he asked, simply extending his left hand. As Deborah watched, Brianna set her hand within his and they walked off together, disappearing below the stairs into the cold room. She could see it would not be long before she would need to have that dress ready, the two were so very suited to one another, she thought. Making a mental note to spend more time in the sewing room, she turned back to the task at hand. She had little to do, since the turkey was already stuffed and roasting, and so she began a batch of bread from the starter in the crock.

It did not take long for the two young people to gather a basket of produce. He took the opportunity afterward to use the bath, while Brianna lingered in the kitchen, and Deborah sensed the young woman wanted to talk.

"My Lady?"

"Aye?" Deborah answered at once as she mixed the flour and other ingredients together for the bread.

"How did ye know ye loved the High Lord? How did it feel?" she asked softly.

"I quickly came to realize after meeting him that he was unique and special," Deborah answered without hesitation. "He was unlike any man I had ever known before; quiet and humble, earnest and ethical, and to say that I found him completely attractive would be an understatement. After we met, I found myself making up reasons to see him and talk to him, much to my own confusion at first until I realized how I felt about him. I pushed his father Drake aside when he was High Lord, just to get to Erinn's side after he was wounded while hunting a rogue bear. It was no easy matter either, as Drake is a very solid man, but his strength seemed to be naught to me, so strong was my desire to get to Erinn. Ask him about it sometime, I would be interested to hear his side of it," Deborah laughed.

"He respects ye so very much," Brianna went on, still speaking quietly. "I shall never be able to win so much from him, as I am not magickally inclined."

"Ye have already impressed him," Deborah laughed, pouring wine for the younger woman and handing her the cup. "He thinks ye are the perfect match for Arthfael, and is already thinking of being a Great-grandfather."

Brianna's cheeks colored bright red as Deborah spoke, and the High Lady reckoned they had talked long enough about the matter. "I would not be too concerned with Drake's wishes. 'Tis yer wishes, and Arthfael's that matter here. Love cannot be dictated or ordered, it either exists between two people or it does not. True, lasting love is rare indeed, and when 'tis found, it should be cherished and nurtured so it grows and flourishes. Ye know what I think?"

"Nay, Madam," Brianna answered.

"I think ye will make up yer own minds about yer relationship, no matter what anyone says or does. Ye both can come to me for talks, either together or separately. I shall hold those talks as private and confidential, 'lest something is within them that affects the Land negatively. I never had anyone like that, and I think 'twould have helped me make my decision ever quicker than I did. Erinn and I were simply meant for each other, and 'twas no keeping us apart. Time will tell if ye and Arthfael have such affection for one another, I am in no hurry and I think neither of ye should be either."

"But My Lord Drake..."

"Wants his family to be large and prosperous," Deborah laughed harder, refilling her own cup. "After so many years of being one of the only Natanleods about, he is delighted not to be alone. Do not let his enthusiasm for the match sway either of ye, take yer time, find out if ye truly make each other happy and if ye can live together peaceably. Formal marriage will wait, after all, Erinn and I were hand-fasted without ceremony."

Brianna digested Deborah's words for long moments, sipping her wine while doing so. Talking to Arthfael's adopted mother was comforting to her in a way she had rarely experienced with anyone else. It felt like one could tell her anything at all, no matter how deeply painful or emotionally scarring. Impulsively, Brianna embraced the High Lady, receiving a firm embrace in return.

"Thank ye, My Lady," Brianna said quietly.

"Ye are most welcome, Dame. And when ye feel comfortable enough to do so, ye could refer to me as yer Mother. If ye are going to be with Arthfael, I would like to think of ye that way. Artos is my only born child, and I always wanted a daughter," Deborah offered kindly, meaning every word.

"Tha…thank ye My Lady!" Brianna replied, bowing slightly before practically running from the room, heading for the guard quarters where she felt most comfortable. Deborah let her go, knowing she must be overwhelmed at the moment and that she only needed time. Meanwhile, she returned to her preparations, sipping cold white wine while doing so, as well as enjoying the occasional pipe of Herb when Drake brought it to her. Erinn was now sleeping on the sofa, and everyone simply let him do so, Deborah covering him with a light blanket as he lay stretched out.

"What did he do?" Deborah asked of Drake as they walked away.

"Slew one of the most powerful Naga High Priests to ever live!" Drake told her. "He was magnificent, my son I mean. I shall tell ye the tale as well as I recall it, and I am certain ye will get further information from him once he wakes," he chuckled. Drake quickly related what had happened up in the ancient dragon's lair, how Erinn had created a magickal bubble around their battle arena and why. When he related how Erinn had taken his head, and how the Lady had come to claim it, Deborah's face took on a look of consideration and a smile quirked at the corner of her mouth.

"So, now I understand the storm's ferocity," she said. "He will be hungry when he wakes, most certainly. I am glad a meal will be ready for him, so he will not have to wait too long."

"Ye are truly the perfect companion for one of our family," Drake smiled fondly. "Ye think of his comfort, his health and welfare constantly, something all men wish their women did," he sighed.

Deborah did not take the bait, reckoning there would be time for such discussions later. He clearly wanted to discuss Jovita, her intuition told her. "He is my husband, his welfare is one of my first concerns and duties. If he is not healthy of body and mind, how can he rule well?" she asked reasonably.

"As I said, ye two are a perfect matching, for which I am very glad. I made the right choice that day."

Deborah's smile was beatific as she offered him a warm embrace, having great affection for her father in law. "Would ye like some wine?"

"Aye, but I need some red," Drake smiled. "Should I bring enough for everyone?"

"I think ye should. Red wine goes well with roasted turkey," Deborah replied.

"I shall bring up a short cask then," Drake replied. "Perhaps ye might have a snack for me before I do?" he wheedled comically. Deborah quickly put together a plate for him out of the prepared sides, asking his opinion of their flavors and textures. Drake made a show of tasting each, chewing thoroughly and swallowing, clearing his mouth with white wine before answering. "All of them are excellent, as always," he pronounced. "I shall take the barley salad down with me, as it always marinates better when cold. What else should be taken to the cold room?"

"Everything else here," Deborah laughed. "I shall assist ye, taking yer age into consideration."

"What is so funny about teasing me about my age?" Drake complained good-naturedly, taking his plate to the sink.

"Because, Father, yer years have nothing to do with yer mental or physical fitness. Ye are an Ascended Being, time has no pull upon ye, even while ye are here in the Land. Knowing that and having the sense of humor I do, 'tis only natural for me to tease ye just a little bit, all in good fun, aye? If I am doing harm, Father, ye should let me know."

Drake said naught, simply laughing softly and offering her an embrace. "Ye are a good woman and I am glad ye are part of our family."

"As am I. Yer cup is empty," she noted, making a gesture and calling a carafe. As soon as it was in her hand, she uncorked it and filled his cup, as well as her own. "To the House, and our family."

"To the Lady," Drake rejoined and they clinked their cups together lightly. "Now, what help might I be to ye?"

"Ye could bring another pipe," she laughed. "Once I put this bread to rise, I shall have little to do except baste the bird, which should be done soon."

Chapter 8

While they enjoyed being with each other, out in the storm a young man wandered, cold and hungry. His clothing was tattered, his boots were worn, but he did not despair. He kept walking, enjoying seeing the wild country around him, hoping he could find a place to call home at last. He had washed up on shore several weeks earlier, just down the beach a bit from someone else. The first man, Liam, had been a liar and a cheat, and had already been dealt with for it. This man was a good man with a golden heart. He had been on the same ship, headed for the New World, hoping to make a new life without his family's reputation hanging over him. The same wave had washed them both over the rail and into the tossing sea before the ship capsized and sank, taking everyone else with her. Two rafts of flotsam provided two bastions of safety in the vast ocean as the current took them along with it, finally leaving them washed up on the outer banks of the Port District, several miles from Erasmus' seat of power. The two men knew little about each other, except that neither cared for the other and their travels through the Land had been decidedly different. While "The Liar" had attempted to take advantage of folk he thought of as less than himself, this young man struck out inland after feasting on the fruit he found along the shore. A few miles of travel brought him to the first small village, and when he wandered into it, he tapped on the first door that looked friendly. An older man opened it and while the young man could not understand the words, he felt the wave of friendliness projected by the homeowner. A gesture to wave him inside, and then a polite escort to the bathing room, where hot water, soap, towels and fresh clothing awaited. After availing himself of the amenities, and gratefully so, he dressed and emerged from the room to find the family waiting for him.

"Can ye understand me?" the older man asked with a smile, and to his shock the young man found he understood the words. "Did ye enjoy yer bath?"

"O!" the young man answered, his shock immense. "I…I do understand ye! What is this place?"

"Welcome to my home," he heard the old man say in a friendly tone. "My name is Albert, and the rest of those ye see around ye are my family; my wife Vera and my sons, Sean and Uwaine. The other two men are Knights from the local guardhouse who I have summoned in accordance with our customs in regards to strangers. I have no doubt ye are a good person, but one can never be too careful here in the Land."

"The Land?"

"Aye, the body of Earth we live upon. A Nation state, such as Spain or England, but we are completely independent of the rest of yer society," the old man explained carefully. "These Knights are here simply to assure ye are not deceiving us, that ye are not a black sorcerer or inhabited by a Naga."

"I do not understand," the young man answered, feeling suddenly very dizzy. Albert quickly came to his side to support him, and assist him to a convenient chair to help him recover. Vera brought a cup of water for him, which he drank thirstily.

"All will be revealed in time," Albert told him soothingly. "Do ye remember yer name?"

"I...I..." the young man stuttered, suddenly realizing he could not recall his name. "I cannot! What is wrong with me?"

"Naught is amiss, except ye are tired and hungry," Albert told him. "I suspect ye were shipwrecked, am I correct?"

"Aye, only myself and one other man were saved, as far as I know," the young man answered, a tear dropping from the corner of his eye. "He was not a very pleasant man, however. I hope he has found a good life here."

"If he was not a pleasant man, he is likely not in the Land at the moment," Albert chuckled a bit, being Druid-trained. As such, he oftentimes knew about news before the postal rider appeared in the village. He was so accurate that people often wagered on it, and an unofficial contest was often sponsored when the rider arrived.

"So tell me, Albert," the man would laugh as he dismounted his horse, bag of posted letters over his shoulder. "What news have I brought?"

Silver coins exchanged hands as he related the news, each item confirmed by the postal rider from his extensive knowledge concerning what was happening all over the Land. It was truly remarkable just how much Albert knew, just from being able to listen in on his brother Druid's thoughts. Everyone knew about Albert's abilities, which is why he was still reclusive. The Nagas had offered a bounty to anyone bringing him in alive for they had wanted to make him one of them in order to use his extraordinary abilities. He had been one of the first to go into hiding, shedding his Druid name and adopting the one he currently wore. Now he regarded the young man in front of him, realizing he was an Outlander.

"Young man, be at ease," he said soothingly, employing some of his less-used skills, those he had learned in the Shrine as a counselor. "Yer full memory will return in time, as always with those who wander as ye do in the Land. The Lady, our Goddess, has brought ye here to see if ye can adapt to life here. She must think ye are someone special to do so, since such occurrences are relatively rare. Come and sup with us, and then we will show ye a bed to sleep in for the night. Ye are welcome to remain as long as ye would like to, and ye may ask me anything ye wish about life here."

That night, the young man enjoyed a simple supper, typical of that served in the farming communities all over the Land, especially at Mid-Summer. Baked chicken, surrounded by vegetables of all kinds, and a starchy tuber he had never tasted before but enjoyed. A salad of cracked barley, marinated in an herbal vinaigrette and flavored with mint, sweet basil and onion stood on the side and the woman of the house served cold tea with chunks of ice floating in it. The young man had never seen a meal like it, and when he finished his plate, he sat there wondering if he could have more. One of Albert's sons, Uwaine, saw him looking longingly at the plentiful food still on the table and leaned over to offer encouragement.

"If we do not finish most of the food on the table, my mother will be concerned that her cooking is unsatisfactory. If ye are still hungry, feel free to ask for more."

"Thank ye," the young man whispered back gratefully before speaking up. "May I have more?"

"Of course, young man," the mother of the house answered, moving to pick up his plate to refill it. He ate hungrily, but with manners, remembering to express his thanks and compliment the meal.

"How may I pay for my meal?" he asked when he finished, wiping his mouth on the linen napkin.

"Ye may go and rest for the night," Vera answered in a tart tone, but the sparkling in her eyes belied it. "In the morning our work will begin again and ye may work with us if ye wish to."

"I do, as I wish to eat again at yer table, Madam," he answered elegantly, wondering where the words had come from. They had just spilled out without much thought, he had simply meant to express his thanks. She smiled and nodded, pointing to the door where his bed lay. Once in the room, he found a stiff brush and a pot of soft, minty smelling paste and wondered what they were for. He tasted the paste, finding it pleasantly sweet and refreshing, and he smiled, for he had finally guessed its purpose. Wetting the brush, he carefully dipped it into the paste, then experimentally passed the brush over his teeth, being careful not to use too much force. He made certain to scrub the surface of each tooth as well as the surrounding gum area, then scrubbed his tongue too, liking how the brush felt on the interior of his mouth. Finally, he used the cup and pitcher sitting there, pouring a bit of the water and rinsing his mouth out with it.

What he expelled had traces of blood in it, so he rinsed again, finding nothing the second time. Resolving to use even less force on the next occasion, he rinsed out the brush carefully, setting it back where he had found it to dry before attending to the rest of his preparations for bed. Walking back into the bedchamber, he found a set of clothing waiting there, and reckoned they were to wear to bed. Delighted at the prospect he dressed quickly, finding the cloth soft and warm to the touch. The bed covers were flipped back and since the night was rapidly cooling, he started by using two of the blankets, retaining the rest for later if needed as he climbed onto the mattress and settled himself comfortably. He laid there, thinking himself most fortunate to find such nice folk so quickly, knowing it would been nearly impossible anywhere else he had ever been before. Sleep came quickly, and he rested extremely well in the comfort of the bed, waking easily before dawn.

When he opened his eyes, he was momentarily confused, and he lay there breathing hard for a moment before he remembered where he was, and how he had gotten there. Once he was calmer, he sat up and looked about, seeing the streaks of light streaming through the seams of his window curtains. A set of clean clothing and a pair of boots stood on the chair at the end of his bed, and he realized the woman of the house had slipped them there sometime during the night. Her stealth had been such that even his sensitive ears had not heard her, he thought with a grin. If he had been at home, he could be dead at the moment due to not hearing her, he thought additionally as he finished pulling on the clean, soft set of unders, then hose, trous and finally the shirt. The boots fit perfectly, as if made for him, he thought, although he recognized they were all hand-me-downs. It felt good to be dressed in farming clothing again, he smiled as he looked at himself. He still missed his family, left behind many years before as he sought to study at learning institutions within the Church.

Now that he was dressed, he was unsure what to do next, at least until Uwaine appeared at his door, also dressed for work.

"First meal is on the boards, and then we have work to do," he said simply. "The day will be hot, we must get as much done before the heat is too great."

"I am ready to work!"

And so it began, the young man's journey across the Land. After that day's work and a full rest that night, Albert presented him with a knapsack at the morning table.

"Ye should be on yer way," he said simply. "My wife and I have packed a small travel bag for ye, with what stores we can spare as well as a change of clothing. Thank ye for yer help today, we are finally ahead of schedule. May I suggest ye make yer way to the Capitol city, where ye can ask to talk to the High Lord about becoming a citizen of the Land?"

"What road should I take?" the young man asked.

"I shall take ye to the gates, so as to show ye the road," Albert offered kindly.

"Yer kindness is most appreciated, Sir," the young man said sincerely. "The bed was comfortable, and the food I have eaten delicious. As I make my way to the Capitol, will I find other opportunities to work for a meal or two?"

"Of course, we of the Land appreciate hard workers, especially now, just before the harvest begins. 'Tis always extra work at such times. May the Lady watch over ye as ye travel."

"Thank ye, Sir, for everything ye have done for me," the young man answered. Albert extended his arm for the grip, and after demonstrating once, the young man understood the gesture to be a common one among men of the Land. It was a good way to show one's good intent right away, he could see that, and decided to adopt it as a way of greeting. Albert watched him walk away, headed in the correct direction and whispered a prayer that the young man would recall his name soon, and that he would find his way to the High Lord.

Weeks passed as he walked along the road, finding work here and there in exchange for a bed and a meal for a few days. Gradually, the speech of the Land came easily to him, and it came to pass that his speech became harder and harder for people to recognize as being that of an Outlander. While the High Lord made his way to the family valley, the young man continued his journey, eventually finding his way up into the mountains and on the road to the family valley. His arrival there coincided with Erinn being there with Brianna, Drake, Arthfael and Deborah, and as soon as the young man wandered into Beri's village, it was clear he was different.

"Excuse me, but is there work to be had?" the young man inquired of Beri. "O! I like yer horns too!" he added, fascinated by seeing the Fae in front of him.

"Ye can see those?"

"O aye, and they are quite lovely and graceful, I might add," the young man answered without hesitation.

"I see," Beri answered, his sense of humor now tickled a bit as the Fae creature sent an alert to Erinn's sleeping mind.

"My Lord?" he inquired, waiting patiently. Finally, he felt Erinn's mind answer his, somewhat sleepily, he noted.

"Beri? What is amiss?"

"My Lord, we have a stranger in the valley. He is standing right here in front of me, apparently unbothered by the fact he can see me as I am."

"He can see ye as a Fae?"

"Aye, and he is undeterred by the horns on my head," Beri chuckled. "I shall send him up the House for ye to deal with. O, and he cannot remember his name at the moment either. He has been in the Land for some time, I think. He is rather ragged."

"Send him to us," Erinn ordered with a chuckle. "We have plenty of food, drink and clothing up here at the House. Perhaps I need to meet this young man?"

"Perhaps so, My Lord," Beri answered in a dignified tone. Turning to the young man, Beri pointed the way and told him that the High Lord was awaiting him up at the family house.

"But, I thought I had to see him in the Capitol city!" the young man answered in a startled tone.

"Apparently, the Lady of the Land is in a hurry to have ye meet him," Beri chuckled. "Be well, young man."

"Thank ye Sir," he answered, shouldering the ragged pack and walking away slowly.

Erinn sat up on the couch, suddenly and fully awake, ready for the coming visit.

"What is amiss?" Drake asked at once, seeing him suddenly sit up.

"We have an outland visitor," Erinn replied shortly. "He is coming from Beri's village, and apparently he can see Fae creatures for what they truly are, horns and all."

Drake's face took on a look of surprised consideration. "An outlander who can see Fae?"

"I am anxious to meet such a young man," Erinn chuckled at his father's consternation. "How many people currently in the Land can do such things?"

"Well my son, anyone of magickal blood can see Fae if they are taught, to be able to see one without training is an extraordinary gift. I shall be interested in his observations of both myself and of ye."

"Why?"

"Because of my true nature my son," Drake chuckled heartily. "Being half dragon would be apparent to any Druid-trained person here in the Land. I know that Nathan was startled when he first met me. What did ye perceive the first time we met?"

"Only that ye were strong, tall and yer aura was extremely powerful, unlike anyone I had ever met before or since," Erinn replied honestly.

By this time, the young man had arrived at the house, stopping for a moment to take stock of the place despite being drenched. What he saw was magnificent, a huge rustic villa home, two stories tall, graced with arched windows and the wide veranda that surrounded nearly the entire ground floor of the house. He walked around the building, unable to help himself, noting the upper patio gracing one of the upper rooms and guessed it was attached to a bedchamber. Erinn and Drake watched him from inside, the young man completely oblivious to their observations as he continued his inspection, finally arriving back where he began.

"My goodness," he thought to himself as he walked to the veranda, seeing a door there. "How many people live here? My whole village back home would likely fit inside the compound I see!"

Gaining the back door, he knocked on the stout oaken door, using just enough force so as to be heard. Erinn opened it, and the young man was astonished to see the shadowy shape of a dragon in his aura.

"My Lord!" the young man addressed Erinn instinctively, not knowing why he would.

"Welcome to my home," Erinn replied in his deep and sonorous voice. "Would ye come inside, 'tis entirely too wet to be standing out there."

"I would be honored," the young man replied, glancing down at his sodden clothing. "But I do not wish to make a mess inside yer grand home."

"Come inside, we will attend to yer sodden condition," Erinn chuckled. "Wife, we have a guest who will need clothing after he bathes!" Erinn turned to call out.

"Very well, what size would ye estimate him to be?" he heard a woman's voice call back, rich and warm to his ears.

"Come and see," Erinn replied, laughing a bit. "My name is Erinn Natanleod, I am the High Lord of the Land. May I present my wife, Deborah Natanleod?" he said as Deborah appeared at his side. The young man could not help himself, he openly stared at the gorgeous woman wearing extremely casual clothing. She wore no cosmetics that he could detect, and her wavy black hair was long and loose down her back.

"Greetings in the name of the Lady," Deborah smiled at the young man, reaching out with her inner senses to ascertain his state. She could feel naught to alarm her, and she could also feel his tension, realizing he understood he was being assessed.

"How did ye do that?" he asked urgently.

"What?" Deborah asked in return, wanting to know the state of the young man's education.

"I felt yer presence in my mind!" he said, his voice anxious and upset. "And 'twas as if yer eyes could see within me! Ye are a witch!"

"Thank ye," Deborah smiled warmly. "In the Land, what ye have just named me is an honorable title. Be not afraid, we are not going to hurt ye in any wise. No one accosted ye on yer road here, did they?"

"N...Nay," he answered slowly as he thought about it. "In fact, everyone was very nice and helpful to me. They offered me shelter, food and work when I needed it, as well as directions to the Capitol city. I have never encountered such friendly, hospitable people, and the food here is extraordinary as well! Am I dead?"

"Not exactly," Deborah laughed. "Come inside before it opens up in another deluge. After a hot bath, and some warm food, we will talk more."

He found he trusted her without knowing why and so stepped over the threshold into the family house, feeling at ease immediately. "Thank ye for yer welcome, Madam. I did not mean to be rude."

"Of course not," Deborah smiled warmly. "Husband, would ye show him the way to the bath? He looks cold and tired."

"Right this way, young man," Erinn chuckled, indicating that the young man should join him. They had nearly reached the door to the bath when Brianna emerged from the barracks and her eyes beheld the traveler, the first outsider she had ever seen. He was filthy from head to toe, she noted at once, but his ginger-red hair could be seen despite it. He was young, perhaps about her age she reckoned, using assessment skills learned in the Amazon fortress. He had blue eyes too, she noted, but they were pale compared to the deep sapphire-blue of Arthfael's eyes. His body was muscular, but thin, and his face was very handsome to her eyes. All she could do was stare for long seconds, finally engaging him in conversation.

"My name is Brianna, what is yers?"

"I do not recall at the moment," the young man answered, casting eyes about the room. When he saw Arthfael, his eyes lingered a bit for the young man was very handsome and it had been a long time since he had sought out a lover. This young man was just his type; athletic, good-looking and clearly intelligent. One had to have someone to talk to after all, he thought, letting his eyes settle on Arthfael's face. I could live with such a gorgeous man, he thought with a sigh.

Arthfael stood there, observing Brianna's reaction to the outlander. He had never experienced jealousy before, but he was certainly feeling it now as he saw how she was looking at the stranger. He thought her expression reflected desire and longing, but such feelings were due to his own growing jealousy. I must put a stop to this, Arthfael thought suddenly as anger boiled up within him. If Drake had not restrained him bodily, he would have walked up to the unfortunate young man and challenged him on the spot.

"Here now boyo," he heard Drake's voice say into his mind. "Jealous are we?"

"She should not be talking to him!" Arthfael answered indignantly.

"Why not? 'Tis just words, naught else. Ye cannot stop her from talking to everyone, ye know, just because ye love her," Drake counseled aloud, keeping his voice reasonable. "She is an Amazon, ye cannot enslave her."

"I do not want to enslave her, but she should not be talking to other men while we are courting!" Arthfael insisted, earning him a slap on the shoulder from Drake.

"Listen to yerself," he growled a bit, so that the young man would hear him. "Jealousy is unbecoming to a Natanleod heir!"

"I bet ye know all about it!" Arthfael lashed out quietly.

"I do, which is why I am counseling ye otherwise," Drake returned seriously, his voice deep and patient. "I almost lost Jovita over jealousy, and I promised myself I would never let myself make that mistake again. If ye seek to keep her for yerself, ye will only force her away. Take my counsel on this boyo, I have lived longer than ye, and loved more often. Ye should take a walk outside, boyo, and cool yer head."

Arthfael glanced outside, noting it was raining harder now than at any other time that day. "I do not want to go out in that!" he replied.

"I told ye, go outside and take a walk," Drake insisted, his face completely serious. "When ye regain yer good senses, ye can return. Ye will not start an incident here, in the family house, while yer father is trying to rest from his labors. Do not indulge yer petty side, ye are simply being selfish."

Arthfael's angry response was restrained by his Grandfather's reasonability, and he feared Drake's martial response enough to take his advice. Stalking away without another word, Arthfael walked in-between Brianna and the newly arrived Outlander to grab his coat off the rack. Brianna had the chance to look at his face, saw the anger there and guessed the cause of it. She followed after him, walking outside behind him and calling his name as she closed the door.

"Arthfael, where are ye going?"

"For a walk, to do some thinking!" he called back, and she could hear the anger in his tone.

"Ye have naught to be jealous about," she called back and he stopped suddenly, turning back to face her.

"What is it about him that ye prefer over me?"

"Arthfael!" Brianna responded, her voice filled with distress. "I do *not* prefer him over ye, but I have never met someone newly arrived in the Land before. I simply wanted to ask him a few questions, I do not want to share the Rite with him! You are overreacting entirely, I do not belong to ye, after all!"

Arthfael paused a moment to take a breath and calm himself before answering. His eyes met Drake's as his grandfather stood on the veranda smoking a sikar and suddenly calm reigned. "Ye are right, Madam," he said simply. "I must apologize for being childish and selfish. Ye are a free woman, ye may speak to any ye wish, whether we are handfasted, married or otherwise. May I ask for yer forgiveness?"

Brianna paused, shocked at his sudden earnestness. Drake stood on the veranda observing, a secret smile on his face. "Ye *are* my grandson!" he thought with satisfaction, watching Brianna walk into Arthfael's arms and snuggle against his chest.

"I never want there to be a misunderstanding between us, Arthfael," Brianna murmured as she was cradled in his sword-hardened arms. "I have chosen ye, and ye alone. Ye suit me, and I am happy when I am with ye. If ye will be patient with me, I shall be so with ye, and we will make a good match."

Arthfael heard her words, spoken softly and tinged with suppressed passion. "I am sorry to be jealous, I simply could not help myself. I shall try my best to be a better man in the future, but I love ye, and wish to be with ye when and only when ye are ready," he said quietly into her ear.

"O Arthfael!" she said in a loving whisper, planting a discreet kiss on his cheek. "Ye are such a good man. I am so fortunate to have found someone such as ye!"

"I am the fortunate one, to have found one such as ye!" Arthfael declared, and while Drake watched silently on the veranda, they shared a kiss of great passion. He said naught, simply walking back into the house, wanting to give them their privacy, and soon the both of them returned to the house, dripping from sodden clothing, but glowing from within.

The young outlander stood there, astonished at the scene transpiring in front of him. As he listened to the conversation, he realized there had been a severe misunderstanding about his interest in speaking to

Brianna. He had thought she might be the handsome young man's sister, and was hoping to find out more about him before making his offer. Now that he understood that she and the young man Arthfael were courting, he felt a moment of panic. He had not meant to interfere in anyone's relationship, he thought, feeling more than a little anxiety. Wanting to clear up the confusion, he approached the group, speaking with great respect and careful words.

"I did not mean to create such havoc," he said sincerely. "But I think the young lady has misunderstood my intent. While she is a very, very lovely woman, it was not her I wanted to speak with at all," he said, turning to Arthfael with a soft expression on his face. "My interest was with ye, young man, but I can see that I must step away from it. Ye both are so very suited for one another, and I would never interfere with true love."

Drake's eyebrows lifted a bit at the young man's words, his surprise at hearing them complete. "How could I have made such a miscalculation?" he thought to himself as he observed the young man. "His aura hid that, even from me? Who is he?"

He turned to the young man and walked to his side, extending his arm for the grip, as he would any other man in the Land. "Do ye remember yer name, young man?"

"I do, my name is Dimitri!" the young man blurted out loudly. "O! I am so sorry, I did not mean to shout, but I have been in yer country for months without being able to remember that."

"Dimitri? Yer name is derived from Demeter, Goddess of Wild Things. Where are ye from?" Drake asked, always interested in such things.

"I come from the Ural Mountains," Dimitri answered, his memories now flowing out. "My family was caught up in the Tsar's latest *pogrom* and only my brothers and I were able to escape. My sisters and my parents are somewhere in Siberia, and I have no hope of ever seeing them again. I was bound for the New World in hopes of simply losing myself in its abundant and verdant forests. Someone like me is always subject to people's dislike and distrust, simply due to who I love."

"Ye will not find it that way here," Deborah spoke out, her heart filled with empathy for him. "People are who they are here, and as long as it breaks none of the Lady's Law, they are free to love whom they will. Ye will find no hatred or bigotry here."

Dimitri's eyes opened wide as she spoke, and he could hear her earnestness. "I hope 'tis true, My Lady," he said slowly and carefully, wanting to be precise. "If so, then yer country would be the only one to practice such tolerance. If only the rest of humanity would do so," he sighed heavily.

"Come, let us get ye bathed and into clean clothing," Drake spoke up. "Supper is cooking, and 'twill be a delicious meal, as my daughter in law is a fine cook."

"I...I may remain among ye, even though ye know all about me?"

"Of course!" Drake chuckled, waving for Dimitri to walk beside him. "No one would censure ye for simply being who and what ye are. As long as ye are harming no one, especially yourself, which our Lady's Law proscribes. 'Tis the only real law we have, here in the Land, and it suits us."

"I like this idea!" Dimitri smiled a bit. The door to the bath opened by itself, due to Drake's abilities and they walked into the steamy room. Drake showed the young man where the towels, robes, slippers and baths salts were, then turned the tap to begin refilling the tub. Dimitri was surprised at the copious flow of hot water, he had never seen anything quite like the boiler arrangement being used.

"How marvelous!" he commented as he looked over the mechanism, seeing how it worked. "Ingenious! However did ye come up with the design?"

"What ye are seeing is common throughout the Land, my friend," Drake chuckled, walking to the wall of glass jars bearing labels indicating the contents. "What scent would suit ye? Roses, lavender, calendula, or a mix of stimulating herbs?"

"I may choose?" the young man asked in amazement.

"Of course!" Drake chuckled a bit. "Ye are a free person, are ye not?"

Dimitri walked to where Drake stood, taking the time to sniff each jar presented to him, finally choosing a mix of lavender and rose. Drake measured the proper amount into the hot water as the tub quickly filled, and soon the room smelled fresh and wholesome.

"Thank ye Sir. I can hardly wait to be clean!" Dimitri exclaimed.

"I shall leave ye to yer bath," Drake told him. "I think ye can manage, aye?"

"O aye!" Dimitri smiled. "Thank ye, good sir. I shall make good use of all the soap I see! O, it all smells so marvelous, I have never seen or smelled anything like all of this!"

"Ye will find this a common thing throughout the Land, young man," Drake replied with a chuckle, leaving the door ajar just a bit, in case the young man needed assistance. Dimitri quickly stripped and entered the bath, easing into the very hot water and relaxing against the side of the tub.

"Glorious!" he thought gratefully, settling his well-tanned body into the water, finding it just a bit above the temperature he was expecting. It was not unbearable, he thought as he began to scrub his hair, as long as I do not remain in the heat too long. After scrubbing his hair twice, ducking under the water's surface to rinse away the dirty lather, he began with the brush and soft soap on his body. It felt wonderful, the sensation of the soft bristles against his skin, and he watched layers of dirt and loose skin float away, spilling out of the tub down a drain to somewhere. Finally clean from head to toe, he leaned back and sipped his wine until the cup was empty, then he hauled himself out of the water, pulling the drain plug and turning off the slow trickle from the boiler.

Turning to the cabinets against the wall, he climbed the two stairs out of the recessed bath to reach them, opening the first one he reached. Inside, he found a stack of thick towels, and when he wrapped one around him, he found himself surrounded by a feeling of luxury and comfort. The towel was soft and fluffy, it soaked up the water off him quickly, leaving him ready to don a robe and slippers, which he found in the next cabinet. Again, the robe was bulky and soft, it invited one to wrap it around one, and when he did he felt it embrace him comfortingly. The knitted slippers were just as soft, when he slipped his feet into them his feet began to tingle a bit, unused to such luxury. When he emerged from the bath, he wore a contended smile on his face, and when the High Lady brought him more wine, he expressed his gratitude.

"Madam, I feel better than I have for many months," he said with warmth in his tone. "But the clothing I was wearing needs to be laundered before I don it."

"Ye are not wearing that outfit again," Deborah declared with a smile. "In fact, I have burnt it so the vermin crawling around on it will not infest my house. I am not being judgmental, I know that sometimes when one is traveling, bathing is difficult to arrange. Come, I shall take ye upstairs to one of the guest chambers, where yer bed is. Ye should be acquainted with how the room is arranged," she invited, indicating the broad and slightly curved staircase. He followed her up, noting the beautiful woodworking of the stairs, a smooth and even curve as it turned to ascend to the top level. He could find no flaw as he ran his sensitive fingers over the surface, it was soft and smooth to the touch, and something he was unused to. In the outside world, the word "craftsman" was bandied about rather loosely as a description of the skill of people. Oftentimes one paid for first quality work only to receive barely that of an apprentice, which was destroying the reputation of the Guilds.

"Here, ye may sleep here in comfort. Welcome to my home, Dimitri of the Ural Mountains. Rest here in peace."

"Thank ye, Madam," Dimitri answered, bowing very low in the style of his people, the Cossacks. They were people from the high meadows, a horse culture of ancient times, finding themselves a bit lost as the world turned from an honorable sense of war to a more savage one. The current Tsar was displeased with their leaders, who were hesitant to join his latest campaign to rid Russia of what he called the "Hebrew scourge," which were called *pogroms*. All of the Cossacks realized such a thing was simply an opportunity to acquire wealth and property by simply removing the owners, which is why they hesitated to join in. Such things had been done to their people in the past, much to the detriment of those who suffered the harsh removals. Oftentimes the former owners were left completely destitute, and were shipped off to work camps in far away, frigid Siberia, never to be seen again, as had happened to his family. He was alone in the world now, separated from all of his family, never to be reunited for fear of attracting the Tsar's attention again. "I am glad to be here in this place, but I must confess that I know not where exactly I am. This place does not appear on any map of Earth I have seen."

"I am not surprised about that," Deborah smiled gently. "We go to great lengths to keep it that way. Ye have seen the maps bearing the illustrations of dragons, and the warning attached to them, aye?"

"Aye!" Dimitri answered, and realization hit him. "Those are true warnings?"

"Aye," Deborah confirmed as she opened all of drawers in the room, showing him the clothing there. "If ye need to don warming clothing, ye will find it here. Supper will be served presently, but only after we have had a full opportunity to relax, chat and possibly share a game of chess or two. My husband's father is keen on the game, and he is very, very good."

"I have played a game or two," Dimitri ventured. "I would enjoy the engagement. What is yer proper title, Madam? I do not wish to offend."

"I am the High Lady of the Land, Deborah Natanleod," she answered without boastful pride in her tone. "I have the honor of being the wife of the High Lord, Erinn ap Drake Natanleod."

"Interesting, ye cite his father, but not yers," Dimitri noted, going being the screen with the set of light, long unders to begin the process of dressing.

"I do not honor my father, who was a traitor and criminal," Deborah answered succinctly. "Nor would I honor my mother, who I would also name as traitor and criminal."

"I meant no offense, My Lady," Dimitri responded at once. "I'm sorry my curiosity has brought up such memories."

"Ye have naught to apologize for, how could ye know?" Deborah smiled warmly, and Dimitri experienced her compassionate, gracious aura. "My dear man, ye are not where ye were at all anymore. The Lady of the Land, who ye would see as the Goddess of all the Earth, has brought ye here for some purpose of Her own. She does this from time to time, bring in people from the outside to offer them an opportunity to pursue a better way of life, seeing them as being worthy. If She sees that ye have such potential, who am I to deny it?"

"O! My Lady!" Dimitri breathed out, astonished at how he suddenly felt about her, as if she were truly his queen. "I shall embrace this opportunity as fully as possible. I have no wish to return to what is out there!"

"Good, then ye have the best attitude towards yer opportunity. Now, when ye finish dressing, come back downstairs unless ye feel tired. If so, please just use the bed, 'tis dressed with clean sheets, quilts and pillowcases. Yer necessity is right through that door, make yerself at home."

"Tha…Thank ye, My Lady!" Dimitri answered, bowing very low.

"We are very casual here at the house, young man," she told him with a smile. "Ye have no need to bow like that each time we speak. I appreciate a friendly atmosphere here at the house, and ye may just call me 'Elder Sister' while we are here. Anywhere else ye will need to use the honorific, as the troops are very strict that everyone in the Land does so. 'Tis simply a matter of respect, and if people cannot honestly address us as such then something is terribly amiss."

"Ye are not noble born!"

"Nay, I am not, although both of my parents claimed nobility. They were not very noble people in how they conducted their lives," she answered simply.

"I am sorry, My Lady, I did not mean to pry."

"Of course not," she smiled warmly. "Now I am going downstairs to tend my turkey. I am certain my father in law has forgotten all about basting it, which will give me the opportunity to point out his lack of attention to detail."

"Yer father in law is not like anyone else in the Land, is he?" Dimitri asked. "His skin has the most interesting luster to it, aye?"

"Ye can see that?"

"Aye, right from the first time I saw him. What is that? And how is it he has a dragon's shadow behind him?"

"Drake is an Ascended Being, a man who has traveled through the rounds of incarnation to leave the physical without dying to do so. He is quite alive, despite not living here full time, visiting from the higher realms at the Lady's behest. His visits are most welcome, as they are usually most timely. I find it interesting that ye noted his aura, not everyone can see him, or discern his energies, especially since ye can see his dragon guardian. Perhaps ye should meet the Elder Brother of the Druids, a group of spiritually inclined scholars, bards, teachers and poets that helps guide young people into their proper life work? Would ye like that?"

"Ye have something like that?"

"Aye, the Guild system in the Land is very advantageous, as young people's talents and skills are found very early, and encouraged to find ways to help develop them. The Druids, and the Temples of the Lady both act as filters for our children, and as soon as their abilities and talents are known, they are offered several paths to follow in order to learn to use them. Aye, ye should meet with Aldridge right away. I wonder if he is busy at the moment?" she thought aloud that last part, sending out her thoughts to the man.

Aldridge was just about to draw his nightly bath when he felt the High Lady's thoughts in his mind, and a faint smile crossed his face.

"Aye, My Lady?" he sent back to her.

"We have a new arrival here in the Land, Elder Brother. He sings very well, and he can see Drake's aura, all of it, and I do mean *all*."

"He can? Well, I should come and speak with him then," the older man chuckled. "Ye wouldn't happen to have an extra bed for an old man at the house, would ye My Lady?"

"We always have room for ye, Elder Brother," Deborah responded graciously, glad he was willing to come assess Dimitri.

"I shall be along soon then," he said in a reassuring tone. It did not take him long to attend to the last few details needing his personal touch, and then he took up his traveling bag, always packed. Moments after disappearing from within his room at the Shrine, he appeared in the common room at the family house in Dragon Valley, startling Dimitri a great deal.

"O!" he cried out when the older man appeared suddenly, without the customary cloud of smoke.

"I am sorry young man," Aldridge apologized at once, offering his arm for the grip. He used this means to quickly assess people's energies by direct contact, being one of those able to "read" people's intentions by doing so. He quickly discerned that Dimitri was no threat to anyone, excepting himself, at least not now that he was in the Land. Aldridge could hear the echoes of older thoughts, ones that would have been considered very dangerous to the young man's wellbeing outside of the Land. Now, he could hear hopeful thoughts, ones that yearned for acceptance and peace, so that Dimitri could simply live his life. "My name is Aldridge, I am the Elder Brother and leader of the Druid Order here in the Land. I am also the Headmaster of our University, and I am here in that capacity. Ye have talents and abilities ye do not know about, and we of the Druids are always seeking out such folk."

Dimitri stared openly at the old man, for despite his long white hair and prodigious beard, he seemed vigorous and sound of mind. In the outside world, men wearing such hair were generally weak and ready to die due to hard work and privation. He had never seen anyone that looked as aged as Aldridge, the man was vital and virile, that much would be obvious to anyone who saw him, Dimitri reckoned. He was also quite handsome, as were all the men in the room, the young man could not help but notice. It was the vitality and robustness that Aldridge exhibited that startled Dimitri the most. In the outside world, men who had gained enough age to wear such white hair were usually on the brink of death from old age, and so Aldridge's appearance mystified the younger man.

"Excuse me, Sir," he blurted, unable to help himself. "But I must ask how old ye are?"

"I have the honor of gaining almost a century of years, young man," Aldridge confessed, wearing a gentle smile.

"One hundred *years*?"

"Such an accomplishment is not unheard of in the Land, young man," Aldridge answered softly, helping Dimitri to calm his emotional response. "Ye have come to a place quite outside yer experience, Dimitri of the Urals. The Goddess of our Land has brought ye here so ye might be free of the harassment and abuse heaped upon people such as yerself, with an opposite incarnation as we call it. Ye are a female soul, incarnated as a man so as to learn what 'tis like to be one. I would estimate that ye have never had such an incarnation before, since ye are having such difficulty adapting to it."

"Adapting?"

"Aye, ye still prefer men in this incarnation, even though ye are a man. Ye do not think of yerself as a male, nor do ye act like one in any manner. I am not accusing or denigrating ye, I am simply pointing out what I see and feel about ye," Aldridge explained patiently. "Daughter, is there red wine available? I have a feeling this explanation will take me more than just few simple words."

Dimitri sat there digesting Aldridge's words, finally realizing he was right about much of it. He had never thought of himself as a male, even as a child he had begged his mother for dresses and pretty things, such as his sisters wore. His father had beaten him many times for it, ending each session with the words, *"Ye are a man, act like one!"* before confiscating the jewelry, perfumes and stolen cosmetics he hoarded and burning any piece of hidden feminine clothing. If it had not been for the *pogrom* that destroyed his family and village, his father would have simply expelled him from the house, ordering him never to return.

Now he found himself confronted by his own nature in a place where he could be what he wanted to be, dress as he wished and consort with others like himself. It was simply overwhelming to him, and he broke down in tears right there beside Aldridge. The older man smiled gently and embraced him, letting him weep against his shoulder for a brief time, until he regained his composure.

"I am sorry about that," he finally said, wiping his eyes with the kerchief Deborah handed him, along with another cup of wine.

"Why should ye be?" Aldridge asked quietly, accepting another cup from Deborah as well, along with the pipe and box of Herb. "People need to vent their emotions, if they build up, a person can become very unhealthy. I would wager ye have never wept in front of anyone, or at least not for a long, long time."

"Ye are right, the last person I cried in front of was my father," Dimitri nodded sadly. "Right after the Tsar's soldiers burnt our house and farm after taking every animal and jar of food from us. It was snowing, and we had no place to go, but the Tsar's men cared naught as they rode away herding our old gentle brood mare and milk cow. We found their hides many days later, and the remnants of the huge party meal the Tsar's soldiers had made of them. At least every bite had been consumed, all that was left was the bones," the young man sighed at the loss of such beautiful and productive animals.

"Ye have no need for such thoughts here," Aldridge reminded him in gentle tones. "Ye will find them fading into the background of yer memory soon enough. Ye should accompany me when I return to the Main Shrine, where the University is. Ye have many hidden abilities and talents, I can see now why the Lady has brought ye to us."

Dimitri stared, his mouth gaping open. An offer to attend University? Such a thing was unheard of for someone like him in the outside world, he had only dreamt of such possibilities in the past.

"I...I could attend such a school?"

"Of course!" Aldridge chuckled, finishing his wine. Deborah was right there suddenly, startling him a bit with her appearance, offering them both more to drink.

"Where did ye come from?" Dimitri blurted before he could stop himself.

"What do ye mean?" Deborah asked softly, a smile upon her face. "I have been here all along, but ye were so deeply involved in yer discussion with the High Druid, ye simply did not notice my approach. I am sorry for startling ye," she said soothingly. "Supper will be served shortly, ye should both go wash yer hands and take a seat at table."

"Aye Madam," Aldridge replied, rising from his seat. "Come lad, ye are in for a wonderful meal. The High Lady is a fine cook."

"Why thank ye, Elder Brother!" Deborah smiled at the compliment. "As I understand it, ye are a fine cook yerself. Someday, perhaps we will prepare a meal together? I would love to work with someone as accomplished as ye."

"Ye mean someone as old as I," Aldridge laughed merrily, engaging her in the game as Dimitri watched, fascinated.

"My Lord Druid, ye are young of heart," Deborah replied in a demure tone, but Dimitri could hear the overtones of humor hiding with it. When she spoke again, he noted that the volume of her voice had increased significantly. "Unlike my Father-in-Law who despite his ascended condition seems to be showing signs of rapid deterioration," she went on. Dimitri watched as Drake's head jerked up a bit at the mention of his name, a slow smile crossed his face, and despite playing a complicated game on the board, Dimitri realized he was paying close attention to what Deborah was saying.

"He knows ye are talking about him," he said quietly to Deborah, receiving a warm smile from the High Lady.

"O, I know he does," she replied. "But ye must understand, 'tis all part of a family game we play. He enjoys the repartee, and I believe that such jesting, as long as everyone understands 'tis all in good fun, keeps the mind and wit sharp. Drake has a wicked sense of humor, honed by many years of war and privation, he needs to have it tickled from time to time, just to remember he has a sense of humor," she explained.

"And it keeps him humble," Dimitri added.

"Indeed so, young man," Deborah smiled, winking broadly before continuing the game. "Are ye ready for more wine Father, or has yer aging body had plenty?" she called out, and he could hear her laughing while doing so.

"I am glad I have so many younger and more able bodied folk about me," Drake called back, barely restraining his own mirth. "Otherwise, I should have to fetch and carry everything myself. 'Tis good to have the young to wait upon those more seasoned than themselves, a humbling experience."

"Well, when ye decide ye wish to expend what strength ye have left in the effort, supper is nearly finished, and ye should take yer place at table," Deborah answered, giggling a bit as she finished her barb.

Drake's face took on a look of comic consternation as he made a show of rising from the couch, slowly and as if he were in great pain. Limping to the table, he slid into his customary seat and tucked the napkin under his chin.

"I am ready for my meal, dear daughter in law," he said in a slightly whining tone, while his eyes sparkled with humor.

"Are ye sure ye can still chew it, or should I cut it up for ye?" Deborah laughed aloud. Drake's laughter joined hers, blending in a pleasant harmony, while Dimitri looked on in amused wonder.

He sat where Deborah indicated he should, tucking the fine napkin in under his chin and waiting patiently for the promised plate of food. He had never before eaten such a meal; the bird was juicy and tender, the stuffing moist and perfectly cooked, the vegetables coming with the meal all flavored with herbs, garlic and olive oil before being roasted. He ate two of the beautifully golden-brown rolls before he realized it, using a third to accompany the rest of the meal. They were so delicious and light, the texture slightly chewy and nutty, he had never tasted anything like them. He sat silently, simply letting himself enjoy a meal for the first time since leaving home, and tears began to roll down his face. Drake simply handed him a kerchief without a word, reckoning the young man was simply overwhelmed with the events of the day.

By the end of the meal, he regained his composure and was chatting companionably with everyone at the table. When Deborah rose to begin clearing, he rose with her to assist, as did everyone else and between their combined efforts, the kitchen was soon clean and ready for the next day. Erinn was nodding visibly again by then, and excused himself to go upstairs for the night.

"Good night everyone. I think I shall remain here tomorrow too, just to finish resting up. Arthfael and Dame Brianna will return to the Capitol tomorrow morning, I need to finish this tour quickly, and I have no time to look after a courting couple while doing so. Such is the province of yer Mother, young man, and I shall leave it to her. I expect ye should go from here directly to the barracks, with no detours, am I understood by the both of ye?"

"I understand completely, My Lord," Brianna responded.

"I do as well Father," Arthfael echoed. "It should take us no more than two days to return to the Capitol, is that correct?"

"Aye," Erinn replied shortly.

"We will not tarry," Arthfael promised. "Good night, Father. Sleep well."

"Good night all," Erinn returned, turning to Deborah. "Are ye sleepy?"

"I was coming with ye, as I am very tired," Deborah smiled, turning to the others. "Good night my son, good night Brianna, I hope the both of ye sleep well. Father, I know ye will remain on guard all night, if ye can stay awake," she smiled at the end.

"O, ye have a harpy's tongue," Drake laughed heartily. "I love ye, Daughter, for being so engaging. Good night."

They watched as the couple ascended the stairs and disappeared into their room, closing the door behind them. Without a word, Arthfael went to the hearth and poked it until it settled, adding a large log or two to keep it going all night. When he was satisfied, he bid Brianna good night and went upstairs to his room, while Brianna retreated into the barracks room, leaving Drake to look after Dimitri.

"I am so tired, I think I shall also sleep Sir," the young man said quietly. "I have much to consider, my life is about to change drastically."

"Yer life changed drastically when ye washed up on the shore of the Land," Drake smiled. "Come on, let's get ye upstairs to yer room before ye fall asleep on yer feet. Ye are practically there now," he chuckled.

"Ye are not uncomfortable being around someone like me?" Dimitri asked.

"Of course not," Drake replied. "I have known many men such as yerself, and many women who only consort with women. It makes no difference to me, as I see everyone the same, especially in martial abilities, which is what is most important to me. No one can control who they love, 'tis a matter between them and their Deity. Everyone in the Land thinks this way, so ye never need worry about censure. Ye will find ye are not alone in the University," Drake replied, simply picking the young man up and taking him to his room bodily. Putting Dimitri down in front of the correct door, Drake smiled and bid him good night. "Sleep well, Dimitri of the Urals."

"I shall Sir," Dimitri answered meekly, impressed by the show of strength exhibited by the older man. "I am very tired."

"I imagine ye are," Drake grinned, opening the door for him. Dimitri walked through it, closed it behind him, and Drake remained for a bit, until he saw the candlelight fade until there was only one remaining. Walking back down the stairs, he took up his usual position on the sofa to meditate and guard the house all night, assuring that everyone could sleep well.

Chapter 9

Dimitri's eyes fluttered a bit before opening fully, and he cast his gaze about the room, recognizing it as the one he had slept in the night before. He had not dreamt last night after all, he realized with delight, he was really experiencing a new life here in this place the citizens called, "The Land."

His stomach rumbled a bit with hunger and he rolled out of the warm, comfortable bed, finding clothing laid out for him. How someone had been in and out of this room without waking him was a wonder, he thought as he went to the necessity to wash the night sweats from his body. Only after he had used plenty of soap and warm water from the kettle over the fire to wash and rinse himself did he dress in the clean set of unders, drawing the soft, comfortable clothing over it, adding the hose and slippers too. Once dressed, he combed his hair free of snarls from sleeping, then rinsed out the comb, setting it on the shelf to dry. It just seemed right to do so, he thought as he did it, as if he had always done so. He flipped the covers back, exposing the sheets he had slept on, letting them air a bit in case they remained at the house another day. Finally, he slipped a robe over his soft, house clothing and went downstairs following his nose, finding Deborah already awake with caffe in hand. She stood in front of the oven, her raven-black hair flowing loose down her back, ready to pull the first tray of simple fruit hand pies as soon as they were ready. He had no sooner gained the kitchen than she was pulling the tray from the oven, and the scent of berries hit his nose.

"Good morning Dimitri," she wished him with a smile. "Ye will find warmed cups over by the sink. Help yourself to caffe or tea, I have both ready. These will need a few moments to cool," she continued on.

"Caffe?" Dimitri questioned.

"Aye, a black beverage of intense flavor and stimulating effect. It comes from the *Land of Mist and Frogs* across the ocean. Here, ye can try mine to see if ye will enjoy it, I just prepared a fresh cup."

"Ye do not care if I sip from the same cup as ye?"

"Why should I? Are ye ill?" Deborah asked in return.

"Nay," he answered simply.

"Then it should be no concern if ye simply sample a taste of the beverage within," Deborah encouraged. "Go on, try a sip. Ye will soon see why I like it."

He sipped carefully from the proffered cup after taking it in hand, then sipped again, swishing the liquid around in his mouth as if he were sampling an unknown wine. The beverage was both strong and sweet, with an undertone of bitterness that appealed to him and a smile crossed his face.

"I like it too! May I have a cup?"

"Of course, and here is the tray of amendments," Deborah told him, waving in the general direction they were located. "If ye have any questions, I am here to answer them."

"Would ye show me how ye amend yers?" he asked shyly. "I did like the way it tasted."

"Of course," Deborah smiled, demonstrating her preferences. Handing his cup to him, she nodded a bit, then turned back to the oven to pull out the next tray of finished pastries, sliding the third and last one into the hot oven. Drake rose from his place at the sofa at just that moment, allowing himself a huge yawn and full, tall stretch to welcome the morning.

"Ah, my Daughter, as usual yer pastries are a welcome treat with my morning cup. Do ye have caffe available?"

"Of course," she answered with a gentle smile, eschewing their word game for the moment. "I have a hot hand pie for ye as well, Father. I have made yer favorite, mixed berry."

"My dear, thank ye!" Drake smiled, genuinely pleased. "Those are my favorites! What needs doing?"

"Naught, that I am aware of," she answered with warm affection. "I simply chose berry, knowing how much ye love the combination of it with yer caffe in the morning."

Drake threw her a long, measuring glance as a slow smile crossed his face and he bent to kiss her forehead in a fatherly fashion. "Thank ye, my dear. I do enjoy such a treat. Join me for a sikar while we wait for yer husband to appear?"

"I would be delighted!" Deborah smiled, genuinely pleased to do so. She liked Drake's company, he was intelligent and well-spoken, and playing the word game for him was an art form. She had learned a great deal from interacting with him all these years, including a great deal of applied strategy. She had watched him wield the power of High Lord with grace and hard diplomacy, sparing no one who had sided with the Nagas and rewarding those who had held faith with the Lady, all the while maintaining a blistering pace of building and repairing all over the Land. She had also watched him train Erinn to follow him as High Lord, so that when the time came, her husband had simply stepped into the role he was born for. She wrapped her robe about her as she followed him into the great room to sit by the glowing fire, and Dimitri trailed after, fascinated to watch their casual interaction. Such a thing would be discouraged completely in the outside world, women were expected to be silent and pregnant, no more. He was certainly glad it was not that way here, women were delightful conversationalists in his experience, but in his world they had not been allowed to speak freely to anyone, especially a man. He watched in fascination as Drake produced two small, dark tubular shapes from his pocket, handing one to Deborah. Dimitri was only slightly startled when Drake produced a tidy flame from his fingertip to light the end of the one in Deborah's hand, and when it began to glow, the warm scent of the tabac tingled his nostrils pleasantly. He had never smelled it before, and he found it intriguing.

"Excuse me, but what is that?"

"They are called sikars and they are made from a plant called *tabac*. Would ye like to try a puff?" Deborah offered at once.

"I would!" Dimitri exclaimed with a bit of excitement. Handing it to him to take a draw, Deborah offered a bit of instruction to the young man.

"Be careful to only draw the smoke into yer mouth, not into yer chest," she told him kindly. "Tabac smoke is quite pungent and can be harsh for someone trying it for the first time.

Dimitri did as she instructed, finding the smoke warm as it tingled over his tongue. He rolled it around a bit in his mouth, finding he enjoyed the leathery, earthy flavor before blowing it out slowly, a smile upon his face. "O my goodness!" he exclaimed with delight. "What a taste to relish! Thank ye, My Lady!" he said, the title coming naturally to him, much to his surprise.

"Ye are most welcome, Dimitri of the Urals," Deborah smiled. "Father, what sounds good for first meal?"

"What about all that turkey left over?" Drake asked in return.

"I think Erinn will need to remain here for another day or so," Deborah responded professionally. "What meat remains on the carcass will make a fine, healing soup when I simmer the bones later. He needs rest and recuperation after dispatching such an enemy in single combat."

"There was not much combat," Drake chuckled at the memory. "He took Enki's head with very little ceremony or warning. It was most satisfying, I must say, to watch his head fly from his shoulders. The look captured there was one of great fear, as if he knew what fate awaits him."

"He does, and thus the fear," Deborah chuckled with him. "Who would not fear the Goddess' wrath after such a lifetime of corruption?"

"Only someone who thought himself above such things," Drake laughed. "No one is above the Lady's Law, NO one."

"The Lady's Law is applied equally to everyone without exception," Deborah observed, suddenly serious. "She cannot be bribed or coerced into a lesser or greater penalty than exactly what someone has earned. In Enki's case, he has earned a harsh repayment, I think."

"Ye are right about that," Drake growled. "After all of the blood he has spilled, his punishment will be severe indeed."

Deborah said no more, wondering if Drake had actually been at the Lady's Court in the Higher Realms to witness Her adjudications. She imagined it as a procession of souls, standing in front of the Goddess one at a time to receive Her verdict and hear their fate. It did not take much to imagine Enki's soul standing there amongst all the others, insisting he did not belong there until he finally was pushed in front of Her.

Across the table from her as Drake observed silently, he saw an expression of intense satisfaction on her face, as if she were truly there watching Enki's soul be judged and sentenced. He shuddered a bit, for even as an Ascended Being, the thought of such an expression being directed at him was a bit terrifying. He had seen what she could do to an enemy, after all, he thought as he let himself remember everything he had seen her do in the last few years.

"O! My pies!" he heard her say, leaping to her feet and walking swiftly to the kitchen to pull the tray from the oven, and just in time too. They were beautifully dark golden brown, or so Drake thought when he came to inspect them.

"Ye have waited exactly the right amount of time, my dear," he complimented, scooping one off the tray onto one of the small plates she had stacked up for the purpose. "I shall let this one cool a bit, however, before I indulge in the succulence of it," he complimented broadly, accompanying his words with an obvious wink. "As for first meal, I suggest yer fine griddle cakes, with some smoked pork belly and fried eggs."

"A fine meal indeed!" they heard Erinn's voice rejoin and the sleepy-eyed man appeared, washed, combed and dressed for the day. Drake observed him carefully, and realized that his son was indeed looking spent. Deborah's assessment of his physical state was spot on, as usual. "Is there still caffe hot?" Erinn continued in a plaintive tone.

"Aye, sit down and I shall bring yer cup," Deborah responded, rising to attend to the task. When she returned, she brought a fresh pot and the tray of amendments with her, so that Erinn could enjoy his caffe at his leisure.

"And is there a sikar for me too?" Erinn asked with a grin.

"Of course!" Drake laughed, handing him one already clipped and ready to light. Erinn produced a flame from his fingertip as Dimitri watched in wonder, thinking that he was in a very marvelous place indeed. Once Erinn was enjoying his tabac, they sat and talked over their plans for the day.

"I am going to remain here for the next few days," Erinn told them both. "I feel very tired, as if I have been at war for weeks."

"I am not surprised after yer encounter with Enki," Drake supplied. "His abilities included being able to siphon off energy from other people, rendering them unable to even move. When ye took him into that bubble, I was concerned for a bit due to that, but ye rose to the challenge as usual. One stroke to take his head, well done boyo."

"I had a good teacher," Erinn chuckled, nodding at his father in respect. "Griddle cakes sound like a wonderful meal, my dear. Can ye remain at least for today before ye must return to yer work?"

"I shall remain as long as I am needed," Deborah assured him. "In fact, I am already planning tonight's meal. How does turkey stew, biscuits and a salad sound?"

"Delicious," Erinn told her at once. "But instead of just making a bowl of stew, perhaps ye might top it with the biscuits for a pot pie?"

"I can do that," Deborah smiled fondly.

"Good, that sounds wonderful!" Erinn replied. "Besides, 'tis an easy meal, which will give us more time to be alone."

Just at that moment, Aldridge appeared, followed by Arthfael and Brianna. Everyone soon held caffe in hand, and those who indulged were offered a sikar as well, while Deborah retired to the kitchen. It did not take her long to whip out a large bowl of griddle cake batter, and Brianna brought her a rasher from the cold room. The young Dame took the chore of cutting the salted meat into thick slices, and soon the scent of it frying set their stomachs all to growling. Dimitri was no exception, and when his platter was set before him, he carefully spread butter and spooned compote in between each cake, settling the two eggs on the top. Having observed the others' habits, he offered a quick and earnest thanks for the meal before picking up the fork and digging in. The flavors of the cakes and the compote together pleased his taste buds at once, and he ate with abandon, observing his manners all the while. He could barely wait to chew the bite in his mouth and swallow it so as to have the next bite until the platter was empty of everything except a few crumbs and splatters of compote.

"How may I help?" he asked as he rose to take his plate to the kitchen.

"Ye can go and get ready to leave," Aldridge told him abruptly. "I have lazed about long enough, I have work to do, and we must get ye settled into the University. Come on, I haven't all day!" he chuckled.

"Aye Sir!" Dimitri replied, making to go upstairs until he realized he had nothing to pack. "I am ready!" he announced.

"Good, I admire alacrity!" Aldridge said, bringing out a laugh from Drake, who used the same phrase often. Dimitri smiled, turned to Deborah and offered an embrace, which was warmly accepted and returned.

"Good fortune to ye, Dimitri," she said quietly into his ear. "Ye have come to a place ye can call home, if ye wish. Take the opportunity to learn and grow!"

"I shall, Madam!" he whispered back. The grip was exchanged with everyone else, including Brianna before Dimitri turned back to Aldridge. "I am ready to go, Sir!"

"Good, come and stand beside me. Ye will feel a rush of cold for a few moments as we travel with the Lady's direct assistance!" Aldridge instructed. Dimitri did so, wondering what he was about, and after a wave of farewell from Aldridge they disappeared suddenly from the common room with no warning. Dimitri felt the intense chill of the instant conveyance from the family house to the Main Shrine, several hundreds of miles away, and when he opened his eyes he saw they were no longer among the Natanleods. The Hall they stood in was huge and vaulted, with living trees standing as support pillars for the huge observation dome above. Sunlight streamed into the interior of the Hall, providing light and warmth aplenty as younger Druids came to welcome their leader home.

"Welcome back Elder Brother!" one of them called out. His name was Quentin, he had been tutor to Artos many years ago. "And who is this?"

"Brothers and Sisters, meet Dimitri, formerly of the Outlands. The Lady has brought him to us for an assessment of his abilities, which we will wait just a few days to perform. We want him to settle in and feel comfortable, all please give him yer welcome!" Aldridge called out in a warm tone. Those gathered under the dome came in twos and threes to welcome Dimitri with warm words, while Aldridge looked on with approval, seeing the Lady's hand at work. "Quentin, would ye get him settled for me?" he asked the younger man.

"Of course, Elder Brother. Which wing would ye suggest for him?"

"Put him in with those seeking entry into the University," Aldridge replied at once. "If he is to become a man of the Land, he should subscribe to the same procedures. Ye will acquaint him with what is expected, aye?"

"Of course, Elder Brother," Quentin smiled, for he had done this task before for others, including Artos Natanleod. As soon as the crowd around Dimitri thinned, Quentin stepped to his side, offering the grip.

"Welcome to the University!" he said with a genuine smile. "My name is Quentin, I am here studying astronomy, navigation and tracking ley lines. Let me get ye settled into a room, so that ye can start adjusting to life here. Ye will be housed in the wing with all those studying for their entry examinations, and I shall help ye get caught up with the others, if ye would like. I oftentimes tutor those needing a bit of extra help."

"O, I would!" Dimitri exclaimed, a bit overwhelmed by his emotions. "O, excuse me! I am just so terribly excited about being able to have schooling again!"

Quentin listened to his voice, heard the raw emotions and, having empathic abilities, wanted to console him a bit. "Ye have no need to apologize," he chuckled, producing pipe and Herb to offer to the young man.

"O! Thank ye!" Dimitri exclaimed again, taking the proffered dosage gladly, drawing the sweet smoke into his chest deeply and feeling the effects nearly at once. Within a short time, he was calmer and could think more clearly, for which he was very grateful. "Thank ye, Elder Brother," he said, the term coming to him easily. Quentin smiled wide at the address, it usually took a couple of sevendays for the title to be used so easily.

"Ye are most welcome, Younger Brother," Quentin smiled. His empathic senses could feel the young man's continued distress, and his counseling skills came into play, reckoning that Dimitri needed to talk. "Ye should know that I am a trained counselor," he said quietly. "Anything that ye and I discuss will be confidential, 'lest it seems ye intend to do some harm. No one shall know aught of our conversations."

Dimitri stopped and stared for a moment, for Quentin's statement seemed divinely sent. He had much he wanted to talk about with someone trustworthy, and Quentin seemed to be that person.

"I am glad to be able to talk to someone," he finally said softly. "Everyone has been so kind to me since I landed here, and now I find myself here, at a school of higher learning as I have always wished. Where I came from, my opportunities were limited by prejudice and bigotry, but it seems as if those walls have been removed suddenly."

Quentin listened to him, and the emotions he heard were tumultuous. In a flash, he realized what Dimitri was not saying aloud and the older man was consumed by a wave of sorrow. It was clear that Dimitri felt guilty for simply being what the Goddess had made him in this life, and Quentin wanted him to realize he had no reason to be such.

"Younger Brother, ye will not find prejudice or bigotry here," he began. "As long as ye are not harming yerself, or anyone else, ye will not find anyone who would despise ye for simply being what ye are. There are many in the Land going through similar lessons, and ye will find them represented throughout the Druid Order, as well as in the Lady's Temples. Everyone has a lesson to learn, and only She can judge if those lessons are being administered and learned correctly. Ye need not be concerned about reprisals or reprimands as long as ye attend to yer lessons and studies with alacrity and attention. Ye are here to learn, after all."

Dimitri's face took on an expression of wonder at Quentin's words. "But ye are not like me, are ye? Yer preference in matters of love is for women."

"Indeed so," Quentin smiled broadly. "But that does not mean I cannot be friends with ye, just because ye seek different comforts. I do not see our different natures as restrictive in our friendships. I have friends of many natures; Elves, Dwarves, Men and Women. We all are simply friends, we discuss the matters of the Land, and we learn the Mysteries together. Who we love is not a matter we argue over."

Dimitri stared openly, hardly able to believe what he was hearing. As Quentin's words impacted him, his face lost its haunted visage, adopting a more hopeful one instead.

"I...I hardly know what to say," he finally whispered.

"Say naught," Quentin told him gently. "Simply accept that yer situation is vastly better than 'twas. Ye should just rest for a bit, ye look tired. Someone will come to fetch ye in time for the next meal. We all eat communally here, ye may sit wherever ye find an empty seat, whether at the Elder Brother's table, mine, or anyone's. When we call ye brother or sister, we truly mean it."

The astonishment on Dimitri's face was clear as Quentin rose from his seat, making his way to the door. "As I said, ye should just rest a bit here where 'tis quiet. Ye will have plenty of opportunities for socializing, but ye are here to learn, aye?"

"Aye!" Dimitri responded. "Thank ye, Brother Quentin."

"Ye are most welcome, Brother Dimitri," Quentin smiled as he responded in a warm tone. "Welcome to the Druid University."

Out the door he went before Dimitri could respond, leaving the young man in a state of wonder. He could barely think as he lay down on the bed, finding it comfortably firm, and before he could stop himself, he was asleep. His last thought before accepting the embrace of sleep was that he was a fortunate person indeed, despite everything that had happened in the past. "Thank ye, My Lady," he thought to the Deity he knew was guiding his life now.

"Ye are most welcome, Dimitri," he heard Her respond.

As Dimitri's life truly began, Erinn and Deborah prepared to relax at the family house in Dragon Valley. They supervised Brianna and Arthfael's departure, Erinn reinforcing his orders to Arthfael and Brianna each privately.

"I am giving ye both the same orders," he said quietly, retaining the air of command. "Ye are both to go straight home to the Barracks and present yerselves to either the War Duke or Knight Commander as soon as ye get there, no matter what time 'tis. NO side trips, no dallying!"

"Aye, My Lord," Brianna replied earnestly. "I shall do exactly as ye are ordering, in the spirit ye are ordering it in."

"Ye are a good Amazon, and an excellent Dame," Erinn replied with a grin, handing her a bundle of smaller sikars. "Watch over Arthfael, he is a Prince of the Land, and his safety is yer concern."

"Of course, My Lord," she replied, tucking the bundle away in her vest. "I would look out for him in any case."

"I know ye would," Erinn smiled. "Have a good trip, and remember, the fishing is excellent this time of year. If ye take the middle fork at the crossroads, ye will find hot springs, food and good camping aplenty."

"Thank ye, My Lord!" Brianna smiled. "I shall remember that, but doesn't that road take a bit longer?"

"Perhaps, but the going is easier, and ye will arrive within an acceptable amount of days as well. If I know ye are going that way, 'twould be a comfort for me."

"Then we will go that way, even if Prince Arthfael does not wish to," Brianna smiled, her voice firm with resolve.

"He will be getting the same orders as ye are," Erinn told her. "The both of ye will have to work together in harmony to make the trip enjoyable for ye both. Ye are taking one large tent, aye?"

"Aye, 'tis easier that way, and we will have room to set up two sleeping areas," Brianna nodded.

"Good, I like a practical woman," Erinn chuckled. "Ye both should be gone before the sun gets too high."

"I am almost ready to go," Brianna responded. "I was just about to go and saddle my horse."

"Go to it then," Erinn said in a gentler tone. "When ye are ready for me to do so, I would like to try out calling ye daughter."

"O, My Lord!" Brianna replied. "That may be a long time."

"As ye wish then," Erinn nodded. "I wish this to be comfortable for ye."

"Thank ye, Sir!" she replied wiping a tear away quickly as her emotions nearly overcame her. He was earnestly offering her the honorific, and she could tell he meant every word he was saying to her. Restraining the urge to simply salute and bolt for the stable, she smiled and offered him the grip instead, which he accepted. When they parted, she for the stable and he to meet up with Arthfael, he took the young man aside for a strict chat.

"My son, I advise ye to follow my orders in this matter. Take the middle fork when ye come to the crossroads, 'tis an easier journey that way. Ye will find more comfort and more food that way than on the other two forks. Go quickly, it should not take more than a few days and nights to get back to the Capitol, and when ye arrive there, go at once to the Barracks. Do not dally, or take side trips. Present yerself to the War Duke, or the Knight Commander, no matter what the hour. Am I understood?"

"Aye, Father. I hear yer orders, and I shall obey them to the letter. Ye need have no worries, Brianna is completely safe with me."

"Of that I have no doubt, my son," Erinn smiled. "Just remember the rules for courting couples here in the Land, and abide by them. Prove ye are a Prince to both her and to me."

"Aye, Father," Arthfael nodded, picking up his knapsack. "Has she gone to the stables?"

"Aye, just now," Erinn confirmed.

"I shall join her there then. Farewell, Father. Rest and take care, ye need have no concerns as to Brianna or myself. We will be perfectly safe, following the route ye have suggested."

"So ye should," Erinn nodded, offering him the grip, then an embrace. Arthfael returned both willingly and with a smile before saying farewell to Deborah and Drake, then stepping out of the common room, heading for the stable. Erinn watched impatiently until the two emerged, which was a much shorter time than it seemed. The two led their horses out of the stable, closing the door behind them then mounting up and galloping out of the courtyard, down the road heading for the main route back to the Capitol.

As she watched them go, Deborah's face took on a look of consideration and she made a decision. Turning to Drake, she took on the air of command before addressing him.

"Knight of the Land, ye have a duty to perform," she said abruptly. "Ye should be about it, watching over the Prince and his chosen mate, aye?"

Drake started a bit and turned to her, a look of appeal on his face. "But Madam, I was going to…"

The look of quiet authority crossed her face, and her foot began to tap on the floor. Addressing him again in more commanding tones, she spoke again. "Ye should be about yer duty, aye?" she repeated more urgently.

"O, very well," he sighed, snapping his fingers. His warrior dress came upon him then, including his cape and bedroll, and with no further words he disappeared from the common room. They only heard the hoof beats of his horse as he galloped after Brianna and Arthfael, already half an hour behind them.

"Now, we are finally alone," Deborah murmured to Erinn. "I think I shall go and draw my morning bath. Perhaps we should have some wine?"

"A fine idea my dear. Today will be a good day for just lazing about the house, I think. Look!" he said pointing. Where it had been bright and sunny, Deborah now saw clouds forming, thick and cold. A breeze sprang up, and she could feel the chill of it coming through the open windows as she rushed to close them.

"My goodness, could it be about to snow?" she thought with alarm as Erinn brought in more wood and stoked the fire.

"The cold stays late and comes early up this far," Erinn observed, walking to the sideboard. He found a full carafe of wine there, and picking up two cups, he returned to the sofa, placing his load on the table. "Come and join me?" he entreated. "It appears we have very little to do outside. The snow will flurry throughout the day, I think." It was not long afterward that the sun was obscured as the wind picked up to a constant pace. Deborah started her turkey stew for that night's meal, noting the tiny snowflakes start falling sometime after noon.

Brianna and Arthfael were well away from the mountains by the time the sun reached its zenith, in fact they were now resting their horses at the crossroads. When they looked back in the direction they had come, they could see the thick clouds and rising fog. A breath of frosty air reached them on the wind and a smile crossed Arthfael's face.

"I think we left in time to avoid being snowed in," he said to Brianna.

"I think ye are right," the young Dame answered, her face showing concern. "We should be on our way, aye? I do not want to camp in the snow."

The road forked into three separate branches at this point, and they were all clearly marked as leading to the Capitol city. However, the outer two acted as conduits to the outer farms and smaller villages, passing through and around many of them. Such a path slowed travel considerably, as it invited side trips to investigate famous battlefields and rebuilt Temples.

"We must take the middle fork," Brianna stated flatly.

"Aye, my Father said that way is the easiest, and provides the fastest road."

"I hear the trip can take as many as four days and nights," Brianna ventured, a note of challenge in her tone. "Has anyone ever ridden the distance in less time?"

"I do not know if anyone has ever tried," Arthfael answered honestly as her tone raise his own sense of competition. "Perhaps we should."

"I favor the idea!" Brianna answered with a grin, swinging up into her saddle and taking up the reins. "Let us ride as hard and fast as our horses will travel, and eat up as many miles as we can. What if we should arrive in less time? Our names will be spoken around the Barracks and we shall have thrown down a certain gauntlet, aye?"

Arthfael chuckled at her enthusiasm as he mounted up and spurred his horse to fall in alongside her. They passed the signpost at a full gallop and the thunder of their horse's hooves could be heard clearly by anyone else traveling. They passed wagons and walking folk all throughout the day, being careful to maneuver their steeds so as not to impede anyone else's travel with their own. It was nearly dark when they finally found a campsite and quickly erected the tent, barely getting it up before the sun fell behind the trees. They were reduced to eating travel rations that night, as it was too dark to even fish.

"We stopped too late," Arthfael observed as he chewed the jerky, wishing for a nice, hot, crispy fried fish. "We should be more observant on the morrow."

"Look how much distance we have covered!" Brianna crowed after clearing her mouth with a swallow of cold water. She was wishing it was hot tea, but a fire could not be lit in the dark. Arthfael of course had forgotten entirely about his magickal abilities, and so had Brianna. If they had remembered, a fire and hot food would have been no difficulty whatsoever. Drake watched them with a grin, thinking they had much to learn about traveling and living off the Land's bounty. He turned the fish in his pan and sipped the tea in his cup, thankful that the Lady's grace had granted him magickal skills.

In the morning, they lit a small fire and heated water for hot tea, which made their morning meal of jerky a bit more pleasant. Arthfael had not slept well at all, having remembered his magickal abilities just before falling asleep. He had spent most of the night chastising himself and was a bit grouchy as he poured water over the coals then kicked them apart to assure they were completely extinguished. Another pan of water from the river made them cold to the touch, he knew then it was safe to leave the place and thanked the elementals for the shelter. The two then took down the tent, packed it away neatly and made ready to depart. Up into the saddles they climbed, noting they were both a little sore from yesterday's ride as they trotted back onto the road and began their mad dash once more. They traveled many miles that day, but were mindful to stop early, especially when a mile marker indicated the presence of a hot spring.

"I would like to bathe tonight, and a hot spring would be perfect," Arthfael proposed. "The fishing is always good in such places too, and a hot meal would be welcome."

"I agree," Brianna replied shortly, her own demeanor a bit grumpy. Once they found the place, they put the pavilion up at once, cleared a place for a firepit and lit a blaze, then went looking for a fishing spot.

"If ye would like to bathe first," Arthfael offered when they found the perfect spot to drop a line in the water. "I shall remain and angle our supper out of the water."

"Thank ye," Brianna nodded. "I shall do so, and when ye return to camp, I shall undertake supper. I remember how the High Lord showed us how to fry fish, and I am confident I can do it."

"I know ye can as well," Arthfael smiled warmly. Just as Brianna walked off, Arthfael's line was hit by a fat trout. The tip of the pole bent to nearly the water's surface as Arthfael attempted to work the fish to the bank. She could see he was completely occupied by the effort and so left him to it, returning to the pavilion and pulling her robe out of her bag. She was determined to be clean that night, she did not like the feel of dried sweat and oils on her nor the acrid smell they created. Whoever had put the sign up for the hot spring on the road had also created marker posts to show the way, and when she found the spring, a huge smile crossed her face. The last marker post was inscribed with a carved dragon, and she wondered if Drake had been here during the war. The spring was certainly large enough for a half dozen large men to use at once, she chuckled a bit as she stripped and stepped cautiously into the hot water. There were places in the Land where crocodiles frequented hot springs, she recalled from her days patrolling with the Amazons. Fortunately, this was not one of those places, and she swam a bit in the hot water before settling in for a long hot soak. She had even brought a bit of soft soap with her, and now she used it to clean herself from top to bottom, including her hair. A last rinse and she was clean, so she stepped from the water and wrapped up in the robe for her return to the camp. She was unaware that Drake watched clandestinely from the trees, so he could assure her safety. He could hardly help but notice she had a fine trim figure, but he found that he did not desire her at all. She was simply not his type, she was too young and inexperienced for someone like him, he laughed a bit to himself as he sat there sipping hot tea from a smokeless fire. Presently Arthfael came along the path, heading for the hot spring. The young man settled gratefully into the steaming water, he was a bit sore from the long ride and thankful they had stopped early that night. He cared little that they would not arrive earlier than the usual time it took to make the journey, he just wanted to enjoy the rest of the trip. As he lay in the hot water, he gave thanks to the Lady for all of her gifts to him, appreciating everything he had now. After washing his hair quickly, he finished by swimming around the hot spring a few times, then pulled himself from the water and wrapped the towel around his loins after drying himself completely. It was getting dark, and he wanted to get back to camp as soon as possible, Drake noted his walking gate was quick as he walked by the hidden position.

"Good lad," Drake thought. "He wishes to return to camp quickly, so she is not alone."

Drake was right about that, Arthfael did not wish to leave Brianna alone to prepare supper. However, as he approached the camp, the scent of frying fish hit his nostrils. When he appeared at the head of the trail to the spring, she was just turning them in the pan and he could see how brown and crispy they were.

"That looks delicious!" he called out as he walked to her.

"Thank ye," she responded, not taking her eyes off the pan. She wanted the meal to be as perfect as possible, and even had foraged some wild greens, which fried in another smaller pan beside the fish. The smell of the food tantalized them as they sat there talking, and as soon as it was properly cooked, she served up the meal on their traveling plates. After a quick blessing, the two hungry people fell to it, devouring everything on the plate except for the bones.

"Brianna, ye cooked that fish perfectly!" Arthfael complimented earnestly. "And the greens too! What a wonderful meal, I could not eat another bite."

"Me neither," Brianna grinned, gathering up the dishes and taking them to wash in the river. Arthfael walked with her and together they performed the task, returning to the camp quickly and leaving the dishes to dry overnight.

"I am very tired," Brianna yawned. "Who will keep watch?"

"I shall!" Drake's voice came into their conversation. "Now both of ye should be abed. Ye are due in the barracks tomorrow morning!"

The two younger people started at his voice, and without hesitation nearly ran for the tent, closing the flap behind them. Both attended to their nightly ritual swiftly, bid each other good night and retired to their separate pallets, while Drake guarded them.

After a good night's rest, the two were up early to dress themselves, then packed up their camp quickly, pausing only to thank Drake for his service.

"Thank ye, My Lord," Brianna said to him before mounting her steed. "I slept well last night, knowing ye were outside the door."

"Good, ye have done well so far young Dame," Drake told her. "I was gratified to see the golden brown color on those fish last night. I know now ye were paying attention. I dislike teaching the same lesson twice."

"Athena was the same," Brianna chuckled wryly. "And when she found herself having to teach a lesson again, she made it doubly memorable."

"I always did like her," Drake sighed. "Go on, the sun is rising. Ye will be late if ye tarry much longer."

"Aye, Grandfather," Arthfael entered the conversation, leading his horse close to Brianna's. "We are going now. Thank ye for guarding us while we have traveled. Was that Mother's order?"

"I was ordered to watch over ye as ye traveled," Drake answered obliquely.

"So, she did order ye," Arthfael surmised. "My Mother has a great deal of influence with ye."

"Ye have seen what she can do," Drake responded dryly. "Such abilities cause me a moment of consideration before I refuse any order. Besides, she was right to assign this task to me, 'tis mine after all. Now, off with the both of ye!" he ordered with a chuckle, disappearing from their sight.

"Come, the sun is almost over the trees!" Brianna urged. "We can make it before first meal is done being served!"

"I am so hungry!" Arthfael exclaimed, leaping into the saddle. "The meal was good last night, but 'twas little of it. I am ready for a good feed, and a long nap, aye?"

"Aye!" she agreed. Off they went after thanking the elementals for the use of the camp, racing each other the entire twenty miles that remained. They rode through the back gate of the city at the same moment, galloped through the back streets up to the barracks and raced through the open stable door, tied with each other. Laughing hard, they both slipped off their sweating horses, embracing the animals with love and affection for their efforts before handing them off to grooms.

"Take good care of them, they have raced home," Brianna told them chuckling. "Is first meal still being served?"

"Aye, and ye'd best hurry! They are serving rare beef!"

"I am ready for a hot cup of caffe and a pastry," Brianna declared. "I can wait 'till second meal if I have that."

"I would like rare beef!" Arthfael chuckled. "Would ye still share my table if I indulge?"

"Of course!" Brianna smiled. The two walked directly to the Knight Commander's office, finding Karpon there already working.

"Good morning, My Lord Commander!" Arthfael and Brianna called out at the same moment, their voices combining together pleasantly.

Karpon glanced up, his face wreathed in surprise. "Where did ye two come from? Is the High Lord alright?"

"Aye, he was when we parted two days ago at the family house," Arthfael grinned. "I believe he and my mother were looking forward to a little private time."

"They deserve at least that," Karpon acknowledged. "Welcome home. Have ye eaten?"

"Not yet, we wanted to make our report as soon as we arrived. 'Twas my Father's wish that we do so," Arthfael told him.

"Well, ye've reported in," Karpon smiled. "Ye'd best get to the dining hall before they run out of beef. I just finished my meal, and 'tis delicious!"

"Thank ye My Lord, we are going there right now," Arthfael told him offering the grip. Karpon exchanged it with both him and Brianna before excusing them, wishing them a good day.

"We better hurry on," Arthfael urged, his stomach growling loudly. "There may not even be pastries left if we do not."

The two of them picked up the pace, arriving at the end of the short line of people still walking through the service line and seeing there was plenty of food available. Once their plates were filled according to their wishes, they found a table among those still enjoying their first meal of the day.

"Good morning ye two!" they heard Ulric's greeting and turned to see the War Duke approaching. "Where is the High Lord?"

"With his wife at the family house," Arthfael answered at once.

"Ah! I see!" Ulric smiled. "Good then, they are safe enough there, I should think. Welcome home to the both of ye. Dame, have ye seen the Knight Commander?"

"Of course, My Lord. We checked in as soon as we arrived."

"Excellent, be sure to see him for yer duty rotation. We have had to change things a bit. Gregorius' wife is with child, at last!"

"I shall have to drop in on them and offer my congratulations," Arthfael nodded, making the mental note.

"The priestesses say at her age it might be difficult, and so I have given Gregorius an extended leave of absence. Tomas and Tomar have stepped in to cover his duties excellently, however."

"If I can be of service, have no hesitation in contacting me," Arthfael offered at once.

"Ye are a good man to offer so quickly," Ulric smiled. "Now, tell me all about the patrol ye were just on. I want to hear what ye have to report."

Arthfael quickly related the entire trip, including Erinn's action against Enki as Ulric listened, completely enwrapped by the tale. When Arthfael finished, the War Duke's face took on a look of consideration.

"No wonder he is at the family house with yer mother then," he said at length. "Very well, I shall not interfere with that. I should not like to earn the High Lady's wrath. Both of ye should be about yer scheduled tasks, aye?"

"Aye, My Lord, after our first meal," Arthfael replied sincerely.

"Agreed, My Lord," Brianna put in.

"Good then," Ulric smiled. He could see how they felt about one another very clearly, but he said naught in the way of people in the Land. Such things were considered to be private, and Ulric was not one to violate anyone's privacy. He walked on then, leaving them to their meal, which was consumed in silence as their thoughts occupied them. Once they finished, they took their plates to the collection area, scraped and piled them with the others, then left the room. Pausing just outside the door, Arthfael pulled Brianna into a side hall, wanting just a few private words with her now that they were home.

"My dear, I shall leave it to ye entirely, how to handle what is between us. Ye may acknowledge it to others or not, I care little. I only ask that ye make time for me if and when ye can, and as often as possible."

"I know not what to do about all of this," Brianna sighed. "I did not anticipate how I would feel upon returning to the barracks."

"How so?"

"I want to be back out on the road with ye, where the rules are more lax," Brianna told him truthfully. "I have never enjoyed a trip more than the last few days. I look forward to spending more time like that with ye in the future, as often as possible. I shall speak to my Captain and ask my sisters in the barracks if they will help me rearrange my schedule to accommodate our being together. I want to make this work, whatever 'tis we have."

"A good friendship, and the beginning of trust," Arthfael smiled, squeezing her hand. "I think 'tis a good start, aye?"

"O aye!" Brianna agreed, embracing him furtively before taking her leave, practically running down the side hall to her chambers. Arthfael watched her go, glad they had chatted briefly before parting. He looked forward to their next conversation already.

Chapter 10

Two days later, Erinn and Deborah parted back to their assignments, she to the building site, and he to the rest of his tour of the Land.

"Ye are not taking a guard?" Deborah asked, with great concern in her tone. As if in answer, Drake materialized in the room, a disgruntled expression on his face.

"Madam, yer biddings and dismissals are sometimes ill-timed," he grouched.

"I am not responsible for how ye manage yer free time," Deborah answered in a mock-lofty tone. "If ye are having such difficulties due to yer advanced age, 'tis the Goddess ye should consult," she finished the barb.

"Ooooo!" he said as if punched in the stomach, but they could hear his amusement. "A low blow, my dear, but very well phrased. I concede the game at this time, reserving the right to re-engage when my duty allows."

"Very well, Knight of the Land," she answered with a wide grin. "As ye wish." Turning to Erinn, she continued, "Farewell husband. I look forward to meeting ye at the turn of Autumn, on the Equinox."

"I look forward to that as well, my dear," he replied, kissing the palm of her proffered hand. "Do not work too hard."

"I was just going to say the same to ye!" she laughed, embracing him and planting a passionate kiss on his lips. "I shall miss ye 'till we meet once more."

"I shall eagerly await that day!" Erinn replied, returning the kiss. When they parted, she simply disappeared, taking her bag and cloak with her, leaving Erinn somewhat despondent for a moment. Quickly recovering himself, he turned to Drake, offering a sikar. "Come, I am eager to be about this tour. The sooner 'tis done, the sooner I can return home."

"I do not blame ye in that," Drake replied, taking the sikar and lighting it, seeing it was already clipped and ready. The two of them took a quick tour of the house to assure all was in readiness for those coming to clean it before taking their leave, closing the door behind them. A brisk walk in the cold morning air brought them to the stable, where horses awaited. It did not take either of them long to dress their steeds, then tidy up the building, readying it for the team of grooms coming to attend to making it ready for use the next time. Once they were outside, Erinn dropped the bar into place, securing the inside against intrusion. Leaning over his horse Ebony's neck, he patted him affectionately before urging him into a gallop, speeding away from the house with Drake beside him. The two mounted men kept pace with each other all the way to the crossroads, made the turn together and continued on their way, heading east and north a bit. The trip to Alom's tabac farm would usually take a week from where they were, but Erinn meant to arrive there much sooner. He and Drake rode all that day, until they reached the next crossroads, stopping soon after they made the turn for the mountains. As they were riding along, a deer crossed the road in front of them and Drake turned instantly, following the beast until it led them to a small clearing with a steaming hot spring.

"Ah, just the place to spend a quiet night!" Drake noted, stepping off his horse. "Just look at that moss, 'twill provide a nice sleeping pad."

"I was not looking forward to sleeping outside," Erinn grouched a bit. "But as ye say, we have a good place with plenty of food about. I think our people have been here before, look at the variety of flowers growing. Not just flowers, but edibles as well!" Erinn pointed out. "Look, ye can see the lamb's quarters, as well as wild mustard greens and lettuces. Father, ye have been here before."

"I have no doubt about that," Drake smiled faintly. "I believe that before I left the Land, my feet had trod nearly everywhere within the Lady's borders. The Nagas were everywhere, after all," he sighed.

"They still are, apparently," Erinn chuckled a bit. "But not because ye were lax in yer duty. They are simply persistence and pernicious, but we are more so. We *will* be rid of them eventually," Erinn asserted, pausing before continuing. "Father, have ye had any word of Artos?"

"Nay, and it worries me a bit," Drake confided. "Yer son is a complicated person, his way of thinking perplexes me in many ways. However, I saw something within him the last time we were together, a strengthening of will and purpose. It seems he has made a decision, my son, and I believe that decision will bring him back to the family soon enough. 'Tis the manner of his return that concerns me."

"It does me as well, I should not like to fight my own son for the High Seat," Erinn confided a deeply held worry. "However, if it becomes necessary, I shall do so, knowing the Lady is with me."

"I would not have liked facing such a choice," Drake said empathetically. "I am thirsty, aren't ye?"

"I am, I was about to make caffe," Erinn replied.

"Caffe? Now, when we are trying to relax and need something cold?" Drake laughed, snapping his fingers. A short keg appeared in the small stream, immersed half way up its side in the glacially icy water two cups sitting atop invitingly. Erinn grinned appreciatively, for his father had simply provided the perfect drink for the rest of the day.

"Thank ye Father, I was considering doing exactly what ye have done," he said gratefully, carefully breaching the keg and pouring the first drops on the ground for the Lady. Afterward, he filled the cups, bringing one to his father and they drank thirstily, for the day was hot and they were parched. "Now, which direction do ye think the hot spring lies?" Erinn asked.

"Ye can follow yer nose to learn that," Drake chuckled.

"And what are we having for supper?" Erinn inquired, sipping his ale.

"We followed a deer in here, but we do not need that much meat," Drake observed. "I shall provide supper, including cooking it. Ye still look tired, which concerns me. Ye did rest up a little bit, even while yer wife was in residence with us?" he asked with comic concern.

"Of course I did!" Erinn replied indignantly, although his eyes sparkled with humor. "She had to sleep too, ye know."

Drake laughed a bit, clapping Erinn on the back. "I shall inquire no further, as 'twould be an intrusion. I am glad ye two get along so very well."

"I am blessed," Erinn sighed. "I think I shall go in search of the spring. I shall mark the way when I find it, I just caught a whiff of sulfur."

"Aye, so did I," Drake nodded. "As I recall, I believe 'tis off that way, across the river. When I was here last, ye could easily step from the spring into the river for a quick plunge, the spring is slightly elevated above the river's edge."

"I am intrigued, is this a natural spring?" Erinn inquired.

"Well, I fixed it," Drake admitted ruefully. "The seating was not very comfortable, and the river water flowed through the spring, cooling it considerably. All I did was simply move the rocks to block off the cold water from the river a bit, and divert it back into the river channel. Be sure ye take a robe and towel with ye."

"I shall simply call it when I need it," Erinn chuckled. "I hope Arthfael remembers he can use magick on his way home."

"He is such a humble young man," Drake observed. "He will likely not remember 'till he gets home to the Capitol. I hope the fact of his new abilities will become second nature to him, as it did for ye."

"I hope I can help him with that," Erinn sighed. "I do not seem to be doing well with my natural son."

"Ye are doing fine, he is being mule-headed and arrogant," Drake pointed out. "And 'tis naught anyone can do about it, he must do something about it on his own. He is as stubborn as Hadrian, and not as good tempered about it."

"Uncle Hadrian was an obstinate man?"

"He was the first born, he inherited all of Father's stubborn nature," Drake replied. Erinn's one eyebrow shot up at the observation, and he added one of his own.

"Hadrian is not the only son of Julius to inherit a stubborn bent, Father," he chuckled. "Fortunately, ye use it wisely and in the service of the Goddess, as did Uncle Hadrian."

"He was a hero, ye know," Drake put in.

"Of course he was! He helped the effort to put the Nagas down as much as anyone or more! Without the two of ye working on the problem one on the scene and one distantly sending energy, the War would have gone on much longer."

"Raad provided the ultimate opportunity for me to act when he unwisely had me declared dead," Drake chuckled, filling his cup by means of his abilities. The cup floated to the small cask, maneuvered itself under the tap which turned open as soon as the vessel settled under it. The cup filled perfectly, leaving a nice layer of foam on the top to seal in the cold, the tap turned off and the cup floated back into Drake's hand.

"Nicely done as always, Father. 'Tis always so easy for ye."

"I am half dragon, my son. Magick would come more easily to me than to most. Ye clearly have no difficulty using yer abilities to yer best advantage."

"I did not create that bubble around myself and Enki," Erinn denied at once, his voice low and quiet. "She did."

"The Lady, ye mean."

"Aye, the Goddess did that. All I did was think I needed to confront him in a place of my own choosing, some place where he could not possess anyone else before I could slay him. The bubble just appeared, but I could feel Her presence."

"She is fulfilling Her contract with ye," Drake stated. "The same contract She has held sacred between our family and Her for all the time since The Landing. She must be very pleased with ye, and how ye are ruling."

"I am honored," Erinn replied humbly. "I only wish to be of service to Her and to the people."

Drake smiled fondly, hearing Erinn reinforce his vows as High Lord right there in the private grove they sat in. Every time, it was sacred, the recitation of the High Lord's vows before the Goddess, and the words were quite simple. They were just what Erinn had stated succinctly, however expressed in a more formal fashion and in full view of Druids, Priestesses and Nobles, as well as those of the people who could be there. The Main Temple's Shrine was always crowded on such days, the people were willing to pack the room tightly in order to witness the High Lord's elevation. When the Goddess' statue, wrapped in dark purple cloth and crowned with Her silver Diadem, had nodded to Erinn, Drake had felt a rush of pride and paternal love for his son. The roar of the crowd in response had been tumultuous, for everyone who had ever met Erinn loved his cool head and warm heart.

"Ye are a golden soul, as is yer wife," he said quietly. "How I was granted such a son and daughter is beyond my comprehension. After all I had to do to win against Raad's evil, I was concerned about my soul. Some of it was not exactly in accordance with the Goddess' Law."

"She seems to have forgiven ye for any of that," Erinn observed, finishing his sikar. "I suggest ye forgive yerself of it as well. 'Twas war, ye did what had to be done to win in the Goddess' name. If ye had not, how many more of our people would be enslaved, or scheduled to be fed to satisfy their monstrous appetites? Really Father, ye should stop lingering on it, ye sound like ye are in yer dotage."

"*DOTAGE?*" Drake objected, rising from the stone he was sitting upon. "My son, ye cut me to the quick! Ye are as bad as yer wife, and her with a harpy's sense of humor!"

"Ye have only yerself to blame for that," Erinn chuckled. "Ye are the one who broke down barriers between the two of ye, and invited her to develop her sense of humor to match yers. Ye should not complain because she sometimes gets the better of ye in the game."

Drake stood there, shock clearly on his face. "She gets the better of me, does she?" he finally said. "We will see about that!"

"She is not cruel, nor disrespectful in her teasing," Erinn reminded. "If she truly had that kind of humor in her heart, she would not be my wife."

"I am sorry, my son," Drake apologized at once. "She does seem to rouse the competitive spirit within me, much as Hadrian did. I truly do love her as a daughter, and think of her that way."

"I know ye do, Father. I simply wanted to remind ye that she is playing the game the way ye have taught her to play with ye. If ye wish to modify it, ye know ye can."

"And have her think she's won?" Drake objected strenuously. "Not for a moment would I consider altering our game! She is just too good with it, and I find that she challenges me constantly."

"As ye taught her to," Erinn laughed softly. "I am going to find that hot spring."

Drake said naught as Erinn walked away, pulling another short sikar from his pocket and lighting it for his walk to the hot water. He reckoned his father simply needed the time to think about the situation, and the need to be clean called to him.

"Oracia," he summoned the elemental within the map in his office.

"Aye, My Lord?"

"Show me where the hot spring is, I do not wish to spend hours looking for it."

As he watched the ground, a faint line of golden light appeared before his feet, leading away from his location as well as back to the camp he had just left. Erinn grinned and followed the track, a minor dragon line amongst many that traced the path that energy flowed through the Land. It did not take him long to find the steaming water in its elevated stone pool, right along the edge of the small stream. As Erinn gained the location, he noted the pool looked suspiciously like one of his father's cooking vessels, raised from the stones that lay along the banks of the river he was fishing out of. The pool was at least five feet deep and seven feet long, providing plenty of space to stretch out to float and let one's body completely relax. Erinn stripped quickly, used the bar of soap in his pocket to wash himself from head to toe before rinsing quickly and then stepping into the pool. The hot water cradled him as he floated, and he let his mind go quiet for a bit, finding the exercise restful. About an hour later he appeared in the camp, carrying his worn clothing and ducking into the tent Drake had raised in his absence, quickly dressing anew in clean unders, his chain mail, then trous, a shirt, hose and his boots before walking back outside. The scent of roasting fowl greeted his nose, setting his taste buds tingling as Drake handed him a fresh cup of cold ale.

"What is on the spit?" he asked, sipping the ale.

"Partridges," Drake answered shortly. "I flushed a covey of them while gathering firewood."

Erinn glanced at the birds, noted the clean cuts on the necks and guessed the manner of their demise. Drake had simply cast his throwing knives skillfully, and from what Erinn observed, he reckoned his father had slain them all without using his magickal abilities. "How many knives did ye cast at once?" he asked, turning back to Drake.

"I cast a dozen," Drake replied shortly as he took a seat back in front of the fire, opening the game bag there. "I still have eight to clean and cook, if ye would like to help."

"I would gladly do so, roasted partridge is one of my favorites!" Erinn declared, noting the additional foraging bags. "Ye have wild greens too, which we both enjoy fried with garlic and olive oil. A wonderful feast, prepared from the Lady's abundance! Thank ye Father, for hunting and gathering while I relaxed."

"It gave me time to consider," Drake replied succinctly. "I must be more cautious about engaging ye in the game. Ye are starting to sound just like yer wife, and one should not have to deal with two at a time in the exchange of wit and banter."

"Are ye telling me I am a worthy opponent then?" Erinn grinned. Drake paused, for he was going to continue on in a different vein.

"I would not have ye for an opponent, my son," Drake replied seriously. "I have seen how ye and yer wife make war, I would not choose to be yer enemy, having seen that. Ye do have my respect, ye know."

"I do?"

"Of course!" Drake snorted. "Would I have allowed ye to become High Lord otherwise? Did ye not wonder each time we engaged in the arena why I pushed ye so hard? I wanted to see yer true potential, yer true temperament and if ye would remain as steady as always even under difficult trial. Ye have done well at every engagement, oral or physical, and I could want no more from ye. The Lady may have other visions, however. When I was here in the Land, I wondered what amount of information I might have access to if I earned my ascension. I have found that I have access to a great deal, as long as it pursues subjects the Lady wishes to talk about. Otherwise, She is silent."

"She is like that here in the Land, Father," Erinn pointed out, finishing with the fourth bird and moving along while Drake talked. "She says what She will, to whom She will. I find Her an enigmatic Deity, to say the least."

"That does not change in the Higher Realms, boyo," Drake sighed, turning to baste the cooking birds with ale, keeping them moist. When Erinn finished dressing out the partridges, he took them to the river to rinse them free of bodily juices. As he returned, he could hear shouts and laughter in the camp, so he picked up his pace considerably, just in case there was trouble. What he found was a patrol of Knights just setting up their camp in the same glade, glad to find company this far out.

"My Lord!" he heard an oddly accented feminine voice. Turning he saw Commander Torvaa, and suddenly he observed the insignias of her corps, the Golden Dragons. "What are ye doing out here?"

"Making a private tour of the Land, Commander Torvaa," he answered, offering her the grip at once. "What are ye doing out here?"

"Routine patrol, My Lord," she answered practically. "There have been reports of strange occurrences in and about Emerald Lakes, and we came to investigate."

"The High Lord has already dealt with the matter," Drake imposed himself into the conversation. "Once more, a follower of the Naga's perverse ways has been met in battle, and overcome."

"O?" Torvaa exclaimed, her eyes upon Erinn. "May we hear the tale?"

"My father tells a better tale than I do," Erinn chuckled, reaching into his pocket and finding sufficient sikars to pass around to the tired men and women. "I shall leave it to his skills to relate what transpired between myself and Enki."

"Enki?" Torvaa said the name with shock and horror. "But Sir, he was one of the worst! He *enjoyed* his malice, and the doing of it!"

"Aye, *was* is the key word here, Commander," Drake chuckled. "Now, after ye've pitched yer tents, tended yer steeds and helped me gather a bit more firewood, ye will have ale and we will feed ye on roasted partridge, fried greens and a tale of battle."

Aye!" they all responded, leaping to the homey task. It did not take long for a large pile of firewood to be assembled and stacked neatly for that nights use, and soon every knight wanting one held a stout cup filled with cold brown ale. Drake put together several more long skewers made from the maple tree close at hand, arranging the birds in threes along their lengths so that they would cook evenly and quickly. Each one was then salted liberally, then Drake quickly ground more peppercorns into a coarse powder, being just as generous with it in his application. While he worked, the thirsty knights gathered around him, gently pressuring him for any details on the High Lord's battle with the Naga lord, Enki. Drake waited until they were all there, including Erinn before he began his tale, while his son simply smoked a larger sikar and sipped his ale. He did not like talking about himself very much, and preferred to let others describe his actions. By the time Drake finished his tale, the first round of birds were cooked to perfection. Drake served a quarter bird with a large mound of fried greens and a wedge of fresh, mealy biscuit on each plate, until only he and Erinn remained to be served. It took very little time for Drake to remedy that situation, and soon all of them were enjoying the crisp, tender bird and the delicious greens, fried in bacon fat and finished with fresh lemons. During his foraging, Drake had found a small wild lemon tree burdened with ripening fruit. They were tiny, but packed with flavor and juice, perfect for squeezing over the dark greens right at the end of their cooking. The meal was delicious and light, allowing easy digestion before retiring, and the troopers all consumed the food with great relish. After thanking Drake for the meal, they gathered around Torvaa for their duty assignments that night.

"I shall take last watch, as always," Torvaa told them with a smile. "Ye all will get a few hours of sleep before we move on. I might even call a halt for the day, I could use a chance to rinse out a few things in my packs," she chuckled.

"If ye walk down the riverside a bit, ye will find a nice hot spring to use for soaking," Erinn advised, standing and stretching. "I need sleep. Delicious meal, Father, as always. I thank ye for hunting and cooking our meal today. Good night all, I shall leave ye to yer duty."

"Good night, My Lord," he heard them all respond as he trudged into the large tent, dropping the tent flap behind him. Once inside, he stripped to his unders, washed his face and neck before pouring a final cup of wine to help him sleep. Piling the pillows of his pallet up to make a backrest, he let himself relax against it, closed his eyes and sent his thoughts out to his wife.

"Deborah?"

"Husband," he heard her response, and noted her exhaustion. "Today has been a long day, but the walls are all up at last. The family will soon be sleeping indoors. I was hoping to complete the entire home before snow flies, but I think we will be fortunate to just get a single level built, with the cold room below."

"If I were that family, I would be grateful to be indoors and safe for the Winter," Erinn replied sensibly. "My dear, sometimes ye expect far too much from yerself. I think ye should be happy that the Obsidian Temple is working again, and that soon 'twill be fully staffed and operational."

"O, I am!" Deborah replied at once. "I was simply hoping to have it all done at once. But we can begin again in the Spring, after the thaw. I must return to the house in the Capitol soon, the harvest is full on and I need to be there."

"Indeed," Erinn agreed, sipping his wine. "I look forward to this private tour being over, so we can be together more often. I love traveling with my father, but I prefer yer company."

"As I prefer yers," Deborah returned with warmth. "I must sleep now, husband. Rest well where ye are, and travel safely on the morrow."

"I love ye too," Erinn told her, his mental voice intense with emotion as her mental presence faded, leaving him alone again. He finished his wine, attended to his nightly routine and turned in, falling asleep nearly as soon as his head touched the pillows. While he slept, the knights walked their guardian routes around the camp, and Drake stood at the entrance to the High Lord's pavilion, assuring his safety.

First meal in the morning came early, a pot of oats and dried fruit served with honey got them all on their separate ways. Drake and Erinn turned for Alom's tabac farm, Torvaa and the Golden Dragons to continue their patrol route. Several days later, the two Natanleod men approached the tabac farm at late morning, and the scent of smoke could be detected.

"Good Goddess, I smell a wildfire!" Erinn shouted out with alarm, urging his horse to a quicker gallop. When they made the turn for the farm, the smell got stronger, and they could see billowing white clouds of smoke, which Erinn noted smelled like a sikar being burnt. "I hope his fields are not on fire!" he thought as he pushed his horse a bit harder, increasing his pace due to his anxiety. Finally, they rode into the courtyard, where they observed the sight of Alom and his staff battling a blaze, standing in a long line passing buckets back and forth between the fire and the well in an attempt to fight the fire. Erinn wasted no time leaping from his horse into the air, transforming into a dragon as he did so, knowing his wings and greater strength would be of assistance fighting the fire. Wheeling about, he found one of Alom's cisterns by the barn and quickly flew to it, hovering long enough to pick up the huge barrel-like container and flying back to the fire with it. Carefully, he began to empty the water onto the flames, while Alom and the rest continued with their buckets, and soon the flames were doused, leaving only the steaming remains of the storage shed. Erinn returned the cistern to its place, so it could refill with the coming rains, then transformed back into his human self as soon as he touched ground.

"Is everyone well? No injuries or burns?" he asked at once with concern.

"Nay, My Lord," Alom answered carefully, still learning the nuances of the language spoken in the Land. "I believe everyone is whole and hale, except for a bit of smoke in the lungs. I think also we have saved the majority of tabac in this fermenting barn, which would be a blessing from the Lady."

"What happened?"

"When the tabac is fermenting, it gets warm. If 'tis not stacked to allow air to flow through, it will ignite the drying tabac easily due to the heat. I shall inquire as to who stacked this part of it, and assure they learn the technique correctly this time," the man assured Erinn. He was still relatively new to the Land, having accompanied a captain and his cargo of tabac and caffe plants as their guardian and caretaker. His accent was warm and rich though, due to his native tongue and Erinn enjoyed listening to him speak.

"I am certain 'tis simply an error due to lack of experience, and since no one is hurt, 'tis no harm done. Since my father and I are here, ye will have extra hands available to assist with the rebuilding of the barn, it should not take overlong to simply repair this. The rest of the barn is unharmed."

"Indeed, My Lord, due to yer extraordinary abilities," Alom smiled. "Come, I was just about to quit for the day. I have cold drink and an antipasto waiting, and I shall only need a moment or two to assure we have enough for all three of us. I recall yer father's appetite as particularly large, especially at this time of the day."

"I work hard," Drake growled a bit, thinking Alom was being critical.

"Of course ye do, My Lord," Alom replied smoothly. "I was simply observing that since ye do work so hard, that yer appetite is correspondingly large. Ye are not a fat man, in any wise."

Drake's brow furrowed a bit, hearing the note of flattery in the man's tone, but he realized that Alom was being artful in his conversation. He had "opened the door" so to speak, inviting Drake to verbally spar with him a bit, playing the game everyone loved in the Land.

"I should hope not," he began, choosing his words carefully. "Such a thing would surely prevent me from returning to the Higher Realms and my Ascended position."

"And we would not wish such a calamity upon the Universe, would we, My Lord?" Alom asked with a straight face. "If ye will come with me, I shall attend to our hunger, and then ye can tell me why ye are here, My Lord."

"I for one, would appreciate the meal," Erinn chuckled, taking a seat. "I have no need to return to the Higher Realms, since my work is here in the Land. And 'tis my work that brings me here, my friend," he went on, transitioning the conversation into another subject.

"Please go on," Alom invited, pouring wine for them all.

"I came to see how yer first harvest is proceeding, but I can see ye have two barns full of leaves already! How close are ye to producing a useable product?"

Alom said naught, a strange expression upon his face as he reached into a side cabinet and pulled out a cedar box. Opening it on well-made hinges to reveal the contents, Erinn laughed aloud, for there were fifty sikars in the box. "I believe we will have yer order filled, My Lord," he said proudly.

Erinn grinned wide, handing one of the sikars to Drake for his testing. "Ye will have enough this year?"

"Indeed so, My Lord, the Lady has been very kind, providing this grant. The soil is rich, the sun is warm, and the rain has been just enough to water the fields all season. What ye see is just one box of many I have ready for shipping to the Barracks, in accordance with our agreement. I have not completely fulfilled our contract, however, but I expect to have no difficulty doing so, especially in light of today's salvation of that barn."

"The Lady is indeed kind," Erinn chuckled, lighting his sikar with a fingertip flame. The sikar he held was nearly black, a rich and smooth variation of the original leaf. It held a darker, richer color and flavor, and it smoked smooth as Erinn drew in the smoke. "I like it!" he declared after a few puffs.

"I do as well, it would suit a stronger drink, like whiskey, very well," Drake added his opinion. Alom smiled, rose from his seat and fetched a stoppered earthen jar.

"Ye'll find the cups behind ye, My Lord," he advised, taking his seat again. Drake wasted no time pulling out the required number and soon they all had a cup of the mellow liquor in hand. Erinn noted that it did indeed compliment the darker sikar well as he enjoyed both at his leisure.

"Why is this leaf different?" Drake asked as he enjoyed his smoke.

"It has everything to do with how the tabac is fermented and aged. I have not perfected the process yet, but I shall in time. It does make a difference, doesn't it?"

"Aye, a good one," Erinn smiled. "What are ye planning for supper tonight?" he asked.

"I had not planned supper as of yet, My Lord," Alom told him. "For some reason, I kept expecting guests, and here ye are. I was never prone to presuppositions before arriving in the Land, could it be that I am developing magickal abilities?"

"Such things are known to happen once a new arrival accustoms themselves to being here," Drake told him. "Ye have naught to fear, and if need be, we can have a Druid come here to instruct ye in their use. The

Lady's Gifts are to be accepted with grace, but 'twill take practice to acquire the skill to use them properly."

"I would be honored to host a Druid here," Alom answered at once. "I have several trees I would appreciate their advice concerning their well being."

"I shall make arrangements then," Erinn nodded, making the mental note. "As for supper, allow me to be of service in that regard? If ye will give me access to yer cold room, I can be about it."

"By all means," Alom agreed easily, knowing Erinn's reputation with cookery. "As I recall, I have a pig down there needing to be cooked."

"Pig?" Drake perked up. "Did I hear aright? A pig needs cooking? Show it to me!" he demanded with a chuckle. Erinn went with him down the stairs, finding the large pig waiting for them, already thawed and waiting on the hooks.

"Have at it, Father," Erinn invited with a flourish. "I must admit that yer roasted pig is better than mine."

"Ye just have not practiced as much as I have," Drake laughed with him. "Very well, I shall use what skills I have to prepare this beast for the spit, if someone will keep my cup full."

"I should be honored," Erinn replied. "Alom, we will need ale, a small barrel of it."

"Ye shall have it," Alom smiled broadly, anticipating a hearty, delicious meal. He also looked forward to learning what made the meat cooked by the Natanleod men so very flavorful and juicy. He had never experienced meat like it before, and wanted to learn to reproduce it. "May I remain to watch the process, perhaps even lend a hand?" he asked.

"Of course," Drake grinned. "My son has business back at that storage barn, aye?"

"Aye, we must assure it can keep the rest of that tabac dry," Erinn smiled. "I shall be back shortly. Father, please do not drink all the ale before I return?"

"Why would ye caution me and not Alom?"

"I know yer drinking habits, Alom's are still a mystery," Erinn replied with a grin, knowing the dig would register.

"And what is amiss with my drinking habits?" Drake demanded, thoroughly amused.

"O naught," Erinn grinned back, continuing the game. "If one is measuring yer abilities as a dragon instead of as a man. I shall see ye both later."

Drake's amusement followed him out the door as Erinn headed for the barn, observing the work already underway there.

"Ho there, perhaps I might be of further assistance to ye?" he called out. "I believe the Lady will lend Her hand too, since this must be finished before dusk. Come, let us work together!"

"Aye!" he heard them reply with enthusiastically. The staff loaded lumber into wagons and brought it to Erinn, he used his abilities to maneuver and secure them enough to keep them together until more permanent means could be put into place. While he did so, the others brought the rest of what was needed to do the job, while others wielded hammers and nails. Finishing by stretching a huge oiled tarp over the gaping hole in the roof, Erinn assured it remained in place by sending their pre-made tack strips up and magickally securing the lot. By then, several hours had passed, and the scent of roasting pig wafted into their noses, carried by the slight breeze.

"We have finished my friends, and since we will have no high winds tonight nor for the next few days, 'twill be ample opportunity to finish what has been started. I am ready for a cup of cold ale, and some Herb to help me relax, are ye with me?"

"Aye!" he heard them respond tiredly, but happily. Erinn passed out the bags and pouches in his pockets, along with the sikars there, until everyone had a reward in hand. Off they went to bathe and change after their long day's labors, while Erinn returned to Alom's house, finding the pig well along in its cooking.

"Tell me ye still have cold ale?" he asked as he sat down heavily.

"Of course," Alom responded, bringing him a cup at once.

"The barn is secure for the night, my friend," Erinn told him tiredly. "Ye will need to get yer people up on ladders over the next few days to finish the roof, but since ye have no high winds coming yer way 'tis ample time to do so."

"Thank ye, My Lord. Yer coming is truly fortuitous," Alom said gratefully. "We would have lost nearly half this year's harvest if ye had not come along."

"Truly we have the Lady to thank then," Erinn smiled, sipping the delicious brown ale.

"My Lord, my bath is available to ye, if ye wish to use it," Alom told him, knowing the habits of those in the Land well by now.

"I would be grateful, I must smell abominable," Erinn chuckled, holding out the cup for more. Alom brought it at once, Erinn finished that cup quickly, and Alom filled it once more. "If ye will show me the way, my friend?" he asked.

"Of course, My Lord," Alom agreed, taking the lead. Down the hall they went past two doors, Alom opening the third. "The tub is in here, and hot water is always available, My Lord. The towels, salts and soap are all along the wall in the cupboards, avail yerself of them. Do ye have a change of clothing?"

"I do," Erinn smiled, calling his bag to him. "Thank ye, Alom. Ye are a good host."

"Thank ye, My Lord!" Alom smiled. "In my lands, hospitality is valued very highly!"

"As 'tis here," Erinn nodded. Alom took the hint and departed, leaving him to his bath, for which Erinn was grateful. He took the opportunity to soak a long time, enjoying a sikar while doing so and sipping the cold ale that refilled his cup each time it emptied. Finally, when he was a bit wrinkled and red, he climbed out of the tub and pulled the drain plug. Reaching for a towel, he dried himself all over with the luxurious length of thick cloth and pulled out his change of clothing to don. It did not take him long to do so, then quickly wash out what he had been wearing, hanging it to dry overnight on the pegs provided. Emerging from the bath, the scent of roasted pig filled his nostrils and a smile appeared. He was very hungry as he hurried to the kitchen, finding Drake in the process of carving the pig onto a large platter.

"Ah, there ye are!" he commented with a grin. "Come, the ladies on the staff have made enough side dishes to round out this meal, including loaves of delicious bread! Come my son, let us partake. I am very hungry!"

"As am I, Father," Erinn agreed, taking his place beside Alom, Drake right beside him. After a quick thanks was offered to the Lady, they all fell to the delicious meal. All conversation ceased as the tastes and textures of the meal satisfied their senses, making their enjoyment complete. Only after the children had been given their second helpings did talk spring up again, and most of it concerned the happenings on the tabac farm. Finally Erinn rose from his seat, after a light cheesecake and berry compote had been served. He offered his thanks for the meal, and for the conversation as well before retiring that night.

"My friends, ye are all working so well together, I have naught to add to it. As such, be assured that yer reward will be plentiful from my hand, and of course, the Lady has already blessed ye. Yer farm works well, Alom, and yer people get along in harmony. I am well pleased."

"Thank ye, My Lord," Alom smiled broadly in quiet pride. "My people work hard, and we get along very well together."

Murmurs of agreement went around the room then, as Erinn bid them all good night, retiring to the bed Alom provided for his use. It was large and comfortable, just soft enough to give support in the right places, and it smelled of lavender and fresh air. He was too tired to even contact

Deborah, due to his magickal exertions that day, and so he let himself drop off to sleep quickly, glad for the rest.

In the morning, he rose and dressed again, leaving the comfort of the room after turning back the covers and removing the sheets he had slept upon, wanting to make it easier for the staff. The scent of fresh pastries hit his nose, along with brewing caffe, his pace increased to bring him into the kitchen area as fast as he could walk. He loved fresh, warm pastries, and when he entered the room he found the cook there just pulling out another pan.

"My goodness, that smells divine!" he commented with a smile.

"O, ye are a flatterer, just like yer Father!" she answered back, turning to face him. "My name is Aceso, and I have known yer Father for many, many years. I would know ye to be Drake's son by yer face alone, ye look just like him. Would ye sit please, and allow me to serve ye this morning?"

"I would be honored," Erinn replied graciously. She smiled with real pleasure as he sat at the table, laying his napkin on his lap as he waited for his plate to arrive. When it did, there was an array of baked goods displayed upon it; apple or berry filled hand pies, almond cookies, a lovely muffin made with shredded summer squash and raisins, and finally a small piece of carrot cake with a thick layer of sweet, soft cheese as a frosting.

"I shall return shortly with yer pot of caffe. And please do not look at me as if I expect ye to eat all of that. Yer Father will be along in a moment or two, I suspect. He has a fondness for enjoying such treats in the morning. Ye two can easily share that plate."

Erinn took up one of the apple hand pies, noting it was still quite warm. Breaking it into two pieces to allow it to cool a bit faster, Erinn attended to his mug of caffe, sipping the first welcome mouthful and thanking the Goddess for it. After a few sips, he reckoned the pie had cooled sufficiently and picked up one of the pieces, mindful of their previous heat. They were comfortable to handle, and so he took a small bite, noting the warmth of the filling at once. It was quite spicy, but in an unusual way, and he wondered what was so different about it. Turning to her, he made to ask as soon as his mouth cleared, finding her supplying the explanation voluntarily.

"I use a bit of mixed ground chilies in my apple pastry filling," she said in a conspiratorial tone. "I like the heat, and I think it complements the apples very well. What do ye think?"

"I like it," Erinn grinned. "I find it an interesting change to what is usually served in the Land. I might make mention of it to my lady when I see her next, if ye do not mind?"

"Of course I do not mind!" Aceso laughed heartily. "My Lord, may I ask, how is Millicent? I have not seen her for so many years. Ye see, she and I trained under the same teacher, in the same kitchen."

"I see," Erinn mused with a grin, continuing to consume the apple pie until it was gone. "I hope ye two got on well?"

"O aye!" Aceso laughed. "We simply cannot work in the same kitchen, as we have very different ideas about how best to accomplish the work. She follows a different path than we were taught, and I have continued to practice what we learned together. The results are basically the same, with small differences to make each unique. When we are not cooking together, we get along splendidly!"

Erinn grinned wider as he began on the next treat, one of the almond cookies. She had put six on the plate, and he had his three consumed before he knew he had even started on the first. They were light, delicious and baked to a crispness that invited them to be dipped into his caffe. He complied with the urge to do so, and was rewarded with a delicious combination of cookie and caffe all at once. He tried the muffin next, expecting to taste vegetable, but finding hints of cinnamon, nutmeg and cloves. It was sweet and slightly spicy, deliciously light and satisfying. He consumed the entire thing, finishing his cup of caffe in the process, and Aceso refilled it without being asked. Erinn amended his cup before continuing with the carrot cake, proceeding with a bit of trepidation as he had grown accustomed to the confection served at the House. The cake was light and moist, well flavored with sweet carrots and spiced lightly to allow the cake to go with any beverage. The sweet, soft cheese spread over the top as an icing seemed to perfectly compliment the cake, even though it was spiced somewhat differently than what he was used to. In all, he found that he had truly enjoyed the entire plate of treats, and told his hostess so.

"My goodness, ye are a fine baker, Madam," he pronounced. "I do not recall enjoying such confections more outside my own home, and I thank ye for them. All of them were spiced alternately than what I am accustomed to, but I find I enjoy the change completely. Thank ye."

"Ye are most welcome, My Lord!" Aceso answered him, bowing low in respect. "I am very glad I have not lost my touch."

Drake appeared just then, freshly washed, shaved and his hair still wet from his bath. "Ah, it smells fine in here!" he commented boisterously, offering Aceso a warm embrace. "I remember how fine yer inn smelled in the mornings, what a shame Raad burned it."

"Aye, but it freed me to be yer ally," Aceso grinned. "The next inn was even better, and the one I opened in the Capitol was better still. Is it still there?"

"The Black Dragon Inn? Aye!" Drake confirmed, accepting the cup of caffe from her. "It has been remodeled recently, and the walls no longer weep along the north side. Ye should come and see it, Barda and Sybelle have done a wonderful job with it."

"Good for them," Aceso smiled. "And Antonina?"

"She has her own house again, and 'tis far finer than the old inn used to be. Everyone wanting a very special meal and entertainment goes there for supper now, even couples celebrating their wedding anniversaries!" Drake supplied. "Ye should come and visit sometime. I am certain quarters can be found for ye in the House."

"We will see," Aceso demurred, and Erinn felt her resistance to the idea.

"When ye wish to visit, the invitation is open to stay with us," he offered graciously, easing everyone's anxiety. "Just let us know ye are coming."

"Of course, 'twould be rude to just drop in," she laughed a bit. "Now My Lord, do ye like yer eggs like yer father does?"

"I do," Erinn smiled. "And I am ready for my first meal too. I wish to be out in the fields early with Alom, and I know he rises early as a custom."

"He might rise later than usual this morning," Aceso chuckled. "He was up late last night inspecting the tabac in the barn that partially burnt. I sleep little these days, and I am aware of his comings and goings. Alom is a good man, he works hard and is respectful of the Lady's ways. He deserves to find a good woman, but that might be difficult due to his looks. I think he is quite handsome, but I am too old. He needs someone his own age."

"I shall speak to my lady about his predicament," Erinn replied sagely. "I am certain she will have advice to offer on the matter."

"Thank ye, My Lord!" Aceso smiled. "Ye do care for the people as deeply as I have heard. In that, ye emulate yer father's example very well, he was willing to give everything to save the people, and save the Land. Drake Natanleod is the ultimate hero of the Land."

"And he has received the reward for his heroism," Erinn heard himself say. "My father is now an Ascended Being, who has been granted permission to come and go in the Land."

"So?" Aceso smiled broadly. "I *was* right! I knew the Lady would grant ye this gift, after everything ye did to save us all!"

"I had to do some horrendous things," Drake replied softly.

"To the enemy, aye, but 'twas war," Aceso insisted. "Ye and I have had this conversation before, while ye healed under my care."

Erinn went on alert at that, he had never heard this tale, and as he watched his father's face, it took on a look of utter seriousness.

"Ye and my father Julius shared that same philosophy about war and what one had to do to win one," he said quietly.

"I know it," she answered, turning to the skillet where some of last night's pork slowly heated on a back burner. Aceso had made a sauce, using the last of Drake's basting base from the night before, shredding a great deal of the pig meat into it until it was thoroughly coated and heated to the right temperature. Now, she took three fresh brown eggs and cracked them one after the other into a hot skillet coated with bacon fat, letting them slowly fry to perfection. Sliding them onto a plate, she heaped the pork beside it, adding a few noodles coated with olive oil and garlic as well as a fluffy fresh biscuit. "There ye are, My Lord. Good morning," she chuckled, setting the platter in front of Erinn. "I shall have yers ready shortly, Drake."

"Thank ye, my dear," he called after her, affection clear in his tone.

"Healing?" Erinn asked quietly.

"I did occasionally get injured badly enough to need a healer," Drake answered without rancor. "The time she is talking about was one of the times I engaged Secundus in a battle of magickal skills. He looked worse than me, I assure ye."

"I am certain he did, assessing by how he looked when I took his head," Erinn answered in a low tone, almost a growl to Drake's ears. Drake's face took on a feral note as he recalled the moment so many years past when his son had cleanly taken Secundus the Sorcerer's head, sounding the end of Raad's rebellious war. When Aceso returned to the table with Drake's platter, the looks on both their faces were as if they were about to go to war.

"Is there danger?" she asked quietly as she put Drake's first meal in front of him. Drake roused a bit, as if returning to himself after a meditation, a sunny smile appeared on his face and he took up his fork.

"Not at all, my dear. May the Lady bless the hands that prepared this bounty."

"Thank ye Drake, for the blessing," Aceso murmured.

"I owe ye that, and more," Drake replied. "If not for yer care, I might have died."

"I doubt that," Aceso laughed merrily. "Ye are half dragon, such a man would be hard to kill. Still, ye were almost dead when ye knocked on my door, then passed out on my stoop."

"True enough," Drake chuckled. "Imagine me waking up to find myself washed and clean, in a clean bed, stitched and bandaged back together, warm and dry. I thought I had passed into the blessed realm for a few moments, especially when ye came to check on me. Ye are still beautiful, ye know."

"O Drake, ye have always been the charmer," she laughed even more merrily. "I know yer heart belongs to Jovita, whether she is with ye or not."

"She is with me, a special grace from the Lady to aid me in my work," Drake told her.

"O, I am glad!" Aceso replied with a smile. "Ye two are so perfect for one another, ye should be together."

"I am glad she is with me too. I always hoped we would be together," he replied honestly. Both of them broke out into merry laughter, exchanging warm embraces as they renewed their friendship.

Erinn watched the interchange, seeing the subtle exchange of energies between the two older people. He realized that this was Drake's way of finishing up business in the Land, and it was clear to him that the Goddess was arranging each of these meetings. Drake's best allies had truly been women, as he had claimed many years earlier, Erinn chuckled to himself. Without women like Aceso, he might not have survived to the end, his thoughts ran on.

"I am very glad that ye and I finally had the opportunity to chat this over," Drake finally said after their laughter had ceased. "I have always wanted the chance to properly thank ye for saving my leg. If not for yer skill…"

"Pish posh," Aceso brushed it off. "All I did was clean it and stitch it together where I could. Yer body did the rest, and I must say, I was amazed that ye were on yer feet within a week. Most men would have been on their backs for at least a month. 'Twas what revealed ye to be Drake Natanleod to me, for only he was reputed to have such abilities. I was so happy ye were not dead, despite Raad's decree."

"He did me such a favor," Drake chuckled low in his throat. "I need some whiskey if I'm going to discuss this," he suggested.

"Very well," she replied, rising and bringing both flask and cup.

"Raad's decree freed me in many ways, mostly from being pursued for the ransom on my head," Drake began. "Once people thought I was dead, I found my passage through the Land became much easier. 'Twas a simple matter to allow my beard to grow out nice and thick, and to let my hair grow long and look a bit unkempt. Drake Natanleod would never let himself be seen looking rumpled in any way, he was a fussy man about his appearance, after all," he laughed heartily, pouring the whiskey into his caffe and adding cacao powder. Erinn noted he was preparing it exactly how Deborah liked hers, and filed it away for later in the game of words. "By the time I rejoined the Black Dragons, I looked nothing like Drake. Only Ironhorse and Fleur knew 'twas me under all that beard and long hair, but Caius kept it completely to himself, much to my relief. He simply followed Fleur's lead, calling me 'Commander' as my title and name. The others emulated him until Drake faded away, and was truly dead, at least 'till he was needed again. That does seem to be a constant theme for me," he continued, trailing off.

"The Lady was with ye," Aceso commented, a bit of awe in her voice.

"As always," Drake smiled warmly. "Now, I must have at the contents of this plate before it gets cold!" he declared, picking up the first treat and digging in. As always, he ate with gusto, consuming nearly everything in front of him, leaving things deliberately untouched in the process. He was of the opinion that wasting food was sinful, and so he always monitored himself carefully, making certain to only bite into what he thought he could finish. "My goodness Aceso, as always, yer food is both familiar and different. I enjoyed that, entirely! Did ye use the rest of my basting sauce to start yers?"

"I did, seeing 'tis a sin to waste good food," she laughed, pouring a bit of whiskey for herself to sip. "I thought I was tasting Julius' cooking for a moment, then realized yers has improved a great deal in the years we have been parted. Drake, ye have become a master of the art!"

"Thank ye, my dear," Drake bowed his head humbly. "I have worked very hard to gain mastery in everything I have been taught."

Aceso shuddered a bit, recalling what his true occupation was during the time she had known him. She had seen his efforts in the workroom and the sight had never left her. It had taken a great deal of mental effort to push the horror of seeing someone skinned alive bit by bit, right in front of her out of her mind. Drake extracted every bit of knowledge and information the poor wretch had to give him before he died however, and where to find the Amazons captured by Raad was something Drake had desperately wanted to know. Three men had died in exquisite agony before the fourth finally told him where they were, and for that, Drake had allowed him to pass on relatively peaceably. Covered in their blood, he had simply cleaned his knives and hands on the dead man's raiment before setting them all alight, leaving them to burn where Raad could find them. With no further words, Drake had taken Aceso to shelter at the Main Temple, using his magickal abilities to do so to save time. He had not paused to change his clothing either, simply disappearing as soon as Elanor took charge of the newly arrived woman. When the Black Dragons had thundered up the pass, what was left of Hadrian's army behind him, he was still wearing the same clothing. After Drake stood forth and held up their collected right fingers to announce the death of Raad's men, the despot's wrath had been savage.

"I want all of those traitors dead!" he had thundered out as Drake's combined attack hit their guardian ring, overwhelming the outer defenses easily. From then on, Drake had simply ridden over anyone in his way to find Jovita and the rest of the Amazons. When he did finally locate them all his heart had nearly broken, finding so many were missing from their number, women Drake had sparred with and drank with in his youth. Now he stood before her an Ascended Being, the first to accomplish the feat for many years in the Land.

"Yer arrival was most timely," Aceso finally said. "I am not certain how many of my sisters would have survived for much longer," she sighed.

Now Erinn understood a bit more about the relationship between Drake and Aceso, the latter had been an Amazon.

"If ye had not brought me those who knew where they were, I would never have found them," Drake told her quietly and the words dropped into Erinn's mind heavily. It had been Aceso who had captured the Naga priests or priestesses to bring into Drake's workroom, and he glanced at her with new respect.

"Ye follow Artemis. Ye acted as his Huntress so that he did not have to risk being seen," Erinn said softly in realization.

"Aye, so I did," she answered with a faint smile. "But 'twas a long time ago, and now I only practice my healing, which I prefer over being a Huntress."

"How often did ye work with him like that?" Erinn asked, unable to help himself.

"More often than I like to recall," Aceso told him seriously. "I do not like discussing those days at all."

"Very well, I shall ask no more," Erinn told her respectfully. "But I thank ye for yer service to the Land."

"Ye are most welcome, I am glad those days are done," she chuckled, standing to pick up their plates.

"We all are, my dear," Drake put in, breaking the tension. "Thank ye for the wonderful meal, I feel like putting in a full day's work due to it!"

"Good, ye can help us finish the repairs on the barn!" Alom's voice came through the door ahead of him, and the smiling man stepped into the kitchen, bathed, dressed and ready for his day's work.

"I would be glad to do so!" Drake declared. "If My Lord Erinn can pause his journey for the day?"

"I can pause for the day," Erinn nodded with a smile. "I want to see the rest of the operation, and meet the staff more personally. Ye have done a marvel here to have so much up and running within a year! Yer people must love ye a great deal."

"I know that I appreciate their work, and that they accept me as one of them," Alom replied humbly. "I am glad to be here in the Land."

"We are glad to have ye here. Now, show me around a bit before we get started on that barn. I would wager we have it nearly completed by tonight!"

"Aye, My Lord," Alom smiled broadly. Two hours later, they were just finishing up the tour in the last and largest barn. This barn housed the finishing process, and was where the sikars were rolled. The scent of good, mellow tabac filled his nostrils as soon as they stepped inside, and for a moment, Erinn was taken back in his memory. With a grin, he recalled the little shop in the Port City where he had first encountered tabac and the delightful treat made from it.

"The scent in here brings back good memories," he said, turning to Alom. "I am reminded of the first time I saw a sikar, during a Wedding Anniversary trip to the Port City. I am anxious to see how yer workshop is progressing."

"Come with me, My Lord. I believe ye will be pleased with my students' work," Alom invited, stepping to the back of the room. Opening a door, he stepped through with Erinn right behind him and the sight that greeted Erinn's eyes was a surprise. There were over twenty people of various ages sitting at the tables, in various stages of learning the process of how to layer the leaves, then roll them correctly, adding the binder leaves carefully around them and wrapping the ends. Some of the people working had a good grasp of the process, others were relearning various stages to improve their techniques. Erinn walked among them, congratulating each on learning as much as they had in such a short time, and adding largesse to prove his words. He received their thanks, and took a few of their better examples to smoke later, meaning to offer a constructive critique. Finally, they headed back to the main house, passing right by the damaged barn, where Drake and his team were almost finished.

"Ye can hardly tell 'twas even damaged, except for the missing paint on the outside!" Alom declared, inspecting the work. "Ye have all done very, very well, to work so fast and so precisely. I am going to speak to Aceso about a special meal tonight!"

"Beef!" came the combined suggestion, and Drake's amusement was clear as he laughed his response.

"I most heartily agree! What say ye, Alom? Do ye have a roast or two in yer cold room?"

"I have better than that, I have a half steer down there," Alom smiled. "And after such heavy work as ye have done today, I think 'twould be an appropriate reward. I shall speak to Aceso at once."

"I can offer my services to cook it," Erinn volunteered. "I have not been working as hard as others have, especially my Father."

"The labor is not overly difficult these days, my son," Drake chuckled. "Even at my advanced age, I managed to keep up with the younger people."

"A blessing indeed," Erinn chuckled with him. "We would not wish that yer diminishing abilities inhibit yer work."

"Ooo…good one!" Drake laughed aloud. "I need something to drink!"

Aceso appeared at just that moment with an ale cart, pulled by a small pony. The cart was outfitted with racks of cups, as well as a reservoir to be filled with chunked ice, Erinn could see it would serve well at any outdoor function.

"Who built this cart?" he asked as Alom served the cold ale.

"I did," he heard the response, turning to find the owner of the voice. A young woman stepped forward, her shoulders brawny and her thighs thick with muscles. "I am the woodworker here, my name is Matilda."

"I am very happy to meet ye, Matilda," Erinn replied, offering the grip as he would to anyone. "Wherever did ye get the idea for it all?"

"Master Alom expressed the desire to have cold ale on the work site, I spent a week or two putting this together. I think it fits the purpose well."

"One pony can easily draw that, even with a heavy keg in it?"

"Aye, I was careful about the balance of the cart. If ye load it correctly, only one pony is required for a load like this. If ye wanted to haul a larger keg, ye would only need two ponies."

"I see! A clever design indeed!" Erinn remarked, walking around the cart and assessing the work. "Would ye consider coming to the Capitol City sometime, and teaching my cart maker to construct one of these? I can think of many, many applications for the Barracks, and for outdoor celebrations."

"Perhaps I might make time in the Winter, after our season has ended," she answered carefully.

"Ye would have my support in such an effort Matilda," Alom told her. "Winter can be a long season out here, so far away from the larger towns."

"I shall consider it then," she agreed, turning to Erinn with a smile.

"I shall inform my lady we will have an additional guest during the holidays!" Erinn smiled back. "Now, what still needs doing here?"

"Naught!" Drake replied. "As Master Alom has already noted, it simply needs to be painted to match the rest of the building."

"Then we are all finished for the day?" Erinn asked.

"Aye!" the collected workers replied en masse.

"Good, then let us retire for the day? I feel the need to relax a bit, aye?"

"Aye!" they responded in a collective roar. The group quickly gathered up the tools they were using, as well as any piece of lumber big enough to be usable, collecting the smaller pieces for firestarters. Carrying it back to the shed used to store the work tools, the items were cleaned and oiled before being put back into the proper places. Erinn approved of such organization, and congratulated them on being so efficient.

"Master Alom's way of doing things fits into the Lady's Land very well, My Lord," one of the workers told him with a smile. "We all enjoy working with him, and all of us are happy here."

"I am glad to hear that," Erinn grinned. "Everyone should be happy with their work situation."

While Erinn celebrated the success of one of his favored projects, Deborah was sweating to complete hers before she had to return to the House in the Capitol city. From sun up to sundown, she worked alongside everyone and anyone she needed to, assuring that Hodor and Olga had a home to live in for the Winter. That would have been a trying test of her skills, but the Lady decided to add a layer of difficulty to the task. Inexplicably and with no forewarning, Druids and Priestesses began to arrive at the Temple, wishing to begin the work of spiritually cleansing and realigning the area around the spire. Indeed, it was explained to her that they needed access to the entire area, including the worksite for their task, and Deborah could not help bursting out in laughter at their suggestion early one morning that the work must cease at once.

"I am sorry, Brother and Sister, but I cannot cease. These people need a home to live in, and I have given my word they shall have just that in time to be ready for snowfall. They have been out gathering what harvest is here and drying it in preparation for lining their pantry, which is very nearly complete. Our work will not go on much longer. Surely, ye can wait to do yer work 'till after the house is finished?" she queried impatiently as they stood in the rapidly warming mid-Summer sun.

"We must begin as soon as possible, My Lady," the two of them answered in unison.

"I see," Deborah observed, her face tightening almost imperceptibly in annoyance. "Let us go and consult with the project Master, and see what his advice is."

Theodosius listened to each of them in turn, finishing with Deborah. When they had all expressed their concerns, he took a sikar out of his pocket, clipped it and turned to Deborah, an imploring expression upon his face. The corner of her mouth lifted in a half-smile and she produced a flame from her palm to light the sikar for him, lighting one for herself at the same time, and offering one to the others with them. The Druid took it, the Priestess shook her head, Deborah offered the flame to the Druid man and as soon as his was lit she quelled the tendril at once, not wanting to tire herself.

"Now that ye all have spoken, 'tis my turn," he laughed softly. "Ye cannot have access to the worksite just yet, Sister and Brother, and let me explain myself. We have tools and work related equipment all over the site, and there are places where one should not walk at the moment. We all know where those places are, but ye would have to be acquainted with them. If ye are concerned so much about the aligning of the area's energies, perhaps ye should start yer work at the Spire? As I understand it, the structure is capable of directing a great amount of the Lady's energies, which could be put to a great many purposes. Is it not so?"

The two spiritual people exchanged glances of alarm, no one was supposed to know anything about what Theodosius was talking about. "Brother..." the Druid man began.

"Aye, I am of yer Order," Theodosius chuckled. "Although, I much prefer the titles of Master Carpenter and Engineer. I left the Shrines because of the many cross alliances that existed during the time before the War. I went to the Guilds, proved my knowledge and was granted a Journeyman's status at once. It did not take me long to earn the next title, and I have been practicing my chosen craft ever since. If ye re-tune that Spire properly, ye might even aid our work speed. It all depends on yer skills and abilities, aye?"

"And the Lady's Will," Deborah put in. "Very well, Sister and Brother, ye have yer task laid out before ye now. I suggest ye get to it. The sooner that Spire is working properly, the sooner the entire area will prosper," Deborah summed it up, making it sound simple.

"My Lady…"

"What?" she answered turning to him as her eyes changed from hazel to amber. "As I said, ye have yer task before ye, and I suggest ye get to it, now. We can use all the aid we can summon to get all of this work done before snowfall, which will be early this year. We must all act with alacrity now, and I must return to my work. Good day."

"G…Good day, My Lady," the two called after her as she turned from the group and walked off, returning to what she had been doing. They turned back to Theodosius and found him ready to return to his work as well.

"Well? Ye wanted direction, ye got it. Ye'd best be about yer work, aye?"

"Aye," the two answered in concert, watching him walk away.

"We must summon more help," the Priestess said softly.

"Aye, we must," the Druid man answered. "The Spire must be cleansed, and we cannot do it alone. I shall contact the Elder Brother to ask for his aid."

"I shall contact Elanor," the Priestess agreed. "We will meet at the Spire before sundown, to discuss what instructions we have received."

"Aye," he nodded, bowing a bit in respect to her. She returned the gesture and they parted to rejoin their own enclaves, sending out their thoughts to each of their hierarchs. Within hours, more Priestesses and Druids began to arrive, all needing to be housed and fed. Deborah's consternation increased, her intent had been circumvented and so now she acted to put it right. Mid-morning approached, and she still had yet to begin her work for the day. Sending her thoughts out to Gwendolyn, now Acting Kitchen Mistress under Millicent's final review, Deborah asked for the help she needed and received it at once.

"Gwen, I am in need of assistance," she stated firmly.

"Aye, My Lady? What service may I render?" Gwendolyn answered patiently, knowing Deborah's ire could be roused easily.

"I shall need several wagons filled with supplies, I have newly arrived Priestesses and Druids needing to be fed and sheltered. I shall contact the War Duke as soon as we finish speaking. I am certain he can assist me with the shelter portion," Deborah answered concisely.

"Aye, My Lady. I shall be certain to pack plenty for the Priestesses, so that their diet may be maintained properly. Should I come along as well?"

"Nay, we have Cyrus here cooking for us, but I know he is running low on supplies. I planned on feeding fifty for the Summer, we have three times that here now."

"I shall be overly generous with the supplies, My Lady," Gwendolyn assured her. "As soon as I have it all assembled, I shall contact ye."

"Thank ye, Gwen," Deborah replied warmly, gratitude in her thoughts. "I can always count on our house in such situations, and I have ye and yer crew to thank for it. I shall have rewards when I return."

"We will expect ye home soon then," Gwendolyn responded with a laugh. Deborah's thoughts withdrew from her mind to seek out Ulric's, finding him working in his office.

"Aye, My Lady?" his thoughts answered hers at first touch. "What is amiss?"

"The numbers of people arriving here at the Temple are increasing beyond our capacity to house them. We will need pavilions, and everything required for people's housing needs at once. Ye should plan on at least two hundred."

"I shall bring enough for three hundred," Ulric responded with a chuckle. "I imagine the news of the Obsidian Temple's reawakening will bring quite a gathering together. We will be generous with our plans."

"Thank ye, My Lord," Deborah answered, relief clear in her thoughts. "If ye would co-ordinate with Gwendolyn, who is already assembling supplies, all should go smoothly. We should have our supplies before sundown, aye?"

"Most assuredly, My Lady, if ye provide the transportation," Ulric laughed.

"Good then, ye know how I admire alacrity, My Lord."

"Indeed I do, My Lady," he responded with great affection. "When we are ready, I shall contact ye."

"Excellent," she answered, and Ulric could hear her sigh. "One more problem solved. Onto the next task then. Good day."

"Good day, My Lady."

He was off then to see to it, including gathering the wagons, teams and drivers to transport the supplies. Each wagon was loaded carefully, so that everything was properly balanced over the axles of the wagons, rather than in the front near the tongue. If the load was done properly, all the horses had to do was pull it, not lift it, and pulling was easier by far. Ulric watched carefully as Knights and Dames loaded each wagon, offering his expertise from time to time when asked, until they had twenty wagons loaded with food, tents, cots with mattresses as well as quilts, blankets and pillows. As well, he sent along two huge wooden tubs and a portable boiler, so that baths could be provided for all. The tubs would also double as laundry facilities, he knew as he remembered to add towels, robes, slippers, soaps and oils to that wagon. Finally, he check over each one before it was covered with a tarp and roped tightly, securing each for its journey through the portal. The sun stood at late mid-day by the time everything was assembled, and Ulric sent his thoughts out to Deborah, feeling her weariness as soon his mind touched hers.

"My Lady, all is assembled," he said quickly.

"Very good, I know I can at least count on the War Duke for his promptness," he heard her terse reply.

"I hope ye will not be wroth with me, My Lady, but I am also sending a few of the Phoenix Guard to be with ye. I am also sending more sikars, and a cask of yer favorite white wine. Should I come along?" he asked.

"I need ye there with both Erinn and me out of the city," Deborah replied. "I thank ye for remembering the wine, I think I shall enjoy a cup or two tonight before supper. Ye are a good man, Ulric."

"Thank ye, My Lady," he replied humbly.

"Warn everyone to keep their horses calm," he heard her say. Moments later, a vast whirling circle of light appeared, opening like an eye to reveal where Deborah stood at the worksite.

"Proceed!" he ordered, watching the first team of horses move through the portal, followed by the next, then by the rest of the line. It did not take all that long for all twenty wagons to trundle through the portal, and with a smile and wave of thanks, Deborah closed it.

Once all the wagons were through, Deborah directed them to various sites all over the worksite, instructing them to begin their work at once. She was especially glad to see the portable boiler and two tubs, a proper bath sounded divine at the moment, she thought. With the wagons had come a full detachment of Knights and Dames, Ulric's addition to security, as well as five members of the High Lady's Phoenix Guard. Those five women came to her at once, saluted and asked where they could be of the best service.

"If ye would coordinate the unloading and dispersal of supplies in the wagons, 'twould be of great assistance," Deborah told her at once. "The rest of ye, see to putting up those shelters. Make sure they are set up to be comfortable and practical!" she called out to the others. "Minerva, would ye please coordinate with Captain Tyrion? I am certain that between the two of ye, everything can be accomplished quickly."

Many of the Priestesses and Druids stepped forward to offer their assistance as well, and by nightfall, only a few pavilions still needed to be raised and supplied. Everyone would sleep indoors that night, Deborah sighed with satisfaction as she watched her Phoenix Guard make themselves at home in her pavilion. By that time, she had bathed and changed into comfortable clothing. Now she held a cup of cold wine in her hand, and a sikar was within reach, an ultimately satisfying end to her complicated day. She could hear those in the camp using the baths, having a cup of cold drink while they waited their turns. It was good to hear them laughing and joking together, she thought, and the whiff of good food cooking floated under her nostrils. Laughter rang out throughout the camp as Knights and Dames quietly patrolled, a sense of calm ran through everyone. They ate together in groups, worked together to clean up after, and bid each other a warm good night while she watched over them, finally seeking her own bed much later.

Over the next few days, a sense of community developed among everyone working, and people let themselves be organized into the work they were best suited for. Oftentimes, Deborah would only have to make a suggestion, and several people would see to it, assuming the responsibility for that task from that point on. The worksite cleared a bit as those involved with the spiritual work attended to it, leaving the carpenters and engineers to finally finish Olga's and Hodor's house. Forty five days later, Deborah escorted the couple and their family to the front door, opening it for them and allowing them to enter first. She followed after, bearing the traditional gifts for a new home; wine, olive oil, a loaf of fresh bread, a jar of honey and several pots of preserves. Deborah had also included a crock of bread starter, a thoughtful gift from one woman to another, as well as assuring that the pantry of the house was fully stocked. Olga and Hodor explored the place as if they had never been there, despite being involved in the process from the beginning, ending their tour by lighting the hearth and setting an image of the Lady upon the mantelpiece.

"O my! Our new house is lovely, husband!" Olga remarked. "I can hardly wait to get the curtains on the windows, and the rugs upon the floors."

"We should get to that then," Hodor smiled warmly. "I would like to sleep in my bed tonight, in my room. What say ye all?"

"Aye!" the children answered. Each went to the room assigned to them, the boys both in one room, and the girls in another. They found their beds assembled, the mattresses upon them, ready to be made up with fresh, clean sheets, blankets, quilts and pillows. Squeals of delight could be heard as the children dressed their beds, anticipating their rest that night. Olga prepared supper on her own stove that night, served supper on their new table with a gaily embroidered tablecloth, sitting upon the new chairs. Afterward, the dishes were quickly washed and left to dry in the dish rack while the rest of the family talked or played chess. Olga and Hodor planned out how to manage the rest of the season to their best advantage, the man of the house hoping for a good store of wild game to offset their winter diet. It was a worry to him, having come from farming stock and preferring to raise all his own meat and produce, but he reckoned the Goddess would provide for them in Her way.

In the morning, Hodor walked to where the lead Knight on the job stood by Theodosius.

"Excuse me, Captain Tyrion?" he asked.

"Aye, Hodor? What might I do for ye?"

"I need to go hunting for my larder. I have a room full of ice blocks waiting for meat to freeze. I was hoping someone with hunting skills would go with me, as I have few of my own. I cannot afford to miss."

"I shall go with ye," Tyrion volunteered at once with a grin. "I am a skilled tracker, and I have taken bigger game on by myself. 'Tis little left for me to do on the worksite, the clean-up has begun already as ye can see. I have the men over there readying yer fishing dock, and some more Knights and Dames are helping to mark out yer new garden plots. If I leave Tristan in charge, I could slip away for a bit. I love spending time in the wildwood."

"Good then," Hodor smiled. In a short time, they were on their way into the deep forest that surrounded the house, headed downriver a bit, away from all the noise and activity. In due time, Tyrion stopped and knelt, peering at the ground intently for a few minutes.

"We should walk away from this area right now," he said quietly. "Those are grizzled bear tracks, and look how huge they are. The two of us are no match for such a beast."

"Lead the way, I am looking for tasty meat," Hodor responded, keeping his voice low as well. The two men walked away from the trail where the bear tracks paralleled it, quickly finding another game trail that held more promise.

"Friend Hodor, have ye ever hunted elk before?" Tyrion asked.

"Aye, not very well however," Hodor chuckled ruefully.

"Just follow me closely, and listen to my instructions. Do not hesitate when I ask for yer help and we will have a fine roast for yer spit tonight!" he chuckled, following the set of tracks. It was not long before they found their quarry, a herd of older bucks traveling together for safety and companionship. One of them was practically grey, and Tyrion carefully sighted his target as the buck stood there, placidly chewing. Only when he was certain of his shot did he release it, the arrow found its mark and the buck was down in two steps. Once Tyrion slit the throat to bleed it, he whispered the prayer common to most hunters in the Land.

"Thank ye Brother Elk, for yer sacrifice to feed the people. None will be wasted. Let yer blood nourish the Earth as a gift to the Lady."

Hodor said nothing, he had heard such prayers before, but never quite so fervently spoken. Tyrion paused for a moment before taking a deep breath and blowing it out slowly, turning to Hodor with a faint grin on his face.

"Ye have field-dressed a beast before, aye?"

"I have butchered my share, I can reckon it out," Hodor answered, grinning back. The two men shared the task and soon had the elk's carcass on a pole between them, returning to Hodor's house as quickly as they could. Clearing the wildwood, it did not take them long to gain the back door of the house, the closest entrance to the cold room. "Let us get this downstairs quickly," the man of the house suggested.

"Aye, the sooner the better," Tyrion agreed, heading for the stairs. Soon, the carcass hung on the corner hook, close the wall of ice that comprised part of the cold room. Tyrion carefully removed a back quarter, helped Hodor heft it upon his shoulder for the return trip upstairs. Olga was there, just finishing a bowl of barley salad, and her surprise was clearly obvious when she saw what her husband had brought home.

"Look Olga!" he said with a grin, accepting the kiss on his cheek she offered. "The Captain and I went hunting for the table, 'twas his shot that brought down this beast."

"We thank the Captain for the contribution to our pantry," Olga answered warmly. "Husband, perhaps ye should offer the Captain a libation?"

"Aye, rightly so!" Hodor smiled, turning for the kitchen and the crockery jug that waited there. "Would ye care for some whiskey?"

"I would," Tyrion smiled. He enjoyed a cup with the man, then rose and bid them good night, uncomfortable in the family situation. His family had not enjoyed such love, which is why he and his brothers were alone in the world. Their father was unhappy that his youngest son Tyrael did not associate with women, and openly condemned him in front of their entire village, exiling him from the family.

"If ye are going to condemn Tyrael for simply being what he was created to be, then ye do not need the rest of us either," Tyrion had stepped up to say, joined by his other two brothers. The three of them had simply packed a single bag, said farewell to their sisters and mother and walked for three days to be off their father's lands, free of his overbearing dominance at last. Fate and fortune had kept them together as they traveled through the Outer Lands, and a shipwreck had brought them to the shores of the Lady's Land. Once there, they had quickly put aside everything they had known to embrace where they found themselves now. All of the martial skills they had learned while traveling came into play as they proved themselves worthy, finally finding themselves attending Drake's first Summer Tournament after the Wars had ended. They had undertaken the trials and passed through to enter the barracks, quickly to find themselves wearing the purple and looking for a troop to join. All of them had chosen the Black Dragons, and their trial to enter had been one of the most unique ever in the history of the elite corps. The three brothers had challenged the entire corps at once in a melee as Drake had watched with great interest and some alarm. They had not only overcome everyone sent against them but did so without harming themselves or anyone else seriously. That had impressed Drake so much he had invited them into the corps at once, and once in the former High Lord had taken Tyrion aside.

"Ye are command material, ye are the eldest, aye?"

"Aye, My Lord. My father trained me to command our house guard. I have always found the martial life to my liking."

"Good, I shall keep that in mind, young man. Know that I am watching, and waiting for ye to prove yerself."

"I shall not make ye wait long, My Lord," Tyrion had promised boldly. He had nonetheless proven true to his word, serving with excellence and patience until tapped for command the first time. Now, he was an experienced Captain, waiting for his chance to command the Black Dragons if possible. If not, then to be its captain, a rank of honor. Entering his tent, he quickly consulted the schedule of guard rotation, noting that the latest shift was now walking the perimeter. Good, he thought with satisfaction, turning to where the wineskin waited and pouring himself a generous cup. A sikar waited there too, providing a relaxing interlude while he prepared for sleeping that night. He was glad to be in the Land, everything he had trained for was now coming into play, for which he was very grateful. Walking to the small altar in the tent, he lit the candle and knelt as was his custom when addressing the Lady.

"Thank ye Great One, for bringing me and my brothers here," he whispered earnestly. "May my service always bring ye honor."

A feeling of all being right in the world descended upon him as he enjoyed the wine and tabac, finally finishing both as night grew darker and deeper. A quick trip to his necessity to attend his nightly regime and then he was between the covers, fast asleep in preparation for the next day.

Chapter 11

A week later, Deborah was ready to depart. Her task was finished, Olga and Hodor's house was finished and ready for the Winter's cold. Their larder was full, their pantry too, and they had plenty of firewood stacked in neat cords. After touring the entire farm, she was satisfied that the couple had been given the start she promised them and gave the order.

"We will return to the Capitol city on the morrow. Give the order to pack and depart. I wish to go as early as possible in the morning. I have much work waiting for me," she sighed.

"What about the permanent housing for the Priestesses and Druids coming to reopen the Temple here?" Tyrion asked.

"Lord Aldridge and Lady Elanor have promised to assure their housing over the severest of the season," Deborah replied, gratefully. "They will not be remaining over the Winter. The work may begin again once the snows have melted. I am grateful to be going home."

The two men smiled at her, respect and love showing clearly on their faces. They had come to admire the High Lady greatly, seeing her administer this task with fairness and alacrity. She had also maintained her good humor throughout, despite the occasional difficulties.

"My Lady is a hard working woman," both men commented in concert respectfully. "We shall have the company ready to move out as early as we can be in the morning."

"Thank ye, both of ye. I shall be certain to speak to the War Duke when we return. Ye have both attended to yer duty excellently, and he should know."

"I appreciate the High Lady's alacrity in the matter," Tyrion smiled faintly, bowing now in respect. Leaving her, they walked back to where the Army waited, giving him his orders as they went. "Pack everything we can tonight, we will be leaving as early as possible in the morning. The High Lady is impatient to return home."

"Very well, Captain!" the young man answered, saluting and sprinting off to pass out the instructions to all. The next day, before the sun rose high at mid-day, they were almost finished loading the last few wagons, while Deborah fidgeted. At last, Tyrion came to her, bowed low and informed her that all was in readiness.

"Good then," Deborah answered him, her smile tight with tension. "Be ready to travel through the portal, I am anxious to be home."

"As am I, My Lady," Tyrion admitted. "Sleeping outdoors for a time can be fun, but I long for my bed."

Deborah's smile widened, she made a gesture and the portal opened, almost exactly where it had manifested to bring them there. The first wagons urged their horses through and soon, the entire cavalcade was moving. "At last," Deborah thought with satisfaction. Waiting until everyone and every last thing they had brought with them was through the gate, Deborah turned to Olga and Hodor, standing there behind her with amazement on their faces. They had seen much magick demonstrated throughout the building of their home, but this manifestation of Deborah's abilities was awe inspiring to them. Deborah went to them, offering warm and friendly embraces, breaking their attention away from the whirling portal of light before them.

"I wish the two of ye all success," she said to them. "Welcome to the Land, Olga and Hodor. May the Winter treat ye well, and if ye have need of aught, ye have only to contact me. Farewell," she bid them, mounting her horse.

"Farewell, My Lady!" the couple called to her, waving with bright smiles as she rode slowly through the brilliant light. As soon as the tail of her horse disappeared within it, the light suddenly ceased, as if a huge candle had been extinguished. The two embraced tightly, turned to the house and began their life together.

"Children come!" they called to their progeny assembled on the front porch. "We should get the nets and see if we can fish a salmon from the river for our supper tonight!" Olga went on.

"I love salmon!" their daughter exclaimed, turning to the house and running for the wooden box where the fishing gear waited.

Far away a light glimmered on an open portion of the road just a few miles from the Capitol city. Wagons and mounted members of the Land's Army began to emerge, gathering in a marching formation. At last Deborah emerged from the portal, where the rest of her group waited.

"Come my friends, let us ride for home!" she called out with joy. "I am ready for a bath, and some real relaxation! Ye have all done well to get this done so early," she laughed, noting the clouds beginning to gather. They were light grey and very fluffy, and as they galloped to the gates of the city, an intensely cold breeze hit their backs. Deborah began to laugh uproariously, they had apparently just beaten the first snow, and as they came to the gate, the first huge flakes began to pour down like rain. They cantered through the city, then down the access road to the barracks, where grooms came at once to take their horses. Stablemen also came to get the teams and wagons, leading them away to a warm barn and good feed.

Deborah hustled everyone inside, pausing to hand out largesse and thanks to all for their hard work before letting them return to their quarters.

"Captain Tyrion," she called out to the young man, who turned at once to face her.

"Aye, My Lady?"

"Thank ye most especially for yer hard work," she said to him. "Ye managed a diverse crew, under arduous conditions, and we managed to finish just in time because of yer skills of organization and inspiration. I wish for ye to take this voucher. 'Tis for a five night stay at one of Nathan's inns, and it expresses my thanks for everything ye did."

Tyrion grinned, took the voucher and tucked into his inner pocket, bowing low afterward. "I am most grateful, My Lady. I have someone in mind to share this with, someone who is very special to me. I have wondered how to make the offer to her, and ye have provided an excellent opportunity for me to take her somewhere very special. Where would ye recommend?"

"I like the Inn at White Sands," Deborah told him. "My husband likes that one too, but I think he prefers Emerald Lakes due to the fishing. However, at this time of year, the heat of the coast is very pleasant. The beach is wonderful for laying out and taking the sun. Also, the tides provide opportunities to harvest shellfish, which ye can cook right there on the beach. Nathan has small shelters set up every so often where ye can get out of the sun and prepare a quick meal from yer catch."

"The lady I have in mind is a Water sign, I often think of her as a mer-woman, especially when she is swimming. I do not know if she has ever been to the coast," Tyrion grinned.

"Then perhaps 'tis time for ye to find out if she wishes to go?" Deborah asked with a smile.

"Aye, My Lady," Tyrion bowed slightly, laughing under his breath a bit. Her sense of humor was delightful, he thought as he took his leave of her, headed to where his lady's room was.

Deborah watched him go, waiting until he disappeared around a corner before continuing on her way to the War Duke's office, finding him there working.

"My Lord War Duke!" she called out in a warm tone.

"My Lady!" he returned, just as warmly, offering an embrace of welcome. "Ye have returned home at last! All is well?"

"Most assuredly," she replied tiredly. "I wish to put in commendation for Captain Tyrion, and his Sub-Captain Tristan. Both men performed above and beyond their original orders, managing a huge and diverse crew of Knights, Dames, Druids and Priestesses without having much warning. Tyrion aided in stocking the family's larder before we left and Tristan was of excellent service to all. How long has it been since a Knight was granted the Lady's Ribbon for Service?"

"Over forty years, My Lady," Ulric answered with a grin. "I would imagine there are even still some made up, and I shall search for them."

"Thank ye, if there are none, then have some made," Deborah ordered tiredly. "I am going upstairs for a quick snack, and then if ye need me, I shall be in my room. I am ready to relax after a job well done. Did ye notice 'tis snowing outside?"

"Then ye managed yer task after all!" Ulric grinned. "Ye need not worry, all is well here in the barracks, and in the house above. Ye have returned home just in time for the slaughter!"

"O have I?" Deborah smiled at the irony of it. "Perhaps I should go in search of my husband then," she laughed softly.

"He is still touring the Land with his Father," Ulric told her. Deborah nodded, she reckoned Erinn could use the time with Drake. Her husband had not had much time with his father before his ascension, she remembered.

Walking slowly up the stairs, Deborah turned left at the top, headed for the kitchen. The smell of jam cooking hit her nostrils, and she could detect the different scents of the fruits; apples, pears, brambleberry, apricots, all cooking in different pots at various stations in the huge kitchen.

"Good afternoon," she called out in a friendly tone, bringing Gwendolyn to her quickly.

"Good afternoon, My Lady! Welcome home!" the large woman greeted, bringing a cup of cold white wine.

"O thank ye, Gwen," Deborah sighed, taking the welcome cup and sipping the delicious, tart flavor. "I see ye have all in hand, and how goes the gardening?"

"The last of the peas, beans and greens have been harvested, My Lady, and the former two are even now drying out there under cover. I had the Knights move the drying tables to the outdoor kitchen area, where we could cover them all easily. I had the Stablemaster bring out the composted straw and heap it over the beetroots, parsnips, carrots and papas, we will gain a few weeks by doing so, aye?"

"Ye have learned my way of doing things very well," Deborah complimented, holding out her cup for more wine. "Is there antipasto available?"

"Also, all of the extra fruit has been squeezed and is aging right now as mead. We will have plenty for the holidays this year, and what is aging now will be ready by Beltane next year! Also, we are making up trays for the herdsmen right now, as well as a big pot of lentil soup. They tell me the slaughter will take a few days longer than usual, and that they have brought in farmers from other districts to assist."

"Good, the people will eat well then," Deborah nodded in satisfaction. "I am going to my room. Will ye send down a small tray for me in a bit? After I have a bite and a nap, I shall come and be of assistance."

"Ye will do no such thing," Gwendolyn objected. "Ye have just returned from a Summer's mission, where ye have been working over hard. Ye are going to yer room, where a bath and bed awaits!" she said, putting a bit of command behind her words. Deborah listened to her, her eyebrows rose at the last of her 'orders' and her face took on a look of amusement.

"Aye, Captain Gwendolyn," she said in a humble, but laughing voice. "I shall hurry to obey!" she went on, a slightly sarcastic tone in her voice. A long moment passed, then Deborah broke out in laughter, holding out her cup for more wine. Gwendolyn grinned wide, poured it for her and offered an embrace.

"I am glad ye are home," she said quietly. "But ye need to rest for a day or two. Go, all is well here."

"Thank ye Gwen," Deborah replied, just as quietly. "I am glad ye are here working with us now. Ye are a treasure."

"Thank ye, My Lady!" Gwendolyn smiled, nodding at the door and handing her a cold carafe. Deborah said no more, simply taking the carafe with her on her way to her room, entering the familiar quarters and closing the door behind her. With a sigh, she walked to the small altar in the room and lit the candle there, offering words of gratitude that her mission was successful.

"I am glad to be home," she added at the end, bowing slightly as an act of reverence. That done she walked to where the bath waited and turned the tap, feeling the steam of the hot water hit her face almost at once.

"Husband?"

"Beloved," she heard at once, finding comfort in the familiar mental tones. "Are ye home?"

"I am, and drawing a bath. Gwendolyn has all in hand, so I am going to relax for the rest of the night. I arrived home to find it snowing, ye know."

"I know it. Alom's farm looks pretty dressed in such a Winter's coat," Erinn chuckled, watching the flakes flutter to the ground, whiskey in hand. "I shall be home within the week, I have found everything to my liking here at Alom's farm. My dear, ye should see it. His crops are lush and green, his farm well-tended and clean. Even his animal barns are sweet to the scent, and such is quite a feat, as I well know. He is an excellent addition to our people, and I am glad the Lady arranged for him to be here."

"I look forward to my husband's return home," Deborah replied shortly, and he could hear her weariness.

"My dear, I am tired too. Ye should indulge in a long hot bath, and eat a good meal. Rest well upon the morrow to let yerself recover a bit. I shall be home soon."

"Good night, Erinn."

"Good night, my dear. Sleep well."

His thoughts left her mind then and she came to herself, seeing that the bath was at the perfect level. Closing the tap, she added the bath salts she loved most, a mix of lavender and roses, then indulged in a long soak. Once she was clean, she drained the bath and dried herself, dressing in comfortable clothing and lighting the hearth against the growing chill in the room. It was not long before she was toasty warm, curled up on the couch with a sikar in hand after enjoying a pipe of Herb, a cup of red wine by her side. While she relaxed, she went over the pile of correspondence assembled for her by Ulric, finding that the exercise relieved anxiety about how much work had piled up in her absence. On the very bottom of the stack was an envelope, and inside that she found a rosette in the Natanleod family colors.

"I found this for ye, Madam, but I think it dates from Julia's reign," the note inside told her. "I suggest ye have new ones made to yer liking. These seem to be a bit outdated and heavy."

Deborah's eyebrows rose at the suggestion made by the War Duke, perhaps she should have new ones crafted, she thought with a faint smile. I shall have to consult with Ulric in the morning to find out what Guild is responsible for making these, if any, her thoughts continued as she took the rosette out of the box. Looking it over quickly, she saw it was broken, and that the back was stained with blood. No attempt to clean or repair it had been done, and Deborah wondered why. Putting her sikar aside for a moment, as well as her wine, she summoned up a bit of her abilities and took the thing into her hand. Almost at once, the image of Drake's father appeared in her mind, and she realized the rosette had decorated the front of his uniform at one time.

"Aye, 'tis true," she heard his curmudgeon's rasp answer her unspoken question. "I managed to earn it," he went on, a wry tone in his voice.

"My Lord, surely ye would have no difficulty in earning such a token?" Deborah asked, waving him to sit beside her, and offering him a pipe.

"Ye are such a kind woman, to give me the honorific," Julius laughed a bit, taking the pipe from her. "I did indeed earn it from Julia's hand, just bare weeks before my death. Secundus took it off my dead body and sent it to his mother like that, an unmistakable message that she was next. How he contrived to startle her horse so that she would fall off is still beyond me, since she was practically a centauress," he chuckled.

"Horses dislike snakes," a female voice answered his statement and Julia appeared. "All he had to do was have one of his slithering allies crawl across the road at just the right moment. The horse reared up, fell back and my leg was caught underneath. Secundus took care of the rest, as I was already fading from shock and the pain of a severely broken leg, not to mention a head injury. 'Twas just that simple."

Julius' face took on a look of great regret, his face tightened a bit and a sigh escaped him. "I should have slain him when he was young. I am the one responsible for all the strife and death."

"Ye are not!" Deborah defended. "Raad is responsible for it, as is Secundus with him. If not for them, the Nagas would have never had the hold on the Land they did. Ye were betrayed from within."

"Aye, which I should have been able to forestall," Julius sighed again, very heavily. "It weighs upon me a bit, that I could not stop it."

"Ye did the right thing, training Drake to take yer place," Deborah stated emphatically. "I loved Hadrian, but he alone could not have defeated Raad and Secundus. It took everyone who labored and fought to put down the Naga threat!"

"Including yourself," Julius pointed out. "If ye had not accepted the power offered ye, Veronica and Spurious would have eventually broken ye. 'Twas their intent all along, to bend ye to the Naga's will, but ye fought them at every turn, even without knowing ye were doing so."

"O, I knew," Deborah smiled, a strange half grin on her face that looked very feral to both of the spirits standing there. "Each time I faced an abuser, my thoughts were that they should receive what they had given, fully and completely according to the Lady's will."

Julius' face took on a look of consideration at her statement, it had not occurred to him that at such a young age, Deborah instinctively had understood how to invoke the Lady's aid.

"My Lord Julius," Deborah began haltingly, hardly knowing how to ask the next question. "This rosette is stained with yer blood, what is it ye wish done with it?"

"Whatever the Lady wills, my dear," Julius answered obliquely, implying it was her choice in the end. "Such a thing is a talisman of great power, and should be kept completely and utterly safe."

"Of course, unless I choose to unmake it," Deborah said aloud, musing over the idea. "I shall consult the Goddess in this, as I am not certain what course to follow. I must say that a great many choices do present themselves at being given such a thing to hold on to."

"Ye will keep it safe, knowing its origin," Julius declared sternly.

"Of course!" Deborah smiled broadly. "The thing is safer with me than with anyone else in the Land, is't so?"

"Indeed so, my dear, since ye are the High Lady," Julius bowed to her a bit, seeing her hair streaking with red highlights right in front of his eyes. "Ye may calm yerself, I am not challenging ye," he said quietly.

"Forgive me, My Lord," Deborah smiled. As he watched, her hair lost the scarlet highlights, her eyes faded from amber to hazel and her skin lost the alabaster appearance that so characterized her transformation. "I mean ye no harm."

"Of course not," he smiled benignly. "Ye are a good daughter of the House, and ye have done our family proud by yer deeds."

"Thank ye," Deborah replied, her voice reflecting a bit of astonishment at his praise, which was a rare thing. "How else may I serve?"

"If ye take that rosette to the Sewing Guild, they will likely have someone skilled enough to reproduce it," Julia put in, rising from her seat. "If ye can find no one, I have the pattern for it in the sewing room at the House."

"Thank ye Madam, I was hoping for that very thing," Deborah smiled. "Ye know how I love to create my own things, keeping in mind both the traditional and the need to progress."

"Which makes ye a great High Lady," Julia complimented. Deborah bowed her head in respect, and gratitude for the accolade.

"And what will ye do with that one?" Julius asked pointedly. "Ye are the High Lady, the thing is yer responsibility."

"I see," Deborah mused, tucking the thing back into its box. "If 'tis my responsibility, I shall attend to it."

"Ye usually do," Julius remarked wryly. "Ye have matured into a fine High Lady, as Drake insisted ye would. My son's intuition has always been something to listen to which is why I knew he, not Hadrian, would be High Lord."

"Hadrian was a good man."

"Aye, he was," Julius confirmed fondly. "But he is not Drake, despite being a fine Natanleod. Drake's abilities are truly extraordinary, as are his son's. Yer abilities, my dear, continue to astonish all of us."

Deborah's eyebrows rose at the revelation, and a half smile quirked at the corner of her mouth. "I am only doing what I have been tasked to do, what ye all have told me I am born to do," she remarked. "That the Goddess continues to bless me I find to be a remarkable thing."

"Good night, my dear," Julius wished her suddenly, rising quickly. Turning to offer a quick and respectful nod of his head, he offered his hand to Julia and they departed, leaving her alone with her thoughts. Deborah's weariness manifested then, she put the last of the sikar aside, finished the red wine in her cup then walked to the necessity to attend to her nightly ritual. It was not long before she was under the quilts, snuggled deeply into their comfort and warmth, drifting off to a restful sleep.

At Alom's house, Erinn woke early, sensing that Deborah was awake as well.

"Good morning beloved," he sent his thoughts to her.

"Good morning," he heard her weary reply. "When are ye coming home?"

Such a direct question piqued Erinn's attention at once. "What is amiss?"

"The slaughter has begun," she answered quietly. "I am up in my sewing room, but I can still hear it."

"My dear, meet me at the family house later today," Erinn chuckled under his breath, knowing how she felt about the process. "I am nearly done here, and I could use some time alone with ye."

"What a wonderful suggestion!" he heard her glad reply. "I shall be there to meet ye, the house will be warm and supper will be cooking."

"Beef?" Erinn requested.

"Steaks or a roast?" she answered.

"Yer choice, I enjoy both. All I want to do is just relax with ye, and enjoy the quiet."

"Very well, my lord," he heard her answer, laughter tinging her thoughts. "I shall await yer arrival."

Erinn felt a thrill of anticipation at the thought of being alone with her for any length of time, and he quickly packed his things, meaning to speed through the last of his tasks at Alom's farm. Looking outside through the window, Erinn could see that all of the wet snow from the day before was nearly melted. Good, he thought, I may proceed as planned. They were hiking up to the mountain plateaus where Alom had planted all of the caffe bushes he had brought with him. Throughout the entire visit,

Alom had alluded that Erinn would be most pleased with the progress he found there. Now Erinn found himself looking forward to seeing it quickly, so he could be with Deborah. Walking out with his bag in hand, he dropped it by the door, rousing Drake's attention as he sat there sipping hot caffe.

"Is yer tour ending today?" he asked.

"Aye," Erinn answered shortly, taking a seat. "Deborah is home and the slaughter has begun. Ye know how she feels about that."

"Aye, so I do. Ye are taking her to the family house, aye?"

"I made the suggestion, and she was in favor of going there," Erinn chuckled.

"Good, both of ye can use the time alone," Drake agreed. "Ye need not summon a detachment of Knights from the Barracks either, since I am already here. Ye will not even see me if ye wish not to," Drake told him seriously.

"All will depend upon my lady's need for privacy," Erinn replied forthrightly. "Come, I wish to get this tour finished. I am anxious to depart."

"I do not blame ye," Drake chuckled.

Alom was treated to a demonstration of how Erinn viewed acting with alacrity. He was marched unceremoniously, but politely, up the mountain path to the upper fields where the caffe beans were now being harvested in the cool misty morning. Alom, sensing Erinn's urgency, walked him quickly through the works, ending at the fermentation area, where the beans were separated from the husks. The young High Lord listened intently and patiently to Alom's explanation of how the process worked until they reached the very end of it, where the beans were laid out to dry before being bagged in burlap and stored.

"The process is more involved than I realized," Erinn smiled when Alom finished and called for the traditional drink, *xocoatl*. "However, ye seem to have it all working well. The caffe we drank this morning is from yer farm, aye?"

"Aye, My Lord," Alom nodded.

"The taste was subtly different, richer and bolder than usual," Erinn commented.

"My people prefer it that way," Alom told him. "As we enjoy the cacao dark and bitter."

"Ye have never tasted it the way my lady Deborah makes it," Erinn replied. "I prefer it that way, a bit sweeter and mixed with good fresh cream."

"I have not had the pleasure of tasting cacao prepared that way," Alom replied diplomatically. "I look forward to the experience."

"Come and visit us during the holidays this Winter," Erinn invited graciously. "Ye will have many opportunities to sample cacao prepared as I have described. Now, the date of my wedding anniversary approaches, my friend and I wish to join my lady as soon as I might. If we are finished with yer tour, and if ye have no further business to attend to here, allow me to provide a quick return to yer comfortable dwelling."

"We are finished here, My Lord," Alom told him.

"Prepare yerself," Erinn smiled, laying a hand on his shoulder. The man felt a long moment of intense cold before they emerged within the confines of his common room. "Are ye well?" he asked.

"Aye, My Lord," Alom smiled wanly, shivering a bit. "At least, I shall be."

"Good. I wish ye good day, Alom. I am serious about ye joining us at the House for the Winter Holidays, if ye can manage to break away from yer duties here."

"I shall give it my best effort, My Lord," Alom answered. "May the Lady watch over ye as ye travel."

"Thank ye my friend. If ye would call for our horses, we will be on our way," Erinn smiled.

It was a short time later when the two horses were led to the door of Alom's house, Erinn and Drake emerged, mounted, waved a final farewell and disappeared in a flash of bright light. When they reappeared a short time later in the courtyard of the family house in Dragon Valley, it was snowing hard. The two stashed their horses in the comfortable stable, assuring they had plenty of food, water and a thick layer of warm straw on the floor of each stall. Stepping out of the stable, they shut the door without locking it, wading through three feet of piled snow to get to the base of the veranda. Opening the door and entering, they found the house was warm and dry, the hearth blazing, the smell of roasting beef heavy in the air.

"Welcome," they heard Deborah say, and she appeared, carrying a cup for each of them. "Look at it, 'tis snowing as if 'twere full Winter out there!"

"So 'tis," Erinn chuckled, taking the mulled wine. "Thank ye, my dear, the hot drink is most welcome."

Drake said naught, simply walking to the barracks door and disappearing into where the accompanying guards would usually sleep. Deborah watched him, her brow furrowed a bit in confusion.

"What is he doing?" she asked Erinn.

"Giving us our privacy, I would imagine," Erinn laughed softly. "He knows full well 'tis our Anniversary."

"Surely, he does not mean to sleep in the guard quarters?" Deborah asked. "He has a perfectly good room upstairs, and he is welcome to come and share company with us, as always. Father, come out here!" she called and Drake appeared in a flash of light, already stripped down to his bare chest.

"What?" he demanded in a startled voice. "I was just about to bathe!"

"Ye are welcome to use yer usual room, Father," Deborah laughed, realizing that she had inadvertently "summoned" him. "I am sorry, I did not mean to be so urgent."

"I can sleep upstairs, like a guest?" he asked.

"Of course, ye are my father in law in this matter. I welcome yer company," she told him seriously. Drake glanced first at Erinn, then back at Deborah before answering.

"Well then, if ye are inviting me to stay," he began, sipping the delicious mulled wine. "I shall gladly accept!"

"Perhaps ye should go and finish yer bath?" Deborah suggested as he stood there bare chested, which showed off his nearly perfect physique. Deborah allowed herself to assess him professionally, and found nothing to criticize.

"I think I shall!" Drake chuckled. "Surely, someone with a kind heart will send another cup or two of this delicious drink to me while I am soaking?"

"We will see if we can find such a person currently in residence," Deborah laughed merrily. "Aren't ye cold standing there?"

"I rarely feel the cold's bite, or the suns heat overly much," Drake told her. "My sensitivity to temperature extremes seems to be much less than 'twas."

"Which would make it easier for ye to go places that exhibit such extremes," Deborah noted. "Ye have plenty of time to soak, supper will not be served for hours," she told him. Drake took the hint and after refilling his cup, he retreated into the steamy depths of the bath, leaving Deborah and Erinn to enjoy each other's company. As soon as Drake emerged, Erinn took his turn and soon he was clean, shaved, dressed and sitting once more in the common room, sipping the delicious mulled wine and now enjoying a sikar.

While they enjoyed the private conversation, far away in Ishmael's home, Artos sat on the floor, repairing his armor again.

"Ye are much too hard on yer equipment boyo," he heard the huge man's voice remark. "Still, today's work was very good. Ye are improving rapidly."

"Thank ye Master," Artos replied simply, concentrating on weaving the links back together with as much skill as he could muster. He now wished he had paid closer attention to Master Argyros' tutelage on the subject, he sighed regretfully.

"Ye are doing a fine job putting that back together," Ishmael finally noted.

"I am not as skilled as my father in such things," Artos answered, and Ishmael could hear his contrite tone. "I should have paid better attention in my youth, this might be going faster if I had."

"Now is not the time to reprove yerself," Ishmael told him. "Yer skills with weaponry are improving every day, yer strength is greater than ever before, and ye have learned to use some of yer magick to assist ye against an opponent. I have never seen anyone outside my own family learn the skills of the "Hashashin" so quickly. Ye will offer a true challenge to anyone ye meet. I can hardly wait to see Drake's face," he chuckled.

"Why?" Artos asked as he twisted the end of the wire around itself, then carefully snipped it, leaving no rough edge to wear against the leather.

"He has always claimed that I could not teach my skills to anyone here in the Land," Ishmael told him. "He does not think much of my teaching ability," he added with a laugh.

"Why not? Ye have done a fine job teaching me," Artos replied, pushing himself to his feet and picking up the mail shirt.

"Ye needed someone who would not put up with yer shit," Ishmael answered seriously. "Since I am not family, I was the perfect person to accomplish what no one else could."

Artos smiled wryly, remembering what extremes Ishmael had gone to while asserting his right to teach the young Natanleod. Some of the bruises were still healing, he went on with his thoughts, slipping on the mail shirt to test his repair work. All seemed to be in order, he noted as he stretched and moved, and when the repair proved to be sufficient to keep the mail all together, he slipped it off again and hung it carefully in the armoire. "Ye are right about that, Master," Artos replied quietly, having learned to keep his voice at a moderate volume. "I was certainly a blockhead."

"That ye were, boyo," Ishmael sighed heavily. "What say ye, shall we visit the hot lake?"

"I would enjoy that, Master, as long as we care for the animals first," Artos replied.

"Of course, go on and get started. I shall contact my local friends and enlist their aid for the next few days. I feel like I need several good long soaks."

"As do I, Master," Artos agreed.

It did not take long for Artos to run through the stable, assuring that each animal had plenty of water and food, as well as clean bedding for the night. When he returned to the house, there Ishmael stood surrounded by his friends, who always seemed to appear out of nowhere. Artos had never seen where they lived, nor a single domestic animal that did not bear Ishmael's mark. He had ceased wondering about it however, preferring to keep his mind on his studies.

"Go on and pack for three days, Artos," Ishmael rumbled as he walked past.

"Aye, Master," Artos nodded respectfully. Walking directly to his room, he grabbed his pack and turned to his clothespress, opening the bottom drawer first for trous and hose. Packing everything in layers according to the order he donned it, he finished with a thick sweater, knowing that Winter was approaching soon. Shouldering the bag, he walked back through the house to where Ishmael stood, and waited quietly.

"Thank ye again, my friends, for allowing me this time. I shall stand in for ye, when it comes time for yers." With silent nods, the people departed to what work awaited them, while Ishmael picked up his bag and put it over his shoulder. "Are ye ready boyo?"

"Aye, Master!" Artos answered with some excitement. He was truly looking forward to spending as much time in the hot water as possible, his body ached from the hard work of the last few months.

"Come then! I too, am anxious for the hot water," Ishmael chuckled. "If ye will provide the transportation?"

Artos nodded, collected his thoughts and concentrated on picturing the placid waters of the lake, reminding himself not to think about when to be there as much as how to be there. In a flash, they were on the shore, at the perfect place to erect their pavilion. Artos looked about, saw the sun was at the right place on the horizon, and breathed a sigh of relief. He had not inadvertently traveled in time, as he had before, only to be reproved by his grandfather for it.

In no time, the two men had their shelter up, their pallets laid out, and a fire crackling merrily. They decided to use the hot water separately, Ishmael going first as was his right as the Master. While he soaked, sipped cold ale and enjoyed both pipe and sikar, Artos quickly netted a few fish for their supper. After cleaning them and leaving the entrails away from the camp for the scavengers, he washed them clean of any remaining debris, then laid them out on a clean towel. Quickly, he sprinkled salt and pepper mixed with ground garlic and dill over them, then glanced about, hoping for a ripe lemon from the trees that peppered the area. Not a fruit could be seen, much to his dismay, and with a sigh he finished preparing them for the pan. Fish was so much better with lemon, he thought, wishing he had a jar of the fish spice mix from his mother's kitchen. Putting the thought aside, he picked up the bag of papas from their stores and quickly looked them over for bruises or other defects, then scrubbing them free of dirt before paring them into squares and putting them in a fry pan with bacon fat. He had just put the pan over the coolest part of the fire when he heard Ishmael approach the camp, singing in his rich bass timbre. The song was ribald and hilariously funny, and Artos could not help but grin at the appropriate moments as Ishmael's voice echoed up the trail.

"Is that supper I smell cooking, boyo?" he heard.

"Aye Master," he responded at once.

"It smells wonderful!" Ishmael complimented upon his appearance in the camp. "How long 'till the papas are done cooking?"

"I have just put them on, Master," Artos replied. "And they are on the coolest part of the cooking surface. They should be finished upon my return to camp."

"And what am I to do with the fish?"

"Naught, Master. I shall attend to that when I return," Artos told him. "Please, just sit and relax while I bathe quickly. I shall not be overlong."

"Good, I am hungry!" Ishmael chuckled. As soon as Artos disappeared out of camp, he pushed the papas completely off the fire, wanting to give Artos the longest soak possible. The lad had worked hard these last few months, and his body showed it, Ishmael thought with satisfaction. Just wait until Drake saw how much Artos' body resembled his own at the same age, the Arab man chuckled with great amusement. It was not long before the young man returned, the towel around his hips and his clean clothing now over his shoulder. Artos' chest had broadened considerably, his shoulders rounded with muscle, his stomach flat and rippled from hours with the blade and other weaponry. Even his muscles moved like cords under his skin, and he walked with grace and balance, like the great puma of the mountains. Ishmael could hardly keep the grin off his face when he imagined Drake's reaction at seeing his grandson again after so many months. Artos had found his own motivation, all Ishmael had done was show him how to accomplish what he wanted to do.

No one in the Land was expecting Artos to be able to do what he did now, and that would be the advantage, at least until everyone had seen the young Natanleod in the arena.

"What are ye smiling about?" Artos asked as he prepared to cook the fish.

"The look on yer grandfather's face when he sees ye," Ishmael laughed. "I am certain he is not expecting such results, not because ye are not capable, but because of yer stubbornness."

"I have tried to amend that," Artos defended himself a bit as Ishmael handed him a cup. "As ye say, Master, strength of mind and will are essential. I have tried to take that stubborn streak and make it an asset, time will tell if I have mastered myself though."

"At least ye are more humble," Ishmael congratulated.

"When a person is confronted by the fact that the person teaching him is vastly superior in every way as far as fighting and hunting skills go, it behooves one to pay attention to what that person is teaching."

Ishmael smiled wide, sat back and sipped his ale, watching Artos grill the fish to perfection before serving it between them. Afterwards, the young man simply heated water and washed the dishes without being asked, then excused himself to bed.

"Sleep well, Artos," Ishmael wished him as he passed into the tent.

"Thank ye, Master. Sleep well when ye do," Artos returned. It was long hours before Ishmael did sleep, his mind turning on his last meeting with Drake, where his Grant had been stripped from him. It still brought a slight tremor of fear to him, the memory of how Deborah's fiery aura had simply appeared around her. It had been as if a huge sun had appeared suddenly, his eyes had been dazzled a bit, and for a moment he thought he was seeing the Goddess Herself.

"Brrr," he finally roused from his reverie, shivering both from cold and from a bit of terror. "I should go get some sleep now, morning is not far away."

Retreating into the tent, he stretched out on his pallet to close his eyes, falling asleep nearly at once. There was no need for a guard here at the hot lake, he smiled as he drifted off. No one with any sense would come to this place, especially with the spiritual guardians the Lady had in place here. Even in the Land, the dead lingered sometimes for a long time. He knew that Drake's family was prone to such things, he had seen and spoken to many dead Natanleods over the years. This place was different, the spirits here were not at such peace due to the manner of their passing. It took a strong will and purpose to avoid their tests, and Artos was just learning the basic skills he needed to do so. Ishmael had no difficulty communing with the dead, being an assassin meant he was very familiar with death and was unafraid of it. Artos was still young, and inexperienced; Ishmael had no idea how he would react when he finally discovered that the "friends" that watched over his house were actually dead. They were all his family, gathered around him for a common purpose, to guard Ishmael and assist his further training. He found it a comfort to be surrounded by most of his family, after all they had been separated much too early by circumstances, he reasoned, letting himself go into slumber.

In the morning, Artos rose first and made his way to the hot lake for an early morning soak. He found several young women there already soaking and called out to alert them to his presence.

"Good morning, Sisters!" he called quietly to them, for he knew they were priestesses from the small local Temple nearby.

"Good morning!" he heard one of them call back. "Come and join us!"

"I shall go a bit further," Artos called back, not wanting to be surrounded by women at the moment. "I like the water a bit hotter than most people."

"I would imagine ye do, Artos Natanleod!" he heard her laughing reply. "My name is Anunit, I am a priestess of the Mother."

"Merry meet, Anunit," Artos called back, seeing a flash of red hair.

"Come and visit me at the Temple!" she offered with much humor.

"I might at that!" Artos called back, enjoying the sound of her laughter. He walked on, finally reaching the spot where the water steamed in the early morning sun, stripped and eased himself into the water, breathing a sigh of happiness.

He was enjoying his time here with Ishmael, he had discovered recently, as his thoughts began to wander. The Master's teaching was unlike anything he had ever experienced before, and the rough camaraderie that had sprung up between them felt like true friendship to him. The two of them had started out on a sour note, but now they worked together nearly seamlessly, any error being on Artos' part he recalled wryly. Rubbing his shoulder, still sore from lessons a few days past, he allowed himself to relax further into the water all the way up to his hairline. The heat embraced him like an extra warm quilt and he let himself relax a bit, much to the benefit of his muscles. As he lay there, he drifted off a bit, and so he did not detect the quiet approach of the young priestess Anunit. She thought to be of assistance to the young prince, seeing his tension behind their earlier conversation. She had a gift for such things, which is why she served at the Temple of Aphrodite.

Artos was blissfully drifting in a light meditative state when Anunit's hands touched his shoulders, and his reaction was immediate. She found herself pinned to the ground, him on top of her with his hands around her neck, squeezing lightly.

"What do ye want?" he demanded roughly.

"I simply came to be of service, young prince," she answered without fear. "If ye have no need of my service, then release me and I shall leave ye. Ye are very heavy, with all those muscles, ye know," she laughed a bit. Artos' eyes widened at her display of fearlessness.

"Ye are not afraid of me?"

"Why?" she asked. "Do ye mean me harm? I was doing no harm to ye, other than startling ye a bit, for which I truly apologize. I tried to make enough noise to alert ye."

"I was not paying attention," Artos replied, not getting off her just yet. "Ye are fortunate that I have been trained well, I might have killed ye for simply touching me. I do not usually enjoy being touched by anyone without my say so."

"I am well aware of how that feels, My Lord," she answered practically. "If ye would get off me now, ye are quite heavy. I am having difficulty breathing."

"O!" Artos exclaimed rolling off her and back into the water quickly. "I am sorry, my dear. I did not realize I was so heavy."

"To someone of my size ye are nearly a giant!" Anunit giggled a bit as she pushed off the ground, getting to her feet. "Do drop by the Temple while ye are here, won't ye?"

"I most certainly shall," Artos rumbled softly as he answered, for his passions had been roused a bit. It had been a long time since he had engaged in the Rite, he thought.

"Good, I look forward to it," she smiled, kissing his cheek before sprinting away. Artos momentarily imagined her as the Huntress Artemis, running through the woods with her deer and his attraction to her increased significantly. He was definitely looking forward to visiting the Temple soon, he thought as he eased back into the water and forced himself to relax again. Soon, he was floating on his back at peace, letting the hot water help his body relax and recuperate from months of difficult training. The sun was peeking over the tops of the cliffs when he finally felt relaxed enough to pull out of the water, laying in the clean sand beside the hot lake to dry off and take some sun. Once he was fully dry, he dressed in clean clothing and walked back to the camp, feeling content. A splash sounded beside him as he walked, he turned quickly, seeing the flash of a large fish emerge out of the cooler part of the lake, where the fresh water stream flowed in. Artos' eyes widened to see one of the biggest trout he had ever seen leap again out of the water, catching a large dragonfly for its morning meal. It did not take him long to scramble down to the stream's egress into the lake, and what he saw there helped him understand why the crocodiles were there. The river mouth was teeming with huge trout, he could see them clearly through the clear water and his mouth watered for a morning meal. Wading into the water, he positioned himself advantageously, waiting to tickle a fish out of the river. It did not take long for him to do so, and soon a huge fish lay there while he rinsed his hands free of entrails and blood, thanking the water spirits and the trout for the meal. Swinging it over his shoulder to carry it, he continued on his way to the camp, finding Ishmael just making caffe.

"Good morning Master!" he called out happily. "Look what I tickled out of the water this morning!"

"Good Goddess, where did ye find such a beast?" Ishmael asked at once, coming to take the fish from him. "He must be close to two stone!"

"I think so too. In any case, 'tis plenty for our first meal. I passed a group of Priestesses earlier, they invited us to the Temple."

"Did they?" Ishmael inquired with interest. "If the Priestesses have offered us an invitation, 'twould be rude not to accept it. We should take them something as an offering, since we have no silver. Perhaps some foraging?"

"An excellent idea, Master!" Artos agreed enthusiastically. Walking into the pavilion, he pulled his bag out and emptied it quickly, intending to use it to forage. When he emerged, he found Ishmael nearly finished with a freshly woven bag, made from the reeds from around the hot lake. "Please Master, share this wisdom with me?" Artos asked in a sincere tone, as he was truly interested. Ishmael said naught, simply pausing his work to show Artos the proper way to begin the project and watching to make certain the younger man understood the lesson. Once he saw that Artos' bag would suffice, despite it being the first time the young man had ever made one, he returned to finishing his own. When both men held large, green bags they struck out together, their sharp eyes scanning the ground for any edible. It did not take long for them to gather wild greens aplenty, as well as edible flowers in abundance, and so equipped, the two men returned to their camp. Stashing the foraging in the water to keep it fresh, they quickly cooked up the fish Artos had caught, eating as much as they could before using the rest as an offering for the scavengers. Once they were done eating, Artos quickly cleaned up their dishes while Ishmael partook of the hot water, returning with wet hair and a fresh shave, which for him was a simple trimming of stray hairs around his beard.

"Are ye ready boyo?" he asked. "The sun is nearly past noon."

"I am ready Master," Artos replied simply.

"Good then, let us be on our way before these edibles wilt any further!"

"Aye Master!" Artos agreed enthusiastically. Their walk to the Temple took only a short time and they were welcomed with smiles and warm embraces.

"Greetings, Master Ishmael and Prince Artos," the Mother of the Temple said when she came to receive them, taking the bags of produce with gratitude. "And thank ye for this, wild edibles are always welcome. Our garden is always productive, but the wild food has a different flavor."

"Ye are so right, Madam," Ishmael smiled broadly.

"If ye will take those to the kitchen, our cook will start supper right away. Ye will stay and eat with us tonight, aye? We have so few visitors, and company is always welcome."

"We would be honored, Madam," Ishmael replied elegantly.

And so they remained, the only guests in the Temple that night. They were royally entertained with songs and amusing stories, then an impromptu performance of Medusa's tale after supper. When the play was over, the Mother of the Temple extended the hospitality of the Lady to them, and both men gratefully accepted.

"Sister Anunit, would ye please see to the young prince?" the older woman called out to her most accomplished priestess. "Make sure he gets to his room and make him comfortable?"

"Of course, Mother," Anunit agreed easily, holding out her hand to Artos. "If ye would please come with me, Prince Artos, I shall take ye to yer room and get ye settled."

"Thank ye, Sister," he said, according to the practices of the Temple, putting his hand into hers. She walked him down a short, quiet hallway, opening a door at the end and indicating he should step inside. When he did, he found the room to be comfortable, decorated in rich primary colors, paintings that showed good skill hanging here and there.

"Ye have a good eye," Artos commented, walking over to one of them that appealed to him and looking it over critically. "I recognize this scene, I was just there this morning!"

"Aye, ye are right," Anunit laughed. "I do love that area of the hot lake, even though the crocodiles lurk there. The scenery is so lush and plentiful, I could hardly resist painting it this Spring. Are yer shoulders sore?"

"Aye, they are," Artos admitted, turning to her. "Do ye have massage skills?"

"Aye, and I enjoy the work. Ye should slip yer shirt off and lay down, so I might begin. Ye look so tense."

"Do I?" Artos asked in return, doing as she asked, then coming to stand in front of her.

"Ye look tense to me," Anunit smiled. "Are ye in the mood for some cold wine? Some Herb?"

"I would like both, they help me relax," Artos answered smoothly, finding the words coming to him easily for the first time in a long while.

"Good. I like a cup and a pipe before I work," Anunit agreed, bringing him the box with Herb and pipe. She was back quickly with a carafe of cool wine and two cups, sitting beside him comfortably. "Ye are in my room, My Lord," she began quietly. "But here, if ye wish, ye can be only Artos. It must be a trial, being addressed with a title constantly."

"I have never thought about it that way," Artos answered, taking the wine she offered him and saluted the Goddess with the first drop. Anunit looked on approvingly as she loaded the oak pipe with fragrant Temple Herb, handing it to him. "But I know I like it when I am with people who do not know I am a Natanleod."

Anunit nodded as he took his puff, handing it back to her, beginning the process of sharing many pipes that night. They finished that one, and one more as well as the first cup of wine before Anunit told him to strip and lay on her bed. She brought out massage oil, setting it on a warmer beside the bed and laying out several towels. Finally, she stripped down to a simple shift and indicated he should turn over on his stomach, so she could begin the massage. He complied, sighing with anticipation as she carefully drizzled the warm, fragrant oil over his back, then applied her hands to spreading it over his skin, letting her fingers run over his taut muscles.

"My goodness, ye have not had a massage for a long time," she commented, beginning her work, rhythmically working her hands over his shoulders. He could feel the slight probing of her fingers, and the release of the tension as she massaged the muscle bundle gently but firmly.

"O, that feels very fine," he murmured as she continued, pressing a bit harder until she discerned his comfort level. "Ye have strong hands."

"I have been giving massages for many years," she answered softly, keeping her voice quiet. "I was accepted into the Temple when I was nine, and my first Temple Mother quickly learned I had an aptitude for massage. Her back would pain her constantly, and I could not stand seeing her stoop over suddenly when the cramping would hit her. I just started running my hands over her back one day, just glad to hear her say how much better it made her feel. It was not long after that one of the older sisters showed me the technique I use now, and I have been doing it ever since."

"Having someone practiced in massage by his side would benefit a man who works with weaponry," Artos commented quietly, nearly asleep due to her ministrations.

"I am not the marrying kind, although if I found the right man, I would be completely true to him," Anunit told him honestly. He was not surprised, seeing that she was Temple trained, to hear her say such a thing. "If love does not keep a couple together, then 'tis not true love."

"I agree," Artos answered softly.

"Ye should just let yerself fall asleep, Artos Natanleod," Anunit told him. Ye are doing yerself no good by fighting it. Would ye like me to stay with ye when I finish yer massage?"

"I would be grateful not to sleep alone," Artos answered honestly.

"Good, I was not looking forward to sleeping in the common room," she laughed softly. He drifted off then and she spent the next hour carefully kneading his back, relaxing every tight muscle she could feel. Once she was done, she quickly wiped off the excess oil from his back and her hands, then attended to her nightly ritual before snuggling into bed beside him. He was warm to sleep next to, she noted, warmer than most men as he reached out for her, drawing her close to him. The warmth felt very good, helping her to fall asleep quickly, and they rested together throughout that night, waking early the next morning. Ishmael waited in the common room impatiently for Artos to appear, glad to see him when he did.

"How are yer shoulders?" he asked.

"Much better Master," Artos answered with a smile. Ishmael's eyes glanced back and forth between the young people in front of him, glad they had found comfort the night before. "I am ready to return to work."

"As am I," Ishmael nodded. "Come then, let us pack our shelter and depart. Thank ye Ladies, for yer hospitality. As always, we are blessed by yer service."

"And we were blessed with yer company in return," the Mother of the Temple answered, completing the ritual. "May the Lady grant ye peace of mind and spirit, 'till ye return to us."

"I pray that day is very soon, Madam," Ishmael answered, bowing low.

"We do also," the handsome woman smiled wide. "All the edibles you brought were most welcome to all of us."

"We would be happy to repeat the offering the next time we come to use the hot lake," Ishmael offered at once.

"Ye are too kind, and we would be so pleased and honored to accept such an offering. Silver is not much use out here," she laughed merrily.

"Done then," Ishmael nodded. "And I suppose ye could use eggs and cheese as well?"

"Such things are always welcome in a Temple, Master Ishmael," the woman answered.

"I shall remember that," Ishmael answered in an intense tone, bowing low once more. Artos did as well, saying naught to Anunit, having done so in his own way earlier.

"Farewell, Mother Elise," the young prince said after he straightened. "I enjoyed my rest last night. Sister Anunit is a skilled masseuse."

"So she is," the Mother smiled wide. "I am glad her skills were helpful to ye."

"They were, I feel much better this morning, and ready to resume my training!" Artos replied with a laugh.

"Very good then, it seems our Temple has been of good service then. Please return soon, yer company is very welcome. May the Lady be with ye both as ye travel."

"And with all of ye, as ye labor in Her service," Artos rejoined. The two men reluctantly departed, headed back for their camp, and when they turned the corner they were confronted by a sight. A huge crocodile was tearing their pavilion to shreds, and Artos could hardly believe the size of the beast.

"How do ye kill something like that, Master?" he asked in wonder, for the crocodile measured three times the height of a normal man of the Land, and had to weigh over a hundred fifty stone.

"With a very sharp blade, boyo. Stand back, I have slain one of these beasts before, without suffering a major injury. Do not let it get away, if it should escape my grasp. The boots one can make from that leather are nearly as good as Naga hide!"

"Aye Master!" Artos agreed, although at the moment he had no idea how he would manage to stop such a huge beast. As he watched however, the frailties of the crocodile became clear. It was slow on land, despite being very agile and swift in the water. It was already angered to the point of violence, which Artos knew Ishmael would use to his best advantage. Indeed, the huge Arab man was now circling the beast, looking for his best opportunity before being seen. He moved slowly, trying to stay out of the beast's line of sight, until finally the crocodile saw him and turned to face him, hissing a challenge.

"Go!" Ishmael ordered firmly, pointing back to the path that led to the lake. "If ye go now, ye will live another day!" The crocodile stopped hissing suddenly, and dropped into what looked like a hunting crouch to Artos. The young man felt a sense of alarm, at least until Ishmael sighed and pulled his belt knife. "Very well, if ye want it this way, 'tis yer choice. Come at me, and let us finish this!"

The huge crocodile lunged at Ishmael suddenly, if it had been in the water, the Hero would have been in considerable danger. As it was, the beast's rage added to his attack speed as Ishmael stepped aside from its mad rush. With a hunter's cry, he leapt upon the crocodile's back, brandishing the sharp blade and leaning over its neck, trying for a jugular slice. The crocodile sensed its danger and fought back, simply crouching and rolling back and forth violently, trying to dislodge the huge Arab man, but Ishmael held on tightly, waiting for his opportunity. Artos watched intently, seeing that Ishmael was more than capable of dealing with the beast, and the prospect of watching him in battle brought a grin to his face. The struggle continued as the crocodile finally gained its legs again and headed for the water as quickly as it could, considering that Ishmael was aboard and weighing it down. Once in the water, the crocodile was in its element and the struggle took on a more violent and urgent tenor. The two of them disappeared under the surface of the water, and Artos sprinted to the lake's edge in case he might be needed. He quickly saw that Ishmael was more than capable of dealing with the beast, the man clung to the crocodile's back with strong legs and a sturdy forearm, the other hand holding the ready blade. As Artos watched, the crocodile showed signs of tiring and then Ishmael, who was holding his breath underwater, took his opportunity. His mighty arm pulled back the head of the beast, exposing the throat fully. A quick stroke with the sharpened blade let loose a cloud of crimson, the crocodile thrashed a bit, its eyes rolled back, then turned on its back, floating to the surface completely dead.

"Master! Are ye well?" Artos called out, wading into the water to help haul the dead beast onto the shore.

"Ye watch yerself, boyo!" Ishmael called back, swimming to join him. "The other crocodiles will come quickly, drawn by the scent of blood!"

Artos smiled a bit, then concentrated his thoughts on the body floating in the water, snapping his fingers suddenly. The beast disappeared from its position, reappearing on the shore in the shade of some trees, much to Ishmael's delight.

"Now we have a proper tithe to offer the priestesses of the Temple next time we visit!" he called out, wading out of the water. "I noted that all of them need new footwear, and Winter approaches. Boots are always welcome in cold weather, aye?"

"Aye, especially if they are lined with rabbit fur," Artos smiled, thinking of Anunit's sturdy feet warm and dry within them.

"Ye will need to snare more than a few to line all of them with such fur," Ishmael pointed out.

"Then 'tis good I enjoy grilled rabbit for supper," Artos returned, a small smile on his face.

Chapter 12

"What is amiss with ye?" Ishmael asked sharply as Artos' thoughts wandered. "Are yer thoughts clouded by a priestess?"

"Nay," Artos answered. "However, I think I understand yer friendship with Madam Antonina now. She is someone ye can simply talk to, aye?"

"Aye," Ishmael answered shortly. Like most men in the Land, he disliked discussing private matters, and Artos was treading on dangerous ground.

"Anunit is like that," Artos agreed, not elaborating further. Ishmael filed the name away for future reference as he turned to look at their shelter, now in ruins.

"I suppose we should return to the house," he sighed with disappointment. "I do not fancy just sleeping out."

"We could return to the Temple," Artos suggested at length. "Or, I could simply repair the thing," he went on, turning to the rent shreds of the pavilion and summoning his energies. In his mind, he summoned up the vision of seeing the tent being rapidly sewn back together, leaving no seams. When the picture was clear, he snapped his fingers and the tent returned to its former condition. Another snap of his fingers and the thing was pitched and ready for occupation, the sleeping pallets inside rearranged with sheets, blankets and quilts. Ishmael watched in fascination, and a wistful sigh escaped him, much to Artos' surprise.

"What is amiss Master?"

"It has always been my fondest wish to be able to do what ye do so easily," Ishmael confessed quietly. "However, such abilities are usually kept from me 'till the Goddess has need of my service and summons me."

"Master, having such abilities is not the answer to all of life's challenges," Artos replied. "However, 'tis a blessing to be used in the service of the Goddess and Her people, and I am grateful for the gift."

Ishmael's eyebrows rose high to hear Artos speak so, it was very mature considering his age.

"Ye sound like yer grandfather," he remarked.

"Then perhaps I have learned something after all?" the younger man chuckled, pulling his own belt knife. "We should start skinning that crocodile. Is the meat any good?"

"If ye treat it right, any meat is good," Ishmael chuckled. "Come then. I intend to take that hide off in one whole piece. 'Tis a difficult thing to master, and I can use yer help a great deal."

The two worked for several hours to remove the entire skin of the crocodile, including the skin around the legs, which Ishmael claimed was some of the softest and finest for gloves or slippers. He then spent his efforts removing the claws from the feet and the teeth out of the maw of the beast, laughing as he did so. Such things were precious to someone like Ishmael, just for their hardness and natural sharpness.

"What will ye use the claws for?"

"Boyo, these are some of the toughest material out there. Ye will see that it makes fine weaponry. The teeth are good ivory, I have made jewelry with it, but it makes wonderful arrowheads. They stay sharp once they are shaped and mounted, and do not break easily. Never waste the gifts a carcass can provide boyo. Even if it is rotting, take a moment to consider what ye can harvest from it. I have sustained myself on animals I have found after a predator has fed, and I have fought off other scavengers to protect my find."

"Anything to survive?" Artos asked.

"If 'tis necessary for ye to live, aye," Ishmael answered definitively, using his own life experience to do so. They spread out the skin to scrape any remaining fat or foreign matter from the inside, then rinsed it in the fresh water, laying it out to dry in the shade. Afterwards, they lit a huge fire using the fragrant cedar lying about on the ground. While it burnt down to hot coals, they collected green branches, stripping them of their bark and sharpening the ends in preparation for their use. Also, they began to cut the crocodile's flesh into evenly sized chunks, putting them in a large bowl with salt, pepper and ground chili powder. Finally, when their fire was at just the right height and had a thick bed of coals, they speared the flesh onto the green cedar branches and set them out around the fire's perimeter. Some were set to cook quickly, but most were set at a height where they would simply smoke and preserve, for wasting such a large amount of meat would surely be a sin. Finally, when they had taken all the meat they could easily remove, Artos sent the rest of the carcass out of the camp with the snap of his fingers. Walking to where it appeared, Artos knelt beside it, and spoke a few reverent words.

"Thank ye brother Crocodile, for the meat ye have provided. Rest now and await yer return to the Land."

Ishmael listened to the young man's whispered phrases, nodding his approval with the act of piety. Leaving the carcass for the scavengers, they returned to tend their fire, sipping ale as they did so until the need for sleep drove Artos to his pallet within the pavilion.

"Wake me in three hours, if ye would please Master?" he asked. "Ye should have a chance to sleep too, especially after yer exertions today."

"Very well, Artos," Ishmael agreed, a smile of pride teasing the corners of his mouth. Artos appeared at the appointed time without being woken, further pleasing Ishmael's sense of pride.

"Thank ye boyo," Ishmael nodded to him as he assumed the guardian stance. "I was getting sleepy. I can tell ye, that smoked crocodile flesh is good eating. Cedar makes for good smoke."

"I shall try some," Artos nodded, feeling his stomach grumble with hunger. Ishmael trudged into the pavilion, dropping the flap closed behind him and soon the candle within winked out. Artos strode to the smoking fire, added a few pieces of dry cedar to it to keep it going before choosing a skewer and testing it for doneness. It appeared to be fully cooked to him and so he nibbled a bit, feeling the bite of the chilies against his tongue followed by the mild flesh of the crocodile. It was a pleasing combination and he quickly finished that skewer, taking another with him as he toured the perimeter of the camp. The night was quiet, the sounds of the area muted, the night sky brilliant with stars and lit by the quarter moon. He remembered why he enjoyed his nighttime observations of the heavens, and he longed to return to the study soon. Not letting himself get distracted, Artos continued on his way until he arrived back in front of the pavilion and assumed his station once more. He continued in this manner, touring the camp every so often and snagging a skewer off the fire as he did so until morning broke. Ishmael emerged from the tent then, yawning and stretching, a wan smile on his face.

"Ready for caffe?" he asked.

"Aye, Master."

"I shall attend to it. How is the meat?"

"I would not have thought that crocodile, which is a meat eater and scavenger, would taste this good," Artos answered honestly. "I enjoy the spice treatment ye have put on it too, the chilies seem to complement the meat very well. I shall remember this combination."

"Crocodile is a good meal, if ye can get past the teeth," Ishmael chuckled. "We will let that meat continue to smoke and dry a bit before we pack it up. The drier we allow it to be, the longer 'twill hold. I noted that the Temple's larder was a bit bare, boyo. Since they do not indulge in meat, we must choose other means. May I impose upon ye to return to the house and bring back some eggs and cheese for the Priestesses?"

"I would be glad to be of service," Artos smiled. "Should I bring aught else?"

"Ye've seen how they live, bring what ye think might help break up their dull lives," Ishmael said. "Why they choose to serve all the way out here is beyond me, but I am glad for their presence."

"As am I," Artos smiled at the thought of seeing Anunit again. "I shall return apace," he told Ishmael as he stood and prepared himself.

"Are ye going now? Before caffe?"

"I shall return soon, and hopefully, ye will still have caffe for me," Artos replied with a grin, disappearing from his sight suddenly. Ishmael smiled wide, Artos was clearly interested in the young, red-haired priestess named Anunit. A good choice, Ishmael thought to himself as he ground caffe and heated water, waiting for his trainee to return. The young woman seemed practical, and her laugh was clear and merry, Ishmael thought she might make anyone a good partner. When the caffe finished brewing, he poured his cup full, amended it to his preference and sat to wait in the morning sun outside of his door. He did not have to wait long, indeed he was just finishing on his own cup of the hot beverage when Artos returned, bearing a large basket filled with items from Ishmael's larder. The older man inspected the basket quickly as Artos served himself caffe, finding that Artos had chosen his offering well, for there were several balls of cheese as well as three parcels, each holding two dozen of large brown eggs. Ishmael saw dried herbs, a jar of dried, ground garlic, one of black pepper and one of pink salt. The entire thing was topped by a large package of roasted caffe beans, and Ishmael frowned a bit when he saw the bundle of sikars included.

"I reckoned that some of the sisters might enjoy a smoke," Artos explained. "As ye said, they live a dull life out here. I shall replace them at my earliest opportunity."

"Very well, I would not share them with anyone other than the Priestesses," Ishmael growled a bit. "Ye have done better than I would have, and I commend ye for it."

Artos bowed his head humbly and replaced the cover on the basket, tying it in place with the cord he had brought. As soon as they had finished their beverage and washed up, the two men took the basket between them and returned to the small Temple. They found the women outside working in their small garden, harvesting the last of their vegetables for winter storage.

"Sisters!" Ishmael called out in a happy tone, getting their attention at once. "We have brought a few things for yer pantry, would ye allow me to cook supper for ye?"

"We would be honored!" the Mother Elise replied, happy for the change of cuisine his cooking offered. "We should cool down some white wine in preparation for this meal, as I recall, Master Ishmael enjoys preparing spicy foods!"

Artos did not see Anunit for a long time, and when she appeared, she seemed surprised to see him.

"Why have ye returned so soon?" she asked, taking a cup of cold wine from him.

"We had gifts to offer, and wished to share supper again," Artos replied truthfully. "I am glad to see ye again, Anunit."

"Do not mistake my reaction," the young woman answered with a faint smile. "I am very glad to see ye again as well. I enjoyed our conversation last night, very much."

"As did I," he returned, offering her a puff of his sikar. With a look of curiosity, she accepted it, looking to him for instruction on how to enjoy it. Artos was more than happy to provide that for her, and soon they were passing the tabac back and forth, truly enjoying the experience of sharing it. They shared the communal supper that night, talking matters of the spirit among them until late in the night. It was very late indeed when Artos noted that Ishmael was not among them. He took the opportunity to speak to Anunit.

"May I join ye tonight?" he implored, extending his hand to her, open palm. "If we only talk together, it matters little. I only know I wish yer company, in whatever way ye would share it."

"Yer words are very eloquent, Artos Natanleod," she answered after a moment's consideration. "I would gladly share conversation with ye tonight, and if 'tis all we share besides more wine, sikars and Herb, I would be grateful."

Together, they walked down the short hallway to her quarters, entering through the door and locking it behind them. After providing cups of wine from her stores, Artos shared his stash of Herb with her before lighting a sikar for them to share. After a short time, she spoke her thoughts aloud. "My time of service here at this Temple approaches its end, and I am considering a myriad of other places in which to serve."

"Would ye consider the Temple of Aphrodite outside of the Capitol?"

"Nay, 'tis much too big for my tastes. I would be required to do much more than simply provide company, and I am not certain I wish to follow that path."

"Have ye heard of Madam Antonina's house?" Artos asked, unable to help himself. Her grace and beauty impressed him, since she did not overly adorn herself. The perfume she used was subtle as well, and he liked being with her. "Her house in the Capitol is the best in all the Land, and she has many women who do not share their beds with those who visit."

"And why would ye offer such a thing?"

"Ye wish to be of service in yer chosen role, and I wish to embrace service in my chosen role," Artos answered honestly. "I think we would benefit by approaching this together, instead of separately. My aim is to win command of the Black Dragons, and I shall need a lady by my side if I manage to do so."

"Lady of the Knight Commander?" she tested it with a grin, handing him a pipe. "I must consider this offer carefully, aye?"

"Aye, if ye accept, ye must win my Mother's approval. She is a hard taskmistress, in every way. However, should ye win her love, she will treat ye as a daughter of the House."

"Daughter of the House?" Anunit asked.

"Aye, 'tis how we talk about our wives in our family. Ye need not take vows with me, I am content with a simple handfasting in the field. Ye content me, and I have not felt this way before about a woman. I have felt the impact of 'The Bolt.' 'Tis not something I think I enjoyed, both times it happened. I feel affection and warmth for ye, and I believe that such feelings will only intensify as time progresses. What say ye, will ye think on it?"

"I shall, most certainly, young Prince," she answered carefully. "Ye have offered a great deal, but I would only wish for yer affection, respect and love. Yer title means naught."

"Ye would be a rare woman to think that way," Artos commented, offering the pipe again. "Which is why I seek yer company."

"We will talk more of all such matters," Anunit smiled, rising from her seat on the sofa and walking into her room. She was only gone a short time, but when she returned, she was much more comfortably attired. "For now, Artos Natanleod, I only wish to share company and talk. Whatever happens when the candles go out is with the Goddess, as it should be."

"Ye are right about that, my lady," he responded, offering his hand to her. She took it, and he turned it so the palm was up, pressing a soft kiss to the center as he had seen his father do so many times. Her reaction was immediate, a slow smile spread over her face as she sat beside him.

"What was that?" she asked, loading the pipe once more.

"My energies touching yers at just the right spot," he summarized instinctively. "We do suit each other, it seems."

"So it seems, my lord," she answered, handing the pipe to him. He produced a fingertip flame, watching her eyes go wide in surprise at the manifestation of his abilities. It gave him a sense of warm satisfaction to be of service to her, and he had an epiphany suddenly.

"I think I understand my parents at last!" he gasped. "I was a bit jealous at their need to be alone together, but now, all I wish is to be alone with ye! I have been such a terrible son at times, but I intend to make it right!"

Anunit smiled, put her arm around his shoulders and drew him in for a passionate kiss. "If ye wish to make what is wrong into right, I would gladly stand with ye."

Several days later, Master and Chela worked in Ishmael's arena, and the elder man noted he was having difficulty keeping up with the younger man. It struck him as odd at first, to see Artos working slightly faster than he could, until he realized the young man had finally integrated more of his magickal skills into his martial ones. He changed tactics then, adopting more of his "Hashashin" techniques, finding that Artos responded in kind without missing a beat. Ishmael continued to increase the pace, working faster and faster until he reached what he liked to think of as a "whirlwind phase," finding that Artos now matched him nearly perfectly. Stepping out of the routine, he took a moment to regain his breath, while Artos continued on, finishing his workout elegantly. When he ceased, Ishmael noted his breathing was controlled and composed, he was not panting or laboring for breath at all. Ishmael's mouth curved into a huge smile of satisfaction, Drake was in for an immense surprise. Indeed, everyone at the High Lord's house was in for the same shock, he reckoned as Artos took up a towel to wipe his hands, then reached for his cup of cold water, draining it in a few sips. After he regained a slower pace of breathing, he wiped his hands and brow again, then tossed the towel into the convenient hamper.

"Master, may I ask a question?"

"Of course," Ishmael rumbled, drying his hands and face after dashing cool water on himself to rinse of the sheen of sweat.

"Is everyone ye call friend hereabouts dead, or are some of them actually living?"

Ishmael grinned wryly, he had wondered when the young man would notice the unusual nature of his neighbors. "If they were in the world outside the Land, aye, they would be dead and wandering. The Lady has granted me a bit of a boon in bringing them here and allowing us to be a family once more."

"They are yer family?"

"Aye, all of them," Ishmael confirmed seriously.

"How is that possible?"

"With the Lady, young Prince, all is possible," Ishmael intoned in a sage tone. "I do not understand it myself, all I know is when I came here and found this place I was alone. As time passed, people began to appear, as if they had been hiding in the rocks, and it took me weeks to recognize them. Imagine my shock at seeing my father and mother again, as well as all of my brothers, sisters and cousins! As I said, I consider it quite a boon to have them about me to counsel and advise me."

Artos stood silently thinking as Ishmael spoke, and realized that the presence of the man's dead relatives was not so strange. After all, his own dead relatives had been counseling him most of his life, he chuckled to himself.

"To have one's dead family return to share wisdom with one is a blessing," he finally said. "I have my own experience with such things, and only now do I realize how fortunate I am. Forgive my question, Master."

"Artos, 'tis naught to forgive," Ishmael chuckled. "I would be shocked if ye did not at least ask about it. Now that ye know, think naught of it. Ye might even find one or two of them offering ye advice on yer form."

"Such advice would be welcome, Master," Artos replied humbly.

As time passed, Artos returned many times to the small Temple to speak with Anunit, and to have her work on his sore shoulders. It was no surprise to Ishmael to find her working in his kitchen one morning, dressed casually enough to alert him she had spent the entire night. She was not bothered by the presence of the others either. Being Temple trained, she simply accepted the situation as it was, asking questions occasionally to increase her understanding of who they were and why they were there. Artos was certainly happier to have her with him, Ishmael noted a few weeks after she arrived. His workouts became even better, he worked harder and experimented more, achieving more and more proficiency as they continued their training. When the envelope arrived from the High Lord's house, containing the invitation to attend the Yule celebration, it was Anunit who suggested accepting it.

"They are yer parents, and the rulers of the Land. 'Twould be simply rude to ignore it, and ye know it well, Artos Natanleod. No matter what dispute ye have with them, Yule is not the right occasion to hold such a grudge. We should go."

Artos' face tightened a bit, for he knew that if he went, there would be a challenge from his Father to face. His mind quickly turned over the suggestion, and he was surprised to find out he was anticipating the contest entirely.

"Ye are right, we should go," he finally said quietly. "I and my father have business to attend. He admires alacrity, as do I."

"Ye have finally gained perspective!" Ishmael declared with pride. "It matters not what challenge ye face with him, he is yer father and ye do owe him. Ye have been trained well, and yer father is not seeking yer life after all. What have ye to fear?"

"Precisely," Artos answered, a strange look on his face. "Besides, there are not many rabbits within the walls of yer valley, Master."

Anunit smiled at his statement, for she was wearing a pair of Ishmael's boots, lined with soft rabbit fur. They were very comfortable and warm, she noted as she wriggled her toes into the luxury. After supper, she retired, leaving Artos and Ishmael to discuss the coming trip.

The Autumn continued to slowly chill the Land, readying it for the Winter's cold to come. Erinn and Deborah returned to the house after their anniversary celebration, quickly attending to any backlog of work needing their personal attention. Erinn spent every morning with Arthfael in the arena, helping to ready him for the coming trials to win command of the Black Dragons, with Brianna looking on. Like most in the Land, the young Amazon was well aware of Erinn's reputation for skill and grace with a blade, but seeing it personally truly brought it home to her. Arthfael's body was laced with small cuts each morning, testimony to how hard he worked, and how hard he was pressing his attack. Erinn looked him over each time, concerned he had not pulled his stroke back enough, and sighing with relief each time he saw that the wounds were merely scratches. Even Brianna took her turn with weaponry against Erinn, for the High Lord wished to assess her skills and abilities. Her talent was undeniable, and in many ways, Erinn noted, she was superior to Arthfael in her ability to attack and pursue. He decided they needed to work together more often, and assigned Ulric the task of finding them a consistent time to do so. Ulric had no difficulty establishing a regular time for the couple, cautioning the both of them against wasting the opportunity.

"The High Lord has arranged for this time of training. I suggest ye use it appropriately," he told them.

"We will not waste it, My Lord War Duke," Brianna assured him with an Amazon resolution.

"Good then, I shall leave ye to it. The time and space in the arena is yers, 'till the High Lord says otherwise."

"Thank ye, My Lord," Arthfael smiled, offering the grip. Brianna also extended her forearm, and Ulric took them both in turn before leaving them to return to his other myriad duties. From that day forward, the two met faithfully each morning at the appointed time, using it to develop their combat skills while working side by side. Their love deepened as well, and soon, Brianna moved her things quietly out of the barracks and up into the main house at Deborah's insistence. Brianna was given a quiet room in the sewing room wing, a place where the sun would provide light and warmth without being overbearing. Arthfael's mother gave the young Amazon free rein in how her quarters were decorated, asking only that some of the more earthy humor items be put out of sight. Amazons enjoyed fun and teasing, and some of the birthday gifts that they handed out reflected that. Usually, they were simple carved items of wood or stone, stylized and hilariously elaborate. Brianna had a large collection of such gifts, being one of the more popular women in the ranks of Dames now that she had overcome most of her negative traits. When she unpacked them, Deborah counted their number and shook her head.

"My dear, I am sorry, but ye cannot display things such as this so prominently in the family quarters," she instructed gently. "I know they are tokens of yer sisters' affections and displays of great humor, but I shall not ask the staff to dust and clean such things. If ye would put them away please, 'till ye have yer shared quarters with Arthfael. Ye and he can decide how best to display them."

"Aye, Madam," Brianna nodded, turning back to the shelf and repacking the small sculptures into their box. "I am sorry, I did not think about it."

"The family quarters are more public than the Barracks," Deborah smiled warmly. "Thank ye, daughter, for yer understanding and cooperation in this matter."

"I wish to be a good Daughter to ye, Madam," Brianna answered earnestly.

"Ye will be a fine daughter," Deborah smiled, embracing her warmly. "Feel free to choose from the stores downstairs for yer furnishings, but I feel as if the Cherry wood set would suit this room best. Come, I shall show it to ye," she invited, holding out a hand. Brianna had become accustomed to being magickally transported by this time and took Deborah's proffered hand without hesitation. In an instant, they were outside the locked door to the furniture storage. Deborah produced the key for it and they entered, leaving the door wide open, and propping it so. It did not take Deborah long to locate the set of furniture she wanted, and as soon as she took the first dust cover off, Brianna saw that the High Lady had been correct in her estimations. The furniture was rippled with dark and light pink streaks amidst the creamy white of the wood, and the crafter had brought out all of the colors as he had shaped and smoothed it. The set included two large clothespresses, a wide armoire, two chairs and a table, as well as two occasional tables and a bed. The bed itself was a four poster, not big enough for a master bedroom, but certainly large enough for a noble daughter's room. Deborah's experienced eye could see it would hold two if necessary, and since Brianna and Arthfael were courting, such things must be taken into account. She had no idea if the two had shared the Rite, and it mattered naught to her. It only mattered that she could see the love and care between them, and how Arthfael looked at his lady, which is how he was referring to her more and more these days.

"I love this furniture!" she smiled, turning to Deborah with excitement. "I have never had anything so beautiful before!"

"I am glad ye like it too!" Deborah smiled. "I shall get some Knights in here to help us bring it upstairs. Wait here," she instructed, disappearing suddenly. Brianna did, standing there for long moments looking about the room, wondering what was under all those covers and in the locked cabinets. Just as she began to fret a bit, Deborah returned with several huge men, all wearing the insignia of the Black Dragons.

"Thank ye again gentlemen, for providing the muscles," she smiled. The men pair off in to teams, arranging themselves around the furniture and waiting for her to nod to them. Once she did, they picked up the heavy piece and disappeared at the snap of her fingers, reappearing upstairs in Brianna's new room. She and Brianna went with the last piece of furniture, the armoire, and once they were upstairs again the Knights helped them arrange the furniture around the room. Brianna was consulted as to placements, the first time she had ever been asked about such things, and she turned to Deborah the first few times, looking for advice.

"I would put the bed over there, where the sun's light is the least," Deborah pointed with a small smile. "I shall have some heavy screens brought up too, so ye can create a separate space around yer bed."

"Thank ye, My Lady," Brianna nodded. "Where would ye put the armoire?"

Between the two women, the furniture was quickly placed around the room in a pleasing arrangement, and then thanks were offered to the men who had helped them. Deborah passed out largesse as Brianna watched, wondering where all of it had actually come from. She had noticed that the High Lord's house in the Capitol city appeared much smaller when observed from outside, and that had roused her curiosity a bit. Now that the Knights were gone, she ventured with her question, hoping that Deborah would not be offended.

"My Lady, why does the House appear so much smaller when viewed from outside?"

Deborah smiled a bit, glad that the subject had finally come up. "Ye must realize that our family is very magickal, my dear. The High Lord's house is as big as it needs to be, when it needs to be. What ye see on the outside is what the Lady wishes to be seen, a simple and circumspect place. Inside however, we can create the house we wish to, and when we have guests we have plenty of room no matter how large the crowd is."

"The house in the family valley, is it the same?"

"Not quite, since 'tis meant as a family only retreat," Deborah answered, glad for her curious nature. "However, if our family grows large enough, I would imagine the house will grow to accommodate that."

"Amazing," Brianna said with awe.

"Indeed, I felt the same way when Millicent explained it to me," Deborah chuckled. "Come, we should go back downstairs and lock that storage room, then I am ready for a cup of cold wine."

"I would like one too," Brianna put in and Deborah embraced her with affection.

"Of course, ye are always welcome to join me, daughter."

The two women disappeared from the room, reappearing just long enough to lock the storage room, making certain no one was inside it first. Afterwards, they walked back up to the kitchen, finding Gwendolyn busy with supper preparations.

"All moved in then, young lady?" she asked Brianna in a warm tone.

"Aye, thank ye Madam," Brianna answered, just as affectionately. Gwendolyn's presence was a comforting one, they knew each other from the Amazon fortress and any hard feelings between them had long ago been forgotten. She heartily approved of Brianna's presence in the House, and looked upon her as part of the Natanleod family already. "What is for supper tonight? May I be of assistance?" she asked.

"Yer offer is welcome, Brianna," Gwendolyn smiled. "As it happens, I have need of someone to take a note down to Klietos in the Barracks Kitchen. Would ye agree to do so?"

"Of course!" Brianna smiled.

"Thank ye, young lady," Gwendolyn answered, nodding in approval. She was always so willing to help, the older woman thought as she wrote out her note in neat script, then folded it and sealed it with her wax stamp.

"If ye would bring his answer back to me as quickly as possible please?"

"Aye, Madam!" Brianna agreed, turning sharply and walking quickly from the kitchen, making the turn for the barracks stairway. After she was gone, Deborah walked around the kitchen, sampling everything cooking for supper.

"Everything is wonderful," she smiled. "As always, the food yer staff turns out is equal to everything served in the past. Have ye heard from Millicent?"

"Aye, she and Typhon are at Emerald Lakes right now. Her last note said she was tired of eating fish," Gwendolyn chuckled. Deborah laughed with her, knowing how men enjoyed putting a line into the water and just sitting to think.

"I am going to my room for a soak," Deborah said to Gwendolyn after their laughter subsided. "Would ye send down an antipasto and white wine?"

"I shall wait awhile before I bring it," Gwendolyn told her. "Ye will want to soak and relax. Here is a carafe of white wine already cold and ready, I shall send more when ye call for it."

"Thank ye Gwen," Deborah said tiredly. "With the holidays approaching, 'tis so much to be done. It appears that most of the noble houses are sending representatives for the first time since Erinn called them together after Drake's ascension. It should make for a merry celebration."

"Indeed so, My Lady," Gwen chuckled, taking that piece of information and filing it away. She would have to alter her plans for the meal now, and a service line would be the perfect answer, she thought with a smile. "We will need every room in the House to be readied, as well as the upstairs bath."

"Aye, so much to be done," Deborah sighed. "If we need extra help, inquire among the staff. See if they have daughters or sons needing work. If they do not, then we will send to the Lady's School for help."

"Aye Madam," Gwendolyn smiled, bowing her head a bit. Deborah took the carafe and cups in hand before leaving the kitchen, turning right and heading for her quarters, already anticipating a long hot soak. When she entered the room, she could hear the water running and feel the steam. Alarm set in, had she forgotten to turn off the tap this morning, she thought as she ran for the tub room, finding Erinn there with a towel wrapped about waist.

"O! 'Tis ye!" she exclaimed with relief. "I thought I might have forgotten to turn the tap off this morning."

"Would ye join me?" he asked in a deep rumble. "We have not seen much of each other of late, and the Holidays are nearly upon us. We will both be very busy soon."

"I shall be delighted to join my lord," she answered with a smile, handing him the carafe and cups. "I have brought drink."

"Excellent, I was about to call for some," he smiled. "And antipasto. I wish to eat supper with ye here, if 'tis to yer liking."

"I would like that too!" Deborah smiled. "The antipasto will be here in a bit, Gwendolyn wanted me to relax and soak. Brianna is now in the family quarters, just a door down from the sewing room. I had no idea that room was so dusty."

"It has not been used for a long time," Erinn pointed out. "Even with the routine cleaning, dust will simply accumulate. Now that it has an occupant, 'twill be cleaner, aye?"

"Aye, my lord," she answered, changing the conversation. "I have been going over the responses to the invitations. It appears that every noble house in every district is sending at least one representative. The House will be quite full."

"Indeed 'twill be," Erinn nodded, pouring the wine and handing her a cup. "Do we have enough people to provide service?"

"I have put the call out to those of the staff with children or other relatives needing work," Deborah told him, loading the pipe from the drawer beside their sofa. "If we still do not have enough, I shall send to the Lady's School!"

"All will be well, my dear," Erinn chuckled, turning off the tap as the water hit the correct level. "I am getting in, I cannot wait to be clean," he said, slipping the towel off and climbing into the tub. Deborah followed him soon after, setting the wine and cups at a convenient place so they could be reached easily. They spent the time talking about the past few weeks, and about the coming holidays until the water cooled. Once they were out, they dressed in clean, comfortable clothing and stoked the hearth, only then did Deborah pull the service cord to call for their antipasto and more wine.

"Ye have made arrangements?"

"I want to remain in our quarters," she told him honestly. "I have hardly seen ye at all for almost forty days."

"Well then, I shall assure that my lady has enough of my company to satisfy her then," Erinn chuckled, pouring the last of the wine for them. As he set the carafe on the table, Gwendolyn's knock came on the door and it opened to allow her entry. She quickly served the snack tray and soup tureen, gathered up the dirty cups and carafe, asked if they needed anything else and departed, leaving them to their privacy. They were not seen until the next morning.

When Deborah rose the next morning, she realized it was exactly two weeks before the Winter Solstice. Guests could start arriving soon, she realized, especially from the furthest flung parts of the Land. As they drank their caffe, her thoughts turned to readying the House, and Artos' face appeared in her mind.

"I have not seen my son for a long time," she said quietly. "Have ye heard anything?"

"I have not, and Father has been suspiciously absent of late, have ye noted?" Erinn asked, feeling relaxed and happy as he glanced outside to see it snowing.

"He will be here for the Holidays, I am certain of it," Deborah laughed merrily. "He loves the Winter Solstice, the time of Yule."

"So he does," Erinn chuckled as Arthfael's knock sounded on the door. The boy had an uncanny knack of arriving at nearly the same time every day, and usually Brianna was with him. It was like that today when the door opened at his gesture and the courting couple entered, holding hands.

"Good morning," Erinn called out. "Sit down and join us, we have plenty to share."

"Thank ye, Father," Arthfael answered, letting Brianna precede him to the sofa and sitting beside her. "What is my schedule today?"

"Ye will be working with me today as we put the final touches on the decorations for Yule," Erinn told him. "Yer mother has arranged for the trees to be brought in, they are ready to be installed throughout the House so they can be decorated. Ye will help me with this, aye?"

"Aye, Father!"

"And where may I be of help?" Brianna asked.

"I am going to open another guest wing today," Deborah put out. "I have counted the responses and totaled the guests, we will need at least a dozen more rooms, especially for the larger families that are coming. Ye will help me with this?"

"I shall be of what assistance I can be, My Lady," Brianna answered sincerely.

"What of Artos?" Arthfael asked suddenly. "Has anyone heard if he will be here?"

"We have heard naught of yer brother since his departure," Erinn grumbled a bit. "I shall not let that stop me from enjoying one of my favorite times of year. If yer brother decides to join us, he will be welcomed."

"Very well, Father," Arthfael answered, realizing the subject was still sore for Erinn.

"He has much to answer for," Erinn added in a quieter tone. Arthfael almost felt sorry for his younger brother as he realized that Artos would be in the arena with the High Lord as soon as he returned to the House.

"Whatever service I can render Father, I shall," Arthfael reminded him earnestly.

"I know ye will," Erinn smiled suddenly, his mood dispelled. "Come, join me in a sikar?"

"Aye Father!" the young man gladly accepted. They sat to enjoy a short smoke, then began moving the potted evergreens into their usual spots all over the house, occasionally using magick when not enough strong arms were at hand. Finally placing the last one, Erinn looked up to see it was already dark outside, and he noted he was tired. Arthfael looked exhausted, he noted with a silent chuckle.

"Come on my son, we have done enough for today," he said.

"Are we done?"

"Aye, we are," Erinn smiled. "I am ready for a long soak, but first some food. I am nigh unto starving!"

"O my goodness, I am too!" Arthfael suddenly realized. They were on their way to the kitchen when they heard Reeves announce the arrival of Tarana and her guard. Erinn sighed, summoned up his energies and told Arthfael to go get his snack.

"What about ye, Father?"

"I shall be fine, just go," Erinn smiled. "Madam Tarana deserves my attention."

"Of course Father," Arthfael nodded, continuing on to the kitchen, finding Brianna there working beside the others. She brought him an antipasto for one and the wine he asked for quickly, squeezing his arm affectionately before returning to what she was doing. As he ate, he could smell all the delicious goodies baking; pies, muffins, cookies, he loved this time of year now that he was free to enjoy it. When he finished, Brianna brought him a piece of mixed berry pie, remaining while he slowly consumed it.

"This pie is delicious," he commented.

"Thank ye, I made it!" Brianna crowed, proud of her accomplishment.

"Ye did? My dear, 'tis quite beautiful. I think the crust is light and flaky, and ye fluted the edges very nicely too. The filling is not too sweet, I can really taste fresh berries!"

"Ye really do like it!" she smiled wide.

"I do!" he said truthfully, taking another bite.

"Would ye like some caffe with that?"

"Nay, but some more wine would be welcome. When will ye be finished here?" he asked quietly.

"I am almost done baking the last round of pies," she smiled tiredly. "I am ready for a soak, and some cold wine. I never appreciated just how hard kitchen work is 'till now, I shall remember to be more respectful of those who labor over our food in the future," she laughed a bit.

"I shall wait to bathe then," he smiled, for communal bathing was common in the Land.

"I should only be a bit longer, if ye will wait?" she asked.

"I will be happy to wait upon ye, my lady," he answered elegantly. She smiled hesitantly before turning back to her work, Arthfael watching her wistfully until she finished. Gwendolyn embraced her warmly, thanked her for her work and sent her out, telling she had done plenty already that day.

"May I return on the morrow? I would love to learn more!" Brianna asked.

"Of course child, ye are always welcome," Gwendolyn told her. Sending her out the door with a large, cold carafe of white wine and two cups, the new Kitchen Mistress of the High Lord's House watched them go, happy for the both of them. They had both been through so much in their young lives, she thought, it was time they found some happiness. A whiff of scorch crossed her nose, she turned in alarm and called out.

"Watch those eggs! We wouldn't want to burn them!"

Brianna and Arthfael retired to the upstairs baths to soak and recuperate from their day of work, discussing the coming Holiday party.

"Father has not discussed what assignment will fall to me during the time the Nobles are here," he began haltingly. "I do not know how much time we will have together."

"We will enjoy what time we have, Arthfael," Brianna replied tiredly. "Would it be possible to dine in one of our rooms tonight?" she asked.

"A private supper? My father and mother enjoy such a thing from time to time, but I do not know if I merit such privilege."

"Can we ask, would it be unacceptable?" Brianna persisted. "I do not feel like being around so many people tonight."

"I shall go and ask when we finish soaking," Arthfael told her. "If plating it causes no difficulty for the kitchen, I can bring the food back with me."

"Thank ye," she said gratefully, pulling herself out of the tub and grabbing a large thick towel, wrapping up in it afterward. "I just do not feel like company. The Holidays are coming and 'twill be plenty of time to enjoy the company of friends, aye?"

"Aye," he answered, getting out of the tub too and wrapping a thick robe around him. "Which room should we use?

"Yers is the bigger of the two," she answered at once.

"Very well, Madam," he smiled, offering his arm. They walked first to her room so she could change clothing, and when she emerged, he noted she had a small bag over her shoulder.

"I might enjoy myself too much and have to sleep on yer floor," she said practically.

"No one will be sleeping on the floor," Arthfael laughed. "The sofa in my room is perfectly comfortable, I have fallen asleep there a few times. I shall just put out extra pillows and comforters and make myself a bed there, if ye should remain."

"Ye are always so good about it," she smiled. "Come, I am ready for more wine, and some Herb too!"

"As am I," Arthfael replied.

While they relaxed upstairs, Erinn and Deborah welcomed Tarana and her team into the house below, assuring they were installed close together as requested.

"Madam Tarana!" Erinn called out when she came through the door. He noted at once the new grey in her hair, and wondered when she would apply for retirement.

"My Lord Erinn, My Lady Deborah," Tarana greeted warmly. "I hope ye have that bath fired up, 'tis blessed cold out there."

"I do indeed have as much hot water as all of ye require. Enter our home in peace, and in the spirit of the Holiday," Deborah welcomed them. "If ye will all follow me, I shall take ye to yer rooms. Supper will be ready soon, we can all just pass through the service line and be at ease."

"I like such a casual service," Tarana smiled, exchanging an embrace with the High Lady.

Laughing as they exchanged news and jokes, the group made their way up the stairs to the rooms assigned to them. Deborah and Erinn left them as soon as they were comfortable, returning to their own quarters filled with the warmth of the holiday. They knew that the next week would be filled with arrivals, welcomes and joy, as every Yule should be.

Far off in the desert, Ishmael and Artos packed their things for their trip to the High Lord's House. Ishmael had simply given his animals to his neighbors, not knowing if he would be returning. It all depended on the High Lady, he thought with a sigh. If she was pleased, he could have his House Grant returned and he could travel wherever he wished to again. If not, she might react to remove him permanently from the Land, something he was very concerned about. Still, the lad needed to go home to prove himself, and Ishmael wanted to see it happen.

"Just about ready?" he called out to Artos.

"Aye Master," he heard the calm response. "I have cleaned up my room thoroughly, and packed everything you have given me, just in case I do not return."

"Very good lad," Ishmael called back. "And what about ye, Anunit?"

"I am ready to go," he heard her quiet voice say simply. Emerging from his room after banking the fire completely and watching it fade out, he looked about one more time to assure everything was in order. Just as he finished, the couple emerged from Artos' room with bags in hand. Ishmael noted Anunit looked very nervous and anxious, he did not blame her in light of her meeting Artos' parents.

"We are ready, Master," Artos said.

"Good, I am ready as well. I love celebrating Yule. Ye realize boyo that as soon as yer father sees ye, he is likely to take ye right to the arena."

"I am prepared for that," Artos replied with confidence. "'Twould be within his right as my father, and as the High Lord considering how we parted."

Ishmael chuckle to himself as he prepared for magickal travel, hoping that Drake would be in attendance at the festivities. Artos had been transformed from a soft weakling to a hard and well-conditioned warrior and Drake had always doubted Ishmael's ability to teach. The Arab man looked forward to watching Artos' perform in the arena, and the look of amazement on Drake's face at seeing him.

"Come then boyo, let us get ye home! If ye will provide transportation and get us as close as ye can, we will find a way to travel the rest of the way," Ishmael grinned, laying down the challenge. Artos smiled back, held out his hand to Anunit and closed his eyes, envisioning courtyard at the House in the Capitol City. Summoning up his abilities, he opened the portal and they walked through, arriving in the middle of a fierce snowstorm. The portal had let them out just a short walk to the front door, testimony to Artos' abilities, and Ishmael grinned wide.

"I shall allow the Prince to precede me," he said. "We will get closer to the door at least that way."

Chapter 13

Artos led the way to the door, fighting the increasing wind and near blizzard conditions until they reached it. He stepped up to it and knocked firmly and loudly, remembering that the House was noisy this time of year. They did not wait but a moment or two before it opened and Reeves peered out, looking at their faces through the driving snow.

"Prince Artos!" he exclaimed, turning to one of his young staff and telling him to bring the High Lord at once. "Come in out of the storm, all of ye, before ye freeze!" he invited, opening the door wide. They entered, standing on the tile Artos remembered well, as the staff came with hot drinks and warm towels. They came with mops too, to wipe up the melting snow that dripped from their coats.

"May we take yer wraps and bags?" Reeves asked courteously.

While the staff greeted Artos, Erinn sat with Deborah smoking a sikar and enjoying a cup of good red wine. He felt Artos' arrival at once, a faint smile appeared and he rose from his seat, finishing his wine in a few sips.

"He is here," Deborah remarked dryly, remaining where she was.

"So he is, and the Hero is with him."

"Hero?" Deborah said in a disdainful tone. "We will see about that. Will ye meet him now?"

"Aye, I see no reason to wait," Erinn said. "I have had one cup of wine, 'twill not diminish my abilities so much that I cannot face my son."

"Mind what he has learned, husband," Deborah warned. "The way of the 'Hashashin' is the way of the whirlwind, 'tis difficult to predict and defend against."

"Ye have been reading?"

"Aye, just in case someone needed to dispatch the Hero," Deborah chuckled. "I never thought ye might need to be warned about yer son's skills."

"We will see," Erinn smiled. Taking his sikar with him, he walked out of their bedroom and down the hall, his entire manner changing as he did so. He would not meet Artos as his father, but as the High Lord, so as to have full access to everything the Lady would grant him. He was not openly armed, as was custom in the House especially during the holidays, he walked with a light footstep and his eyes constantly moving as Drake had taught him. His heart leapt a bit when he saw Artos for his son was tanned and muscular, his muscles long and lean. A young woman stood beside him, her hair of russet hue and of course, Ishmael stood behind her, silently waiting.

"Artos, my son, welcome home," he called out when he was close enough. "And who is this beautiful young woman with ye?"

"Thank ye for yer welcome, Father," Artos answered humbly. "I would like ye to meet my lady, Anunit."

Erinn smiled wider, his face took on a softer expression as he turned to her, extending his hand for hers. "Welcome to the High Lord's House, Anunit. Merry Yule."

"Merry Yule, My Lord," she answered, in a slightly husky voice. She was experiencing all manner of emotions, mostly fear, and her hand shook a bit as she reached for his. When his hand took hers, she felt it was warm, with calloused earned from years of wielding a blade. His face was kind, and he was very handsome, an older version of Artos. As he stood there, everyone bowed low, and he knew Deborah had followed him. He released Anunit's hand and turned to greet her, concerned at her expression, and the color of her hair.

"Hello my son," she said softly. "Welcome home. I am glad ye have come for Yule. I was concerned ye would not. Who is this?" she finished, turning her head to observe Anunit.

"Mother, I would like to present my lady Anunit," Artos replied evenly.

Deborah looked at Artos, then to Anunit, sizing her up with an assessing expression. "Ye are a Priestess of the Temple," she finally said.

"Aye, My Lady, I was," Anunit answered. "When Artos made me the offer, I went to the Temple Mother and resigned from service. I only wish to serve him, and our family, if ye will accept me."

"Well spoken, young woman. Ye will come with me and we will talk a bit. Have ye eaten?"

"Not yet, My Lady," Anunit answered honestly.

"Wait," Erinn said sternly. "I have business with my son first. Come Artos, walk with me to the arena. Ye have explanations to offer."

"Aye, so I do," Artos nodded. Picking up his bag, he removed his blade and scabbard strapped to the top, putting it on his back. "I am ready."

"Good, let us not waste time. Ye know how I admire alacrity."

"Aye, so I do," Artos smiled. His father had changed little as far as he could see, but he would not allow his ego to blind him as to Erinn's abilities. Drake had trained him personally, and his father's magickal skills might still outstrip his, Artos quickly assessed the situation as Ishmael had taught him.

Erinn watched him thinking, heard his thoughts and said naught. He wanted to see what Artos had been trained to do, in fact he was looking forward to meeting him, since Ishmael had trained him. Deborah was not the only one who had been reading, Erinn grinned to himself, and reading was only one step in learning. The High Lord had a few tricks up his sleeve, just in case he needed them, he thought to himself as they arrived in the Barracks and began to walk through.

Ishmael made to follow them, only to find himself magickally restrained. He looked up and met a set of amber eyes, and realized the High Lady was the reason.

"Ye will come with me!" she stated quietly. "I do not trust ye. I have read that some of the 'Hashashin' are mind workers, able to manipulate people's thoughts and perceptions. As far as I know, ye have trained my son to assassinate my husband in the arena, so it looks like a tragic accident. How can I be certain of yer motives?" she mused aloud. Her face lightened, a smile appeared and her hair finished turning scarlet red as she spoke the next words. "Knight of the Land ye are summoned to appear!"

A puff of thick smoke and Drake appeared in front of her, accoutered for war, helm in place and sword in hand. "What is amiss?" he asked at once. A smile played at Deborah's mouth as she answered.

"I wish ye to accompany this one to the arena, where the High Lord and his son are about to cross swords in a test of skills. If he is manipulating Artos, ye are to slay him on sight. Do ye understand?"

"Aye Madam," Drake growled, turning to Ishmael. "Is this true? Have ye been working with his mind?"

"ME?" Ishmael objected strenuously. "I do not train the mind that way, my specialty is the body and weaponry. Even if I did do such things, I would not have practiced it against the young prince. I am no fool, I am well aware that *she* would know," he finished, pointing at Deborah. "I desire to walk as a free person in the Land again, and I have only done as I was asked to do by the Goddess. Artos has been trained to bring out his natural skills and abilities, the style he exhibits is his own, however. I look forward to seeing the results, as I would think ye would be, Drake Natanleod."

Drake felt caught between two loyalties, he stood there for a moment before gesturing to Ishmael. "Come then, let us see what ye have wrought. And who is this delightful young woman?" he asked, catching sight of Anunit.

"My name is Anunit," she answered in a quiet voice. Drake Natanleod, she wondered. He was reported to be dead, despite the news of his ascension. As a Temple Priestess, she was fascinated by such a prospect, and when he reached for her hand, she was shocked to feel living skin.

"I am an Ascended Being, I am not dead," he said to her with a faint smile. "How people continue to believe that ridiculous rumor of my death is beyond me. Would ye like to see the contest?"

"I would, My Lord," she answered carefully. "If the Lady will allow me to watch, I would like to see Artos in the arena. I swear, I have no mental influence over my lord. He makes up his own mind about things."

Something in the way Anunit made her statement caught Deborah's attention. It was how she used the term "my lord," the High Lady considered, turning it over in her mind a few times. It hit her as they reached the top of the stairs down to the Barracks, she and Artos were together! She cared little if they had shared the Rite or not, her son had finally picked a woman he could not overwhelm with his aura. Deborah could feel the young woman's presence, calm reigned inside and out, except for just the slightest trace of concern due to the coming contest.

"My son has made a good choice," she said simply as she walked beside Anunit. "Yer name is associated with Venus, a Goddess of Love and Desire."

"Indeed so," Anunit nodded. "In my former work in the Temple, it was important to have such a name. When the Elder Sister accepted me into the Temple, she gave me this name. I have grown to like it, and would like to keep it."

"Ye are Anunit as far as I am concerned," Deborah responded, knowing that the Priestesses often changed names when they changed Temples. "I look forward to talking more with ye."

"I am at the High Lady's disposal," Anunit answered humbly. The two women, accompanied by Drake and Ishmael, walked through the barracks into the viewing seats around the arena. Deborah walked directly to the family box and took her seat, indicating that the others should join her. When Ishmael sat, she turned and fixed her gaze upon him.

"If ye have been toying with my son's mind ye will pay the price!"

"Aye, Madam," Ishmael responded calmly. "I look forward to the return of my Grant, so I might walk as a free man once more."

"We will see about that," Deborah responded. He noted that her hair did not return to its usual raven-black, and that her eyes were still burning amber. He said no more, simply turning his attention on the sandy circle below, waiting for his chela to prove himself.

Erinn and Artos walked onto the sands, turned and exchanged the grip, as was customary at such occasion. Both men wanted a fair fight, the grip reminded both they were men of the Land, as well that they were father and son. Erinn walked over to where his usual arena blade sat waiting, then turned and watched Artos draw his personal blade from the back scabbard he wore. Very well, Erinn thought with resolution, ye have chosen the hardest test. Focusing his mind, he summoned his war blade and when it appeared in his hand, he began to slowly work with it to limber and warm his muscles. Artos did the same, and for long moments, their routines were very similar, but as the younger man worked the differences in style became apparent. Erinn simply concentrated on his own work, watching Artos do the same. At length, the two men turned to each other at the same instant, noting the synchronicity of the moment.

"Ready then, my son?"

"Aye!"

"Come at me then, and let us see what ye can do!"

Ishmael sat up on the edge of his seat, craning his head for the best view. Drake sat right between him and Deborah, blade in hand, his eyes watching for any sign of influence from the Arab man upon the young prince. Anunit watched with a passive face, but Deborah watched her fingers tremble a bit before she clutched them into fists. So, she is concerned, but for whom, Deborah wondered as she put her attention back on the contest.

"Be safe, husband," she sent to him.

"I shall be," she heard him say confidently. "He has not learned so much that I cannot overwhelm him. My skills have been honed by war and combat, his in the arena. No matter what Ishmael may have taught him, I was trained by Drake, who is an Ascended Being now. I think I have the better education, and I am High Lord on top of all of that. Unless 'tis the Lady's Will that I should step aside, She will be with me."

"So be it then," she said with a sigh.

"Have no fear, ye and I will be sharing pipe and a sikar later, in privacy," he sent to her, along with a burst of his love for her.

"I look forward to it, My Lord," she answered. "I have made a new style of comfortable clothing, I was going to show ye the first set I made tonight."

"I shall make this short then," he chuckled into her mind.

With no further word, Erinn stepped into the arena, walking to the center. Artos joined him and they crossed blades, Ulric appearing suddenly at the entrance to the contest floor.

"Hold there! Ye'll need a Marshall!" he called out.

"Aye, so we will," Erinn nodded. "Is this agreeable to ye, my son?"

"Aye, 'tis. We would not wish any stain upon this contest, no hint of wrong."

"Indeed not," Erinn replied, brandishing his blade. Artos grinned and for a moment, Erinn saw his son young again before he composed his face for battle. So, ye are still in there, Erinn thought as he watched Artos heft his sword and cross his, barely touching it.

Artos watched his father's face compose into icy calm, but he had seen that before, many times. It did not deter him or dismay him as it had in the past, he felt confident and strong, able to keep pace with his very accomplished father at last. When Ulric's arm dropped, he leapt at Erinn full force and the High Lord smiled to feel his strength, muchly increased from their last encounter. Good, he thought, perhaps the lad can bring me a challenge at last!

The force of their blades striking together rang throughout the Barracks suddenly, every warrior within knew the sound well and what it meant. They filled their cups to take with them, making their way from the common room and dining hall to the workout arena. They were all surprised to see Artos there, many of them hardly recognizing him due to the arduous conditioning he had gone through in the desert. Those who did recognize him at first wore looks of shock and surprise, for where the young prince had been slightly soft before, he was hard now. Both men worked without shirts, exposing their upper torsos to everyone's view and allowing comparisons between their physiques. Erinn's was tight and composed, the result of hours and hours of self-discipline in the arena and a more careful attention to his diet. Artos' body appeared to be a bit more athletic than warrior, but he was quick and strong, making up for any lack.

As those in the Barracks began to gather, Erinn saw his opportunity and increased the pace of his work. Artos effortlessly and immediately responded, a smile appearing on his face.

"I was hoping ye would want to work faster," he remarked.

"We can work as fast as ye can stand," Erinn returned without panting. Artos was amazed, his father's body was hard and rippled, even more so than he remembered. Clearly, his father had not ceased his search for perfection, Artos realized as Erinn picked up the pace again.

Drake watched intently, looking for any sign of communication between Chela and Master, finding none. He kept his senses keen though, in case Ishmael's skills had developed beyond Erinn's, which he doubted seriously. As he watched the contest, he could see that Erinn was not laboring at all. His breathing was even and calm, his eyes alert, his reflexes quick and responsive, everything he should be, Drake thought with satisfaction. When Artos tried the first few feints and distractions, Erinn deflected them away easily, smiling as he did so. Artos attempted to get around him, finding only steel in his way and his father laughed a bit, simply exhilarated by the challenge.

"Ye have learned a great deal, my son!" he sent to Artos' mind. "I am pleased!"

"I have not yet begun to show ye what I have learned," he heard Artos respond coolly. With no further conversation, Artos disappeared into a whirling cloud, as if he had become one of the dust swirls that frequented the desert. Erinn grinned wide, he was exhibiting some of the "Hashashin" knowledge imparted to him by Ishmael, something Erinn had anticipated. The books he had read hinted that one simply had to discern the pattern of footwork being used and interrupt it suddenly in order to overcome the user. Erinn employed the art of pursuit, using his own feet in an attempt to distract his son and finding Artos was not fooled. He continued the well-practiced pattern despite anything Erinn did, and so the High Lord changed tactics, drawing from his years fighting in war. He increased the pace of the bout to the point where he could barely be seen, a smile crossed Artos' face and he too, simply worked so quickly he could barely be seen. The ringing of their swords could be heard in ever increasing speed too, until it sounded like one continuous note ringing in the small space. Within the light cloud of dust, Erinn and Artos strove against each other without even scratching one another.

Erinn's delight was immense, his son was better than ever before. It was as if Ishmael had tapped a resource deep inside Artos, releasing what had always been there. He watched Artos launch flurry after flurry of cuts and slices, which would have decimated anyone else not capable of deflecting the furiously powerful blows. Artos suddenly seemed taller, and Erinn realized he was calling his magickal abilities into play. He responded in kind and Artos was soon looking up at his father as if he were a young boy again as Erinn's height grew to match his. Erinn increased the size of his weapon, and Artos followed suit, it was as if two small giants were now contending in the middle of the arena. The ground trembled under their feet, the sound of the whirlwind around them roared and the ringing of their blades harmonized like a set of well-tuned bells. Everyone in the arena sat silently watching, awestruck at what they were witnessing. The battle between the two Natanleods was epic, it would be talked about for years and years to come, Erinn realized. Artos' reputation was forever changed now because of this battle, no one would remember what he was before, and Erinn saw the hand of the Goddess entirely in the affair.

"So, ye took him away to train him and help those in the Barracks to forget him, only to bring him back as a quickly maturing Natanleod heir," Erinn thought to the Goddess.

"I did, because he would not listen to anyone else, not even ye, not even Drake. I knew he had chosen a harder path, and Ishmael was the perfect individual to provide that. He was not swayed by his relationship to the boy, he treated him as if he were just any chela, as he should have been all along. Look at their faces, all of them around him now," She entreated and Erinn took the moment, seeing the awestruck expression on nearly every face present. "He wishes to lead the Black Dragons. They will follow his orders, knowing his might and intelligence because ye have allowed him to prove it this night. I suggest ye get back to celebrating Yule, and welcome yer son home."

"As ye wish, My Lady," Erinn answered, a grin appearing. Artos saw it, his brow wrinkled a bit with questions and Erinn simply thought back to him. "Would ye like to quit now?"

"Are ye tired?"

"Nay, but I am thirsty and 'tis Yule. I have guests to entertain. Look around ye, look at their faces, they see ye completely differently than before. If ye wish to try for Knight Commander, ye will be welcomed now rather than simply tolerated because ye are my son. I am very, very proud. Ye have done extremely well. Ye are strong and fast, yer approach is smart and practical, ye are better now than ye have ever been before, do ye not see it?"

"I do, and I am honored that ye do too," Artos replied slowly, as if thinking over every word while they continued to exchange furious blows. "I am thirsty, and 'tis Yule, as ye say. Perhaps we have done enough?"

"I think so," Erinn chuckled into his mind, whirling out of the exchange. Artos continued until he completed the routine, coming to a sudden stop at the end and standing their breathing rapidly but not panting for air. Erinn walked to him at once, offering the grip in congratulations.

"Well done, my son!" he called out with joy in his voice. "I am pleased with what ye have learned. Welcome home!"

"I am glad to be home, Father. I must say that without Ishmael ben Cain's training, I would not be what I am. He lost his Grant because of my request, Father, may it be reinstated?" Artos asked at once, sheathing his sword and kneeling at Erinn's feet. The spontaneous act of humility further impressed each and every Knight and Dame in the arena, they waited breathlessly as Erinn considered finally turning to where Deborah sat, her hair brilliantly red.

"What say ye, My Lady?" he called out, his breathing completely regular. "Our son's training is very impressive, and his attitude is muchly improved due to the training he has received in the desert. Has Ishmael ben Cain earned back his House Grant?"

All eyes turned to the seats where Deborah sat and she rose from her seat, gesturing for Ishmael to do the same.

"Come with me, Ishmael ben Cain," she said, her voice deep and resonant. He did as he was bidden, taking her proffered hand, Drake right behind him and the three of them disappeared, reappearing on the arena floor so that Deborah stood beside Erinn.

"Was training my son difficult?" she asked kindly.

"At first. He was very headstrong, Madam," Ishmael answered. "However, so was I when my father first started with my training. The young prince is intelligent, his mind reckons things out quickly and he generally reacts practically when confronted to act. He kept pace with the High Lord for over half the hour, something not easy to do, aye? His body has been cleansed inside and out, so he could begin anew, and just look what he has accomplished! He looks like a young Adonis!"

"Indeed he does!" Erinn put in. "Did ye see him move, My Lady? He is quick and agile, as he should be. The Hero's training has done him a world of good."

"Hero?" Deborah demanded, her tone heavy with affront. "Who has accorded this criminal with such an accolade?"

"His deeds in the past won him that title, My Lady," Drake added his voice to the matter. "Without him, the Black Dragons would have all been sacrificed to Enki's demonic Naga possessor, and I might not be here at all. I gifted him a House Grant before to thank him for my life, for my men's lives, and for everything he has done in service to the Lady since I have known him. Surely, he might have it renewed because of his service to the young Prince of the Blood?"

Deborah appeared to pause in thought for a moment, and as they watched, her hair lost most of the scarlet color, and her eye color dimmed considerably. Ishmael's breath caught in his throat as she held out her hand and a column of flame appeared in the palm, could it be that his service had merited such a reward, he wondered. As she stood there, palm extended and wreathed in flame, an elegant scroll materialized. The flames around her palm faded out, leaving the scroll lying there, a ribbon of House colors tied around it. Ishmael knelt at her feet, head bowed, hoping the Lady would be kind once more.

"Ishmael ben Cain!" he heard her say, but it was as if there was more than one person speaking. "Rise to face me!" He did as he was commanded, bringing his deep and liquid brown eyes into contact with her slightly amber ones. "Aye, My Lady?"

"Will ye swear to serve the Lady of the Land and House Natanleod for the rest of yer days?"

"I do swear service and allegiance to the Lady, and Her representatives, the Natanleods!" he answered, his voice strong and rich. Everyone in the arena heard it, and knew they were witness to a very special event.

"Then receive this Grant as a life gift from our House, so that ye might travel the Land as a free man. Ye will find it pays for housing, food and transportation anywhere in the Land 'tis presented, to any merchant or farmer or Guildsman. Thank ye, Ishmael ben Cain, for training my son and helping him to find his way," she intoned, handing him the simple scroll, edged with silver.

"I was honored and pleased to be of service to yer house, and to the Lady of the Land in this regard," Ishmael answered humbly, taking the scroll from her hand. Untying it and unrolling it, he read over it, seeing that everything she had said was included in the writing, and that it was signed with her sign, overlaid with the Natanleod seal.

"Take good care of that," Deborah smiled. "It must last for a long time."

"I shall care for it as a precious thing, since it comes from thy hand, My Lady," he said elegantly, bowing very low in respect.

"Now, as I recall, we have a party going on upstairs," she laughed, breaking the solemn mood. "I suggest we rejoin it. Husband, are ye ready for more wine?"

"Very ready," he answered with a smile. Taking the scabbard off his back, he used his abilities to send the weapon back to its storage area, replacing his shirt and tucking it in to the top of his trous. "Come my dear, the wine awaits!"

She smiled and took his hand to walk back through the Barracks, the both of them distributing small packages of largesse as they went. Wishing them all good night, the group walked back upstairs, where the music was just beginning.

"I must rest a bit before I dance," Erinn smiled as a server brought them wine.

"We need not dance at all," she whispered to him, her hair now raven black once more, and her eyes returned to their usual hazel grey. "My son is home, and he has brought his lady with him. I must get to know my son again, and acquaint myself with Anunit."

"She is a beautiful young woman," Erinn noted as Artos stopped one of the staff laden with full cups of wine, taking one for the young woman beside him and one for himself.

"Indeed so, and Temple trained. She will not be easily treated lightly, nor will he be able to dominate her," Deborah smiled. "The conversation we have shared so far has been good, and I look forward to seeing her in the sewing room."

Erinn produced a sikar for the both of them, clipped them and lit them, handing one to her and sitting back against the back of the chair. "He is good, my wife, very good. Artos has improved so much, 'tis a little frightening."

"We will see how much he has improved," Deborah answered, watching as Arthfael and Brianna came to greet Artos and Anunit. "He was so jealous of Arthfael, so angry that he had a brother. I hope all of that has been resolved." As they watched, the two brothers embraced heartily and warmly, as if Artos had truly missed Arthfael's company. They introduced their ladies to one another, the two women exchanged warm embraces and the four paired off to head to the wine cask.

"It certainly appears that our natural son has accepted our adopted son as part of our family," Erinn mused, watching it.

"So it does, but we will see. I hope it all works out," Deborah sighed, sipping her wine. "I am glad to see ye are unhurt, My Lord."

"Artos had no chance to hurt me, my dear," Erinn smiled a bit. "And he did not wish to either. Our son's entire attitude has changed for the better, and I am grateful. Perhaps he will simply embrace his role in the family now, and stop pushing his responsibilities aside."

"Husband, 'tis Yule," Deborah said suddenly. "We should put such thoughts aside 'till after the holiday. Look Cadoc and Aphrodite have arrived! I am going to meet them and make sure they get upstairs. I shall return apace."

"Hurry back," Erinn smiled, kissing her palm. "Ye know how I value alacrity."

"Of course, My Lord!" she said, laughing merrily as she swished off, sikar and wine in hand. He watched her go, glad she was with him, until Drake sat beside him.

"Ye think his attitude has truly changed?" Drake asked.

"Ye would know, ye are the Ascended one, unless yer facilities are beginning to fade due to advanced age," Erinn answered, chuckling a bit.

"O! Ye are as bad as yer wife!" Drake exclaimed quietly, laughing while doing so. "Yer wit continues to improve."

Finis

Made in the USA
Coppell, TX
11 November 2021